Southern Ghost

ALSO BY CAROLYN G. HART

Death on Demand
Design for Murder
Something Wicked
Honeymoon with Murder
A Little Class on Murder
Deadly Valentine
The Christie Caper

Southern Ghost

Carolyn G. Hart

BANTAM BOOKS NEW YORK · TORONTO · LONDON · SYDNEY · AUCKLAND

SOUTHERN GHOST
A Bantam Book / July 1992

BOOK DESIGN BY GRETCHEN ACHILLES

Library of Congress Cataloging-in-Publication Data
Hart, Carolyn G.
  Southern ghost / Carolyn G. Hart.
    p.   cm.
  ISBN 0-553-07392-3
  I. Title.
PS3558.A676S67   1992
          813'.54—dc20   92-2543
                                  CIP

Published simultaneously in the United States and Canada

Bantam Books are published by Bantam Books, a division of Bantam
Doubleday Dell Publishing Group, Inc. Its trademark, consisting of the
words "Bantam Books" and the portrayal of a rooster, is Registered in
U.S. Patent and Trademark Office and in other countries. Marca
Registrada. Bantam Books, 666 Fifth Avenue, New York, New York
10103.

PRINTED IN THE UNITED STATES OF AMERICA

BVG   0 9 8 7 6 5 4 3 2 1

In love and gratitude to my wonderful agent,
Deborah C. Schneider.

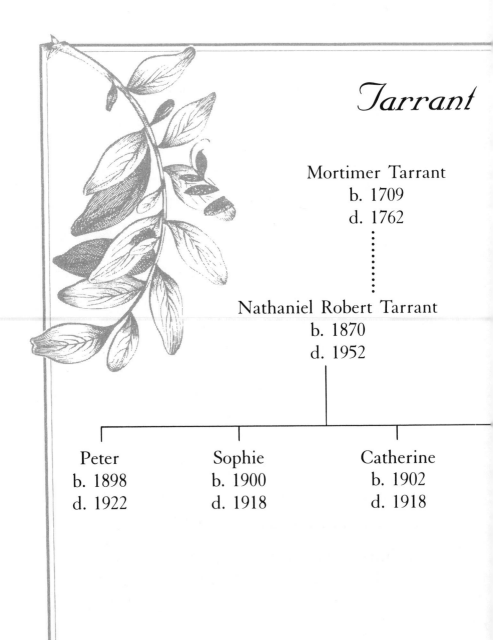

Tarrant

Mortimer Tarrant
b. 1709
d. 1762

Nathaniel Robert Tarrant
b. 1870
d. 1952

Peter	Sophie	Catherine
b. 1898	b. 1900	b. 1902
d. 1922	d. 1918	d. 1918

Family

m. Jane Malcolm
  b. 1720
  d. 1753

m. Rachel Wallace
  b. 1874
  d. 1911

Abigail	Augustus m. Amanda Brevard
b. 1905	b. 1907 b. 1918
d. 1942	d. 1970 d. 1971

Milam m. Julia	Whitney m. Charlotte	Ross
b. 1942 b. 1944	b. 1945 b. 1945	b. 1949
		d. 1970

Melissa	Harriet Elaine	Courtney
b. 1969	b. 1972	b. 1970
d. 1971		

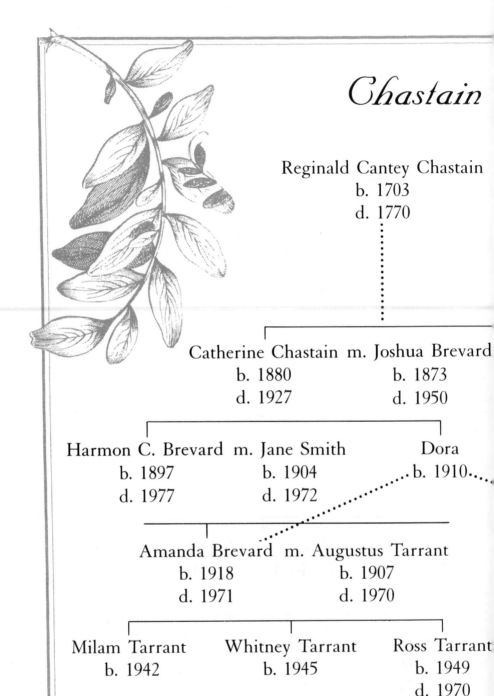

Chastain

Reginald Cantey Chastain
b. 1703
d. 1770

Catherine Chastain m. Joshua Brevard
b. 1880   b. 1873
d. 1927   d. 1950

Harmon C. Brevard m. Jane Smith   Dora
b. 1897   b. 1904   b. 1910
d. 1977   d. 1972

Amanda Brevard m. Augustus Tarrant
b. 1918   b. 1907
d. 1971   d. 1970

Milam Tarrant   Whitney Tarrant   Ross Tarrant
b. 1942   b. 1945   b. 1949
                                      d. 1970

Connection

m. Martha Corey
  b. 1710
  d. 1762

Albert Chastain m. Ann Bolt
  b. 1890   b. 1897
  d. 1960   d. 1924

Borden Chastain m. Ruth Hass
  b. 1924   b. 1930
  d. 1982   d. 1982

Sybil Chastain Giacom
  b. 1953

Chapter 1.

Had he lived to be an old man, Ross Tarrant's face, stripped of every vestige of youth and joy, would have looked much as it did in that last hour: brooding pain-filled eyes deepsunken, grayish skin stretched taut over prominent cheekbones, finely chiseled lips pressed hard to prevent a telltale tremor.

Slumped wearily in the battered old morris chair, a man's chair in a man's retreat, he stared at the pistol, horror flickering in his eyes like firelight against a night sky.

The sound of the motor reached him first, then the crunch of tires against the oyster shells.

The door was locked.

But it was no ultimate defense.

Ross knew that.

As the throb of the engine died and a car door slammed, Ross reached for the gun.

"Ross." A commanding voice. A voice he knew from childhood, from crisp winter mornings when the men zigzagged across a field and lifted shotguns to fire at the flushed quail.

The gun was heavy. So heavy. Ross willed away the unsteadiness of his hand.

He was Ross Tarrant.

His mouth twisted bitterly.

Perhaps not an officer and a gentleman.

But he was Ross Tarrant, and he would not shirk his duty.

At the first knock on the door, the gun roared.

Chapter 2.

Sybil Chastain Giacomo would always catch men's glances and inflame their senses. Especially when the unmistakable light burned in her eyes and she moved sensually, a woman clearly hungering for a man.

Always, it was a young man.

But, passion spent, the latest youth sprawled asleep beside her, Sybil slipped from beneath the satin sheets, drew the brocaded dressing gown around her voluptuous body, and prowled restlessly through the dark house, anger a hot scarlet thread through the black misery in her heart.

Chapter 3.

Despite the fitful gleam of the pale April moon, Tarrant House was almost completely hidden in the deep shadows of the towering live oaks. A wisp of breeze barely stirred the long, dangling wisps of Spanish moss. A single light shone from a second-story window, providing a glimpse of plastered brick and a portion of one of the four huge Corinthian columns that supported the elegant double piazzas and the pediment above.

Pressed against the cold iron railing of the fence, the young woman shivered. The night pulsed with movement—unseen, inimical, hostile. The magnolia leaves slapped, like the tap of a woman's shoes down an uncarpeted hall. The fronds of the palmettos clicked like ghostly dice at some long-ago gaming board. The thick shadows, pierced occasionally by pale moonbeams, took the shape of hurrying forms that responded to no call. She stood alone and alien in a shrouded, dark world that knew nothing of her—and cared nothing for her. The scent of magnolia and honeysuckle and banana shrub cloyed the air, thick as perfume from a flower-strewn coffin.

"Ohoooh!"

Courtney Kimball drew her breath in sharply as the falling moan, tremulous and plaintive, sounded again; then, her eyes adjusted to the night, she saw the swoop of the owl as it dove for its prey. One moment a tiny creature moved and lived; the next a scratching, scrabbling sound signaled sudden death.

But nothing could hold her gaze long except the house, famed as one of the Low Country's loveliest Greek Revival mansions, home for generation after generation of Tarrants.

The House.

That's how she always thought of it.

The House that held all the secrets and whose doors were barred to her.

Courtney gazed at the House with unforgiving eyes.

She was too young to know that some secrets are better left hid.

Chapter 4.

The tawny ginger tom hunched atop the gravestone, golden eyes gleaming, muscles bunched, only the tip of his switching tail and the muted murmurs in his throat hinting at his excitement.

The old lady leaning on her silver-topped, ebony cane observed the ripple of muscles beneath the tom's sleek fur. She was not immune to the power of the contrast between the cat, so immediately alive, and the leaf-strewn grave with its cold, somber headstone.

Dora Chastain Brevard stumped closer to the monument, then used the cane's tip to gouge moss and dirt from the letters scored deep in granite.

ROSS CARMINE TARRANT
January 3, 1949–May 9, 1970
Taken from His Family
So Young
in a
Cruel Twist of Fate

As she scraped, a thumb-size mouse skittered wildly across the grave. The cat flowed through the air, smooth as honey oozing from a broken hive, but he was too late. The frantic mouse disappeared into a hole beneath the roots of a huge cypress. The feline's tail switched in frustration; then, once again, he tensed, but this time, despite the glitter in his eyes, the cat didn't pounce.

The sluggish, slow-moving wolf spider, a huge and hairy tarantula, would have been easy to catch.

But the ginger tom made no move.

Did the prowling cat know that the slow-moving arachnid possessed a potent poison? Or was it merely the ever-present caution of his species, the reluctance to pounce upon an unfamiliar prey?

The cane hissed through the air.

Miss Dora gazed without expression at the quivering remains of the spider. She wished she could as easily dispose of the unexpected communication that had brought her to this mournful site.

Chapter 5.

Max Darling whistled "Happy Days Are Here Again" as he turned the Maserati up the blacktop toward Chastain. He was looking forward to the coming meeting with more excitement than he'd felt in a long time. In his mind, he heard once again Courtney Kimball's intriguing voice, young but self-possessed, a little breathy, very South Carolina.

He walked into the new waterfront restaurant and his spirits rose when vivid eyes sought his in the mirror behind the bar. The young woman who swiftly turned and slipped down from the stool and walked to greet him, a graceful hand outstretched, would capture attention anywhere.

Max was assailed by a mélange of immediate impressions: remarkable blue eyes, a beauty at once apparent yet elusive, a projection of confidence and dignity. But, paramount, was her intensity.

Her first words caught at his heart.

"I need you."

Chapter 6.

Annie Laurance Darling put down the telephone at the front desk of Death on Demand, the loveliest mystery bookstore this side of Atlanta, and didn't know whether to laugh or cry.

Whichever, she had only herself to blame.

Who was always exhorting her husband to apply himself, to work hard, to devote himself to duty?

She, Annie Laurance Darling. Although, in truth, she had eased off recently, ever since Max began to avoid talking about his office. She had stopped asking about his cases or lack of them, concerned that she might have hurt his feelings with her well-meant admonitions to hew to the course. She hadn't pasted any helpful dictums to his shaving mirror for at least a week. (Amazing—and soul-satisfying to strivers—the encouraging mottoes intended for underachievers: *The early bird gets the worm. Little by little does the trick. Put your shoulder to the wheel. Toil, says the proverb, is the sire of fame.*

Under the influence of poverty or of wealth, workmen and their
work are equally liable to degenerate. . . .)

Obviously, however, her efforts had not gone unap-
preciated; witness the call she'd just received from Max. So
now that Max was involved in a case, how could she complain?

"Dammit, Agatha, you'd think he could arrange work
for office hours!" Annie slammed her hand down on the
countertop.

The sleek black cat atop the bookcases devoted to Agatha Christie lifted her elegant head to stare with unblinking
amber eyes at Annie. (Was it simply coincidence that the cat
considered these particular shelves to be her own or were
there matters involved here beyond ordinary human understanding?)

"And what's so confidential he can't even tell his own
wife?"

Annie heard the hurt in her own voice. And what was
so urgent, so important that Max had called to say he
wouldn't be home for dinner—and not to wait up for him
tonight. She glanced toward the front windows. She'd just
put up the CLOSED sign and was tallying the day's receipts
while waiting for Max to walk down the boardwalk from
Confidential Commissions, one of the more unusual busi-
nesses on the South Carolina resort island of Broward's
Rock. Annie always thought of Confidential Commissions as
a modern-day equivalent to the good offices performed by
Agatha Christie's detective of the heart, Mr. Parker Pyne.
Max rather liked that analogy, but he was also quick to point
out that he was neither a private detective nor a practicing
lawyer, but merely a consultant available to those with problems outside the ken of the licensed professionals.

It had become a happy ritual, the two of them coming
together at the close of the business day, each with much to

tell. At least, she always had much to tell. But this week Max had said even less than usual. In retrospect, she realized he'd been quite closemouthed, merely observing that things were picking up at the office. Of course, Annie'd swept right on with her reports, how Henny Brawley, her best customer, had sent a postcard from England to report on her tour of Shrewsbury Abbey, the home of Ellis Peters's incomparable Brother Cadfael *("Annie, I actually saw the small altar to St. Winefride!"),* and how busy it had been in Death on Demand —*"Would you believe a busload of clubwomen from Charleston?"*—since Ingrid Smith, her chief assistant, was bedridden with a spring flu.

Annie felt deflated, a suddenly empty evening ahead. Max hadn't even said where he was going. Dusk was falling, and soon the air would cool sharply. Nights could be shivery in the spring despite the reassuring harbingers of the new season: the call of the chuck-will's-widow, the rachet of swamp frogs.

"I wonder if he has his sweater with him?" Her voice seemed to echo in the empty store.

Agatha yawned, a nice equivalent to a human shrug, then rose, stretched, and dropped to the floor to pad lightly down the central corridor toward the back of the bookstore.

Annie followed, pausing to alphabetize several titles in the Romantic Suspense section: *My Cousin Rachel* by Daphne du Maurier, *Danger in the Dark* by Mignon Eberhart, *Widows' Plight* by Ruth Fenisong, *Alive and Dead* by E. X. Ferrars, and *The Clue of the Judas Tree* by Leslie Ford.

"Max was so abrupt, Agatha. And abstracted." She put the latest title by Elaine Raco Chase face out. "Like he was talking to a stranger."

Agatha waited imperiously atop the coffee bar, which offered customers a different blend every day (Annie's favorite, of course, was Kona) served in mugs bearing the names

of famous mysteries and their authors. Annie offered Agatha
a fresh serving of dry food, received an unequivocal feline
glare in response, and quickly reached for a can. Agatha did
not tolerate frustration well. It was wise, Annie had decided
after applying Mercurochrome to numerous scratches, to satisfy Agatha's needs, wants, and desires promptly. And, if she
thought hard about Agatha, she wouldn't mull over that
odd, unsatisfactory call from Max.

As she emptied half the can into Agatha's bowl, she
remarked conversationally, "I have to hand it to you, Agatha, you're one of a kind."

And so, she thought with admiration, were the tales of
tangled lives and thwarted passions created by the authors
featured in this month's watercolors. As Agatha contentedly
ate, Annie concentrated on the pictures on the back wall over
the fireplace, the better to avoid other thoughts.

In the first painting, a slender young woman in a night-
gown and housecoat stood midway between the living room
of the playhouse, where flames flickered in the fireplace, and
the indoor swimming pool. She stared in horror at the body
lying next to the pool, so close, indeed, that one arm dangled
over the side. The dead woman was middle-aged and expen-
sively dressed. Her heavy blond hair, usually worn in a coronet braid, spread loose on the tiles.

In the second painting, the gully was choked with vege-
tation, honeysuckle and wild grape, dogwood and redbud,
flowering shrubs and looping vines. A small area, down one
side of the gully, showed the effects of many trampling feet,
the grasses bent, vines torn away. An attractive middle-aged
woman watched in dismay as a younger woman reached
toward a blood-spattered clump of Spanish dagger to pick up
a black satin ribbon with an old-fashioned Victorian gold
locket. The locket's front decoration was a spray of lilies of
the valley, the stems and leaves made up of tiny encrusted

emeralds, the bells of pearls. A bowknot of rubies tied the spray of flowers.

In the third painting, a young woman, terror on her face, stared at a fog-wreathed, grim, gray Victorian house. A bloody kitchen knife was impaled in the front door. Six old-fashioned oval portraits circled the house. Each was named. The portrait at the top, labeled Pauline, was of a middle-aged woman with old ivory skin, black eyes, black hair in bangs, and a cold and unfriendly gaze. Clockwise were Sophie, plump, overrouged cheeks and blond hair piled high with too many curls; Anne, short curly black hair with distinctive wings of white at the temples and a warm smile; Elise, elegant and lovely with haunted eyes; Marthe, pleasant looking with a good-humored grin; and Rose, young and vulnerable with blue eyes and shiny brown hair.

In the fourth painting, the skyward gleam of the Bentley's headlights pierced the inky darkness of the night, cruelly illuminating the fatal embrace of the Bentley and the Mercedes as they arced over the side of the cliff to plummet down into the rocks and the sea below. Two men and a woman watched, transfixed. In a hollow nearby, the little boy wrapped in a man's coat didn't stir from his unnatural sleep, despite the noise of the crash and the frenzied licking of his face by a large mongrel dog.

In the fifth painting, there was a strange tableau in the exquisitely appointed museum room with its array of gorgeously restored Egyptian antiquities. A young woman with dark eyes, olive skin, and a heart-shaped face framed by masses of thick black curls raised a mace as the handsome older man approached. Coming up behind the man was a figure clothed all in black with a gun held firmly in one hand.

Generations of readers loved these gothic adventures. Perhaps she should pick out one of her old favorites and take it home to while away the empty evening hours while her husband pursued the work ethic. (Max?) Not, of course, that she had to have dinner with Max every night to be happy, but . . .

Annie glanced up at the rows of cheerful mugs with the titles and authors inscribed in bright-red flowing script. She needed a mug that would brighten her empty evening. Perhaps Margaret Scherf's first Martin Buell mystery, *Always Murder a Friend.* Or Annie's favorite by Constance and Gwenyth Little, *The Great Black Kanba.* How about the zany humor in *Lion in the Cellar* by Pamela Branch? Or would her spirits improve if she spent an hour with Ellie and Ben in *Mum's the Word* by Dorothy Cannell?

"Perhaps," wafted the husky voice, "I am somehow lacking."

Annie damn near jumped out of her skin. Jerking around, she gazed into limpid dark-blue eyes. "Where the he—Laurel, where did you come from? I didn't hear the door." Annie tried not to sound too startled and accusing, but, honestly, if Laurel didn't stop materializing without warning . . .

Her mother-in-law gave a lilting sigh. Anyone who didn't believe sighs could lilt just hadn't dealt with Laurel. The lucky devils.

Her alarm past, Annie surveyed her gorgeous—yes, that was the only appropriate descriptive adjective for Laurel —mother-in-law and smiled. How did Laurel manage always to appear young, fresh, and vibrant, no matter how bizarre her getup? On Annie, the baggy tweed suit and mottled horn-rims, along with a stenographer's notebook and freshly sharpened No. 2 pencil, would have looked like a grade school librarian's trophies from a rummage sale. On Laurel, the effect was enchanting. The horn-rims gave a piquant accent to her elegant patrician features and shining golden hair (Dammit, how could anyone look so marvelous with hair drawn back in a tight, no-nonsense bun?), the droopy tweeds fell in becoming folds against her svelte figure.

"You see, I have to wonder if it's me," Laurel continued earnestly. "Annie, would you say that I am not *simpatico*?"

Annie's smile broadened to a fond grin. "Laurel, nobody would say you are not *simpatico*." And also flaky, but this thought Annie didn't share. Off-the-wall. Just one step (which way?) from certifiable. But, always and ever, *simpatico*—to people, to animals ranging from anteaters to dolphins to whales, to situations, to the whole damn world, when you came down to it.

But those dark-blue eyes, so unnervingly like other eyes that lately, when business was mentioned, slid evasively away from her own . . . Annie struggled back to the present, determined to focus on Laurel.

". . . have always tried to be so open to experience, so *welcoming*. If you know what I mean?"

Annie deliberately turned her thoughts away from Laurel's five marriages. And why, after so many trips to the altar, was Laurel persisting in not marrying their neighbor, Howard Cahill, who would be such an attractive father-in-law, so stable, so respectable?

". . . so *disappointed* when Alice didn't come."

It was not the first time in their acquaintance, which was surely long in content if not in time, that Annie was left staring at Laurel in hopeless confusion.

Alice?

Who was Alice? Had they been talking about someone named Alice?

"Alice?" she murmured uncertainly.

"Oh, my dear." A wave of a graceful hand, the pink-tinted nails glossed to perfection. "Certainly you know all about Alice."

Alice Springs? Alice in Wonderland? Alice Blue

Gown? Annie pounced on the latter. "Alice Blue Gown?" she proposed hopefully. It was just offbeat enough to be the answer.

But Laurel was pursuing her own thoughts, which, understandably, could well occupy her fully. Annie had seen the day when Laurel's thoughts had occupied many minds more than hers. But it was better not to dwell upon the past. Though that period—the one with saints—had held its own unique charms. It was at moments such as this, indeed, that Annie herself was likely to call upon the excellent advice of Saint Vincent Ferrer. *(Ask God simply to fill you with charity, the greatest of all virtues; with it you can accomplish what you desire.)* Annie surely needed heaps of charity in order to attain patience, a definite requisite for an amiable relationship with her mother-in-law.

". . . thirteen times backward. I know I did it right. I was counting." Laurel gnawed a shell-pink lip in perplexity. "Annie, do you suppose I could have miscounted?"

"Certainly not," Annie assured her.

Palms uplifted, despite the notebook and No. 2 pencil, Laurel exclaimed, "Then it's quite beyond me! Because Alice definitely didn't come."

Annie decided to explore this cautiously. "You were expecting her?"

Her mother-in-law dropped the notebook and pencil on the nearest table, opened her carryall, and pulled out a sheaf of Polaroid pictures, the bulky self-developing camera, and several road maps. "It just came to me—you know the way things do"—an enchanting smile—"that it would be so *useful* to take photos on the spot. And, of course, if anyone should be there, how wonderful to be able to show skeptics. *Seeing* is, as someone once said so cleverly, *believing*." The golden head bent over the pile of photographs. "I'm marking the exact date and time on the back of each picture. It's easy as pie with the tripod and one of those clever electronic controls—so magical, just like the television remote—so I can be in the pictures, too." She beamed at Annie and handed her a photograph.

Annie was halfway to a smile when she felt her face freeze. Oh, God. It looked like . . . Surely it wasn't . . .

"Laurel." Annie swallowed tightly and stared at the photo of——

". . . really, one of my better pictures. Of me, don't you think?"

——Laurel gracefully draped on a marble slab atop a grave, chin cupped in one hand, smiling wistfully toward the camera.

"It would have been quite *perfect* if Alice had come." She stepped close beside Annie, and the scent of violet tickled Annie's nose. "See. There's her name. That's all they put on the slab. Just 'Alice.' "

"Alice," Annie repeated faintly. "She's dead?"

"Of course she's dead!" Laurel exclaimed. "Otherwise," she asked reasonably, "how could she be a *ghost*? And it would have been so convenient! It would be so easy to visit her often. It's a delightful trip from here to Murrells Inlet, and the All Saints Cemetery is lovely, Annie, just lovely. So many people have seen Alice after circling her grave thirteen times backward, then calling her name or lying atop the slab. I did both," she confided. A sudden frown. "Perhaps that was the problem. Too much. But"—a winsome smile replaced the frown—"I took some lovely notes." She patted the notebook in satisfaction. "I do intend to devote a good deal of space to Alice. After all, it's such a heartrending story, a young woman in love, separated from her beloved by her family because they thought he wasn't suitable, spirited away from her beloved home to school in Charleston. One final night of gaiety at the St. Cecilia Ball, then stricken with illness and when they brought her home, they found her young man's ring on the pale-blue silk ribbon around her neck, and her brother took it and threw it away, and while she was dying and delirious she called and called for the ring. Is it any wonder," Laurel asked solemnly, "that Alice is often seen in her old room at The Hermitage or walking in the gardens there? Everyone *knows* she's looking for her ring." A gentle sigh, delicate as a wisp of Spanish moss. "Ah, Love . . . Its power cannot be diminished even by the grave."

If there was an appropriate response to that, Annie didn't know it, so she tried to look sympathetic and interested while glancing unobtrusively toward the clock.

Of course, anyone attuned enough to subtleties to seriously expect to communicate with ghosts wasn't likely to miss a glance at a clock, no matter how unobtrusive.

"Oh, dear, I had no idea it was so late. I must *fly*." Swiftly, those graceful hands whipped the photographs, camera, and maps back into the embroidered carryall. "My duties are not yet done for the day." Laurel backed toward the storeroom door, smiling beneficently. "Give my love to dear Max. I know you two would adore to have me join you for dinner, of course you would, but I do believe that mothers, especially mothers-in-law, should remember that the young must have Their Own Time Together. I try hard not to forget that. Of course, with my commitment to my Work, it's unlikely that I should ever be underfoot." Laurel had backpedaled all the way to the storeroom doorway. "I do believe my book shall be quite unique. It's just a scandal that South Carolina's ghosts have yet to be interviewed. Can you believe that oversight? All of these books are told from the viewpoint of the persons who saw the ghost and I ask you, should they be featured just because they happen to be present when a ghost comes forth—that's a good term, isn't it"—

the doorway framed Laurel's slender form for an instant—
"perhaps that should be my title, *Coming Forth*. Oh, I like
that." She was out of sight now, but the throaty tone, a
combination of Marlene Dietrich, Lauren Bacall, and wood
nymph, carried well. "Do have a delightful dinner, my dar-
lings." The back door opened and closed.

It seemed awfully quiet after Laurel was gone.

Annie, of course, had had plenty of time to call out and
say Max wasn't coming home for dinner tonight and she and
Laurel could drop by the Club.

It wasn't, of course, that she didn't want to tell anybody
(and especially not Laurel?) not only that Max wasn't coming
home, but Annie didn't have any idea where he was.

Or with whom.

The South Carolina Low Country has many charms—a se-
ductive subtropical climate with a glorious profusion of plant
life including flower-laden shrubs, lush carpets of wildflowers, and seventy-five-foot loblolly pines, abundant
wildlife ranging from deer to alligators, and an easy-paced
life-style characterized by graciousness and the loveliest accent in all of America—but the coastal road system, once off
the interstates, is not one of them. The narrow two-lane
blacktops curve treacherously through pine groves and skirt
swamps, affording few chances to pass.

Max leaned out the window of his Maserati, straining in
vain to peer around the empty horse trailer bouncing behind
an old Ford pickup. Every so often he glanced at the clock in
the dash. Events had conspired against him. The ferry was
late leaving Broward's Rock. He'd chafed at the delay; then,
once on the mainland, he'd realized he'd better stop for gas.
Laurel was in the habit of borrowing his car and this time
she'd returned it with the gas gauge damn near a dead soldier. The little country gas station, perhaps not a good

choice, had been jammed. He wondered if the attendants were selling drugs on the side or maybe the crowd had something to do with the cerise cabin festooned with streamers advertising "Tanning Booths." So much for bucolic innocence.

Every minute lost made Max more frantic, even though he was sure the deaths Courtney Kimball had asked him to investigate were exactly what they appeared to be, just as he'd told her in the report he made yesterday. When he'd concluded, she'd asked sharply, "You didn't find anything out of order? Anything at all?" He'd spent several hours in dusty records at the county courthouse, studying files from the coroner's office. They confirmed the information he'd found in old news stories. That's what he told Courtney. She looked at him, her eyes dark with unhappiness. "There has to be a way—" She broke off, seemed to acquiesce, paid his fee. He'd thought that was the end of it.

Until the call this evening, the shocking, incomplete call. Words tumbled over each other, frantic and incomplete: "Help . . . got to have help . . . the cemetery . . . Ross's grave . . . oh, hurr—" And the line went dead.

He'd dialed her number.

No answer.

Ring after ring.

And now, this damn truck—impatiently, he swung out the nose of the sports car, then yanked hard right on the wheel.

A Mercedes blazed past in the facing lane, horn blaring.

Fuming and chafing, his eyes watering from the pickup's bilious exhaust, Max finally found clearance to pass. The speedometer needle raced to the right. That broken cry, ". . . oh, hurr—" Help? What kind of help? The fear in her voice spelled danger. The Maserati plunged forward, born to race.

·   ·   ·

Annie's hands gripped the telephone like a vise, but she had her voice under control. Just barely. "No, Cynthia, none of Max's sisters are in town."

Cynthia waited for amplification.

Annie smiled grimly and uttered not another word.

"Oh, well." A sniff. "I just thought it had to be one of Max's sisters when I saw him at that wonderful little restaurant in Chastain Monday. You know, the new one with the Paris chef. Especially since the girl was blond and *gorgeous*."

Blond and gorgeous.

"And I was so *surprised* not to see you there." A saccharine laugh.

"A business lunch is a business lunch," Annie said lightly, all the while envisioning excruciating and extensive torture suitable for the middle-aged owner of the gift shop around the corner whom Max had rebuffed at the annual merchants' Christmas party. Cynthia had been snide ever since. "Besides, I've been tied to the store since Ingrid's been sick."

"Oh, that awful spring flu . . ."

Annie doodled on the telephone pad—Cynthia's pudgy, beringed hand took shape. With a flourish Annie added an upward swirl of flame from matches jammed beneath the fingertips.

It was fully dark by the time the Maserati screeched to a stop beside the church. Max grabbed the flashlight from the car pocket, then flung himself out of the car. He thudded toward the massive bronze gates of the cemetery. As he shoved them open, the car lights switched off behind him.

The golden nimbus of light from the nearest street lamp offered scant illumination, succeeding only in emphasizing the shifting mass of darkness beneath the immense, low-limbed live oaks with their dangling veils of Spanish moss. The narrow cone from the flashlight wasn't much help. Beyond its focus, the crumbling headstones, many awkwardly tilted by roots or undermined by fall torrents, were dimly seen patches of grayness. Leaves crunched underfoot. A twig snapped sharply. Max stopped and listened.

"Courtney? Courtney?" he called softly. "Miss Kimball?"

Palmetto fronds clicked in the freshening breeze.

A bush rustled, and the thick sweet smell of wisteria enveloped him. The lights of a passing car swept briefly across the graveyard.

A raccoon scampered atop a marble burial vault.

An owl in a live oak turned glowing eyes toward him.

He looked down and took a reluctant step forward. A silky strand of Spanish moss brushed his cheek, as gauzy and insubstantial as a half-forgotten memory.

The swinging arc from the flashlight illuminated a cloth purse, half open, lying on the leaf-strewn path next to the Tarrant family plot. The beam steadied. It was an unusual purse with pink and beige and blue geometric patterns. The day he'd first met Courtney Kimball, she'd placed it on the bar when she opened it to reach inside for her checkbook.

The policeman's head swiveled around at the muted roar from the television set flickering in the corner of the station house, then swung back to face Max. "Home run." His stolid voice was surly.

Max was damned if he was going to apologize for interrupting a man obviously more interested in Braves baseball than a missing woman.

"Look." Max didn't try to keep the urgency out of his voice. God, how much time had passed? He'd called out for Courtney Kimball, searched as well as he could in a dark landscape that swallowed up the fragile beam of his flashlight, then, grabbing up the purse, he'd run to the nearest house and asked the nervous woman shielded behind a chained, partially open door for directions to the police station. It had taken another six minutes to get here. And now, this dolt wanted to watch a damn ball game. "We need to get men out there to—"

"Cemetery at St. Michael's, right?"

Finally, finally. "Right."

The policeman—his name tag read SGT. G. T. MATTHEWS —fastened faded blue eyes on Max. "Let's see your driver's license, mister."

"Oh my God, this is a waste of time. We've got to—"

"License, mister." Matthews stuck out a broad, stubby hand, palm up.

Time, time. Everything took time.

Max clenched his fists in frustration as Matthews laboriously wrote down the information from the license.

When the sergeant finally looked up, his gaze was still skeptical. "Okay, Mr. Darling. Let's see if I got you right. You had a date with this woman—this Courtney Kimball— in a graveyard."

"Not a date. A business engagement." Even as he spoke, Max knew how odd that sounded.

"Oh, yeah, excuse me. A business engagement back by the mausoleum with the broken palm tree. I believe that's what you said." Narrowed eyes now. "Mighty peculiar place to conduct business, Mr. Darling."

"I suppose there was something Ms. Kimball wanted to show me at the Tarrant plot." Max tried to keep his voice level, his temper intact. "She was scared. She called me and she was scared as hell. The call broke off. I don't know why or how."

The policeman rubbed his nose. "No phone booths at the cemetery. If she was scared, needed 'help,' why didn't she tell you to come where she was? Why the cemetery?"

"I don't know." Max spaced out the words. "But she

did. I came as fast as I could, but when I got there, all I found was her purse, flung down on the path. Now, what does that look like to you?"

"Looks like the lady lost her purse," the sergeant said mildly. He held up a broad palm at Max's fierce frown. "Okay, okay, we'll check into it. We'll be in touch, Mr. Darling."

Max almost erupted, but what good would it do? With a final glare at the uncooperative lawman, Max turned away. He banged out of the station house and slammed into his sports car. He hunched over the wheel. What the hell should he do now? Obviously, it was up to him. Would it do any good to check Courtney Kimball's apartment? Max didn't feel hopeful.

But it was better than nothing.

That took time, too. He had Courtney Kimball's address, but he didn't know Chastain. He didn't find any help at the nearest convenience store or at the video express, but an elderly woman walking two elegant Afghan hounds finally came to his assistance.

"Oh, you're very close. That's still in the historic district. The half number probably means a garage apartment. Turn left here on Carmine, go two blocks, turn right on Merridew, young man. It should be in that block."

It was.

A street lamp shone on a bright-white sign: THE ST. GEORGE INN. A lime-green dragon lounged upright against the crimson letter *S,* his tail draped saucily over a front paw.

Max hurried down a flagstoned path past a shadowy pond to the back of the property and an apartment upstairs over the garage. No outside light shone, but lights blazed inside and there was a murmur of sound. Voices?

Max took the outside stairs two at a time, relief washing through him. Maybe it was going to be all right. Maybe it was a lost purse, just like the cop suggested. After all, Max had been late—though not that late—but Courtney Kimball was a driven woman. Certainly in the brief contact they'd had, Max had recognized a strong will. There was, in Courtney's single-minded concentration on the Tarrant family, a chilling sense of implacability. Just so did the narrator seek to find the secrets of the House of Usher.

At the top of the stairs, he realized two disturbing facts at the same time.

The door was ajar.

The voices, impervious to interruption, flowed from a television set.

Max knocked sharply. The door swung wide.

The voices—amusing light chatter from an old movie —continued unabated, as unreal as a paper moon, masking the absolute quiet of the unguarded apartment.

Max stepped inside. "Courtney? Courtney, are you—"

Disarray.

A hasty search had begun. Cushions littered the floor. Desk drawers jutted open. Papers spewed from a briefcase tipped over on a coffee table. But across the room sat a Chippendale desk, its drawers closed, and through an open door, Max glimpsed a colonial bedroom, the four-poster canopied bed neatly made, the oxbow chest undisturbed.

A search begun. A search interrupted?

He called out again.

The flippant voices from the television rose and fell.

If Courtney Kimball was here, she couldn't answer.

Chapter 7.

Annie recognized him at once and knew his arrival meant trouble.

Chastain Police Chief Harry Wells wasn't a forgettable man, not from his slablike face to his ponderous black boots, now solidly planted on her front porch.

Wells hadn't changed a whit since she'd last seen him. His wrinkled black jacket, white shirt, and tan trousers were just as she remembered. The crown of his white cowboy hat was as smooth and undented as a river-washed stone, and his rheumy, red-veined eyes surveyed her like a hangman measuring rope.

Annie didn't hesitate. "What do you want?" she demanded.

Dislike flickered in his eyes. Dislike and a flash of malicious pleasure.

Annie braced herself.

"I'm investigating a disappearance in Chastain, Miz Darling." Wells's words had the lilting cadence of South

Carolina, but even that glorious accent couldn't mask the threat in his tone. "Your husband's involved. I want to know about this woman he was meeting." His eyes clung to her face, greedy for her response.

The blows were so rapid, Annie felt stunned and sick.

Woman.

Chastain.

Disappearance.

Max.

Only the adrenaline flowing from the shock of Wells's unexpected appearance kept her on her feet.

That and hot, swift, unreasoning fear.

"Max! Where is he?" She gripped the door for support.

"He's safe enough." Wells's voice scraped like a rusty cemetery gate. "Right now he's in the county jail. Under arrest as a material witness. Who was she, Miz Darling?"

When she didn't answer immediately, the burly police chief leaned forward. It was, she remembered, a favorite trick of his, using his commanding height to intimidate. His sour breath swept over her. "So you didn't know about her. Well, that doesn't surprise me, Miz Darling. I understand she's good-lookin'. A mighty cute blonde. The kind a man would go a far piece to keep his wife from finding out about. Thing is, those kind of women get insistent, say they're going to tell the man's wife—"

Later, Annie was proud of her quickness because she understood in a flash: Wells was going to accuse Max of an affair and blame the disappearance of this woman—what woman, oh Max, what woman?—on Max's determination to keep the truth from her. But despite the shock, there was an immediate, elemental response too deep for words. Annie couldn't know the truth of anything—except Max would never injure a living soul.

Not Max.

Never Max.

She clapped her hands to her hips and thrust out her chin. "Get real, Wells." Her voice dripped disgust. "Max had a business engagement this evening. If some client's in trouble, if something's happened to her, it's because of the problem she brought to him. And no, I don't know what that is. Or who she is. Or care. I run a bookstore, Chief, and I don't try to work two jobs. Max takes care of his own business. But I'll tell you this, you're wasting your time talking to me. Did you say she's disappeared? Then you'd better get back to Chastain and start looking for her—and listen real hard to what Max has to tell you." With that she turned and marched back into the house.

Wells started to follow.

Annie yanked her coat out of the front closet and scooped up her purse from the hall table. "Nobody asked you in," she snapped, facing him in the doorway like an outraged terrier staring down a mastiff, "and I'm leaving."

"Now wait a minute, Miz Darling." He backed out onto the porch, his face turning a choleric purple. "If you won't cooperate with lawful—"

"You don't run a damn thing on Broward's Rock." She slammed the door. "If you try and detain me, I'll file the biggest lawsuit for illegal restraint you've ever seen." She marched down the steps, heading for her Volvo. "See you in Chastain, Chief."

By the time a sleepy magistrate agreed to release Max on his own recognizance, there were no more ferries to the island. They found a motel, The Pink Flamingo, on the outskirts of Chastain. As the door shut behind them, Annie glanced at the clock on the bedside table. Almost three A.M.

"The sorry bastard."

Annie knew who Max meant. The brief drive from the jail had consisted of one furious diatribe by Max.

Max gave her an exhausted, despairing look. "God, Annie, this is a mess."

"We'll handle it." She reached out to take his hand.

He looked down abruptly and smiled, the first smile she'd seen since he'd been ushered out of his cell.

Annie smiled in return. This was Max, her Max. "Tell me."

He gave her hand a hard squeeze and nodded, then dropped wearily into the bedroom's sole chair. Annie propped up some pillows on the lumpy bed and curled up to listen. It didn't take long to tell: the original assignment, his report, tonight's phone call, the purse at the cemetery, Courtney's apartment.

He popped up and began to pace the small confines of the motel room, the old wooden floor creaking beneath him. "I started looking for Courtney. It didn't take long to be sure she wasn't in that apartment. I was heading for the phone to call the cops when this voice yelled, 'Hands up,' and I turned around to look into the barrel of the biggest damn gun I've ever seen. It was my old friend, Sergeant Matthews." Scowling, Max flung himself down again in the chair. "So I guess I've got to give the Chastain cops some credit. Matthews brushed me off at the station, but he did come to check Courtney's apartment. Of course, he won't listen when I say that's what I was doing, too. Hell, no. He decides I'm 'acting suspiciously' and there's evidence of a crime scene—did he think I trashed the damn place? So I wind up in jail. And I'm the one who got the cops stirred up! Can you believe it?" His voice rose in outrage. "Anyway, it was about an hour later that Wells lumbered in."

"Chief Caligula," Annie said resentfully.

That brought another brief smile, quickly gone. Max's eyes narrowed. "Here's where it gets interesting." A speculative note quickened his voice. "Wells asked why I was meeting 'the missing woman' in the cemetery."

Annie rolled to a sitting position and slipped her arms around her knees.

Max leaned forward. "Now, listen closely, Annie. I'm going to tell you exactly what I told Wells. Okay?"

"Sure." She didn't understand her role yet, but Max obviously had something in mind.

Max's tone was formal. "On Monday, I received a call from a woman who subsequently identified herself as Courtney Kimball. She inquired about the kinds of projects undertaken by Confidential Commissions."

Max had chosen his words carefully in dealing with Wells. The sovereign state of South Carolina has very particular requirements for the licensing of private detectives, several of which Max could not meet (two years of work in an existing licensed agency or two years as a law enforcement officer), and Max was not licensed to practice law in South Carolina, which eschews reciprocity with other states (South Carolina has no intention of making it easy for retired lawyers from other climes to pick up some pocket change). Wells would dearly love to nail Max for acting illegally in either capacity. The chief still harbored resentment against both Annie and Max from their encounter several years ago during the Chastain house-and-garden tour mystery event that turned to murder.

"I told Wells how I explained to Ms. Kimball that the objective of Confidential Commissions was to provide information and solace to those in the midst of trying times." A bland enough statement that nowise, Max would protest, could be equated to the investigative efforts mounted by private detectives or the counsel proffered by practicing attorneys. "I made it clear that Ms. Kimball asked me to do a historical survey, and I was happy to be able to advise her that I would do my very best to be helpful."

Annie grinned. She wished she could have seen Wells's face.

"I met her Monday at La Maison Rouge in Chastain. She asked me to do two things—"

Annie held up her hand and reached for her purse. When she had a pad and pencil in hand, she nodded for Max to continue.

"One. To find out every possible detail in regard to the deaths of Ross Tarrant and Judge Augustus Tarrant, both of which occurred on May ninth, 1970, in Chastain.

"Two. To determine all the persons living in or present in any capacity at Tarrant House on Ephraim Street in Chastain on May ninth, 1970."

Max's eyes gleamed. "Up to this point, Wells just listened. No expression, of course. I've seen faces at Madame Tussaud's that looked more alive. Until"—Max struck the chair arm sharply—"I mentioned the Tarrants and Tarrant House. All of a sudden, it was different. Damn different. Wells picked up a cigar and lit it, taking his time. He looked at me through a haze of smoke and asked—and here's exactly what he said, Annie—'Who the hell is Courtney Kimball?' He didn't ask me a damn thing about the Tarrants or whether I'd found out anything about their deaths or the people at Tarrant House that day. Oh, no. All of a sudden, he wanted to know about Courtney. That's when he turned hostile and started making cracks about me and my 'relationship' with her, saying I'd be a lot better off if I told the police what had happened to her and stopped trying to create some kind of mystery. Not having slept entirely through Criminal Law, I decided to stop being so damn helpful to the constituted authorities and refused to say another word. So Wells dumped me in jail—"

"And came to the island to see how much I knew."

Max looked at her with startled eyes. "I hadn't stopped to figure out how you turned up with the magistrate. I called you and there wasn't any answer so I called Howard Cahill and asked him to get his lawyer for me." Then the import of her words struck. "Did the sorry bastard imply I was having an affair with her?"

Max's outrage made Annie feel warm and cossetted.

"Don't worry," she said blithely. "I told him you had a business engagement with her."

Max's grin made him look like Joe Hardy (all grown up and sexy as hell) after a winning touchdown. "That's telling him." But the grin didn't touch the dark core of worry in his eyes. He smacked his fist in his palm. "The hell of it is, Wells is concentrating on me. Nobody's doing anything about Courtney."

Annie heard the anguish in his voice. A business engagement, she repeated to herself. That's all that it was. Max was here now with her, loving her. That didn't mean he couldn't be concerned about others.

Courtney Kimball.

Wells wanted to know who the hell she was. Annie made a wreath of question marks around Courtney's name on the pad. Frankly, Annie shared Chief Wells's interest. But she had another question that mattered even more to her. "Max, why didn't you tell me about this assignment?"

Her charming, unflappable husband looked, in turn, sheepish, uncomfortable, and embarrassed.

Very un-Max responses.

Annie tried to keep on breathing evenly.

As if it were just a casual question.

"Well"—it was the closest to hangdog she'd ever seen him—"you kept encouraging me to get involved in an interesting case, and, the thing about it is, I didn't want to get your hopes up that I was into something big. When I finished checking on the Tarrants, everything looked on the up-and-up so I decided not to mention it at all—since it didn't amount to anything."

Dark-blue eyes looked at her mournfully.

Once again, Annie didn't know whether to laugh or to

cry, but she knew one thing for certain: Never again would she exhort Max to work harder.

"Max, I'm never disappointed in you. And," she added a little disjointedly, "it certainly has turned into something."

The worry was back in his eyes, but it was okay now. Now she could ask, "Who is Courtney Kimball, Max?"

He ran a hand through his thick blond hair. "The hell of it is, Annie, I don't have any idea."

"Then I think," Annie told her husband gravely, "we'd better find out."

Annie was glad she wore her hair short, but, even so, without a dryer and using the motel soap (no shampoo), she was certainly going to look totally natural, as in moderately unkempt. It didn't help to pull on yesterday's clothes. The pale-yellow cotton pullover was okay, but the madras skirt looked like something Agatha would happily have nested in. Max had slipped out early. His goals were to buy shaving cream, razor, toothpaste, toothbrushes, et cetera, and to call his secretary, Barb, who would activate the answering machine at Confidential Commissions and take over at Death on Demand in Ingrid's absence. Max won Annie's heart anew when he returned with coffee and a biscuit with sausage for her. The coffee was acceptable, although not, of course, on a par with that at Death on Demand or at the Darling house on Scarlet King Lagoon.

He also brought in a file marked "Courtney Kimball."

Annie took the thick manila folder and looked at him in surprise.

"Barb's terrific. I called, and she brought it over on the first ferry. Said to tell you to relax, she'd take care of everything at the store and get some chicken soup to Ingrid, too. Now"—he was brisk and organized—"I want you to dive into that file. Maybe you can find something I missed."

Annie put the folder down. "What about you?"

"I'm going to get some answers out of the Chastain cops. Whether they like it or not."

As the door closed behind him, Annie almost called out. But Max would surely be careful. The chief was a tough antagonist. She took the file and her coffee and settled in the chair. The file contained:

The Tarrant Family History
Guide to the Tarrant Museum
Copies of several newspaper stories on the deaths of the
    Honorable Augustus Tarrant and his youngest son, Ross,
    on May 9, 1970.
Photographs of Ross Tarrant's grave and of the urn
    containing the ashes of Judge Tarrant.
A photograph of Tarrant House.
A monograph on Tarrant House.
Photographs of Judge Tarrant and Ross Tarrant.
A list of persons likely to have been in Tarrant House on
    May 9, 1970.

Annie started with the photographs.

Judge Augustus Tarrant, in his black judicial robe, looked sternly down from the bench. His was an aloof, ascetic face, somber gray eyes, a high-bridged nose, hollow cheeks, a pointed chin, firm, pale lips pressed tightly together. There was no vestige of warmth in his gaze.

Annie would not have wished to be charged with a crime in Judge Tarrant's court.

This was a formal studio portrait.

There were almost a dozen newspaper photographs. Annie particularly studied two of them. One showed a smiling Judge Tarrant—it could have been a different man—

handing a trophy to a teenage girl. The congratulatory smile softened that stern face. The caption reported: *Judge Augustus Tarrant presents the Class of 1969 valedictorian, Serena Michaels, with the National Honor Society trophy.* In the second photograph, Judge Tarrant, unspeaking, head high, was pictured brushing through a crowd of reporters and photographers on the courthouse steps. The caption reported: *Judge Augustus Tarrant declined to comment as he left the courthouse after giving the maximum sentence possible to David Wister Marton, a longtime friend and former state representative convicted of bribery. In a nonjury trial, Marton was judged guilty of accepting money from the Lumont Construction Company in return for achieving passage of legislation favorable to the company.*

So the Judge was not a good old boy.

Good for the Judge.

Tough shit for Marton.

The photographs of Ross Tarrant were much more appealing. Annie studied the lively freckled face—a blond cowlick, merry blue eyes, an infectious grin—and realized her own lips had curved in response.

She thumbed through a sheaf of photographs: Ross astride a chestnut jumper at a horse show with a group of girls waving and calling to him; Ross, one of five sunburned happy faces on a tip-tilted catamaran just beyond the surf; Ross with his arms around two pretty girls, one dark, one fair, both laughing up at him; Ross in tennis shorts and shirt standing on a scuffed clay court, holding his racquet like a rifle. In a formal studio portrait, Ross wore full cadet regalia and stared straight into the camera. But wasn't there just the hint of a smile at the corners of his mouth and a dancing light in his blue eyes? Over the years and the gulf that could not be crossed, she felt a sense of loss that she'd never known him. She would have liked him.

Annie replaced the photographs and picked up the copies of the news stories from the *Chastain Courier.*

Prominent Family Loses Father, Son in Double Tragedy

The Honorable Augustus Tarrant, 63, suffered a fatal heart attack Saturday after learning of the death of his youngest son, Ross, 21, in an apparent shooting accident.

Harmon Brevard, Ross's grandfather, found the body of The Citadel senior at the family hunting lodge on Deer Creek in late afternoon. After calling authorities, Brevard went to the family home, the well-known Tarrant House, to inform the family.

Judge Tarrant collapsed upon hearing the news. The family physician, Dr. Paul Rutledge, was immediately summoned, but the jurist died before he could be hospitalized.

Funeral arrangements have not yet been announced.

The father and son were members of one of Chastain's oldest and most influential families. Tarrants have played prominent roles in Chastain and in the history of South Carolina since Mortimer Tarrant arrived in Chastain in 1735. Family members have led efforts to preserve historic sites in and around Chastain.

Judge Tarrant was the son of Nathaniel Robert Tarrant and Rachel Wallace Tarrant. He was born in 1907. A 1928 graduate of The Citadel, he received his law degree from the University of Virginia. In 1937, he married Amanda Brevard of Chastain. Judge Tarrant served in the Circuit Solicitor's office from 1931 to 1936. He joined his father's firm, Tarrant and Tarrant, in 1937 and practiced there until the outbreak of World War II. Judge Tarrant served in the infantry during the War, rising to the rank of lieutenant colonel. He returned to private practice until he became a circuit judge in 1950.

Ross Tarrant was born Jan. 3, 1949. An outstanding student at Chastain's Wellston School, he was an honor student at The

Citadel and would have been graduated this spring.

Judge Tarrant is survived by his wife, Amanda, and two sons, Milam and his wife, Julia, and Whitney and his wife, Charlotte.

Annie sighed. What heartbreak. Two in a family lost the same day. Poor Amanda Tarrant. Her husband and youngest son dead with no warning, no preparation.

Tragic, yes. But what in that family tragedy prompted a young woman to hire a private detective twenty-two years later? (Annie called a spade as she saw it. She didn't have to pretend about Max's occupation, no matter how Max avoided the appellation of private detective.) Why did Courtney Kimball hire Max? Who was Courtney, and why did she care about the deaths of Judge Tarrant and his youngest son?

Annie carefully reread the article, then skimmed the other news stories and the formal obituaries. The facts remained the same. The only additional information concerned funeral arrangements.

She studied the newspaper photograph from the May 12, 1970, *Chastain Courier*. The mourners wore black. They stood beneath umbrellas in a slanting rain among a gray and cheerless sea of tombstones. A veiled woman leaned heavily on the arm of a young man.

The caption read: *The family of Judge Augustus Tarrant and Ross Tarrant bade them farewell Monday at graveside rites in St. Michael's Cemetery. The judge's widow, Amanda, walks with her oldest son, Milam. Also pictured are Mrs. Milam Tarrant, Mr. and Mrs. Whitney Tarrant, and Mr. and Mrs. Harmon Brevard.*

Annie concentrated. Mr. and Mrs. Harmon Brevard? Oh, of course—Amanda's parents, grandparents of Ross, Whitney, and Milam.

The veil hid what must have been the grief-ravaged face of Amanda Tarrant. Her son Milam had the stolid look of a man enduring great pain. His wife's face was white and pinched. Whitney Tarrant frowned, the kind of frown a man makes to hold back tears. His wife, Charlotte, pressed a hand against her mouth. Harmon Brevard stared grimly at an open grave site. His wife touched a handkerchief to her eyes.

A sorrowing family.

Annie riffled through several more stories and found nothing that changed the import of the initial report.

She returned the photographs and clippings to the file and picked up *The Tarrant Family History* and *Guide to the Tarrant Museum,* both cream-colored pamphlets with crimson printing. A yellow tab on the outside of the history carried an inscription in Max's handwriting: *Received from Courtney Kimball.*

Annie looked through the *Guide to the Tarrant Museum.* She was startled when she realized the museum was housed in former slave quarters toward the back of the Tarrant grounds. Wow, this was Family and History in capital letters, although it was clear, despite the obviously biased introduction by Mrs. Whitney Tarrant, its founder, that the museum housed some interesting and valuable collections, including playbills from early traveling shows. *The Orphan or the Unhappy Marriage* was presented in 1735, shortly after its initial production in Charleston. In 1754, a traveling troupe put on *A Bold Stroke for a Wife, The Mock Doctor,* and *Cato.* The museum housed the personal letters of Hope Tarrant, who spent her life opposing slavery and was one of the earliest to speak out in South Carolina, along with Angelina and Sarah Grimke. Copies of many of the various Chastain newspapers from 1761 to 1815 were featured. (Three had belonged to Tarrants, of course.)

Annie put down the guide reluctantly. A hodgepodge, yes, but such an interesting mélange from the past.

The Tarrant Family History was also written by Mrs. Whitney Tarrant. Was she perhaps a trifle obsessive? Annie skimmed the introduction: . . . *distinguished family from the outset of Mortimer Tarrant's arrival . . . the author's aim is to provide ensuing generations with a record of bravery, devotion to duty, and honor . . . gallantry both in war and peace . . . exemplary conduct which can ever serve as a shield in good times and bad. . . .*

The introduction was signed by Mrs. Whitney Tarrant and dated September 14, 1987. In parentheses following the date, it read: *Marking the two hundred and fifty-second year of the Tarrant Family in Chastain, South Carolina.*

Annie raised a blond brow. My, aren't we proud of ourselves! But she turned to the first page and dutifully began to read.

"Chief's not in." Sergeant Matthews's pale eyes returned to the papers on his desk.

Max leaned on the doorjamb and drawled, "No doubt he is leading a posse in search of wrongdoers even as we speak."

The sergeant looked up, blinked once, then ostentatiously began to straighten the papers before him.

"Any trace of Courtney?" The drawl was gone.

Matthews ignored him.

Max crossed the brief space to the desk in two strides, leaned over, and knocked sharply. The papers quivered.

Sergeant Matthews's head jerked up, and his pink cheeks deepened to tomato. "You want to go back to jail?"

"Jail?" Max exclaimed. "Jail? In law school, I must have missed the section where it's against the law to undertake polite intercourse with the properly constituted authorities of a municipality."

As always, the magic reference worked. Max almost felt a moment of shame and wondered anew at the undeserved deference paid—even if grudgingly—to anyone possessing a law degree.

"The chief'll be in around ten."

"That's all right. You can help me." Max's tone was brisk. "What progress has been made in the search for Courtney Kimball?" At Matthews's look of dogged resistance, Max continued crisply. "I want everything that's part of the public record."

He knew damned well the sergeant wasn't certain what constituted a public record.

Max didn't enlighten him.

When Annie closed the cream-colored pamphlet, she knew with certainty that Mrs. Whitney Tarrant was not going to be a bosom chum. Annie was willing to bet that Charlotte Tarrant was extremely serious, extremely humorless, and quite boring. *The Tarrant Family History* resounded with grandiloquence: the Tarrants were not only a leading Family, but they always "enjoyed prominence in Society even among their own kind." Of course, in Texas, Annie's place of origin, it mattered most how a man conducted himself today, not where he came from or who his family was. In fact, it was still not considered mannerly to ask where people came from, a harkening back to the days of the Old West when a man might not be exactly eager to reveal his past. Now, as then, it was the present that counted.

However, there were glimpses of the past that not even Charlotte's labored prose could trivialize.

The heartbreak when five daughters—Anna, Abigail, Ruth, Margaret, and Victoria—were lost to yellow fever in 1747.

The loss of a younger son, Edward, his wife, Emily, and their three children in a storm at sea when he was taking them to safety in Philadelphia as the Revolution began.

With her husband, Miles, gone from Chastain to serve in Sumter's army, his wife, Mary, sallied forth to oversee the outlying plantations. Mary managed a bit of work for the Revolution as well, smuggling papers or food, information or boots, whatever the moment required. Her devotion to her infant nation was repaid with grief: Miles perished in a British prison camp just two weeks before the end of the war.

But happier days were to come. The land overflowed with plenty when Tarrant rice was sold in every market at home and abroad and wealth poured in. Oh, the dances and the convivial dinners when nothing was too grand for guests. These survivors of war and deprivation embodied in their lives the ideals for which they had fought. Of first importance was a man's honor.

The code of chivalry was understood:

A man's word was his bond.

A woman's name was never uttered except with respect.

A promise, whether wise or foolish, must be kept.

A man must always be prepared to fight for his name, his state, or his love.

Tarrant men died in duels in 1812, 1835, and 1852. Michael Evan Tarrant was seventeen years, three months, and two days of age when he bled to death "near the great oak on the bluff above the harbour after meeting in combat in an open field." Another, Roderick Henry, shot his own gun into the air, refusing, he said as he lay dying, to permit another man to make him into a murderer.

Tarrants had survived or been felled by warfare and pestilence. Then came fire. Tarrant House, the first structure on the present grounds, burned to the ground in 1832. All were rescued from the inferno except Catherine, the mistress of the house, a victim of paralysis. Catherine was tragically trapped in her bedroom on the second floor.

A daughter, Elizabeth, defied her family and eloped with a young man from Beaufort. Her father wanted her to marry an older widowed planter. The breach between Elizabeth and her family was never healed.

South Carolina on December 20, 1860, was the first of eleven states to secede from the Union.

Four Tarrant sons perished in The War Between the States: Philip, twenty-five, at Fort Beauregard in one of the earliest engagements; Samuel, twenty-two, who drowned trying to run the blockade; and William, nineteen, of yellow fever at Manassas. The second son, Robert, twenty-four, was a graduate of West Point, who served in the Union Army. During the third year of the War, he made his way through the lines to come home as he'd heard his sister Grace was ill with typhoid. His father, Henry, home with a wound suffered at Chancellorsville, met him at the door and refused him entrance. They struggled. Robert was stronger and he pushed his way past to go upstairs to his sister's sickroom. There was a gunshot. Robert fell on the stairway landing, mortally wounded. A dark stain marks the top step, and no manner of scrubbing has ever been able to remove it. During the long war years, the women of Tarrant House cut up curtains to make clothes, tore down the copper gutters, which were melted and used for torpedoes, took in sick and injured soldiers and nursed them back to health or buried them. But one by one came the news of the deaths of the sons of the house. Henry Tarrant did not recover from his wound, though some believed he died of a broken heart. His widow, Emma, and their remaining son, Thomas, by guile and wile, despite the loss of all the outlying plantations, somehow managed each year to pay the taxes and so were able to hold onto Tarrant House.

Quiet years followed after the War. Then in 1895, Nathaniel Tarrant wed a wealthy young woman from Detroit. One son, Peter, was disowned in 1920, his name never spoken. It was said that he ended his short life in Paris, a painter. He was Augustus Tarrant's older brother. Augustus had three sisters. Two, Sophie and Catherine, were lost in the great flu epidemic of 1918. His other sister, Abigail, scandalized the family by going to work for a newspaper. She married a foreign correspondent in 1933 and for almost a decade letters with exotic stamps arrived at Tarrant House erratically. She was killed in the bombardment of Singapore in 1942.

Annie felt awash with tragedy. Certainly, the death of Ross Tarrant in a gunshot accident and the Judge's demise were part of a long chain of bloodshed and sorrow.

And why had any of this mattered to Courtney Kimball in the Year of Our Lord Nineteen Ninety-Two?

The wooden front porch was painted white. A green wooden swing hung at one end. Wicker chairs were interspersed with potted ferns. The white paint of the frame house glistened and had almost certainly been recently applied. Although converted now from a private residence, the St. George Inn was an excellent example of the typical Chastain house: freestanding on a large lot among magnificent oaks, a two-story, frame construction on a brick foundation. Wide porches across the front extended around the sides, and huge bay windows rose from floor to ceiling.

Beyond the screen door, the front door was open wide, as it had probably stood in good weather for two hundred and fifty years, to take full advantage of the prevailing southeasterly breezes.

Max poked the doorbell beside a smaller sign with the insouciant dragon.

"Come in," a woman's deep voice ordered.

Max obeyed, stepping into the dimness of a wide hall floored in gleaming heart pine. The wallpaper, green, dark brown, and rose, pictured Greek ruins amid trees that looked vaguely like eucalyptus.

Through a door to the right, a remarkably large

woman rose from behind a delicate Chippendale desk. Smiling, she walked toward Max. "I'm Caroline Gentry. Welcome to the St. George Inn. How may I help you?"

Her voice was a rich contralto. It matched her size—almost six feet—and bulk. She had large, expressive brown eyes in a heart-shaped face and dark-brown hair in a tidy coronet braid. Garbed in some kind of loose-flowing black dress, she stood as straight as a statue.

Max introduced himself. "I'd like to rent a room for myself and my wife for several days, if you have a vacancy."

But Mrs. Gentry was staring at him, her eyes suspicious. "I saw you," she said abruptly. "Last night. When the police came to my garage apartment."

He met her gaze directly. "That's right. I came here to look for Ms. Kimball. She is a client of mine—and she didn't show up for an appointment."

"In the paper this morning, it said she'd disappeared. So why do you want to come here? Why do you want to stay at my inn?" She folded her arms across her solid midriff.

"Because I don't intend to leave Chastain until I've found her." Max's eyes never wavered. "I don't care how long it takes. And here's where she was staying. Maybe I can learn something from that, from you."

"I don't know anything about her. I'd never seen her before in my life until she came here Monday." Her deep voice was angry.

"Did she tell you anything—"

"I showed her the apartment. That's the only time I ever talked to her. If I'd had any idea she was going to get in trouble, I'd never have let her in. This kind of publicity can ruin an inn. I've already had three cancellations since the paper came out this morning. A wedding party."

"Mrs. Gentry, the sooner we find Ms. Kimball, the better off you'll be. Give me one of those cancellations."

It hung in the balance, but finally, grudgingly, she nodded.

Max had one more question as he filled out the registration. "Do you know why Ms. Kimball came here? Why she picked this place to stay?"

Her dark eyes were unreadable, but the moment stretched until Max knew there was an answer. He waited, scarcely daring to breathe.

She picked up the registration slip, then said abruptly, "She said Miss Dora told her to come here. Miss Dora's—"

Max nodded, completed the sentence. "Miss Dora Brevard."

He and Annie first met Dora Brevard when Annie put together the mystery program for Chastain's annual house-and-garden tours one spring.

Miss Dora, who knew everything there was to know about Chastain. Max felt a stirring of hope.

By the time Annie finished reading the monograph (also authored by Charlotte Tarrant) on the history of Tarrant House, she had a good understanding of how to make tabby for foundations (a combination of oyster shells, sand, and a lime obtained through the burning of oyster shells), the popularity of Corinthian capitals, and the reason for the ever-present pineapple motif (pineapples indicated prosperity and hospitality). As far as she could tell, the important point about Tarrant House was that it had stood in all its Greek Revival glory on that lot since 1840, and was one of the few homes in Chastain still in the hands of the original family.

But, shades of Laurel, if she could be permitted that phrase, Tarrant House did have a very interesting background in ghosts.

Background in ghosts? Of ghosts?

Annie was unsure how to say it.

Laurel would know.

The telephone rang.

Startled, Annie knocked over her almost—but not quite empty—Styrofoam cup.

The phone continued to ring as she bolted to the bath and grabbed up a face towel to mop up the coffee, saving *The Tarrant Family History* from desecration.

Another peal of the phone. Was Max once again being permitted a single call?

"Hello." She tried to sound in command, ready for anything.

"Dear Annie."

God, it was Laurel. Which was almost spooky. Except surely there was an obvious and rational explanation. Laurel must have called Barb, Max's secretary, to track them down. However, Annie would have remarked upon the coincidence of Laurel calling at the precise moment Annie was thinking of her, but Laurel's words riveted her attention.

"You are feeling beleaguered! That is evident from the strain in your voice. My dearest, I have called to offer my services and I *shall* come. Even though it will require an ambulance. I cannot—"

"Ambulance! Laurel, where are you? What's wrong? What's happened?" Annie moved the file away from the damp spot on the desk.

"A *minor* contretemps." For once, the throaty voice lacked its usual élan, verging indeed upon embarrassment. "I am in Charleston, surely one of the loveliest cities of the world and filled with the *most* hospitable, charming people, most of whom are quite sophisticated about the specters in their midst, such as dear young Dr. Ladd at the house in Church Street and the rattling wheels of Ruth Simmons's coach on Tradd Street. I am confident that all true Charlestonians would agree that it is permissible to resort to deceit when obdurate personalities thwart reasonable goals."

"Laurel"—Annie said it gently but firmly—"in words of one syllable, what happened?"

Shorn of elaborate circumlocution, Laurel's recital boiled down to trespassing late at night upon posted property, entering a condemned building, tumbling down ramshackle stairs, and severely spraining not one, but both ankles. "I quite fail to understand the exceedingly unpleasant response of the property owners, who have refused to cooperate with psychical researchers despite the fact that a most delightful and energetic ghost is reputed to have lived there. At least, we are almost *certain* this is the right house. The story goes that a little girl, Lavinia, came there to live with two old aunts after her parents died. Lavinia enjoyed the third floor—I was on the third floor when I fell—such a long way down—and one day as the poor child ran up the steps, she was surprised to hear running steps beside her. Well, the long and the short of it is, though she never saw anyone, Lavinia realized the steps belonged to a ghost, whom she called Pinky. Now, Lavinia and Pinky had such fun together. They danced and ran and skipped. But, as happens to us all, Lavinia grew up—and she met a young man in whom she was very interested. Of course, the first thing she did was to tell Pinky—and I'm sorry to report that Pinky was *most* jealous, and now instead of dancing feet there were ugly stamps. Temper, you see. And he rapped angrily on the walls and tossed objects about." (Obviously, despite the name, Pinky was a boy ghost.) "But Lavinia was in love. Finally, when Pinky's temper didn't improve, Lavinia told him to go away and never come back.

"Silence. No more companionable footsteps. Pinky was gone. Lavinia—such a kindhearted girl—tried to coax him back, promising they would always be friends, even though she dearly loved Kenneth and they were going to marry. But Pinky didn't return.

"It was a lovely wedding in the front parlor. That night she and Kenneth came upstairs to her room for their honeymoon. That was the custom then. When they were ready for bed, Kenneth turned down the oil wick and all of a sudden there were great raps and stamping and clothes flew about. Kenneth jumped out of bed, turned up the wick, and looked about in astonishment. Pinky yanked on Kenneth's nightshirt. It was then that Lavinia explained to her bridegroom about her ghost. Kenneth was as aggravated as could be. Lavinia tried to persuade Pinky to be a good ghost and, finally, she laughed and said they'd just have to put up with it, that's all they could do. And so, they began their new life together. The three of them."

"Three," Annie said ominously, "is a hell of a crowd."

"Oh, I rather thought Lavinia was a dear—making room in her life for everyone."

Annie wasn't going to pursue this conversation. As far as she was concerned, conjugal frolics definitely were limited to two. She almost said so, then decided to get to the heart of the matter.

"Both ankles?"

"I am *prostrate*. However, nothing shall keep me from Max's side when he is in need. As soon as I talked to Barb this morning—my dear, she's having such fun at Death on Demand, playing with Agatha and reading—my duty was clear. I shall order an ambulance immediately and come to Chastain." Rustlings of an uncertain nature sounded on the telephone line. "So difficult to keep one's papers in order when confined to bed. But now I have paper and pen. Where are you in Chastain?"

"Oh, Laurel"—and if ever Annie had sounded heartfelt it was at this moment—"I cannot tell you how your devotion to duty touches me and how much it will mean to Max, but clearly it is your responsibility to stay in Charleston. Don't you feel that it was meant that you should have an uninterrupted period of quiet to ponder the wondrous information you have collected and perhaps to make a substantial start upon your book?"

"Can you dear young people cope without me?" Laurel obviously had her doubts.

"Laurel"—Annie felt as if she had been inspired—"we shall call upon you, yes. But not to come here. After all, we are in communication at this moment, even more closely than those who have gone before communicate with we who have come after." Even if she had to say so herself, this was an especially nice touch. "We shall call you daily and share our investigation with you and you will be able to provide leadership and encouragement."

Laurel's satisfied murmurs were as liquid as the call of mourning doves. They parted with mutual protestations of affection, respect, and good intent.

Annie was grinning as she returned to her papers. Funny, the way Laurel had phoned just as Annie reached the part about the ghosts of Tarrant House. For a split instant, Annie felt the sting of guilt. Wasn't it heartless not to share that surely fascinating information with their own intrepid ghost-seeker? But there would be ample opportunity during the calls aimed at keeping Laurel safely in Charleston.

Besides, right now, Annie was more interested in flesh-and-blood Tarrants, especially those who had been in Tarrant House the day Judge Tarrant and his youngest son died.

Annie picked up that list.

PERSONS KNOWN TO HAVE BEEN IN

TARRANT HOUSE

MAY 9, 1970

Judge Augustus Tarrant, 63

Amanda Brevard Tarrant, 52

Harmon Brevard, 73

Ross Tarrant, 21

Milam Tarrant, 28

Julia Martin Tarrant, 26

Whitney Tarrant, 25

Charlotte Walker Tarrant, 25

Dora Brevard, 61

Lucy Jane McKay, 48 (Cook)

Enid Friendley, 39 (Maid)

Sam Willingham, 44 (Butler)

May 9, 1970. A traumatic day for the Tarrant family. How would those still alive remember those hours?

Nineteen-seventy. Annie was six years old. She didn't know now how much she truly remembered of that spring and how much she had learned in later years. But there were words that still struck a chill in her heart and would forever cast a shadow in her mind.

Kent State.

That was 1970 to Annie. She remembered her mother staring at the flickering black-and-white television, tears running down her cheeks.

8 A.M., SATURDAY, MAY 9, 1970

May sunlight sparkled through the open French doors on the ruddy richness of cypress paneling. But neither shining sun nor gleaming wood dispelled the cool formality of the study, musty leather-bound books, crossed swords above the Adam mantel, a yellowed map of early Chastain framed in heavy silver. The room echoed its owner, the books precisely aligned, the desk top bare, the sofa cushions smooth. Judge Augustus Tarrant tolerated disarray neither in his surroundings nor in his life—nor in the lives of his family.

The Judge sat behind the desk as he sat behind the bench, his back straight, his shoulders squared. He scowled at the newspaper. This kind of rebellion couldn't be tolerated. What was wrong with some of these college administrators, giving in, listening, talking? As for closing campuses, that was surrender. It was time to face down the mobs, time to jail those dirty, violent, shouting protesters. Burning the flag! Refusing to serve their country! Who did they think they were? He wished some of them would come before his court.

You had to have standards.

Standards.

Amanda's face, her eyes red-rimmed and beseeching, rose in his mind.

Rage swept him.

Chapter 8.

Max knocked again. "I can't believe she isn't here." He rattled the huge brass knob. "It's not even nine o'clock yet.
Where can she be this early?"

"Out looking for a fresh supply of eye of newt," Annie
suggested as she pressed against the screen to peer into Miss
Dora's unlit dining room. "Or simply disinclined to answer
the door."

"We'll come back." He said it aloud and a little louder
than necessary for Annie to hear.

If the old lady was inside, listening . . . Annie suppressed a shudder. She couldn't think about Miss Dora without remembering embittered old Miss Havisham in *Great
Expectations*, a withered old spinster living among the dust
and decay of her broken dreams.

The cordgrass in the salt marsh rippled in the breeze. Fid-
dler crabs swarmed on the mud flats. The exquisitely blue
sky looked as though it had never harbored clouds, though

the evidence of March rains remained in overflowing drainage ditches on either side of the asphalt road. Thick, oozy-green algae scummed the stagnant water.

Annie welcomed the rush of the mild spring air through the open windows of the Maserati. There was an aura of decay and stagnation about Miss Dora's house, a sense of secrets long held and deeply hid. Had Courtney Kimball knocked on that door? What would have brought her to Miss Dora? Had Courtney stood on that porch, young and alive, intent upon her own mysterious goal only days before? Annie shivered.

Raising her voice to be heard over the rush of wind, she asked crisply, "What about next of kin?"

"The sergeant got real cagey there." Max fumbled in the car pocket, retrieved his sunglasses, and slipped them on.

Annie admired that familiar, so-handsome profile, thick blond hair now attractively ruffled by the wind, the straight nose, firm chin, good-humored mouth. A mouth now tight with worry and irritation.

The Maserati picked up speed. "It's like there's some kind of conspiracy to keep me from finding out anything about Courtney. But at least I got the name of her family lawyer out of Matthews." Max honked at a scrappy-looking black pickup nosing out of a side road. "Honest to God, doesn't anybody down here know what a stop sign's for?"

Absently, Annie defended her adopted state. "I've seen some pretty lousy driving on the back roads of Connecticut." But she was puzzling over Max's information. "A lawyer? Why a lawyer? I mean, usually the cops direct you to a parent or a husband or brother or somebody in a family. Why a lawyer?"

The Beaufort law offices of Smithson, Albright & Caston occupied a—what else?—antebellum buff brick home. (The tasteful bronze plaque noted that the Franklin Beaumont House was built in 1753.) Six Corinthian pillars supported three piazzas.

A chestnut-haired receptionist smiled a sunny welcome as they stepped into the enormous hallway that divided the house.

"I called earlier." There was no mistaking the intensity in Max's voice. "Please tell Mr. Smithson that Max Darling and his wife are here to talk to him about Courtney Kimball." Under one arm, Max carried the file that Annie had studied at the motel.

At the mention of Courtney's name, the young woman's smile fled. "Oh, yes," she murmured. She kept her voice even, but curiosity flared in her eyes. She led them swiftly up the paneled staircase to the second floor and paused to knock on white double doors. She opened the right-hand door. "Mr. Smithson, Mr. Darling is here." As she stood aside for them to enter, she stared at them openly. Annie could feel that avid glance as the door closed behind them.

A slender man in his early sixties with a silver Vandyke beard rose from behind an enormous mahogany desk and hurried toward them. His patrician face was somber, his eyes fearful. "Courtney—is there any word?"

"Not to my knowledge, sir," an equally somber Max replied.

"I had hoped . . ." The lawyer paused, pressed his lips together, then held out his hand to Max. "Roger Smithson."

"Max Darling. My wife, Annie."

"Please." Smithson gestured toward a pair of wing chairs that faced his desk.

When they were seated, the lawyer returned to his desk; then, still standing, he stared down at them, his face intent, suspicious. "On the telephone, you claimed that Courtney hired you."

Max met the penetrating gaze with equanimity. "Courtney hired me on Monday." He opened the folder and drew out a slip of paper. He rose and handed it to Smithson.

"That's Courtney's signature," the lawyer acknowledged gruffly after a moment. Handing the paper back, he pressed a hand to his temple, as though it throbbed. He looked old and weary. "I talked to the authorities in Chastain this morning. They found Courtney's car late last night at Lookout Point on Ephraim Street."

Annie knew that area well. The graveled lot on the point afforded a glorious view of the swift-running, silver river beneath. Across the street from Lookout Point was the squat, buff-colored Chastain Historical Preservation Society, which Annie had good cause to recall with clarity. She'd had her first encounter with Miss Dora there when she'd come to Chastain to plan a mystery program for the annual house-and-garden tour, a mystery program marred by murder. Rising along the river were some of the stateliest old homes in Chastain, including Tarrant House and Miss Dora's home.

"And Courtney?" Max asked eagerly.

Smithson gripped the back of his desk chair. "The car door was open." The lawyer swallowed once, then said starkly, "There are bloodstains in the car. On the front seat, the driver's side." His voice was impassive, but the hand on the chair whitened at the knuckles. It took a moment before he was able to continue. "But not a great amount"—he faltered—"of blood."

"Bloodstains . . ." Max's face tightened. It was bad enough to find an abandoned purse. Worse to investigate a ransacked apartment. But blood . . . Max took a deep breath. "No trace of Courtney?"

"None." Smithson's face was gray. He pulled out the chair, slumped into it. "I warned Courtney not to go to Chastain."

Annie looked at him sharply. "Why? Did you think something would happen to her there?"

His head jerked toward Annie. "God, of course not. I would have stopped her somehow, if I'd had any idea. It never occurred to me she would be in danger. But I know— I think lawyers know better than most—that stirring up the past is a mistake. People don't expect it. They don't want it. But to have Courtney disappear—I never expected that."

"What did you expect?" Max watched him closely.

"Perhaps some unpleasant surprises. That's what I told Courtney. To expect unpleasant surprises. I told her she was a stubborn little idiot if she went to Chastain. And now . . ." He rubbed his eyes roughly.

"Why did she go?" Annie asked gently. "What was so important, so urgent, so critical that she felt she had to go there?"

He stared at the two of them with reddened eyes. Finally, abruptly, he nodded. "I tried to tell the police this morning, but they wouldn't listen. They said they had a suspect." The lawyer's eyes fastened on Max. "They said Courtney was running around with a married man." For an instant, his gaze narrowed. "They're talking about you, aren't they?"

Max nodded impatiently. "Sure. For the same reason they wouldn't listen when you tried to tell them why Courtney came to Chastain. They don't want to hear anything connected with the Tarrant family."

"The Tarrant family." Smithson said it without warmth, indeed with anger. "Old sins cast long shadows. I don't know, you see, what the truth is, I don't know what happened or why—but I know part of it and I can guess part of it."

He leaned forward, looked at them searchingly.

It was very quiet in the elegant office, an office, Annie

thought, that had rarely contained so much raw emotion, an office more suited to low-voiced, gentlemanly conferences, to the planning of wills and the ordering of estates. A pair of dark blue Meissen urns decorated the Adam mantel with its delicate stuccoed nymphs and garlands. The central panel of the mantel showed a fox hunt. A law book was open atop an Empire card table that sat between huge windows with jade-green damask drapes. A handsome mahogany secretary was open. A fine quill pen rested beside a filled cut-glass ink-stand, as if waiting for a country squire to take his place to write in his plantation records. Cut-glass decanters sat on a Chippendale sideboard. A cut-glass bowl on Smithson's desk held jelly beans.

"All right." His voice was crisp now, decisive. "I'll tell you what I know with the understanding"—he paused, his eyes still probing theirs—"with the understanding that find-ing Courtney takes precedence over everything else. Is that a deal?"

"That's a deal," Max said quickly.

Smithson smoothed his beard and leaned back in his chair. "Very well. I have to go back some years. Twenty-two years. At that time, I represented the Kimball family, as had my father and my grandfather before me. Carleton Kimball and I were at the university together. We were boyhood friends before that. Carleton married my cousin Delia. A happy marriage. But there were no children. Both Delia and Carleton were only children. Not even nephews and nieces to love. They wanted children desperately, but finally, they didn't talk anymore about when children would come, and the years were slipping away.

"That was the situation in 1970. In December of that year, Carleton and Delia left town rather abruptly in mid-month. I saw them the evening before they departed. And I will tell you, as the father of five children, that the possibility my cousin, then in her early forties, might have been nearly full-term pregnant never occurred to me. I was astonished when Carleton and Delia arrived back in Beaufort just before Christmas with Courtney."

His face softened in remembrance. "They were enormously proud of their new daughter. Through the years, I tried several times to talk to Carleton about Courtney, but he always cut me off. He was a genial man, but this was one topic he would not discuss. The last time I brought it up, a few years before his death, I told him that if any question ever arose about Courtney's parentage, it would be important to have adoption papers to prove she was indeed his daughter at law. He answered simply, 'Courtney is our daughter.' Their wills specifically provided for Courtney to inherit the bulk of the Kimball estate, which was considerable. And, finally, after time, I didn't think about it anymore. Carleton died when Courtney was seventeen; Delia died this March. Courtney came into her inheritance. There were no other surviving relatives."

Max went straight to the point. "You don't believe she is the Kimballs' natural daughter."

"No." A glint of humor. "Germaine, my wife, was pregnant too many times. It's there, the way a woman carries herself, the look in her eyes. But, more than that, Carleton and Delia were both big people. He was well over six feet, Delia must have been at least five seven. Tall and big. And dark. He had swarthy skin and Delia was olive skinned. They both had coal-black hair and dark-brown eyes."

"Oh, I see." Max turned to Annie. "Courtney's slim and small boned and very fair skinned with blond hair and blue eyes. Like Laurel."

Annie shrugged. "Brown-eyed people can have blue-eyed children. It's rare, but the gene for blue eyes is recessive and it does happen. And lots of children and parents don't look at all alike."

The lawyer was quick to agree. "Oh, I know. We have a redheaded son and there hasn't—officially—been a redhead in the Smithson family in two hundred years. Germaine gets a bit touchy about the usual kind of jokes people make. So yes, it could be. But that isn't all. That isn't even most of it." Smithson absently straightened his perfectly aligned desk blotter. "There's a matter of personality. Do you have children?"

"Not yet." Max flashed an ebullient glance at Annie.

Her eyes narrowed. Not yet. She wasn't ready yet.

"Hmm. Well, let me say simply that heredity can't be denied." Smithson glanced at the row of photographs on his desk.

"That's for sure," Max said emphatically. "I have three sisters."

Annie could appreciate the wealth of emotion in Max's voice. Certainly only heredity could account for Deirdre's penchant for marriages (four to date), Gail's devotion to causes (the only California mayor to parachute into the midst of a North Carolina tobacco auction with a sign declaring SMOKING KILLS), and Jen's free spirit (Bella Abzug with beauty). And they all knew whence sprang these militantly unconventional attitudes.

Annie usually forced herself to avoid lengthy contemplation of this subject. After all, Max wasn't spacey. But sometimes, his dark-blue eyes were uncannily like those of Laurel. . . .

"Environment can play a major role," Annie said determinedly, quashing the thought that she was whistling in the dark.

"Certainly," Max agreed. But he didn't look at Annie.

The lawyer nodded slowly. "Yes, that's true. But the core of personality—Carleton and Delia were both extremely serious, extremely intense. Carleton was an excellent tax lawyer, cautious, conservative. He enjoyed Double-Crostic puzzles. He collected train memorabilia. He wasn't an outdoor man or a sportsman. He was not well coordinated. Delia was interested in family history. She collected snuffboxes and china plates. She never engaged in a sport in her entire life."

"And Courtney didn't fit?" Annie asked.

The lawyer looked at her appreciatively. "Precisely. Now, I want to be clear. Carleton and Delia adored Courtney. She was the delight of their lives. But they always seemed fairly astonished by Courtney and her enthusiasms." He reached for one of the silver-framed photographs on his desk and turned it toward them. "This is my youngest daughter, Janelle. Janelle never saw a dare she didn't take, either. She and Courtney were inseparable growing up. They won the state junior doubles championship in tennis two years running. They both played field hockey. Watching Courtney play field hockey almost drove Delia and Carleton mad with worry. She broke her left arm one year, a collarbone the next. Courtney plays to win. She loves jumping." He looked at them doubtfully. "Horses." They nodded. "And she has a stubborn streak. If anybody tells her she can't do something, well, that means she'll try doubly hard to do it. She was suspended for two weeks her senior year because she climbed to the top of the town water tank and attached the school flag to it." He returned the photograph to its place.

Annie was just a little surprised at the admiring light in the lawyer's eyes.

He reached into the cut-glass bowl for a handful of jelly beans and popped several in his mouth. He pushed the dish toward them, but they shook their heads. He continued, a bit indistinctly: "Courtney was an excellent student, both here and at the university. She majored in archeology, got her private pilot's license, and spent summers at digs in Peru.

Delia and Carleton never enjoyed traveling outside the United States. They always worried about the water, the political situation, and the food. But they were never able to say no to Courtney. They never understood her, but they loved her. And when Courtney has an enthusiasm, it's like a spring tide, there's no holding her back. She lives every day as if it were the most glorious, the most exciting, the most wonderful day in the history of the world."

The light in his eyes died away. "I'd never seen Courtney subdued until last week. I thought the child was sick when she first came in. She didn't give me a hug, the way she always had. She just walked to that chair"—he pointed toward Annie's chair—"and sat down and looked at me, as if she'd never seen me before, as if everything here was strange to her. She had smudges under her eyes, as if she hadn't been sleeping well for some time. She looked straight at me and, without any preliminaries, said, 'I want to know the truth about my parents. My real parents.' "

He pushed back his chair and strode to the fireplace. For a long moment, he gripped the mantel; then his hands fell away and he turned toward them, anguish in his face. "I couldn't tell her! God, I couldn't tell her—and she was so sure I would know, so certain that all she had to do was ask me—and I had nothing to give her. I should have made Carleton tell me."

Annie understood his regret, but that wasn't what mattered now. "How did Courtney know Delia and Carleton weren't her parents?"

"She was clearing out Delia's papers." He stroked his beard. "I have to wonder, you know, if Delia intended for Courtney to know. Courtney was going through her mother's things, packing a lot of them away, boxing up clothes to give to the Salvation Army. She found a blue silk letter case in Delia's bedside drawer. And in it, Courtney found a letter—a letter that made it clear that her father was Ross Tarrant."

"And her mother?" Annie asked.

"No hint. At all."

That was all he knew.

The lawyer gave them a copy of that letter and Max added it to the file. But, when they stood to go, Max had one more question.

"Just for the record," he said quietly, "where were you, sir, from approximately four yesterday afternoon to, say, ten o'clock last night?"

Smithson stiffened. Bright patches of color stained his pale cheeks above his beard. Then, abruptly, he nodded. "Fair enough, Darling. I was in conference with a client from shortly after four until almost six. I had a quick dinner at the cafeteria across the street because I'm on the city council and I had to be there for a meeting at seven. The meeting didn't end until eleven-thirty." A dry smile. "Zoning generates enormous excitement." He reached for a pad from his desk, scribbled names and numbers on it. "You can check these." The angry patches faded away. He reached out, gripped Max's hand. "I'm very fond of Courtney. You'll find her, won't you?"

Max pushed open the gate to the St. George Inn, holding it for Annie. In the street behind them, a car door slammed. Running footsteps thudded on the sidewalk.

"You! Hey, you!"

They paused and turned.

Annie felt a swift thrill of fear, because this was a man out of control. He was young—probably her own age—the kind of person who normally would be immediately accepted, well dressed in a pale-green, crisp summer cotton suit, well groomed with short auburn hair, unobtrusively attractive with open, frank features. But his necktie was bunched at his throat, his suit jacket swung unbuttoned, a red gash on his chin from a shaving cut still dimpled with blood, his brown eyes flared wide and wild, and his chest heaved as he struggled for breath.

"You—you're Max Darling?" He was at the gate now, and no one existed in the world for him at that moment but himself and Max.

Max nodded and his accoster grabbed his jacket with a shaking hand. "Goddammit, where's Courtney? I'll *kill* you if you've hurt her, I swear to God I will!"

His eyes full of pity, Max stood unresisting in the young man's grasp. "I'm looking for Courtney, too. My wife and I both are."

Annie chimed in and that got his attention. "Listen, my husband had nothing to do with Courtney's disappearance. She hired him to find out about her family, and we're doing everything we can to find her. Don't waste our time. And don't waste your time! Do you know who's trying to hang her disappearance on my husband? The police chief! He wants to keep everything quiet for the Tarrants. Courtney hired Max to find out what actually happened the day her real father died. We're still trying. If you want to find Courtney, the best thing you can do is make sure the Chastain police do their work."

Finally, he calmed down enough to listen. They took him to their suite and, while Max made coffee, they heard his story. His name was Harris Walker, and he was a young lawyer in Beaufort (Ogilvy, Walker & Crane).

He paced up and down in their suite. "I've known Courtney all my life. She lived next door." The shadow of a smile. "Irritating little kid, always hanging around the big guys, wanting to do whatever we did. I always called her Skinny. Drove her crazy." He looked at Annie with eyes that held a thousand memories, and Annie winced at his pain.

"Bullheaded when she was a little kid. Bullheaded now." His chin quivered. "I told her that. I told her to *burn* that goddam letter. What difference did it make who her dad was? It was a long time ago. It was other people's lives. It didn't have anything to do with us. But she was set on coming over here. So she hired you." He looked at Max. "Now she's gone, nobody knows where. What the hell are you doing about it?" He was combative again.

When Max finished an account of the past twenty-four hours, Harris scowled. "Jesus, you haven't accomplished anything, have you?"

He didn't wait for an answer. He took a gulp of coffee and banged his cup down on its saucer. "Listen, I'm going back down to the river. And I'm going to round people up. Start a real search. Goddammit, it doesn't do any good to talk to people. We have to look."

After Walker slammed out of their suite, Max reached for the phone. "Going to call Barb," he said briefly to Annie.

Annie dropped into a needlepoint chair and picked up the family tree of the recent generations of the Tarrants, but she listened to Max's conversation.

"We're in a race against time, Barb, and we need more help. I've heard about a pretty good private detective in Savannah, Louis Porter. Hire him." Crisply, Max described Harris Walker. "Yeah, that's right. Harris Walker. I want everything possible about him—and I want to know where he was from four o'clock on last night."

Annie shivered. Surely not.

". . . and get Porter busy on the people who were in Tarrant House on May ninth, 1970. You'll find the list in the Kimball file. Okay. Anything from your end?" Max leaned back against the bolster on the four-poster mahogany bed, then immediately sat up straight. "I'll be damned. Now, that's interesting. Annie and I went by her house this morning. Okay, Barb, we're on our way."

Annie put down the sketch of the family trees.

"Come on, Annie. Miss Dora has sent a royal summons."

"About time you got here." The tiny figure in the long black bombazine dress and high-topped black leather shoes was the Dora Brevard Annie recalled, without pleasure, from previous meetings. The reptilian black eyes with their flicker of intelligence and disdain gazed commandingly at them. Shaggy silver hair streamed from the sharp-boned, wrinkled face. Half-gloved, clawlike hands grasped the familiar silver-headed ebony cane.

The old lady turned and led the way with surprising speed across the age-smoothed heart pine hall into a drawing room where time had stood still for a century. *Bois-de-rose* silk hangings decorated the floor-to-ceiling windows. Two baluster-stemmed Georgian candlesticks rested on either side of a Queen Anne gaming table. For how many generations, Annie wondered, had the table stood on that same spot? And had the golden-cream candles been there for years and years, too? A Georgian settee was to the left of the fireplace, two Georgian chairs to the right, with a soft rose Aubusson rug between. The elegant Georgian mantel shone as white as an egret's wing. It was a beautiful room.

Miss Dora sped to the nearest chair, inclined her head briefly toward the settee, and waited until they sat opposite her, for all the world, Annie thought resentfully, like children called to account by a strict headmistress.

"Well?" The sturdy cane thumped sharply on the floor.

"You wanted to see us, Miss Dora," Max prompted.

Her glittering eyes settled coldly on his face for a long

moment, then she reached into a capacious pocket and, with a rustle, pulled out a square of neatly clipped newsprint and thick-lensed pince-nez. She perched the delicate gold-rim glasses on her nose, held the clipping close, and began to read in her sandpapery voice:

Heiress Disappears; Police Are Puzzled

A Beaufort heiress, Miss Courtney Kimball, 21, has been reported missing, according to Chastain police.

Police Chief Harry Wells announced today that a Broward's Rock businessman, Maxwell Darling, had an appointment with Miss Kimball on Wednesday night, and that Darling came to police with Miss Kimball's handbag claiming he found it at the site of their scheduled meeting, but that Miss Kimball never arrived.

Miss Kimball's car, a 1992 cream-colored BMW, was found by police late last night at Lookout Point. Bloodstains were found on the front seat.

Chief Wells said Darling was held for questioning when police discovered him at Miss Kimball's apartment Wednesday night shortly after he had reported her missing to police. The apartment showed signs of a search.

Chief Wells reported that the police laboratory confirmed the stains in the car are from human blood.

Darling was released late Wednesday night on his own recognizance.

Efforts by this reporter to contact Darling, owner of Confidential Commissions, a personal consultation company on Broward's Rock Island, have been unsuccessful.

An all-points—

Annie couldn't take any more. She jumped to her feet. "That louse. That rat. That slimebag—"

"That will do, Annie," Miss Dora snapped. "It won't help to have a hissy fit at Harry Wells. The damage is done. Your young man is in a pack of trouble, and you both might as well get ready to face it." There was more than a hint of satisfaction in her thin voice.

Annie opened her mouth, looked into Miss Dora's penetrating, raisin-dark eyes, and abruptly sat down.

"Good. I'm glad to see you can sometimes be sensible. Now," Miss Dora cleared her throat, "to continue":

An all-points bulletin has been issued. Miss Kimball is described as a slender, blue-eyed blonde. The missing woman is the daughter of the late Mr. and Mrs. Carleton Kimball of Beaufort, one of that city's oldest and most prominent families. The family attorney, Roger Smithson III, declined comment today on what might have brought Miss Kimball to Chastain.

Miss Kimball arrived in Chastain last week, renting an apartment unit behind the St. George Inn. Mrs. Caroline Gentry, owner of the inn, said, "Oh, this is so shocking. Such a charming young woman. She said she was in Chastain to do research on her family history."

Miss Dora removed the pince-nez, folded the news clipping into a neat square, and returned both to her black bombazine pocket. She whipped the cane up and pointed it peremptorily at Max. "Why was Courtney meeting you?"

"I had undertaken a commission for her, Miss Dora." Max looked intently at the old lady. "The landlady at St. George Inn said you recommended the inn to Courtney. That means you and Courtney met. Why?"

Miss Dora's eyes sparkled. Her sudden cackle made Annie's spine crinkle.

"Not so mealymouth as you look, are you, young Max?" The cane dipped, as if in reluctant recognition that she had met her equal. "Polite enough, but nobody's fool.

Yes, I can see why you might wonder. Well." Miss Dora sat upright in the prim chair, her shoulders as straight as any soldier on parade. There was a contained ferocity eerily like that of obsessive Miss Rosa Coldfield in *Absalom, Absalom!*, Annie thought with a shudder, remembering William Faulkner's splendid novel of gothic passions and doom. "There's more to this than meets the eye. Much, much more."

"Do you know who Courtney's parents were?" Annie interjected impulsively.

The shrewd black eyes focused on Annie. "That's the question, isn't it?" And she cackled again.

"Miss Dora, you know more about Chastain than anyone." Annie felt as if she were on the verge of great discoveries. "Do you know what happened to Judge Tarrant and Ross Tarrant and—"

Miss Dora thumped the cane once, resoundingly. "Just wait, young miss. That's you all over, fly off like a flibbertigibbet chicken trying to go after all the grain at once. That way, you end up with nothing. First things first." She pursed her lips into a tight bow. "There is evil abroad." Her whispery voice was as low and deep as water rushing through a cavern. "I won't have any more misery. Too much misery's been visited already."

The old, implacable voice hung in the elegant room like the echo of funeral bells. Miss Dora's face, crosshatched like parchment, looked for all the world like a skull unearthed from an ancient grave.

Annie shivered.

Abruptly, the tiny old lady was on her feet. The black cane swept toward them. "Come with me."

Annie and Max looked at each other in surprise as she darted out into the hall, then hurried to follow.

Miss Dora thumped down the central hallway to an

enormous door. She pulled the silver handle and stepped out onto the back piazza.

As she and Max joined their elderly hostess, Annie's eyes widened. For a moment, she had no thought but for the beauty that lay before them. The magnificent garden reached all the way to the river, a paradise of scent and color. Delicate lavender wisteria bloomed against mossy brick walls to either side. A glorious profusion of azaleas, pink and rose and crimson and purple and yellow and white, ran in dazzling swaths all the way to the cliff's edge.

She started when Miss Dora's wiry fingers fastened on her wrist.

"These homes along the bluff"—the cane swung in an arc to her left—"were built when the river was king. This" —her silver head jerked to indicate the wide door behind them—"was where visitors were welcomed. Oh, the excitement when the wide-bottom canoes came into view, the eagerness with which they awaited the latest news from Savannah—the price of rice, the most recent ship from England, who the governor favored, what lovely daughter would wed and whom—gone, all gone. Only the ghosts remain."

Her voice sank at the last into a husky, chilling whisper.

"Sometimes—when the wind is right—you can hear laughter and the clink of glasses and faintly—very faintly— strings from a harpsichord."

The breeze rustled the leaves of the nearby magnolia. Suddenly, the sweet scents from the garden—from the magnolia and the wisteria and the banana shrub and the thick white blossoms of the pittosporum—caught in Annie's throat, choked her.

The cane thumped against the wooden porch. The cold fingers tightened on Annie's wrist. "Ghosts." Ebony eyes looked from Annie to Max. "Are they real? Or are they memories? I didn't hear the cry the night Amanda died."

Was the old woman mad? Was she caught up in a family's demise, chained to memories of graves and worms and epitaphs?

Miss Dora's mouth trembled. "My favorite niece. Such a pretty, lighthearted girl. Everyone was surprised when she married Augustus Tarrant. He was close to thirty and she a girl of eighteen. Everyone said what a fine man, what a good man. True enough. But too old to marry a young girl. And three sons so quickly. She moved through the days and years quietly. Then, it was like a second youth, that year before Ross died. Amanda bloomed. A light in her eyes, a smile on her lips. But when Ross died, the light went out and she was an old woman. I would see her in the evening, walking along the bluff. . . ." The cane pointed toward the river. "They found her body at the foot of the cliff, a year to the day that Ross died."

Miss Dora loosed her pincer-tight grip on Annie and placed both hands on the silver handle of her cane. She stared toward the river, her face wrinkled in misery. "Sometimes at dusk or early morning, fog boils up from the water. It billows over the azaleas, swirls up into the live oaks." The silver head nodded. "That's when they see Amanda, walking on the path at the edge of the bluff, dressed all in white to please Augustus." It was said so matter-of-factly that it took a moment for its import to register.

"They see Amanda?" Goose bumps spread over Annie.

Miss Dora's unblinking eyes never wavered. "They say her soul can't rest, that she's looking for Ross." A sudden cackle. "But he's not there, is he? Ross is in the graveyard. I went there last week and looked at a young man's grave. Twenty-one. Too young to die. An accident. That's what they said at the time. Well, that had to be a lie, do you know that?" She stamped the cane on the porch and started down the broad wooden steps.

Annie touched Max's arm. "Max, she's . . ."

The old woman turned, stared malevolently up at them. "I'm what, young miss?"

Annie swallowed. She couldn't have answered had her life depended on it. Was this how the second Mrs. de Winter felt when she faced the cold emnity of the housekeeper at Manderley?

But Max wasn't daunted. "Miss Dora, are you saying Ross Tarrant was murdered?"

The old lady gave an appreciative nod. "You can follow a thread, can't you? Trouble is"—another shrill burst of laughter—"nobody knows the truth. But you're going to find out," and the cane pointed squarely at Max's chest. "Because Harry Wells is sniffing after you, young man. He wouldn't pay me any mind when I told him about Courtney Kimball coming here. Harry said Amanda acted real funny a few weeks before she died, everybody knew it, and he was as sure as a 'coon dog after a possum that Amanda just walked right off that cliff, driven mad by grief. He's right about one thing. Amanda wasn't herself when she wrote that letter—"

"The letter to Delia?" Annie demanded. The letter was a fact, something to hold onto in the welter of emotion and inference created by Miss Dora. The letter and Courtney coming here, that was what mattered. As for Amanda's ghost, who knew what kind of turmoil existed in Miss Dora's mind?

"Yes'm, that letter. Date's on it and everything. Amanda wrote it. I know her handwriting." The old mouth pursed, and she stared at them grimly. "Amanda wrote it one week before she died."

"The letter in the blue silk packet." Max was making sure.

White hair shimmered in the sunlight as Miss Dora nodded vigorously. "Saw it with my own eyes," the old lady said fiercely. "Harry Wells can't say that letter doesn't exist. But he won't pay it any mind, even though Amanda wrote that her son Ross was innocent and that someday, if ever Delia told Courtney about her parents, she was to tell her, too, that 'they lied about her daddy. Oh God, Delia, they lied about Ross.' " The last, the part that Miss Dora was recalling from the decades-old letter, was said in a high, clear tone completely unlike Miss Dora's. With a prickling of horror, Annie realized Miss Dora was mimicking Amanda Tarrant, speaking in a voice not heard since a grieving mother was found at the foot of a cliff.

"How did they lie?" Annie whispered. "Who lied? What happened to Ross Tarrant?"

"If I knew that, do you think I'd have called you here?" Miss Dora snapped. "That's for the two of you to discover." Her eyes darted from one to the other. "And you'll start here —tonight."

The neatly folded newspaper lay near the front of the desk. Judge Tarrant finished reading the plaintiff's brief and returned it to the file. The work of a second-rate, jackleg ambulance chaser. Obviously, the plaintiff had been negligent, and the mill shouldn't bear any expense for the injuries. A summary judgment would answer. He lifted his head and squinted as he thought about his order. Anger still smoldered deep within, but he was a man who would never let his personal feelings distract him from his work. His cold, sunken eyes swept past, then returned to focus on the Sargent portrait of his mother, painted when she was a girl of seventeen. She wore a white organdy dress and, in her hands, held a closed pink parasol. The sudden softness in his melancholy brown eyes merely underscored the severity of his features, a long supercilious nose, gaunt cheeks, thin firm lips, bony chin. With that haunting sense of loss that had never left him, he stared across the sunlit study at the oil portrait above the Adam mantel. He had been only four when she died. She was a faint memory of warmth and softness and the scent of roses, a mystic sensation of safety and goodness and well-being. She had been the mother of five children but he could not—

had never—pictured her in a passionate, sweaty embrace.

What kind of difference might it have made to two generations of Tarrants if he had seen his mother as a woman, not a Madonna?

Chapter 9.

Max didn't need to glance at his watch. He'd been sitting in the dusty, spittoon-laden waiting room of the Chastain courthouse for almost an hour, waiting for His Highness, the chief, to deign to see him. He forced himself to remain at ease in a chair harder than basalt. He hated every ponderous click of the minute hand on the old-fashioned wall clock. It was late afternoon now, almost exactly twenty-four hours since that frantic call from Courtney.

Blood on the front seat of her car.

Dammit, where was Wells?

And where, dear God, was Courtney?

Annie was lousy at geometry and worse at what math teachers so endearingly call story problems. So her sense of accomplishment when she held up two sheets of paper, the Tarrant Family Tree in one hand and the Chastain Connection in the other, was monumental.

Because this was essential.

She and Max could easily slip into a morass of confusion if they didn't get a good sense of who was who both now and then.

Now she could see at a glance how Miss Dora figured in and why Courtney had come to see her.

Courtney knew from the letter to Delia that her father was Ross Tarrant, which made Judge Augustus and Amanda Tarrant her paternal grandparents. Miss Dora was the sister of Ross's maternal grandfather (father of Amanda), and, therefore, Amanda's aunt and Ross's great-aunt. It was interesting to wonder why Courtney chose to visit her father's great-aunt. Why not her father's brothers? She and Max needed to pursue this.

The laboriously drawn family charts also revealed, to Annie's distinct amusement, that Miss Dora was related—a cousin of sorts—to Chastain's naughty lady, Sybil Chastain Giacomo, whom Annie and Max had met a couple of years ago during the house-and-garden mystery program. No wonder Miss Dora took Sybil's lustful life-style so personally. Not, of course, that Annie cared at all how attractive Sybil was to men, even to one particular blond whom Annie cherished.

Annie forced her mind back to relationships (other than carnal). After all, she wouldn't have to deal with Sybil during this visit to Chastain. In fact, Annie fervently hoped the incredibly gorgeous mistress of another of Chastain's storied homes was at that moment far away. Far, far away. Maybe at her villa in Florence.

Annie double-checked her dates and put the sheets on the bedside table. She chewed on her pencil point for a moment, then marked a series of lines, connecting Dora to Amanda (and thereby Ross) and to Sybil.

The phone rang.

As she reached for the receiver, Annie was suddenly

certain of her caller. But she refused to accept this intuitive knowledge as a presentiment.

". . . do hope that *dear* Dorothy L. is being cared for, as well as Agatha."

"Laurel"—Annie was outraged—"of course they're both fine! Barb's going by the house morning and evening to feed Dorothy L. And Dorothy L. purred like a steam engine when I went by the house this afternoon to pack a couple of suitcases." Annie felt no need to elaborate on her packing objectives, which included not only clothes and toiletries, but a coffeemaker, two pounds of Colombian Supreme, and a container of peanut butter cookies. She'd stopped by Death on Demand, too, and borrowed two coffee mugs, one inscribed in red script with *The House on the Marsh* by Florence Warden and the other with *The Circular Staircase* by Mary Roberts Rinehart. After all, even armies maintain troop morale with food. Besides, did Laurel think she and Max were cat abusers? Who could possibly forget Dorothy L., a cat with more self-esteem than Nancy Reagan and Kitty Kelly combined. And not, as habitués of the bookstore knew, exactly a bosom companion of Agatha, Death on Demand's resident feline. Sometimes separate maintenance is an inspired solution.

". . . surprised that I don't know of a single cat!"

Annie knew she'd missed something. Laurel knew many cats in addition to Agatha and Dorothy L. Could this be selective memory loss? What might it augur for the future? Would Laurel soon begin dismissing from her memory persons, as well as cats, for whom she didn't cherish an especial passion? Such as Annie?

". . . it's curious to me because they are the *most* empathetic of creatures, as we all know. Instead, there is this huge white dog, apparently not the least bit charming. In fact, he quite terrifies travelers on the road that passes by the ruins of Goshen Hill near Newberry. And has been doing so for more than a hundred years. But I simply don't understand why not a *cat*! However, it isn't mine to criticize the workings of the other world; it is mine simply to report, and I did think, Annie, you would find it interesting to know that Chastain is quite a *hotbed* of ghosts!"

Oh, of course. No ghost cats. A ghost dog. And a hotbed of ghosts in Chastain. Since most references to ghosts with which Annie was familiar stressed the icy coldness that enveloped those in close proximity to otherworld visitants, Annie thought the term "hotbed" a curious word choice, but she had no intention of delving for the reason, ostensible or unstated.

"Annie, are you there?"

"Oh, yes, of course, Laurel. I was merely considering the question of no ghost cats."

"My dear child"—a throaty sigh—"how like you to focus upon a philosophical aside. Your concentration here should surely be on the ghosts associated with Tarrant House."

It was difficult not to be offended. After all, it was *Laurel* who had brought up ghost felines or their lack, not Annie.

Annie counterattacked. "Oh, sure," she said offhandedly, *"those* ghosts. We know all about them. The ghostly gallop heard when the moon is full is Robert Tarrant rushing home to see his sick sister. And no amount of scrubbing has ever been able to remove his bloodstains from the step next to the landing. And everyone knows about Amanda Tarrant walking along the side of the cliff by the river."

"Oh." The simple syllable sagged with deflation.

Annie felt an immediate pang of shame. How could she have been so selfish? Poor Laurel. Confined to bed, no doubt her ankles throbbing, reduced to phone calls (although Annie did remember that Laurel had elevated this means of communication to an art form), how could Annie have been so callous? "But I'm sure you have a much better sense of what these appearances mean," Annie said quickly.

Laurel was never quashed for long. "Certainly there is *that.*" The husky voice was emphatic. "And I know—because I've developed such rapport—that these spirits are tied to Earth because of the trauma involved in their leave-taking. Such *heartbreak* for a family. The War, of course."

Annie raised a sardonic eyebrow. Was Laurel aspiring to true southernhood by referring to the Civil War simply as the War?

"Three sons lost fighting for hearth and home, the fourth lost through a father's uncontrolled rage—and you know the guilt and misery that must have stemmed from such an act." Her tone was funereal. "One can only guess at the kind of passions aroused that day when Robert came home—only to shed his heart's blood on the very steps he'd lightly sped up and down as a beloved child."

For just an instant, Annie experienced a wave of sadness that left her shaken. She could see the father's distraught face, feel Robert's determination, hear the sharp crack of a pistol shot.

"Laurel," she cried. "That's dreadful."

"Oh, dear Annie, you feel it, too!"

Annie looked down at the sketch pad beneath her hand. Most of the sheet was taken up by notes she'd made concerning the Tarrant and Chastain families. It unnerved her to see that she'd also drawn a cat with a quizzical expression, a dog with his lips drawn back in a ferocious snarl, and a stairway with a dark splotch near the landing. Dammit, she wasn't a Ouija board!

". . . so disturbing to all the family that Ross and his father had that hideous quarrel on the day both died."

"Quarrel!" The pen in Annie's hand scooted along the page as if possessed, leaving a trail of question marks. "What quarrel? How do you know?"

"Obviously, my dear." The husky tone was just this side of patronizing. "As a *competent* researcher, I do seek information from those still inhabiting this earthly vale. It should be apparent to the meanest intelligence that I can't communicate in *person* with figures involved in events where the primary participants are now on the Other Side. Although one has heard of astounding success with channeling. But rather a different objective, don't you think? It was séances in the nineteen-twenties and -thirties. But so many *did* turn out to be contrived. So disillusioning for true believers. I know that Mary Roberts Rinehart—such an adventurous woman, especially for those days, nurses' training in the most arduous early days of nursing, camel journeys, *rugged* camping, even going to war—cast a jaundiced eye upon the results. I for one—"

"Laurel." It was not permissible to snarl at one's mother-in-law. Annie knew her tone was just short of offensive. "Who told you Ross and his father quarreled that day?" Annie's pen was poised to write.

"Why, Evangeline Copley, of course. And it does seem to indicate almost a Direction from Beyond that in inquiring about Tarrant House ghosts, I should obtain this snippet of information, which obviously is of utmost interest to you."

Evangeline Copley.

Frantically, Annie scrabbled through her sheets of notes. Who the hell was Evangeline Copley?

Annie's silence revealed her ignorance.

"A next-door neighbor to the Tarrant family. Miss Dora directed me to her." Laurel's tone was as smug as Agatha's bewhiskered expression upon consuming salmon soufflé. "*Dear* Miss Copley was ninety-nine last Sunday. An

avid gardener. She was spraying her marigolds with nicotine
—those dreadful red spiders—on that Saturday, the Saturday in question, of course, May ninth, 1970. Miss Copley
heard Ross and the Judge shouting at each other! The bed of
marigolds was just on the other side of the wall separating
the properties. The quarrel occurred in midafternoon. Ross
slammed out of his father's study and ran down the back
steps into the garden. What happened after that is unclear,
but I shall continue to seek out the truth from my sickbed.
Not about that quarrel, intriguing as it may be to you and
dear Max as you pursue earthly goals, but about the renewed
activity on the supranormal plane. Ghosts are walking once
again at Tarrant House. Just last night, Miss Copley saw a
figure in white deep in the garden at Tarrant House. A view,
you know, from her back piazza. I hereby designate you,
dear Annie, to serve as my agent on the scene. Do not let a
single opportunity escape you. Seek out the events of that
tragic Saturday as I shall continue to pursue the visitations
that have resulted. We have here a great opportunity to demonstrate the *reason* that ghosts exist, and perhaps, if we learn
enough—if we ascertain the truth of that day's occurrences
—we shall discover whether public understanding of a
trauma rids a site of the unhappy spirit. I depend upon you.
Tally ho, my dear."

    Annie replaced the receiver, then stared at the mute
instrument thoughtfully.

    A figure in white deep in the garden at Tarrant House?
Miss Dora, too, had spoken of that dimly seen specter.
Swirling fog, the old lady had harrumphed.

    Annie knew that's all it was, of course.

    It couldn't be anything else.

    She rose and walked to the door. Opening it, she saw
that twilight was falling.

    She and Max weren't due at Miss Dora's until eight

o'clock. Max, of course, would be back from the courthouse soon, but it wasn't far to Miss Dora's. Only a few blocks. Turning quickly, she found a clean sheet of paper, scrawled a note, and propped it up where Max couldn't miss it.

The cat's pleasure in toying with a mouse is enhanced when the mouse lunges and twists and tries to escape. Max maintained his casual air of relaxation as he leafed through the three-month-old *Sports Illustrated,* and he evidenced no impatience or irritation when Chief Wells's office door finally opened, more than two hours after Max had arrived for their scheduled appointment.

Wells loomed in the doorway, an unlit cigar in his mouth. He gave Max an indifferent stare and made no apology for the delay, mumbling indistinctly, "Oh, yeah. You're here. I've got a few minutes." He turned away.

Max dropped the magazine on an end table and strolled into Wells's barracks-bare office, which contained a steel-gray desk, an army cot against one wall, a shabby leather chair behind the desk, and a hardwood straight chair facing it.

"Any word on Courtney Kimball?" Max asked.

Wells sat down heavily behind the desk. He dropped the cigar stub in the green-glass ashtray. Near it was a single brown manila file folder. Wells pointed at the chair facing the desk. It sat directly beneath a glaring light that hung unshaded from the ceiling.

Max casually shoved the chair from beneath the light and dropped into it.

Wells's obsidian-dark eyes glinted; then he creaked back in his oversized leather chair. He absently touched an old scar that curved near his right cheekbone. "No word. You ready to tell us where Miss Kimball is?"

Max ignored that. Instead, he looked pointedly at his

watch. "It's getting late, Chief. Yesterday at a few minutes after five, Courtney Kimball phoned me. Nobody's heard from her since. So far as I know, nobody's seen her since. I've always understood that if a missing person isn't found within the first twenty-four hours, the likelihood of turning up dead runs about ninety percent."

"I don't like your face, Darling. I don't like your mouth. And I don't like this setup." The chief's hard-edged face looked like a gunmetal sculpture. "We've dragged that damn river all day and into the night and all we've got are old tires and logs. It's costing the county a fortune. I don't think she's in there, Darling. Something stinks here, and I think it's you."

"Wrong again, Wells. When something dead's dug up, it smells rotten—and that's what's happening here. Let's go back twenty-two years, Wells. Let's go back to May ninth, 1970." Max reached into his pocket and pulled out a small spiral notebook. He flipped it open. "Oh, by the way, I thought you might be interested to know that I have a new client."

Wells waited, his unblinking black eyes never leaving Max's face.

"Miss Dora Brevard has employed me." It felt like slapping an ace on a king.

Wells folded his massive hands across his chest. He'd played a little poker himself. "Miss Dora doesn't know what she's doing."

Max met the chief's pit-viper gaze without a qualm. "Oh, yes, she does. She told me to tell you, she very specifically told me to tell *you* that the truth had to come out."

Wells reached for his tin of chewing tobacco, pulled out a thumb-size plug, and stuffed it in his right cheek. "Twenty-two years ago." His voice sounded like stone grating against steel. "I'd been chief for six years." His jaw moved rhythmically, the scar stretching; his dark eyes were cold and appraising. "I grew up here in Chastain. My people have been here for two hundred years. I know the Tarrants. The Judge was a fine man."

A grating voice giving that accolade now; earlier an old lady's whispery voice.

"A hanging judge." There was no mistaking the approbation and respect. "Judge Tarrant expected men to do their duty, wouldn't accept excuses when they didn't."

A fine man.

A hanging judge.

Max scrutinized that heavy, slablike face. "What really happened to Judge Tarrant?"

A flicker of what might have been a smile touched Wells's somber mouth. "That was a damn long time ago, Darling," he drawled. He was very relaxed now, his big arms resting loosely on the armrests, his jaw moving the tobacco between phrases. "Only reason I recollect anything at all is because I thought a lot of Judge Tarrant. Since it was natural causes, there was no reason for my office to be involved. You see, in South Carolina when a doctor is present at the time of death and can certify the cause of death, no autopsy is required. That was the case with the Judge. Seems that when he was told about young Ross's accident"—was there just a hint of stress on "accident"?—"the Judge took bad real fast, and they called for his doctor—he only lived a couple of doors away—and he got there just before the Judge died. Damn sad situation. Since it was natural causes, I had no call to go to the house, and I had my hands full, dealing with young Ross's body. But you're all fired up to know everything about that day—a tragic day for a fine family—so I thought maybe it'd cool you down if you saw how the investigation into Ross's death was conducted. I went down to the dead files in the basement and got the folder on Ross.

You're welcome to take a look at it. There's an empty office across the hall. When you finish with this"—he lifted up the manila folder—"you can return it to the desk sergeant." He pushed the file across the desk and stood, his craggy face expressionless, his dark eyes amused.

It was the longest speech Max had ever heard from him.

The lying son of a bitch.

The evening breeze rattled the palmetto palms and the waxy magnolia leaves, but it wasn't strong enough to disperse the sweet smell of the magnolia. The huge tree, full of fist-size blossoms, crowded the end of Evangeline Copley's back porch.

It was fully dusk now, the shrubs indistinct against the darkening horizon.

Annie knew she was trespassing. But no one had answered her knock at Evangeline Copley's house—and what could it hurt if she just slipped toward the back and took a quick look around?

Although every twig underfoot—she was carefully walking to one side of the oyster shell path—cracked as loud as a circus cannon, Annie reached the back of the house without challenge.

No lights shone in the back of the house either. Annie began to breathe a little more easily, though her hands were damp with sweat.

The garden stretched before her, a jumbled mass of scented shadows. An ivied wall stretched between the Copley garden and the Tarrant grounds.

Evangeline Copley, Annie thought, is a liar.

Miss Copley certainly couldn't have seen into the Tarrant gardens from her own garden.

Stealthily, Annie crept up the back steps to the piazza. All right, that explained it—now the Tarrant grounds were visible. Annie strained to see through the thickening darkness. She looked toward the river. Toward the back of the garden rose a marble obelisk, spotted with moonlight. The wind stirred the leaves of nearby trees, making the branches creak, sounding almost like far-distant cries.

Annie felt the skin of her skull tighten.

Suddenly, with no warning, Annie smelled freshly turned earth—the unmistakable odor of a new grave, deep and pungent. But it wouldn't be the smell of a grave, not really. It was just a trick of the wind, sweeping the scent from Miss Copley's garden. That's all it was.

She didn't believe in ghosts. She did not. She wouldn't run away. In fact, she would go down into the garden. She walked stiffly down the steps, heading for the gate in the wall that led to the Tarrant grounds.

Annie followed the path. Shrubs rustled. Palm leaves rattled. She approached the gate, treading cautiously. But, of course, there was no one to hear her. Still, she slipped up to the gate and peered through the bars. The shadows were so deep now and so dark that it was hard to separate trees from shrubs. Then, she held her breath for a long moment. There was a flash of white near the obelisk. Just that, a quick flash, and nothing more. Now it was dark, all dark.

But there had been something there.

Something.

She heard a lilting call: "Amanda, are you there? Amanda?"

And another faint, high, pleading call. "Amanda? Amanda?"

Annie wanted to run, yet she had the terrified instinct that she would never be able to run fast enough. But she burst on down the path, stumbling over uneven flagstones, pushing away trailing vines. When she reached the path along the bluff, she saw the bobbing lights out on the river, and drew courage—there were people out there. They would hear if she shouted. Then, with a shiver, she realized that the lights marked the continuing search for the body of Courtney Kimball.

"Annie, what's wrong? What happened?"

"Nothing." She closed the door to their suite behind her and avoided looking at Max. She didn't believe in ghosts—past, present, or future. She glanced in the girandole-topped, gilt-framed wall mirror opposite the chintz-covered couch where Max was awash in a sea of papers. She did look a little pale, and she'd snagged some hibiscus in her hair during her pell-mell dash through the Copley garden. "I took a wrong turn coming back from Miss Copley's." It took a moment to explain Miss Copley. (Annie left out the part about ghosts; what mattered was the quarrel overheard between the Judge and Ross.) "We'll have to talk to her."

Unspoken was her firm decision to make that visit during daylight hours.

Although, of course, she did not believe in ghosts.

"A quarrel between the Judge and Ross! Annie, good going." But Max was still concerned about her. "You look kind of ragged."

The phone rang.

Annie rushed to answer it, glad for the diversion.

Barb chirped in her ear. "Honestly, Annie, you do lead the most interesting life." Max's secretary sounded genuinely impressed. "Sara Paretsky's publisher just called to ask if you would like to have her for a signing in July, and I told her we'd love to. Then Henny's postcard came. She visited the Wood Street Police Station where Inspector Ghote arrived early for the international conference on drugs in *Inspector Ghote Hunts the Peacock* by H.R.F. Keating. Henny wrote that she's using the *Mystery Reader's Guide to London* by Alzina Stone Dale and Barbara Sloan Hendershott, and she says it's wonderful. Doesn't that sound like fun? I'd love to always work here—but I do have to tell you that Agatha's been in a *nasty* humor. I mean, I don't suppose she actually *objects* to being petted—"

Annie could see trouble coming. Agatha had fierce opinions indeed about human hands and when they were welcome. But Annie didn't want to hurt Barb's feelings.

"—and I was just smoothing her coat when she *flew* to the top of Romantic Suspense and leveled the display—"

Annie pictured the books, *The Woman in White* by Wilkie Collins, *The Simple Way of Poison* by Leslie Ford, *The Chinese Chop* by Juanita Sheridan, and *The House of a Thousand Lanterns* by Victoria Holt.

"—Really, Dorothy L.'s much more appreciative."

Annie began to feel far away from the Copley garden. It always made her feel good to think about Dorothy L.'s enchanting purr.

"But anyway, I just called to give you the preliminary report from Louis Porter. He rang up a little while ago to give me some preliminary stuff, and I thought I'd better get it right to you."

Annie covered the receiver. "Barb's got some stuff from the PI for us." She pointed at her sketch pad. Max handed it to her. Flipping to a fresh sheet, she made notes as fast as she could.

". . . and that about wraps it up. Oh, yeah, Annie, Mr. Porter said he'll fax a bunch more stuff tomorrow."

"That's great, Barb. Thank you, and thanks for taking care of the store." Annie wriggled her shoulders to loosen tight muscles.

"No problem. It's fun—except I sure wish I had more time to read. Talk to you tomorrow," and the connection was broken.

Max looked at her in anticipation.

Annie took time to pour a steaming cup of coffee, then began to read from her notes:

PRELIMINARY REPORT FROM LOUIS PORTER:

One. *Judge Augustus Tarrant.* Died May 9, 1970, at the age of 63. Death certificate indicates cardiac arrest, signed by Dr. Paul Rutledge (died March 3, 1987). Judge Tarrant had an excellent reputation as a fair though stern judge and was considered a legal scholar. His opinions are cited even today for their clarity and reasoning. He was an authority on maritime law as it affected South Carolina litigants. According to all accounts, he was stern, unemotional, reserved, dignified, disciplined, hardworking, devoted to his family, an excellent shot, an accomplished horseman, an avid golfer.

Two. *Ross Tarrant.* Died of accidental gunshot wound, May 9, 1970. Well-liked by his contemporaries, a leader in the cadet corps at The Citadel, a superior athlete. Accustomed to handling firearms.

Three. *Amanda Brevard Tarrant.* Died in a fall from the cliff path behind Tarrant House May 9, 1971. Contemporary newspaper reports imply suicide, hinting at her deep depression over the deaths of her husband and son the previous year on the same date. Her death was officially termed an accident by the medical examiner, Dr. Paul Rutledge.

Four. *Harmon Brevard.* Died of lung cancer July 18, 1977. Father of Amanda Brevard Tarrant, grandfather of Ross Tarrant, brother of Miss Dora Brevard. A hard-drinking sportsman, owner of several plantations. Ebullient, determined, stubborn, domineering. Once he made up his mind, impossible to sway. Good-humored unless challenged.

Annie paused for an invigorating gulp of coffee. These precise, unemotional reports from Porter put everything back into perspective. These people were all dead and gone, and, despite Chastain's reputation as a haven for ghosts, Annie felt confident she wouldn't have to mingle with them at Miss Dora's gathering tonight. But that didn't hold true for the remainder of the thumbnail sketches, so she'd better concentrate.

Five. *Milam Tarrant,* the oldest of Augustus and Amanda Tarrant's sons. He is 48. At the time of the Judge's heart attack, Milam was employed as a junior vice-president at the Chastain First National Bank. He resigned that post the week after his father's death and he and his wife, Julia, and daughter, Melissa, moved out to a Tarrant plantation, Wisteree. Milam is a painter, specializing in still lifes. He has sufficient family income that he hasn't had to depend upon his paintings for income. Local artists consider him a second-rate dilettante. Since the death of their only daughter in a drowning accident, both Milam and Julia have avoided most social occasions. His relationship with his family is strained as he is openly contemptuous of his younger brother, Whitney.

Six. *Julia Martin Tarrant.* Now 46. Almost a recluse. Reputed to have a drinking problem. Spends most of her time gardening. Have been unable to discover any close friends.

Seven. *Whitney Tarrant,* 46, senior partner of Tarrant & Tarrant. Primarily a business getter for the firm. Reputed to be lazy, easily bored, petulant. Difficult to deal with. Plays golf several times a week. He and his wife, Charlotte, are among the social leaders of Chastain, entertaining several times a month. One child, Harriet Elaine, reportedly living in Venice, California.

Eight. *Charlotte Walker Tarrant,* 46. Author of *The*

Tarrant Family History. House proud and family proud. Very active in the Chastain Historical Preservation Society. Masters bridge player. Collects antique plates. Considered an authority on Low Country history. Reputation for snobbishness. Enjoys golf, horseback riding.

Max checked the clock. "We'd better get ready to go."

Annie put the notepad on the coffee table. "I wonder what Miss Dora has up her bombazine sleeve?"

As they walked swiftly through the dark streets, the shadows scarcely plumbed by the soft gold radiance of the old-fashioned street lamps, Annie clung tightly to Max's hand. For comfort. Because she kept seeing young Harris Walker's stricken face. Where was he now? Did he still carry hope in his heart? Or was despair numbing his mind?

Max strode forward like a gladiator eager for combat. When he spoke, it sounded like a vow. "I don't know how or when, Annie, and it may not happen tonight, but I'm going to rip this thing open, no matter what it takes."

She looked up at him, Joe Hardy mad as hell, his handsome face grim and intent.

"Lies, lies all over the place." He bit the words off. "Was there anything in the police report about Ross quarreling with his father that afternoon? No. Not a word. Not a single word. Just a bland statement. 'Subject found dead of a gunshot wound at the family hunting lodge at shortly before five in the afternoon.' Have you ever heard of anybody going hunting alone at five o'clock on a Saturday afternoon?"

What Annie knew about hunting could be summed up in one word: nothing. So she just murmured a noncommittal "Hmmm?" and hurried to keep up.

"As for the autopsy report—body of young, white, healthy male, a bullet wound to the right temple, evidence of contact from powder burns, powder residue on the right hand. That doesn't spell accident to me." They turned the corner onto Ephraim Street. The river, dark and quiet, ran to their right. "But if it was suicide, why not say so?"

"The Family," Annie said with certainty, taking a little hop. There was a pebble in her right shoe, but now was not the time to deal with it. She tried to avoid limping. "Can't you imagine how upset everyone would be? And in a small town like this, people would keep it quiet. But suicide doesn't jibe with the letter Amanda Brevard sent to Courtney's mother. Amanda wrote that 'Ross was not guilty.' Not guilty of what? Not guilty of suicide? Does that mean that he was murdered? Or was it an accident, after all?"

Max shook his head impatiently. "I don't know, but I'm going to find out."

They passed three of Chastain's oldest and loveliest homes, which Annie had come to know well when she provided the mystery program for the annual house-and-garden tours. Next came the Swamp Fox Inn, now under new management. It had been freshly painted. Annie glanced from the former tabby fort that served as the headquarters of the Chastain Historical Preservation Society across the street to Lookout Point, where Courtney Kimball's abandoned car had been found. No lights bobbed on the river tonight.

A single dark figure stood at the cliff's edge, staring out at the swift river.

"Max." She heard the tightness in her voice.

At his glance, she pointed across the street.

Max's stride checked. "Walker," he said quietly. Abruptly, he reached out and wrapped a hard arm around her shoulders and held her tight for a long moment.

Annie understood.

Max gave one more look toward the river, then said brusquely, "Come on."

This was where Ephraim Street dead-ended. They curved left onto Lafayette Street. The river curved, too, but here it was hidden behind the houses on Lafayette Street. Now the beautiful homes were to their right. The river— and the path where Amanda Brevard had fallen to her death —ran behind the elegant old houses. They passed Chastain House, with its remarkable Ionic columns and gleaming white pediment. It blazed with lights. Annie frowned at the luxurious classic Bentley in the drive. So Sybil Chastain Giacomo was in residence. Annie's hand tightened on Max's arm.

He mistook the pressure and slowed, looking down.

Annie pointed at the next home. "There's where Miss Copley lives."

Then they reached Tarrant House, huge and dark behind its enormous bronze gates.

"You could practically fit Sherwood Forest in there," Annie murmured. She slipped off her right shoe, shook out the pebble, and put it back on.

Max stared somberly at the old mansion. "If those walls could talk . . ."

A car passed them in a hiss of tires, turned in next door.

Miss Dora's guests were beginning to gather.

Max took her elbow. They walked swiftly up Miss Dora's drive. Despite the light showing through chinks in the shuttered windows, the old tabby mansion, deep in the shadows of a phalanx of live oaks, had the aura of a ruin, as gloomy as the burned-out shell of Thornfield. An owl hooted mournfully.

Annie was swept with dark foreboding.

Amanda Tarrant's portrait, made for Mother's Day, sat on her dressing table. It pictured a cameo-lovely woman with smooth magnolia skin and gentle blue eyes. Rich auburn hair framed her oval face in luxuriant waves.

Amanda reached out, picked up the frame, and stared at her image. Her eyes smeared with tears, and she turned the frame facedown. She huddled in the chair in front of the ornate rosewood dressing table in a room fragrant with the lily of the valley perfume she always wore, and, unwillingly, almost in disbelief, looked in the mirror. Mirror, mirror . . . She couldn't look like that! She couldn't! Her hair in blowsy disarray, her eyes wild and filled with misery, her lips trembling . . . And she couldn't stop the little hiccups of distress or control the jagged rhythm of her breathing. She lifted a trembling hand to touch the bright-red mark on her cheek where Augustus had struck her. That was hideous, but worse, much worse, was the threat he had made, his voice as cold as death.

She might as well be dead.

Suddenly, the perfume she loved so much seemed overpowering, threatening to choke her. Striking out, she overturned the ornate crystal scent bottle. It shattered into sharp fragments, and perfume spread across the gleaming dressing table. She scarcely noticed the cut on her palm and the blood mingling with the scent.

Oh, God, what was she going to do?

Chapter 10.

Annie knew the outcome of the gathering at Miss Dora's couldn't be predicted, but her first shock came when she and Max entered the elegant, austere drawing room and Sybil Chastain Giacomo flicked her an incurious, bored glance, then focused on Max, her dark eyes suddenly alive and lusty. A quiver of a smile touched those full, sensuous lips.

Annie felt her cheeks flush. What was Sybil doing here? Sybil lived just two doors away from Miss Dora, but that, of course, was irrelevant to this evening. Or was it? Shrewd old Miss Dora never acted without reason.

But there'd been no mention at all of Sybil in any of the materials about the events at Tarrant House on May 9, 1970.

Sybil wore a green, décolleté gown. *Very* décolleté. She was a striking, vivid figure against the cool ivory of the walls. An aura of wildness invested Sybil's every glance and every throaty remark with a current of fascination. Her presence dominated the room. Each woman and each man was acutely aware of her flamboyant, unrestrained sexuality.

Sybil knew it, of course, knew and took some pleasure in it, although her brown eyes held a depth of unhappiness that no momentary pleasure could relieve.

Miss Dora, her ever-present cane tightly gripped in her left hand, thumped across the floor to Annie and Max. "You know Sybil."

Sybil moved closer to Max and gave him her hand. "Not nearly well enough. But perhaps we can remedy that." Sybil gave him a come-on-over-tonight-honey look, ignoring Annie altogether.

It only added to Annie's fury that Max, dammit, was enjoying every second of Sybil's high-voltage performance. It would serve him right if Annie abandoned him to Sybil for the rest of the evening. He might learn something about the old adage that those who play with matches can bloody well get singed.

But there were no flies on Miss Dora. Somehow—Annie wasn't certain how—Sybil was bypassed, and she and Max were on a circuit of the room with Miss Dora. "My young friends from Broward's Rock, Max and Annie Darling," Miss Dora announced to each family member in turn.

Milam Tarrant was minimally polite but obviously uninterested. His long—by Chastain standards extraordinarily long—blond hair curled on his collar like that of an Edwardian dandy. He wore a pink dinner jacket that didn't hide a heavy paunch.

Milam's wife, Julia, smiled pleasantly but her eyes had the lost and lonely look of a neglected child. Her evening dress was old and shabby, its once vibrant black dulled to the color of a winter night sky.

Weedy, aristocratic Whitney Tarrant, whose high-bridged nose and pointed chin were replicated in the family portraits, held Annie's hand a trifle too long in a moist grip.

Annie fought away the desire to wipe her fingers when they were free.

Whitney's wife, Charlotte, gave Annie and Max a brief nod and a supercilious smile. Despite her dowdy white evening dress, Charlotte exuded the self-assurance of a woman supremely certain of her social position.

Conversation was politely formal: the unseasonably sultry weather, concern over the safety of Savannah River water for drinking ("How can we ever feel safe with that damned nuclear weapons production plant upstream?" Whitney demanded), the plans for the summer regatta. Annie was glad when Miss Dora promptly led her guests in to dinner, though she heard Sybil's caustic, "No drinks first? God." The dining room was gorgeously appointed, the crimson damask curtains a dramatic counterpoint to the deep emerald green of the walls. They sat around a Hepplewhite dropleaf table on Hepplewhite shieldback chairs. On a Sheraton sideboard, a large Georgian silver bowl and tea service glistened in the light from the enormous crystal teardrop chandelier.

Annie was delighted that Sybil was seated as far from Max as possible. Miss Dora, of course, was at the head of the table. At the other end was Milam. Sybil sat to his left, and Max was at Miss Dora's right.

That was on the plus side.

On the minus, Annie had Whitney to her right. Was he deliberately pressing his knee against hers? She pulled her leg away. But he moved his leg, too. Annie's eyes narrowed. She remembered a request she'd heard Gloria Steinem make once in a speech: "Do something outrageous. Tell him to pick it up himself." Annie gripped her shrimp cocktail fork, dropped her hand sharply to her right, and poked.

Whitney gave a small yelp, which he unsuccessfully tried to smother.

Max looked sharply down the table. Annie spread her right hand to indicate all was copacetic, but she hoped Whitney was aware of the dark look he was receiving from her husband. She turned to Whitney and smiled sweetly. "I'm *so* sorry. It just got away from me."

In a very different way, Annie was just as aware of Julia on her left. Julia's thin arms were pressed tightly to her sides until the wine was served. As soon as her glass was poured, she grabbed it and gulped the wine.

Miss Dora saw it, of course. But instead of the quick condemnation Annie expected to see in those raisin-dark eyes, there was only sadness.

Sybil ignored her wineglass and asked for bourbon.

On the plus side was the food (the shrimp fritters were beyond belief), quickly and competently served by a young maid, who watched Miss Dora with wide eyes to make certain the chatelaine was pleased.

From the first instant, Miss Dora directed the conversation, drawing out each in turn. Sybil almost looked happy as she described her visit last week to Boca Raton. "I played tennis all week, every day, all day long." That accounted for her air of vigor and health despite the haggardness in her eyes. But she drank bourbon steadily through dinner and only toyed with her food.

Milam ate greedily and there was a smear of butter on one finger. He shrugged away Miss Dora's question. "Last week—oh, nothing special." He reached for another roll. "I finished a painting." He gave her a sardonic smile. "You wouldn't like it. It's a plantation all bright and shiny and freshly painted, but when you look close you can see the maggots and snakes, and if you look very hard at the live oak trees and the strands of Spanish moss, you can see faces, some black, some white. The face of a slave girl who has no choice when the master—"

His sister-in-law gave him a look of utter loathing. "Milam, it's downright tacky how you act. The Family—"

"Fuck the Family, Charlotte."

There was an instant of appalled silence.

Charlotte's pale-green eyes bulged with outrage.

Whitney's face twisted in a petulant frown. "I'll thank you not to be vulgar and insulting to my wife, Milam." There could be no doubt about Whitney's lineage—the long nose, sharp chin, dark eyes—but his was a second-rate imitation of the Judge's vigorous and commanding face. Whitney's chin was weak, and his eyes slid away from Milam's challenging glance.

Sybil threw back that mane of glorious hair and hooted with laughter. "Way to go, Milam honey."

All of these exchanges were in the cultivated, lovely accent that Annie had enjoyed hearing ever since she came to South Carolina. The smooth-as-honey voices made the rudeness even more shocking.

Miss Dora ignored the exchange. The only indication she'd heard was the slight increase in volume when she spoke. She spooned a mound of peas. "And what can you tell us about your week, Whitney?"

Uneasiness flickered in his pale-brown eyes.

Annie sipped her chardonnay and waited. Whitney must have been easy meat for teachers when he was growing up. She'd never seen anyone so transparent. It made her— and, she was certain, everyone else at the table—wonder what the hell he'd been up to. Though Whitney was such a drip, it probably didn't amount to much.

"Whitney?" The old lady put down her spoon and fixed him with a penetrating gaze.

"Uh, the usual, Aunt Dora. The office, some golf. Charlotte and I went into Savannah for the symphony." But something lurked in his eyes, eyes that wouldn't meet Miss Dora's.

The old lady looked at him speculatively.

Charlotte preened. "I'm on the Women's Committee, of course. Why, we've worked so hard to gain support for the symphony. Such long hours. Of course, I never mind the effort. I'm happy to be able to—"

"Spare us, sweet Charlotte." Sybil yawned. "Good works are excessively boring when recounted. Especially by the self-satisfied doer."

Charlotte turned an ugly saffron. "If it weren't for those of us who dedicate ourselves to preserving and maintaining our glorious heritage, it would be destroyed by those to whom the past—"

"—is past." Sybil raised an elegant black eyebrow. "Grow up, Charlotte. This is the last decade of the century— the twentieth century, not, for Christ's sake, the nineteenth." She crumpled her napkin and dropped it beside her plate. "Jesus, tell me about the museum, how important it is." A wicked light danced in her eyes. "I know, let's have a special display of chamber pots, really bring back the essence of the old South."

Miss Dora watched them, like an owl surveying rabbits.

"Our civilization will be destroyed if we don't hold onto the values of those who came before." Charlotte quivered with outrage. She lifted trembling fingers to the heavy roped gold necklace at her pudgy throat.

Milam's full mouth spread in a grin, not a pleasant one. "Civilization," he mused. "Tell me about it, Charlotte. Tell me about the slaves. Not dependents, honey. Call a spade a spade. Let's look at how it really was. Tell me about the slaves, and the poor whites, and the plantations and later the mills where little kids worked twelve-hour days. Tell me about civilization, dear sister-in-law."

Whitney's chair scraped back, and he started to rise. "That's enough, Milam. Shut your mouth."

"Milam. Whitney."

Miss Dora didn't need to say more. Milam looked down at the table, his face suddenly sullen. Whitney sank back into his chair.

The old lady nodded and the maid began to clear the table. "Sullee made Key-lime pie for us tonight. Now, Charlotte, tell us about your week."

The pattern was clear enough by now. But what did Miss Dora have in mind? Obviously, Annie was not the only guest who wondered. And all of the family members, except poor quiescent Julia, shot an occasional wondering glance at Annie and Max. Who were they? Why were they here? It was obvious that this was no ordinary dinner party. It was almost as if they were in a class, and Miss Dora was calling upon each member to recite.

And now it was Charlotte's turn. She flounced a little in her chair, torn between exercising her anger at Milam and responding to Miss Dora. But it was no contest. "It was such an important week, Miss Dora." She smoothed her faded blond hair, and the carnelian ring on one finger glowed a rich rose. "We've raised enough money to start reconstruction of Fort Chastain. Why, you know how important it was in the Battle of Chastain. That's where William first joined his company. And at one time Henry was in command there. When it's rebuilt, we can climb to the ramparts and look out over the river—just like Henry and William."

As the maid brought dessert, Julia held up her wineglass to be refilled. When the glass was full, she downed the contents in one swift, practiced motion.

"Hot damn, Charlotte," Sybil drawled. "Won't that be the day! Climb that rampart, honey, wave that—"

Annie glanced down the table at Max. He was looking bland, but laughter danced in his eyes.

"Sybil." There was impatience more than anger in Miss Dora's voice.

Sybil shrugged.

Annie also noted that Max didn't miss the languid movement of that shapely figure.

Thinking of shapely figures, Annie was tempted to refuse the dessert. But as a guest . . . The Key-lime pie was so good Annie enjoyed every bite despite the charged atmosphere of the dinner party.

"All right, Aunt Dora. I'll be good." Sybil's carmine-red lips curved in an unrepentant grin. "But, just between us, don't you think it's stupid when someone whose people don't amount to a hill of beans gets so almighty excited when they connect up with an old family?" The question was addressed to Miss Dora, but its impact was calculated. Sybil's derisive glance raked Charlotte.

This time Charlotte ignored Sybil, but the flush didn't fade from her heavy face.

Miss Dora was already turning to Julia. "And your week, my dear?" For the first time, her voice was gentle.

Julia licked her lips and squeezed her eyes in concentration. "Week?" She blinked owlishly.

Abruptly, Annie realized that Julia was drunk as a lord, which made Annie wonder how much Julia'd had to drink before she and her husband ever arrived at Tarrant House.

"Oh, Julia had her usual week," Milam intervened. "She likes to—"

"Let Julia tell me, Milam." Miss Dora reached out a clawlike hand to pat Julia's arm.

Annie wondered if the thin woman beside her even noticed, or if she was so anesthetized the touch went unremarked.

Julia gave Milam a suddenly sweet smile. "S'funny. Came in for bulbs." She stared intently at Charlotte. "You always said okay. You weren't home. I went down to the beds near the 'b'lisk."

Charlotte understood. "Certainly, Julia. The iris beds near the obelisk." Annie didn't perceive kindness in Charlotte's response, merely the clearing up of a tidy mind.

"Last night." Suddenly Julia's eyes filled with tears. "I saw Amanda."

Someone drew a breath in sharply.

Annie looked quickly around the table.

Miss Dora's wizened face was alert.

Milam reached up and tugged at the gold stud in his left ear.

Whitney's black brows drew down in a tight frown.

Charlotte's hand clung to her necklace as if it were a lifeline.

Sybil's amusement slipped away, and her face held no hint of her usual spark of deviltry. "Don't cry, Julia. It's all right." She spoke gently, as if to a child.

The tears slipped down Julia's thin face, unheeded. "I tried to run after her. I called for her—but she wouldn't stay." Julia stared hopelessly at the old lady. "Why did Amanda have to die? Amanda and—"

"Come on, Julia." Milam pushed back his chair and was at his wife's side. "Let's go upstairs for a few minutes. Come on, now."

As they walked away from the table, Milam holding her elbow, Miss Dora called out, "When you come downstairs, join us in the drawing room, Milam." And to the other guests she nodded. "We shall have coffee there." She inclined her head and rose.

Miss Dora led the way, her cane a swift staccato accompaniment to her steps. They all followed, of course, Sybil carrying along her half-full tumbler of bourbon.

The three-tiered crystal chandelier illuminated every corner of the spacious drawing room. Annie admired the lovely Meissen china and the elegant silver coffee service. At

Miss Dora's nod, Charlotte took her place behind the coffee table to serve. For the first time that evening, Charlotte looked happy, her green eyes glowing. She served very prettily, her plump, beringed hands adept. Her pleasure in her role was evident.

Annie, unaccustomedly, took both sugar and cream.

Max shot her a quizzical glance.

Annie ignored him. She suddenly felt she needed every bit of extra energy possible.

Miss Dora waited until Milam and Julia slowly came down the mahogany stairs and joined them. Milam shepherded Julia to a secluded seat in a corner beside a jardiniere with a leafy fern and brought her a cup of coffee. He put it on the Queen Anne table next to her chair.

The old lady took her place in front of the fireplace, hands clasped on the silver knob of her cane, and faced her seated guests scattered about the drawing room. Annie was glad Max sat next to her on the Georgian settee.

Despite the muted richness of her rose gown, Miss Dora had a funereal air. Her ancient, sharp-featured face settled in implacable lines, eyes hooded, lips pursed, arrogant chin thrust forward.

Slowly, one by one, voices fell silent.

Miss Dora looked at each of her invited guests in turn. In a doomsday voice, she pronounced their names, clearly a roll call. "Milam. Julia. Whitney. Charlotte. Sybil."

Sybil's intelligent eyes appraised her. "You're on the warpath, aren't you? Who's in trouble? Is it Milam for attacking icons? Or maybe it's poor dear Julia who starts the day with a glass of vodka neat. Or is it Whitney for grabbing a little ass when poor Charlotte's not looking? Or Charlotte for that god-awful pretentious piece of crap she wrote about the Tarrants? She oh-so-conveniently left out all the drunks and the black sheep and especially the Tarrant who was playing both sides against the middle during the Revolution, à la the revered and very clever Ben Franklin. Or am I the one on the spot?" She flashed a wicked grin. "But you know what I like, Miss Dora. I could have brought him tonight, but this crowd's a little old for Bobby. He's a sweet young man."

"How can you be so disgusting," Charlotte hissed. "To consort with mere boys." Her pale-green eyes glistened with dislike.

"The usual term is 'have sex,' Charlotte. Although I don't suppose it's an activity you enjoy. Not high-class enough. And Bobby's nineteen." Sybil's smile would have embarrassed a satyr. "That's old enough. Believe me."

Miss Dora's eyes, dark as pitch, turned to Sybil. They were for an instant filled with pity.

Sybil saw that, too. She sat very still in the gilt Louis Quinze armchair, every trace of mocking amusement erased. Slowly she lifted the glass to her lips and drank, focusing on that physical act.

Miss Dora's eyes lingered on Sybil yet an instant longer; then the old woman spoke in measured tones. "I have called all of you here because I intend to institute a court of inquiry, prosecuted by me, into the events of May ninth, 1970."

It should have been ludicrous, the old, hunched figure, the thin, age-roughened voice, the grandiloquent pronouncement. It was, to the contrary, majestic. Tiny and indomitable, the moment belonged to Miss Dora.

The silence was absolute.

Anger.

Shock.

And fear.

Annie could feel raw emotion in that elegant room.

But from whom?

Milam's heavy face twisted into a scowl, every trace of sardonic lightness gone.

The fragile coffee cup in Julia's hand began to shake. Clumsily, she put it down on the Queen Anne table.

Whitney's thin face had the look of a fox hearing the hounds.

Charlotte's social smile congealed into a blank, empty mask.

Sybil's face crumpled. She turned away and came up blindly against the mantelpiece. Both hands gripped it. She stood with her back to them, her smooth, ivory shoulders hunched, then whirled to face Miss Dora.

"Ross," she cried brokenly. "You know how it happened, you old bitch. It shouldn't have happened, but it did. An accident. Ross and I . . ." She looked about with glazed, uncomprehending eyes. "That's when everything went wrong, and it never came right again. Never. I still don't know why he went out to the lodge. He was supposed to meet me at the bottom of the drive. I was there," she said forlornly, years of grief weighting the words. "I waited and waited—and then Daddy found me and . . ." She broke off. Sybil's bejeweled hands clenched. There was more than grief, there was anger that could never be answered, the fury at fate that had robbed her of the man she loved. Annie thought she'd never seen Sybil look more lovely . . . or more dangerous.

"I saw you and Ross in the garden that afternoon," Miss Dora said gently.

For an instant, the years fell away and Sybil looked like a girl again, young and in love and breathtakingly beautiful. "One last kiss—it was so light, just the barest touch. We thought there would be time for all the kisses in the world." The brief illusion of youth fled, replaced by the sorrow-ravaged yet still gorgeous face. Sybil's bitter eyes raked the room. "Why couldn't it have been one of you? Why couldn't it have been Milam? Or Whitney? They aren't a quarter the man Ross was. Ross was—" She swallowed convulsively.

"Oh, God, he was wonderful. Young and strong. And a *man*. He knew how to live—and none of you has ever lived, not the way Ross did. He could laugh and make love and ride a horse and be brave and gentle and kind and rough. Oh, dear God, what irony, what sick and puking irony that he should die and any one of you live." Years of anger corroded her husky voice.

Annie reached out and took Max's hand and held it hard. Max watched Sybil, his dark-blue eyes somber.

"How *dare* you talk like that!" Charlotte, her voice high with anger, her plain face livid, turned to Miss Dora. "You make her hush up right this minute. We don't have to sit here and be insulted. Why, Whitney and I—"

"You and Whitney will do as I say," Miss Dora snapped.

Charlotte looked as though she'd been slapped. Her head jerked up, her mouth opened, but no words came. Then, her shoulders slumped and her eyes fell before Miss Dora's unbending gaze.

"Of course we will, Miss Dora." Whitney's voice was placating. "But the past is past. Dad and Ross—that's been over and done with for more than twenty years. There's nothing to be gained by discussing it."

Charlotte lifted her chin. "A tragic day," she said loudly. But there was no sympathy in her voice. Annie heard instead the oily complacency of a chorus in a Greek tragedy. "A double loss for poor Amanda."

Julia buried her face in her hands for a long moment, then struggled up from her chair and moved heavily toward the sideboard, one hand outstretched for the cut-glass decanter.

Milam bowed toward his great-aunt. "What an exquisite sense of drama you possess," he drawled. His green eyes glittered with malice; his plump face was once again amused. "But the difficulty is, you face a dead end. No one will ever know more about that day because the principals are all beyond this earthly vale of tears."

"I will know more." The old woman spoke with utter confidence.

Again, taut silence stretched.

"You see," the whispery voice continued, "no one has ever questioned the official version, Ross dead of an accidental gunshot wound; Augustus dead from a heart attack upon hearing the shocking news." She smiled grimly, her ancient face an icy mask of contempt. "All of you—except dear Sybil, of course—were in Tarrant House that day. Whitney, how did you learn of Ross's 'accident'?" Her voice lingered deliberately on the final word.

Whitney stood with his hands clasped behind him, rocking back and forth. He had the wary look of a man suddenly confronted with a minefield and ordered to cross it. He cleared his throat. "Grandfather told me."

Annie's mind went back to her painstakingly inked family trees. That would be Harmon Brevard, Amanda's father.

"What time was that?" Miss Dora's question was rapier-quick.

Whitney looked confused.

"It's disrespectful to the dead." Nervously, Charlotte pleated her white chiffon skirt. "Miss Dora, this is dreadful, like pulling and picking at bones."

But Miss Dora ignored Charlotte's shrill protest. The old lady's imperious gaze never left her great-nephew's face.

Whitney moved restively. "God, it's been twenty—"

"*Whitney,*" Miss Dora said sharply.

Whitney moved restively, then glanced uncertainly toward his brother.

Annie squeezed Max's hand. How revealing! Whitney, the member of the bar, the substantial brother, still deferred to his older brother, whom Annie had supposed to be the weaker personality of the two. Or was that just society's prejudice taking over, the assumption that a lawyer of substance in a community would, of course, dominate an older, unconventional sibling.

Milam sniggered, breaking the silence. "May as well give up, brother dear." He fluffed the thick blond hair over his collar. "Aunt Dora always did have your number. Oh, well, I don't suppose it matters after all these years. Why not let the truth come out—"

"Milam, *no!*" Charlotte importuned. Panic shrilled her voice.

"Truth!" Sybil said harshly. "What truth?" In the light from the glittering chandelier, her eyes glowed a hot, deep black.

"Your sweetie pie shot himself all right." Milam's light, high voice held a sickening note of satisfaction. "Suicide in the first degree, my dear Sybil. That's why dear Papa dropped dead—he and Ross had enjoyed a hell of a nasty little scene and—"

Hands raised, Sybil launched herself with a deep cry. Her fingernails raked Milam's face, scoring crimson slashes on both cheeks.

Milam stumbled backwards, swearing and awkwardly struggling to push away Sybil's slender, green-gowned body.

But it was Julia's drunken voice that cut through the sound and fury and brought a terrible quiet to the drawing room.

Julia stood at the sideboard, pouring brandy sloppily into a cut-glass tumbler. She plunked down the decanter and picked up the glass in her trembling hand. " 's true, Sybil. Because it was the same gun, you know. Ross took the gun that killed the Judge and used it on himself."

Sybil tore free of Milam's grip and whirled to face her distant cousin's wife. "The gun that killed the Judge? Jesus Christ, Julia, what are you saying?"

Whitney lifted his hand to knock at the door of the study, then let it fall. He felt, at the same time, hot and uncomfortable and cold and sick. He hadn't hurt the firm. Not really. To be thrown out, to have nowhere to go—once again he could hear his father's icy, contemptuous voice, "A lawyer's conduct must always be above reproach." *Christ, hadn't he ever wanted a woman like Jessica? Whitney pictured his father's thin, merciless, ascetic face. His shoulders slumped. He turned. Blindly, he walked away from the study door.*

Chapter 11.

"Julia!" Milam's voice was still high, but shorn of mockery, his tone sharp, urgent, imperative.

Julia clutched the tumbler of whisky in trembling hands and looked at her husband uncertainly. "Truth, Milam." Her voice was slurred; her mouth quivered. There was a smear of crimson lipstick on one cheek. "You said we'd tell the truth."

"Let her speak, Milam." Miss Dora stalked between them.

But he refused to look at his great-aunt. "She's upset. We're going home," and he took a step toward Julia.

Miss Dora's cane slashed upward, barring him from touching his wife. "No, Milam. Not yet. Not until we know precisely what occurred that day. Julia, I want you—"

Sybil flew past them both. Her strong, beautifully manicured hands clutched Julia's thin shoulders. Bourbon spilled down the front of Julia's dress, and the tumbler crashed to the floor. "Who shot the Judge? When was he shot?"

Julia stood helplessly in Sybil's grip. She blinked. "I tol' you. You asked me. I tol' you. *Ross* shot him. That's what happened, he left a note and—"

Sybil let go of Julia and in a swift explosion of rage struck the drunken woman across the face.

Julia wavered unsteadily on her feet and began to whimper. Her arms hung straight and limp. She didn't touch her cheek.

Miss Dora swung toward Sybil. "Enough. Get back, Sybil. Now."

But Sybil, of them all, was not cowed by Miss Dora. Ignoring the old woman, she spat at Julia, "*Never!* Ross never shot his father; Ross never killed himself. Never." Her voice was as deep as a lion's roar and as full of danger. "Lies, all of it, lies."

"You weren't there, Sybil." Whitney nervously smoothed his thinning hair. "What were we going to do? Nothing would bring Dad or Ross back. They were both dead; we had Ross's note. Did we want to be entertainment for the tabloids? What would that have done to Mother? Dr. Rutledge agreed. It wasn't even that hard to do. The bullet" —his voice shook—"left only a small slit in Dad's coat and most of the bleeding was internal. The bullet lodged in his chest. There was no indication at all, other than the entry wound, that he'd been shot. I helped Dr. Rutledge put a fresh shirt and coat on him, and when he was taken to the funeral home, the director was instructed to cremate him immediately."

Annie, still holding tight to Max's hand, looked from face to face.

Miss Dora, her dark, hooded eyes glittering, pursed her mouth in concentration.

Charlotte's plump face was pasty, like uncooked dough left to rise too long.

Milam banged his half-empty tumbler of whisky onto the Queen Anne table and pulled Julia into the circle of his protecting arm. The bloody scratches on his cheeks were in shocking contrast to the flippant pink of his dinner jacket. Julia slumped against her husband. Milam took the handkerchief from his pocket and brushed at the tears on her red-splotched cheeks, then pressed it against the wet front of her dress. Bright drops of blood welled from his scratches.

Sybil's glossy-black hair rippled as she shook her head from side to side. "No. You don't understand, Whitney, Ross and I . . ." She pressed her fingers against her temples for an instant, then, her lovely face hard and resolute, demanded, "When was the Judge shot?"

"Oh, for Christ's sake, Sybil, let it go." Milam glared at her. "It was a fucking mess. We did the best we could."

Annie tensed, wondering if Sybil would fly at him next.

Miss Dora, too, obviously feared another explosion. She spoke quickly, her raspy voice commanding. "Sybil, come stand by me. I promise you that we shall pursue this."

Sybil resisted for a long, tense moment. Then, with the contained ferocity of a caged tigress, she moved to Miss Dora's side. But her angry gaze probed each Tarrant in turn.

Charlotte rose and stepped forward. "Miss Dora, I *beg* you—"

Miss Dora lifted her voice to override Charlotte. "I assure all of you that I have good reason, which I shall reveal in due time. Now, we shall proceed in an orderly fashion." She fastened her icy, uncompromising gaze on Whitney. "I wish a clear, concise outline of that day's events."

Whitney once again darted an uncertain glance at his older brother. Then he said sullenly, "I agree with Milam. I don't see any point in—"

"Whitney."

Grudgingly, he began. "We didn't know what had happened for a while. At least, I didn't. I was in the garage. It was about four o'clock. I heard a bang. But it didn't seem all that close. And I was on the far side from Dad's study. I heard it, but I didn't think much about it. I suppose, if I gave it any thought at all, that it was probably kids down on the river. Anyway, it must have been about ten, fifteen minutes later that Ross ran into the garage. He looked—wild. And he was carrying Dad's gun, the one Dad brought back from the war. It was crazy. He was supposed to be at school, and, all of a sudden, here he was in the garage, carrying Dad's gun. I asked him what the hell he was doing. He just stared at me as if he'd never seen me before. I can't describe that look. God, it was awful." Whitney swallowed and licked his lips. "Ross ran to his car. He was out of breath, like he'd run for miles. There was sweat on his face. Then he kind of mumbled, 'Tell them I've gone to the lodge,' and he jumped into the car and roared out of there like a bat out of hell."

Milam took over impatiently. "Jesus, Whitney, you never could get to the point. Who gives a damn what he looked like? Look, Aunt Dora, it's simple and stupid." There was no remembered horror in Milam's voice; he was disdainful. "Ross and Dad had a hell of a fight about three-thirty. You could hear Ross shouting and Dad had that cold, clear voice he used on the bench. You know what I mean. Like God making a judgment from on high, and sweet Jesus, you better listen. Ross should have known better. What a goddam do-gooder. So they mowed down some students at Kent State! Why should Ross put his ass in a sling? Hell, he could've graduated and gotten his commission and applied for transportation or the quartermaster corps or someplace where he wouldn't have been shipped off to Nam. If he couldn't stick that, he could've 'accidentally' shot himself in the foot! Whitney and I did Air National Guard, sweeter than honey. Funny thing is, Dad wasn't fooled, but we had legally met our obligations, so he let it lie. But Dad was always so goddam proud of Ross. A cadet colonel, another in the long line of Tarrant gentlemen-soldiers. So, I thought it was pretty funny when Ross finally bucked the system. He yelled at Dad that he wouldn't serve, he wouldn't graduate from The Citadel, and if he was drafted, he'd go to Canada. So the old man about had a stroke and he told Ross he was disowned, to get out of the house and never come back. Dad said Ross had no right to the name, that Tarrants were men of honor and principle—"

"That's what Ross was," Sybil cried passionately. "Not like you and Whitney. Ross never ran from anything. He never hid. He did what he thought was right—and everyone knew that war was hideous. The day the National Guard killed those students—oh, God, they were walking to class!" A generation's lament rang in her voice. "Ross brooded about what had happened all week. Campuses closed all over the country. People marched. Ross came home Saturday morning; he'd made up his mind. He was quitting. He wouldn't take his commission. He told his father. They quarreled, but Ross was determined. That's when he met me in the garden and we planned—" Tears edged down her cheeks, streaking her perfect makeup. "Whenever spring comes, I remember that day. We stood in the sunshine and it was warm against us and he held me and I smelled the honeysuckle and the roses. He kissed me and I ran home to gather up my things. We were leaving." She glared at them defiantly. "The car was his. He worked summers and earned the money for it and he had some money saved and so did I and we were going to run away and be married. I waited for him—and he didn't come. He didn't come." The agony of empty years and lost dreams and a crippled heart echoed in the simple declaration.

Charlotte stood with her arms tightly folded across her

ample bosom. "Ross was always a hothead. None of it surprised me." She looked disdainfully at Sybil. "You know what he was like—he always had to have his own way. Spoiled rotten, that's what Ross was." Her voice rose suddenly, turned strident. "And Amanda was always on his side, against Whitney and Milam. As if Ross were better or—"

"That's enough, Charlotte." Whitney cleared his throat. "Point is, Sybil, Ross shot Father—"

"No. He wouldn't have." Sybil stood firm, chin lifted, and there was total certainty in her eyes and her voice. "Ross was upset, yes, but we were leaving. It was all decided. Why would he shoot the Judge? There was no reason."

"You were in the garden," Miss Dora said crisply. "You said good-bye and were to meet again—"

"In only a few minutes," Sybil cried. "Just long enough to gather up some clothes and meet him at the gate."

Charlotte smoothed her hair, her composure regained. "Ross probably went back into the house to get some of his things and the Judge saw him and told him to leave and Ross lost his temper. Ross always acted like Tarrant House belonged to him and not the rest of us. He was crazy about the house. Maybe he decided the Judge had no right to throw him out." She shrugged. "What difference does it make? We all know what happened, Sybil."

"I don't care what you—or anyone—says or will ever say." Sybil spoke jerkily. "But I knew Ross. I *knew* him. He would never have shot his father—and he would never have killed himself. That was a coward's way out—and Ross was never a coward."

Miss Dora said quietly, "You are quite correct, my dear child. Ross was a brave young man. A very brave and gallant young man—but he did indeed take his own life. My brother —Ross's grandfather—went to the hunting lodge that day.

The next day Harmon related to me what had happened. Harmon told me that when he arrived—it was late afternoon by then and the shadows were thick and it was cool and quiet on the front steps—he called out to Ross and tried to open the door, but it was locked. He rattled the knob—and there was a gunshot. He ran to the back of the lodge but that door, too, was locked. Harmon took a log from the woodpile and used it as a battering ram and broke down the back door. Ross was there, sitting in the old morris chair. And he was dead. The front door was still locked."

Sybil reached out, clinging to a chair for support. Annie had never seen a woman so pale, as if all the blood and life had drained away. And, no matter what Sybil had become, Annie's heart ached for her.

"So we know—we have the word of a witness—what happened to Ross." Miss Dora's face was grim. "But that does not end our quest tonight. We still must determine when—and how—the Judge's death occurred."

"No." Sybil clasped her arms tight across her body. "That's wrong, wrong, wrong. I'll never believe it. Ross was brave, I tell you, brave and—"

Miss Dora nodded. When she spoke it was directly to Sybil and her voice had a gentleness Annie had never heard. "Yes, Sybil, Ross was brave and gallant. You will understand that even better when we are done. For now, Sybil, I want you to listen. No matter what is said or done, we cannot change the past. But my hope is that we can lay to rest the misery that past has visited upon us and"—she paused and looked at each of the Tarrants and her voice hardened—"that we can prevent evil from again warping and destroying the life of this family."

A sense of inexorable judgment emanated from the old woman, much like Miss Rosa Coldfield's unbending, almost demented determination to vanquish Thomas Sutpen.

Annie's eyes were focused on that narrow, intelligent, determined old face. Later, she would regret that she had not been quicker to look about the room. Would there have been a flicker of fear—or fury—on one face?

For when she did look, masks were in place: Whitney wary, Charlotte tense, Milam sardonic, Julia withdrawn.

Abruptly, Miss Dora pointed her cane at Max. "Proceed."

The silence was abrupt. All of the family members stared at Max and Annie. She realized that in the heat of their quarrels, they'd almost forgotten their presence. And now, not only did they remember there were strangers within the gate, they were shocked and enraged to have Miss Dora invite Max to take part. The Tarrants looked at Max with varying degrees of hostility and outrage.

Milam glared at Max, then turned to his great-aunt. "What business is it of *his*?"

"*My* business, dear Milam," Miss Dora said briskly. "I have commissioned Mr. Darling to assist me in my inquiry."

Annie kept her face blank, but she was irritated at not being mentioned. The sexist old hag.

Max didn't waste time. "Mr. Whitney Tarrant, when did you hear the shot?"

Whitney threw back his head like an irritated horse. "Enough is—"

"Whitney, you will cooperate with Mr. Darling. And" —a grudging addition—"Mrs. Darling." Miss Dora lifted her cane, pointing it at each Tarrant in turn. Her black eyes snapped angrily.

Milam said brusquely, "Oh, Christ, Whitney, go along. Or we'll be here all night." He walked to the sideboard, poured himself a tumbler of whisky, and picked up a fresh glass for Julia and filled it. She took it greedily and withdrew to the brocade-covered chair by the fern.

"I was in the garage. I told you that," Whitney said sullenly. "It was just a minute or two after four when I heard the shot."

Max turned to Charlotte. "Mrs. Tarrant?"

Charlotte glanced at Miss Dora. "I was . . . I think I was arranging flowers. Roses, white roses. The ones planted by Great-great-grandmother Tarrant. We were to have a dinner party that night. I remember I'd bought a new frock for it, and, later, I never could bear to wear that frock. I was in the garden shed."

"The time?" Max prodded.

"It was just after four." She spoke precisely, carefully.

"You're sure?"

"Why, yes. I looked at my watch." There was growing assurance in her well-bred voice.

"Why?" Annie asked.

Charlotte's chin jerked up. Annie could see outrage in her eyes. Obviously, the chatelaine of Tarrant House wasn't pleased at having to submit to Max's questions, but just who the hell did Annie think she was?

"Why?" Miss Dora repeated sharply.

Charlotte lost her composure. "This is simply unendurable. I will not continue this idiotic charade—"

Miss Dora fastened her steely, implacable gaze on Charlotte.

It was a battle of wills.

The outcome surprised no one.

Charlotte licked her lips. "I don't know why I looked at my watch. But I did. And I can swear it was just after four o'clock."

"Actually, Charlotte's right, for what it's worth." Milam sounded bored. "I heard it, too. A couple of minutes after four."

"Where were you?" Max inquired.

"Upstairs." Milam once again reached out for Julia's

empty glass. He returned to the sideboard, generously re-filled it, and took it back to his wife. Julia grabbed it and tipped it to her mouth. Her husband's eyes watched her sadly.

"And you, Mrs. Tarrant?" Max asked gently.

Julia Tarrant blinked, then looked toward Max. "That day—" She drank again and there was only a little left in the glass. "I'd been upstairs." Tears spilled down her cheeks. She made no effort to wipe them away. She sat there and wept, silently.

Max looked helplessly at Annie.

"Julia," Annie said tentatively.

Slowly, the older woman turned her head. "You have a soft voice. Like Amanda."

Annie hesitated, then plunged ahead. "Did Amanda hear the shot?"

A cunning smile lifted Julia's lips, yet the tears still slipped down her cheeks. She emptied the glass, looked at it regretfully, and put it on the Queen Anne table. "Trying to trick me!" She waved a finger waggishly. "Can't trick me. I'd just heard the grandfather clock. Boom. Boom. Boom. Boom. So it was just after four o'clock. So loud. I put my hands over my ears." Waveringly, she lifted her hands and clapped them to her ears. Then she slid them over her face and hid her ravaged eyes. A shudder shook her frail frame. "Awful. Awful. Awful."

"Julia!" Miss Dora's cane thumped the rich old carpet.

Julia's hands fell away, her head snapped up, and she stared, eyes wide and vacant, at Miss Dora.

"You heard the shot?" Miss Dora's stare demanded an answer.

Annie found it hard to believe the words meant anything to Julia, so glazed and blank was her face, but, slowly, unhappily, she nodded.

"It's a dead horse—" Milam began angrily.

Miss Dora held up a hand, her eyes glittering with satisfaction. "You all agree then, that the shot occurred at shortly past four that afternoon. Whitney? Charlotte? Milam? Julia?"

Each nodded acquiescence, reluctantly. Whitney massaged his temple as though his head ached. Charlotte clasped her hands together so tightly her rings must have bruised her fingers. Milam stood stiffly by the fireplace. Julia stared morosely into her empty glass.

Miss Dora used her cane as a pointer. "How many shots, Whitney?"

"Why, one. Just one." He looked surprised.

"Charlotte?"

"One, of course." Her tone was pettish.

Miss Dora eyed her thoughtfully. "You would have heard had there been more than one?"

"Certainly." Charlotte obviously felt on safe ground here. "I must have been among those nearest to the study— and I think the study window was open. Why, of course. That's why it was so loud. I was so startled, I dropped the vase. And it broke. I was so upset—and that's why it took me a minute or two to come into the house—not, of course, that I had any idea at the time that something dreadful had happened. As I came into the house, Julia ran past me, her face as white as a sheet." She shot a tiny, vindictive glance toward her sister-in-law.

"One shot, Aunt Dora," Milam interposed gruffly. "Sorry, it wasn't the Wild West that day."

"One shot," Julia said with great precision.

Miss Dora nodded regally. "That is my recollection, too. I did wish to verify it, to make certain of my ground."

There was a note in her voice that commanded attention.

Every eye in the room focused on the implacable old lady.

She did not disappoint them.

"Yes. I heard the shot. I was at the gate into the Tarrant House garden. But I had stopped for several minutes because I did not want to interrupt what was obviously a very private and personal meeting between Ross and Sybil. And I hesitated yet a while longer after you departed, Sybil. I wished to give Ross time to regain his composure. I had just raised my hand to push through the gate when Ross and I heard the shot—at just after four on the afternoon of May ninth, 1970."

Julia squeezed her eyes closed and bunched her hands over her ears, but the Judge's cold, scathing tone filled every crevice of her mind.

"You aren't fit to be a mother. You have forfeited every right."

It was as though her mind was a cavern, a hideous, damp, dark place and his words echoed, louder and louder, ". . . right . . . right . . . right . . . right . . ."

"If I could, I would remove Melissa from you altogether." *The Judge paused and when he spoke, his tone was venomous.* "Milam has always demonstrated utter lack of judgment. His selection of you as his wife confirms that."

Julia wanted to scream, to cry, to run, but there was no escape, just as there had never been an escape from her father.

"I can see no good solution, but I have decided that you and Melissa will return to your parents. That should direct the course of your behavior and provide Melissa with a stable background."

Somehow, never looking toward the Judge yet so horribly aware of his malevolent gaze, Julia stood

*and moved jerkily toward the door, her mind a
maelstrom of horror and sick fear and frenzied
determination.*

She had to save Melissa.

Her baby. Oh, Jesus God, her baby . . .

Chapter 12.

Miss Dora dominated the elegant room and her shocked guests. "A single shot." Those reptilian eyes flickered to each face in turn.

"But that means . . ." Julia's slurred voice trailed off.

The others said nothing—and that in itself was an admission: they believed Miss Dora. They had to believe her. She might be old, she might be imperious, she might be unpleasant, but she was totally competent, capable, and cognizant.

"Christ." The shock in Milam's voice was mirrored on every face.

Charlotte's plump face was bewildered. "I don't understand." She reached out, held to Whitney's arm.

He murmured a meaningless "It's all right, Charlotte." But it wasn't all right, and he knew it. His eyes had the look of a man who'd been jolted, his very foundations shaken, and Annie knew Whitney was recalling that afternoon and trying to incorporate this piece of information that destroyed for all time a family's pained acceptance of tragedy.

"I knew it," Sybil cried. "Miss Dora, I knew it couldn't be Ross." Then her face fell. "But, why would he—oh, God, Miss Dora, Uncle Harmon must have been wrong—" She seemed to hear and understand her own thought for the first time and the enormity of it transformed her into a raging Fury, her splendid eyes flashing, her lovely face twisted into a mask of hatred. "One of you. One of *you!*" Her fierce gaze probed each in turn, Whitney so clearly shaken by Miss Dora's disclosure, Charlotte seeking reassurance, Milam's face blank with shock, Julia fumbling for comprehension.

"Sybil, listen to me closely." Once again, Miss Dora spoke gently. "My brother, Harmon, was no fool. I realized at the time that he was not telling me everything. Harmon would go to great lengths to protect the Family—but he would not have connived in hiding a double murder. Harmon knew how Augustus died. Harmon made the decision to mask that murder. Harmon personally handled all of the funeral planning and oversaw the removal of the bodies that day. We know from what Whitney told us that he and Harmon worked together to dress Augustus. Harmon would only have done so had he felt the murderer was beyond justice. So we can, in the main, accept much of what Harmon related to me that next day: Ross left a note; Ross killed himself."

"But Ross *didn't* kill his father." Sybil's tone was bewildered. "You know that. So why would Ross leave a note confessing to a murder he didn't commit? Why would he kill himself when his grandfather came to the lodge?"

"Because he was determined to accept responsibility for his father's murder." Miss Dora said it quietly.

Annie shivered. She could not even imagine what

would have propelled Ross Tarrant to make such an awful sacrifice.

Sybil swept a hand through her thick black hair. "That's crazy. Ross was never crazy. Don't you see, Uncle Harmon had everything wrong—"

"Oh, I understand," Charlotte said in a rush, her words tumbling eagerly. "Amanda! It had to be Amanda! She and Augustus had quarreled, I know that. It must have been Amanda!" She looked from her husband to her brother-in-law. "Don't you see? That explains everything—Ross came into the house and found his mother in the study with Augustus. Maybe she was still holding the gun. Of course he would take it from her and send her upstairs and then he would run with the gun. Maybe he was going to hide it. And when he got to the lodge, he realized that the police would come and even if he said he did it, his mother would step forward and confess. But if he died—then why would she speak out? His death would protect her."

They all stared at Charlotte.

In Miss Dora's bright, dark eyes, there was grudging respect.

Sybil blindly sat down and stared sightlessly at the cold fireplace. "Ross loved his mother. Oh, my God."

Whitney cleared his throat. "I can't believe Mother would—but if Ross didn't shoot the Judge, why else would he kill himself? Oh, Christ."

"Not Amanda," Julia murmured blearily.

"My conclusion"—Miss Dora thumped her cane—"is that Charlotte perceives correctly one aspect of that dreadful day: Ross Tarrant indeed took his own life late on the afternoon of May ninth, 1970, and can be adjudged a gallant and honorable and loving son. I have no doubt but that some scene such as that envisioned by Charlotte did indeed occur; Ross was convinced of his mother's guilt."

"So this bloody little exercise of yours, dear Aunt Dora,

has been for naught." Milam grabbed his half-full tumbler from the table and lifted it. "On behalf of your grateful and admiring family," he said furiously, "may I thank you for this scintillating evening of civilized entertainment—and for Christ's sake, don't invite us next time." He downed the whisky, slammed the glass onto the table, and turned to his wife. "Come on, Julia."

"Milam, my inquiry is merely beginning." Miss Dora responded imperturbably, indifferent to his sarcasm. "Surely you understand that I would not call you here tonight merely to reopen wounds. Were Amanda the guilty party, there would be no need for an inquiry. But Amanda was not guilty. Ross was in error, an error which proved mortal for him and which has caused enormous pain and anguish on the part of those who loved him."

Milam glared at Miss Dora. "What the hell do you have up your sleeve now?"

"Mother didn't do it." Whitney's relief was enormous. Then, his shoulders sagged. "But, God, that means we don't know who killed the Judge."

Miss Dora reached out to take Sybil's hand. "I am afraid, my dear, that the road you travel is to be more difficult still. I know that you have courage. Will you join me in a journey filled with travail?"

"Nothing worse could happen to me than has already happened," Sybil said dully, the muscles in her face slack from misery.

Miss Dora gave Sybil's hand a quick squeeze, then loosed her grasp. "You will need all of your strength, my child."

Annie stepped closer to Max. It was comforting, in the midst of this puzzling—no, frightening—exchange, to be close to the most reassuring person she'd ever known. But even Max, his brows drawn in a tight frown, looked uneasy. What next, for God's sake?

"I don't understand." Charlotte's voice rose queru-
lously. "What does Sybil have to do with any of it?"

Miss Dora ignored Charlotte's question, but she gave
her full attention to Charlotte. "You are an intelligent
woman, Charlotte, intelligent, perceptive, responsible."

Charlotte accepted the accolade with a complacent nod,
and some of the strain seeped out of her face.

"So"—it was a hard-edged, jolting demand—"why
haven't you called the police to offer them information about
Courtney Kimball?" Miss Dora's obsidian eyes surveyed
Charlotte like an alligator eyeing a succulent cottonmouth.

Charlotte's mouth moved, but no words came. Pudgy
fingers clawed at her necklace.

If the atmosphere of the room had been tense before,
now it was surely electric.

An odd wheezing sound emanated from the old lady.

Annie looked at her in concern, then realized Miss
Dora was amused.

"Cat have your tongues, all of you? You know who I'm
talking about, each and every one of you. The young woman
who's opened this all up again—she's the reason we're here
tonight. And she's the reason I won't let this drop until we
know the truth. Because one of you"—there was no laughter
now on that wizened parchment face—"one of you may
have taken another life—and this time I won't tolerate it. Do
you hear me?"

"Who?" Sybil asked. "What are you talking about, Miss
Dora?"

"Pretty girl." Julia wavered unsteadily. "Came out to
Wisteree on Monday. Told her how nice Amanda was. Her
grandmother."

Spots of color burned in Charlotte's cheeks. "Nonsense.
She showed me a copy of that letter Monday, too. For all we
know, she found a letter from Amanda to her mother and
copied the handwriting. I don't care what kind of heiress she

may be, that doesn't mean we can let her make up stories about us. There is only one Tarrant grandchild, our daughter, Harriet."

Julia giggled. "And Harriet doesn't give a damn." At Charlotte's enraged glare, Julia tried to stifle her little hiccups of laughter. "Don't care. It's true. Want truth? Bet you don't even know where Harriet is."

"Harriet will come home someday. And no impostor is going to take her place," Charlotte said stiffly.

"I don't understand any of this." Sybil looked from Charlotte to Miss Dora. "Who are we talking about?"

Whitney intervened impatiently. "Christ, Sybil, don't you ever read the newspaper? The girl who's disappeared, the one who claims Ross was her father."

Every muscle in Sybil's body hardened. She stood for an instant as if turned to stone, but her eyes, wild, shocked, stunned eyes, huge and imploring, clung to Whitney. "Her father!" Abruptly, as if launched from a catapult, she was across the room, clutching her cousin's arm. "A girl who says Ross was her father?"

"That's what she said, Sybil." Pulling free of Sybil's grasp, Whitney glanced toward his wife, then continued defiantly. "Attractive young woman. Though I suppose that's neither here nor there. She claimed to have a letter from Mother saying that Ross wasn't guilty, that no matter what anyone should say Courtney should know that her father was innocent. She gave me a photocopy of the letter—" He looked briefly at his wife. "It sure looked like Mother's handwriting, but everyone knows Mother wasn't herself— before she died."

"Courtney." Sybil's voice shook. "When was she born?"

"How in the world should we know?" Charlotte said irritably.

"*When* was she born?" Sybil cried desperately.

"December twelfth, 1970," Max said quietly.

"December twelfth . . ." Tears spilled down Sybil's cheeks. "December twelfth—oh, Jesus, they lied to me. They lied to me! They said she was born dead. Oh, God, I heard her cry. I told my father I heard her cry, and he said I was wrong. He said it was another baby. Oh, God, they took my baby away from me."

As the front door of Chastain House closed behind Sybil, Max took Annie's hand. They walked in silence down the broad steps and along the moonlight-dappled drive toward the street.

"How could they?" Annie tried hard to keep the tremor from her voice. She didn't succeed.

Max slipped his arm around her shoulders. "It was a different day, a different age. And this was a conservative family in a small town."

She repeated it. "How could they?"

"Her father dead; her mother seventeen and unmarried." Max took a deep breath. "Annie, they thought they were doing the best thing for the baby and for Sybil."

"God." Annie stumbled to a stop and looked back toward the Greek Revival mansion. "Max, will she be all right? Shouldn't we stay?"

"She didn't give us a choice," he said dryly.

At Miss Dora's brusque command, Annie and Max had walked home with Sybil. Or tried to. Sybil had plunged ahead of them, taking a dark shortcut that she knew, and they had trouble following. But they were close behind when she stormed up her front steps, unlocked the door, and paused only to say, her face grim and stricken, "Tell them— tell them I will find her. I will. And if anything's happened to her, I'll spend the rest of my life finding the one who hurt her. Tell them that," and she'd slammed the door behind her.

Partway down the drive, Annie stopped again and looked back. Lights blazed from almost every room in the Chastain mansion. "Max, I don't think we should leave her alone."

Max gave Annie a quick, hard hug, then turned her once again toward the street. "Sybil will survive this night," he said quietly. "She's a survivor. She has to come to terms with the most shocking revelations she's ever faced. We can't help her do that. No one can. But tomorrow, tomorrow she'll see us. Because she'll want our help in searching for Courtney."

Slowly, reluctantly, Annie walked with him down the drive.

The oyster shells crunched beneath their feet. The far-away, mournful whistle of a freight train mingled with the nearby hoot of an owl.

Annie shivered. The night was cool and damp, the shadows ink dark, the rustles of the shrubbery disquieting.

"Max?" Her voice was thin. "Do you think Courtney's dead?"

Her question hung in the air.

He didn't answer, but his hand tightly gripped hers.

Annie felt better when they walked into their carefully appointed suite at the St. George Inn. The crimson coals from a discreet fire glimmered in the grate. The Tiffany lamp cast a warming glow over the chintz-covered sofa. The spread was invitingly turned down on the four-poster rice bed, and foil-wrapped candy in the unmistakable shape of truffles waited on the plump pillows.

As Max put on Colombian decaf to brew, Annie picked up the envelope lying on the coffee table. It was addressed to them in Barb's free-flowing script.

Dear Annie and Max,

What a day! For starters, the PI from Savannah dropped by and we have a date to go bowling tonight. Honestly, Max, do you believe in fate? He's really neat —kind of like Michael J. Fox, that cutie, all grown up —maybe forty-something. And he's really come up with the goods for you and Annie. I put the folders with all his stuff on your table—

Annie looked at the stack of folders piled on the replica of a pine plantation desk near the kitchenette.

—and I'll fax you some more stuff tomorrow. You'll find the fax behind the chaise longue in the bedroom. I paid a bonus to get the phone installed and turned on today. Also, I wangled about a half-dozen pictures of Courtney Kimball from friends, schools, etc. Isn't she pretty? Gee, I hope you find her okay. But it's scary, isn't it? More than twenty-four hours now.

Everything's super at Death on Demand. Except I think maybe Agatha needs counseling. I was reading about these cats in New York and they go to a psychiatrist and maybe you could get a long-distance consultation. I'd swear that Agatha actually threatened me! I know that sounds crazy—

Annie didn't think so. She'd known Agatha to be in a mood.

—but when I was fixing an anchovy pizza for lunch, Agatha jumped up on the coffee bar and tried to snag an anchovy, so, of course, I gave her a push—

Annie could have written the rest of the scenario herself. One did not shove Agatha.

—and I swear she growled and raised her paw at
me! And, Annie, she wouldn't get down until I put a
couple of anchovies in her bowl. Have you ever had a
cat give you an I-don't-give-a-damn look and refuse to
budge? Other than that—

Annie decided she would have to instruct Barb without
delay that what Agatha wanted, Agatha got. Otherwise,
many unpleasant and rationally inexplicable events would
occur—books randomly knocked down from displays, customer lists shredded, claw marks on collectibles (Annie'd had
to knock fourteen dollars off the price of an otherwise vf
copy of *Murder with a Theme Song* by Virginia Rath), and
once—and Annie had no explanation for this—the utter disappearance of a miniature replica of the famed Edgar
awarded annually at the Mystery Writers of America ban-
quet. Annie was confident Agatha couldn't have removed it
by mouth (it was ceramic and so offered no toothholds) or by
paw (she was smart but didn't have opposable thumbs).
Nonetheless, the miniature was nowhere to be found. Annie
consoled herself with the thought that life did hold its little
mysteries as well as its big. (Two socks go into a washing
machine, one comes out; you are wearing your oldest, sorri-
est sweat outfit and the first person you see in the grocery is
a) your priest, b) the hunk you've hankered to impress, c) the
banker you approached for a business loan in your niftiest
little black suit; late for a job interview on the fourteenth
floor, you find the elevator is broken so you arrive in the
office with a cherry-tomato face and a respiratory rate quali-
fying you to blow up the balloons at the annual company
picnic.)

—everything's going fine. I put Henny's latest postcard on top of the folders. Gosh, if some people don't

have all the luck! Anyway, hope you and Max are fig-
uring out what happened. We had two calls today from
the *Atlanta Constitution* and one from the *New York
Times* and one from AP. I put out a news release that
said Max was pursuing late-breaking developments and
hoped for an early and successful conclusion to his investigation. Was that okay?

Next to her flamboyant signature, Barb had penned a
happy face wearing a deerstalker hat.

"Milk?" Max asked, his hand on the small refrigerator.

"Milk and sugar both." Why did she still feel so cold
inside?

"Coming up."

He brought the coffee on a tray—this was a suite with
every refinement—with the cups and saucers, sugar bowl
and milk pitcher, and a plate full of peanut butter cookies.

Annie grabbed her cup and handed Max the message.
As he started to read, she said, "I hope Barb had fun bowling."

"Barb always has fun," he answered absently. He settled
beside her on the cushioned wicker couch, the note in one
hand, his cup in the other.

Annie picked up Henny's postcard.

Dear Annie,
X marks the spot.

Annie turned the card over and spotted a red *X* inked
beside St. Paul's Cathedral.

I actually stood at the very spot where Charlotte and
Anne Brontë stayed when they came to London to see
their publisher in 1848! They stopped at the Chapter
Coffee House which was at the entrance to St. Paul's

Alley, just by St. Paul's Churchyard. Can you believe it? In transports of joy, yours, as ever

—Henny.

They were both smiling as they put down the respective missives. Annie drank the clear, fresh coffee, munched on her cookie, and felt the icy core inside beginning to warm.

Max picked up the top folder and opened it. He drew his breath in sharply, then held up, for her to see, a photograph.

Annie put down her coffee cup. She shivered. No, the coldness hadn't gone away.

Courtney Kimball's blond hair was drawn back in a ponytail. Barefoot, she wore a floppy shell-pink T-shirt, and faded cutoffs. She leaned forward to balance on the uplifting catamaran, the carefree grin on her face and the luminous shine in her eyes the essence of summer.

"Oh, Max." Annie's voice broke. "We *have* to find her."

Charlotte gazed complacently at the gilt-framed oval mirror that hung in the hallway near the door to the study. Such a lovely mirror, though the glass now was smoky with age. There was a story that a handsome British officer had given it to the mistress, Mary Tarrant. She'd accepted with many pretty protestations of appreciation and accepted from him also a pass through the British lines, which she used to smuggle quinine to her husband in a prisoner-of-war camp. Sometimes Charlotte felt that she glimpsed another face there, brown hair peeping from beneath a dainty lace cap, high cheekbones, and a generous mouth. Charlotte smiled at her fancy and nodded in satisfaction at her own reflection, her hair drawn back in a smooth chignon, just the trace of pale-pink lipstick, no other makeup. The Judge admired restraint. Charlotte's glance swept the hallway, the glistening heart pine flooring, the Chinese print wallpaper, the magnificent mahogany stairway, the marble bust of Homer on a black oak pedestal. The bust of Homer had been brought home from Athens when Nathaniel and Rachel honeymooned there. She brushed her finger over the cool stone. Tarrant House. She belonged here. She and the Judge held the same values. Not like Julia. Julia didn't understand the importance of family. Julia didn't appreciate continuity, the thrill of

pouring tea from a china service brought from London for Christmas in 1762. Julia didn't deserve to be mistress of Tarrant House. With a final approving look—the pale-blue chambray of her dress was perfect—Charlotte turned toward the study.

Chapter 13.

The wail of the sirens and the ring of the telephone registered at almost the same time in Annie's sleep-numbed consciousness. She fought to wake from the bone-deep sleep of mental and emotional exhaustion.

The telephone shrilled again. The siren's cry became a shriek.

Annie came flailing out of bed and banged her knee into the chaise longue. Max rolled out from his side and knocked over a chair.

Max flicked the light switch just as Annie's pawing hands found the telephone.

She knew before she lifted the receiver that something terrible had happened. Good news doesn't come over the telephone in the middle of the night.

"Come at once." There was both anger and chagrin in Miss Dora's pronouncement. "A fire at Tarrant House." And the connection was broken.

• • •

Annie stumbled over a fire hose.

"Lady, get out of the way!"

"This way, Annie." Max held her elbow. They back-tracked, skirting the far side of the two fire engines, then cut across the street to the west side of Tarrant House.

Flames danced against the night sky. Smoke billowed high.

"Max!" Annie strained to see. "It doesn't look like it's the house. It's *behind* the house."

When they reached the garages, the site of the fire was clear. Straight ahead, past an herb garden and a huge rose trellis and a garden shed was yet another structure and it was afire.

Whitney and Charlotte Tarrant stood beside the ga-rages. Whitney gripped his wife's arm tightly. "Charlotte, you can't go in. You can't! God, look at it—"

Flames wreathed the wooden structure. Sparks swirled upward, creating whirling plumes of light. Flames leapt and danced as boards crashed. Smoke eddied, darker than the night.

Annie could feel the heat from the flames.

"It's a total loss." Whitney coughed as a wave of smoke swept them.

In the fitful light from the leaping flames and the back-wash of light spilling from the house, Charlotte's face was dead-white and stricken. She was too distraught to realize that the tasseled tie of her peach-silk robe dragged on the ground and that her silk gown gaped.

"The papers, the family papers," she cried, her voice hoarse with despair. "The records! Whitney, do something! They must save the papers. The diaries." She struggled to be free. "Let's tell them George might be in there," she said feverishly. "Then they'll have to go in, won't they? We could say those are the servants' quarters. They were once. How will they know any different?"

"Don't be absurd, Charlotte." Whitney shook her.

"George?" asked Annie.

"The gardener," Max explained. "His father was the butler—"

Miss Dora joined them, looking more witchlike than ever in the wavering firelight. "And Sam's father before him and his father—they used to live there. Charlotte remodeled the whole shebang, turned it into the Tarrant House Museum." The old lady pointed with her cane. "Slave quarters once. Call 'em dependencies now." A dry wheeze might have been sardonic laughter. "Pretty words don't make pretty deeds." Miss Dora's silver hair shimmered in the glow from the flames. She stared at the fire-engulfed structure, her wizened face grim and thoughtful.

Whitney turned and glared at the three of them. His gaze fastened on Annie and Max. "This is private property—"

Miss Dora waggled her cane. "Here at *my* request, Whitney."

A wall collapsed. Sparks spewed skyward.

"The papers," Charlotte moaned. She sagged against her husband. "Oh, God." It was a heartbroken wail. "My thimble collection."

"The papers." Miss Dora's voice was speculative. "Inclusive, weren't they, Charlotte?"

Charlotte half-turned. "Oh, Aunt Dora, it's a tragedy, a tragedy! Mary's diaries, the letters she received from her husband from the English prison, the records of the baptisms and burials, gone, all gone."

"But more than that," Miss Dora mused. "You saved everything from this century, too, didn't you, because someday, God forbid, they'll be writing about us. All of Augustus's papers. And I suspect, Amanda's too."

Charlotte's eyes flared. Whitney's head jerked toward the old woman.

In the silence that fell on the small group, the sound of the fire intruded, the crackle, hiss, and roar, the brusque calls of the firemen, the thump of their running feet, the crash of falling timbers.

Miss Dora looked from Charlotte to Whitney, then toward the flickering flames. "A murderer moved in the quiet of this night to search out and destroy. But I shall prevail."

Annie didn't know which was most ominous, the voracious destructiveness of the fire or the inimical certainty in that whispery voice.

"So, you think it was arson." Annie's eyes ached with fatigue. She watched with approval as Max poured coffee into their cups. She needed every ounce of energy the world's finest brew could provide. Although they'd gone back to bed after the fire was extinguished, she'd smelled smoke for the rest of the night and tossed and turned restlessly. She had a sense of time speeding past and she and Max trying desperately, frantically to capture a dangerous and wily opponent before it was too late.

Too late for what?

Wasn't it almost certainly too late for Courtney Kimball?

So why this unremitting sense of urgency?

Was it the fact of the fire, the reminder that death and destruction could strike at any time?

Was it Miss Dora's parting injunction? As they'd turned to go, she called after them, "Quickly, we must progress quickly."

Or was it the fear that murder wasn't yet done?

Max nodded as he speared another piece of papaya (which Annie found about as tasty as chewing on the plastic handle of a toothbrush). "Not only does the inn provide an excellent breakfast with the room, but look at this terrific assortment of fruit. Annie, we must start having this at home."

Annie drank more coffee and reached for another peanut butter cookie.

A little indistinctly, Max continued. "Sure, it's arson. Didn't you smell the gasoline?"

She realized suddenly that she had indeed smelled gasoline. "No wonder the flames spread so fast." She sprinkled brown sugar on her oatmeal. "It's infuriating to think we were that close to finding things out, and the murderer's outwitted us."

Max poked the serving spoon in the bowl of fruit, looking for more papaya wedges, but settled for honeydew. "No, that's not true." He was emphatic and utterly confident. He flashed her an upbeat smile. "In fact, the murderer made a mistake—a big one. Look at it this way: just because we're going to Tarrant House today doesn't mean we would have asked about the recent family papers or learned that they, too, were stored in Charlotte's personal museum, or, even if we'd learned about them, that we would have made them a top priority. So, the murderer did us a big favor. The fire makes it damn clear we have to scratch and scratch to find out more about Augustus."

Annie reached for more brown sugar. "Why Augustus?" She thought it through. "Why not Amanda? She's the one who went over a cliff after writing a letter stating Ross wasn't guilty."

Max looked at her in surprise, then nodded agreement. "Sagaciously put, partner in crime."

Annie tried not to look too pleased. Of course, Agatha Christie's Tuppence Beresford often saw more ramifications than her husband, Tommy, but it made for marital harmony to be tactful.

The phone rang. Annie glanced at the time. Almost eight o'clock.

"Hello." Max tucked the receiver against his shoulder and poured fresh coffee. "Yeah, Barb. Great. Let's hear it."

Annie finished the last scoop of oatmeal and watched as Max scribbled notes.

Hanging up, he said briefly, "Harris Walker. Porter checked, Walker's in the clear. Played golf Wednesday afternoon, two rounds, didn't come in off the course till seven. Had dinner at the grill with one of his foursome. No chance he could have been in Chastain."

Annie pictured that desperate, frantic face. She wasn't surprised, but she was glad.

Max took a gulp of coffee and looked up at the mantel clock. "We need to hurry, Annie."

She understood. It was already Friday morning. Courtney had been missing since Wednesday night.

If they were to find her, it had to be soon.

On her way out of town, Annie slowed the Volvo and turned onto Lookout Point. She wasn't sure why. She couldn't have recognized the jaunty MG parked there. But perhaps her heart knew.

Oyster shells crackled beneath the tires. She drew up beside the MG. Jerkily, the man slumped asleep over the wheel raised his head and stared at her blankly. Then Harris Walker's bleary eyes snapped wide. "Courtney? Have you—" But he didn't have to finish his question. The hope on his haggard, unshaven face seeped away.

"No. I'm sorry. But we're doing everything we can." Swiftly, Annie reported all she and Max had learned.

Walker listened, staring out at the river. A boat was underway now, a heavy net lowered for dragging. The young lawyer rubbed at a bristly jaw. "All right. Thanks." He closed his eyes briefly, then, in futile, violent anger slammed a fist against the steering wheel, over and over again.

Annie winced, but he gave no evidence of the pain he must have felt.

"Tarrant House." That was all he said. But his eyes were bleak and merciless.

Annie checked the road map spread on the car seat beside her and hoped that she wasn't hopelessly lost. She spotted a road marker listed in her directions (four miles to the earthworks of Fort Welles). So far, so—

The car phone rang.

Annie involuntarily flinched. She wasn't yet accustomed to carrying Ma Bell with her wherever she went.

"Hello?" Odd not to answer, "Death on Demand, the finest mystery bookstore this side of Atlanta." She felt a pang of homesickness. A Friday morning in the spring—there would be beaucoup tourists. The island was at its loveliest now, with mild, temperate, gloriously sunny days. And so many wonderful new books to sell, new titles by Susan Dunlap, Randy Russell, and Nancy Pickard, a bookseller's dream come true.

". . . so *sad!* Only four weeks of happiness, and then such trauma."

Annie made a comforting noise and slowed for a school zone.

Laurel sighed. "At least the wedding itself was glorious."

Annie almost inquired whether it had been a three-ring circus, then thought better of it. No need to hurt Laurel's feelings. And certainly, Annie took great pride in the fact that her own wedding, though assisted by Laurel, had been quite tasteful. She contented herself with a murmured "Hmm" as she picked up speed and began looking for her next checkpoint.

"Edingsville Beach, across from Edisto Island, of course. Before the War." The husky voice flowed like honey.

Annie hadn't asked, but it was nice to know.

"The wedding was at St. Stephen's. It united two great island families when Mary Clark wed her cherished sweetheart, Captain Fickling. Oh, they had a glorious feast—oyster pie, mincemeat, rice cake, ginger pound cake, and syllabub. Four weeks after the wedding, Captain Fickling set sail for the West Indies. Mary awaited his return eagerly. The days passed, and his ship was overdue. The sea swells began to rise, the sky darkened, the wind howled. A huge hurricane struck the island, causing great devastation. Mary was astonished to have survived. The next morning, she went down to the beach and saw the flotsam and jetsam sweeping in. Then Mary saw the body of a drowning victim. She ran out into the water to pull in that sodden form—and it was her husband. She gave a great cry of despair. Even today visitors to the strand of beach that remains have been known to see Mary plunge into the water and hear her heartbroken cry when she recognizes her adored husband."

"How hideous." Annie's hand tightened on the steering wheel. Despite her resolve not to be affected by Laurel's recitations, Annie couldn't avoid a shudder.

"Ah, yes. The further I delve into this rich history, the better I understand our ghosts." Laurel spoke with great confidence. Dr. Laurel Darling Roethke, Ph.D. in ghostology.

Annie knew she was being led down a garden path (What was there to understand?), but she couldn't resist. "Oh?"

"It's as simple and clear as dear Alice Flagg's grave." The implication, of course, was that any damn fool should understand.

"Oh, yes, of course. Certainly. I quite agree." Annie slowed. Yes, there was the country grocery noted in her directions. The name fascinated: The Mata Hari Meat Market. No way she could resist stopping there on her return to ask why.

The line crackled.

Annie grinned. Teach Laurel to one-up past a certain point.

But Laurel was always graceful in defeat. A light trill of laughter. "So lovely to deal with an intellectual equal. And how are you this morning, dear?"

So Laurel wasn't going to share the simple yet evident reason for the existence of ghosts. At least not today.

"Trying to find out more about the murder of Augustus Tarrant." Annie checked her mileage counter. Another mile and a half past the grocery, she would turn right.

"Murder!" Laurel exclaimed.

Annie was too well-bred to gloat openly about knowing more than Laurel. Amiably, she brought her mother-in-law up-to-date on the results of Miss Dora's dinner party, evincing not even a *soupçon* of superiority.

"Good heavens!" Laurel exclaimed. "Ross dead by his own hand and blamed for his father's murder! My dear, no wonder ghosts walk at Tarrant House." Laurel's husky voice took on sepulchral overtones. "Such trauma. Such despair. Such misery. Perhaps I should put aside my work here and join you and dear Max. A *pallet* on the floor would be more than ample and I—"

"Dear Laurel." Annie braked sharply to make her turn. She'd almost missed her turn. The Volvo jolted down a rutted dusty gray road beneath an overhang of live oak limbs. "I would never forgive myself for interfering in the creation of the definitive book, *Ghosts of South Carolina, from Earliest Times to the Present.*"

"Oh." A thoughtful pause. "There *is* my book."

Annie pressed her advantage. "You know how publishing is, Laurel. If an idea strikes one author, why, it will strike another." (There was the year Joan Hess, Marian Babson, and Carolyn G. Hart all did murder weekends.) "You dare not lose time—or a book just like yours will come out."

"Not *just* like mine, Annie. You don't understand. My book is truly original, and . . ."

Annie saw the sign for the Mt. Zion Baptist Church— one mile. She slowed the car, looking for a spot to park.

". . . I know absolutely no one else will have a chapter on— Perhaps I should be discreet." Laurel's husky voice fell to a whisper. "Telephones. Electronics. All that ether out there. Someone might overhear." She rebounded ebulliently. "Annie, you are such a *dear*. Such a *fount* of wisdom. *Arrivederci,* my sweet."

Annie was smiling as she replaced the receiver. How nice it was for Laurel to have an enthusiasm . . . at a distance.

There were no turnoffs and she didn't want to park at the church. Pulling over as far as she could on the narrow, dusty road, Annie idled the motor and hoped no traffic would come for a minute or so.

She picked up the top folder on the stack in the passenger's seat. Usually, she and Max studied background information before starting out, but this time, they'd split the list of those to be interviewed and taken the materials along. She knew it was one more evidence of their urge to hurry, hurry, hurry.

Flipping open the folder, she read:

LUCY JANE JEMSON McKAY—Born April 23, 1922, on a Beaufort County farm to Lola Wayne and Henry Jemson. Fifth of nine children. Attended rural schools, completed eighth grade. Worked on her parents' farm, married Edmond McKay June 5, 1939.

Moved to Chastain, began working in the kitchen at
Tarrant House as an assistant to the cook, Anna Duvall. Four children, Samuel, Elijah, Preston, and
Martha. Husband killed in action in the European the-
ater, World War II. She became chief cook at Tarrant
House in 1944 on the retirement of Mrs. Duvall and
remained at Tarrant House until 1985 when she joined
her widowed son, the Rev. Samuel McKay, as his
housekeeper. A member of the choir of the Chastain
Emmanuel Baptist Church for forty-six years. Matilda
Weems, who sang with Lucy Jane for most of those
years, describes her as "Busy! Land sakes, you don't
find any flies on Lucy Jane. Cooking, canning, cleaning,
sewing, gardening, Lucy Jane does it all and she hasn't
slowed down a particle since she was a girl. She's one
no-nonsense woman. Raised those children by herself
after her man was killed in the war—they were just
babies then—and she wouldn't hear of anything but
good from every one of them. Samuel, he's a preacher,
Elijah is a cook like his mamma, Preston's a teacher at
the high school, and Martha's a nurse. They all married
and had families. Course, Samuel lost his wife and
that's why Lucy Jane lives way out there in the country
now, helping him. I miss her in the choir. Can't nobody
else sing 'Amazing Grace' like Lucy Jane. She's mighty
proud of her children, though she won't let on. Says
it'd give them the big head. She doesn't believe in complaining and won't put up with complainers. She has a
deep laugh and she loves to let it ring out, says the
world was meant for laughter, not tears."

Annie closed the folder. She was looking forward to
meeting Lucy Jane McKay.

As Max hurried up the sidewalk toward the yellow stucco
building on Federal Street that housed the law offices of
Tarrant & Tarrant (though Whitney was the only Tarrant at

present in the firm), he reviewed what he had just read about Whitney Tarrant: Forty-six. Middle son of Augustus and Amanda Tarrant. Good health. Good credit. Income from law firm erratic, not impressive; lives on inherited wealth. A social leader in Chastain. Plays golf at the country club every Wednesday afternoon and on both Saturday and Sunday. Consistently shoots in the eighties. Likes to play skins. Wins and losses even out. A complainer, nothing ever quite suits. One of the New South's strong Republicans. Hostile to unions. Episcopalian. Opposed to women priests, ordination of homosexuals. Reputed to have an eye for the ladies. Rumored to have had several affairs over the years, usually with women met through his work with the Chamber of Commerce. No suggestion divorce ever contemplated. Apparently on good terms with his wife, Charlotte. No public quarrels, except for their disagreement over their daughter, Harriet. Active in the bar association. Considered a lightweight lawyer, good at bringing in clients who are subsequently handled by his younger partner, Richard Parks. As one older lawyer remarked, "The old Judge would have a seizure if he saw Whitney in action. Whitney's all mouth, no show. No substance there—and lazy to boot." Another said, "You have to be damn careful with Whitney. He'll always cheat just a little bit." A former lover snapped, "The only thing Whitney ever loved was Whitney." His daughter, Harriet: "Pop? Oh, Christ, what can you expect of anybody who'd be fool enough to marry Charlotte? Pop and male black widow spiders have a lot in common. Though he did stand up to her for me—once. Maybe once is enough."

Max passed the ground-floor jewelry store and opened the door leading to the stairs to the second and third floors. Though the walls were painted a modern cream, the wooden stairs, the steps worn in the center, revealed the building's age.

On the second floor, Max entered a law office that

looked as though it had been there since the building was built in the 1880s—and it probably had. Old wood paneling, old wooden floor, worn Persian rug, its rich colors muted by age. The door creaked as Max closed it behind him.

The young receptionist damn sure hadn't been there since the 1880s. As Max stepped inside, she smoothed glistening platinum hair and smiled brightly at him, and it was a smile that said a lot. Max was glad Annie wasn't there to see it.

"Good morning. May I help you?"

"Yes. I'm Max Darling. I'd like to speak to Mr. Tarrant." Max took out his card and scrawled: *Miss Dora sent me.* "If you will give this to him, I would appreciate it."

Miss Dora's name continued to work magic, which came as no surprise to Max. As he followed the receptionist into one of the inner offices, the tight frown on Whitney Tarrant's face came as no surprise either.

As the door closed behind his receptionist, Tarrant eyed Max coldly. "You've obviously taken advantage of an old woman's foolish credulity. I owe my great-aunt every courtesy, but I don't owe you a damn thing—and I want to make it clear that I'm violently opposed to your meddling in our family affairs."

"Murder can cause worse than meddling. I'd imagine you'd rather talk to me than to Chief Wells." Max gestured toward the red leather chair that faced Tarrant's beautifully carved desk. "May I?"

Tarrant stared at him. "Chief Wells?"

"Miss Dora has informed him of last night's revelations." Max looked at him inquiringly. "I'm surprised you didn't call him yourself."

"But—" Whitney's eyes shifted away from Max. Better than anyone else at Miss Dora's, Whitney, as a lawyer, knew there was no statute of limitations in regard to murder. "Yes, yes, I see. Of course, we will have to think back." His glance became wary. "Yes, I see. Go ahead, then, sit down. But I can't give you much time. I have to be in court at ten."

Max thought this was probably invented on the spot. Whitney was definitely an office lawyer, though his walls were decorated with prints of English barristers. It was assuredly an impressive office. An Aubusson rug stretched in front of the massive desk, a pair of matching Chinese Lowestoft gamecocks rested at either end of the bookcase behind the desk. A French Empire clock dominated the mantelpiece above the Georgian fireplace. A small, spider-legged circular table, its antique patina gleaming, sat in front of the fireplace. One wall held a gun collection: a musket, two sets of silver-plated dueling pistols, a Colt Model 1860 revolving pistol, a Spencer rifle, and a Springfield carbine.

Max looked the collection over. A gun lover. A weak-chinned gun lover. But guns couldn't help Whitney now.

Max leaned forward in his chair and spoke briskly. "This is your chance to stand up and be counted, Mr. Tarrant. Do you want to find your father's murderer or not?"

"Of course I do," Whitney snapped. "Though I still have to wonder . . . perhaps Miss Dora was wrong about the time and seeing Ross."

Max didn't bother to respond to that weak ploy.

Tarrant abandoned it, too. He straightened the single stack of papers on his desk top. "I just don't see—I mean, that leaves Milam and Julia and Charlotte. And Lucy Jane, the cook, was around somewhere. And Sam, the butler. And the maid. God, what was her name. Tiny little thing who always moved real fast. Oh, yeah, Enid." His head lifted. "I can't believe it! It couldn't be one of them!"

Max pulled out his notebook and flipped over several pages. "Is there anyone who you know for a fact could *not* have done it?"

"How would I know that?" the lawyer asked, puzzled.

Max glanced at the notebook. "Last night you said you

were in the garage when you heard the shot. That's some distance from the house. Maybe you saw someone just before or just after the shot and that would place them too far from the study to have committed the murder."

"No." That was all he said. Even an office lawyer knows that simple answers are best.

Max looked at Whitney until the lawyer's gaze slid away.

"All right, then. Let's go back to the garage. You were working on your car?" Max put a minuscule note of doubt in his voice. "You often worked on your car?"

"Uh, no." Whitney moved restively in his leather seat, and it squeaked.

"But that's what you were doing that afternoon?" Max pressed.

"Yes." Whitney clipped the word off and glared at Max.

Unabashed, Max asked, "What kind of car was it?"

"Oh, God, let me think. Damn long time ago. Oh, yeah, yeah, we had a 1968 Pontiac."

Max let the answer hang. It wasn't the kind of car to excite devotion. Finally, he said, "All right. You were in the garage with your car. What were you doing to it?"

Whitney shrugged. "Cleaning it out. We'd been out to the country on a picnic the night before and it had a lot of stuff in it."

"What time did you go out to the garage?" Max held his pen over the notebook.

Whitney folded his arms across his chest. "How should I know? Oh, hell, I don't know. I don't remember. What the hell difference does it make?"

"It's necessary to pinpoint exactly where everyone was at four o'clock. When we know that, we may be able to show that one or more of you couldn't have been in the study and murdered the Judge." Max had no idea whether this concept was true, but he felt damn certain there was something Whitney didn't want to reveal. Whether it concerned the garage, his own actions, or his father's murder was impossible to tell. "So"—Max tried a persuasive smile—"could you see anyone else from your vantage point in the garage?"

Whitney drummed his fingers irritably on the desk top. "Look, Darling, it's twenty damn years ago! And I was cleaning the damn car. I wasn't rubbernecking out the window."

"The garage has a window?" Max wished that he had scouted out the garage before coming to the Tarrant offices. He could have been much more precise and demanding in his questions.

"Oh, yeah. Several. And—" Whitney stopped. A startled look crossed his face. He frowned, then shook his head.

"You saw someone?" Max demanded quickly. "Who? Where?"

But Whitney was absorbed in his memories. He was obviously turning an idea—and a worrisome one—over and over in his mind.

Max asked again. "Who did you see?" He felt an urgency, a sense of excitement. Maybe, finally, something was going to break.

"Who did I . . ." Then Whitney focused on Max. The lawyer's face hardened. It was as if a shutter came down in his eyes, and they were as bright and hard and unreadable as agates. "I didn't see a damn thing." He repeated it emphatically. "I didn't see a damn thing." There was a ring of truth in his voice. "Because there wasn't anything *to* see." He shoved back his chair and stood. "It's too long ago. Either Ross did it—or we'll never know who did it. And I'm out of time. Let's make it quick. I was in the garage. I didn't see a damn soul until my brother came slamming in and that was ten minutes after the sound of the shot. At least ten minutes.

I didn't leave the garage during that time or shortly before that time. I sure as hell didn't sprint into the house and shoot my father."

Max slowly stood, too, and tried to look benign. "Mr. Tarrant, please be assured that our objective is to unearth the truth, not trouble innocent parties. But until we learn what really happened that afternoon, we have to ask questions, questions that I hope you will answer frankly. For example, will you tell me what kind of terms your father was on with the other members of the family?"

A mirthless smile pulled down the corners of the lawyer's mouth. "Terms? His own terms, Mr. Darling. My father—" He took a deep breath. " 'Judge' was what we called him, Mr. Darling. All of us. Even my mother. The Judge ruled. It was that simple."

"Had you talked with him that day?" Max kept his eyes on Tarrant's face.

"Just a good morning at breakfast," Whitney said carefully.

Whitney wasn't a talented lawyer. His suddenly smoothed-out expression was patently contrived. He wouldn't have fooled a jury for a minute. He sure didn't fool Max.

"Breakfast? Oh, I see. Were you and your wife living there on a permanent basis?" It wasn't quite an idle question, but the response surprised Max.

Anger and, even after all these years, embarrassment flashed in the attorney's eyes. "I was a young lawyer. I was just starting out." His tone was clearly defensive. "I didn't have the income to afford a home. Besides, Charlotte loved living at Tarrant House."

"Did you?" Max asked quickly.

A dull flush stained Whitney's cheeks. He didn't answer.

Max tapped his notebook. "I have some figures here—your family is quite well-to-do. Couldn't your parents have helped you and Charlotte with a home—or made one of the plantations available?"

"That's an offensive question, Darling." Whitney walked to the door and flung it open. "And I've got better things to do than be insulted by you."

Max stood his ground. "Did the Judge refuse to help you? Did he insist you earn enough money to support yourself outside of family income? I understand he never accepted money from his parents."

Whitney's bony face twisted in a furious scowl. "Get the hell out, Darling. Now."

Enid Friendley tapped politely on the door to the Judge's bedroom though she knew he was in his study. At the expected lack of response, she turned the heavy bronze doorknob and entered. As she moved swiftly around the room—Enid always moved quickly, though she begrudged every step in the service of this house—she dusted efficiently and thoroughly and savored the pleasure she felt when she saw that the carved mahogany box was no longer in place atop the Judge's dresser.

Chapter 14.

The Mt. Zion Baptist Church glistened in the early-morning sunlight. A cemetery adjoined the church, the plots beautifully cared for. The frame church had recently been repainted and was a dazzling white. The frame house on the far side of the church also sparkled with fresh paint. White and red impatiens grew in profusion in the front bed. Crimson azaleas flamed along the side of the tiny house.

Annie pulled into the shell drive. The slam of her car door sounded shockingly loud in the placid morning quiet.

As Annie approached, the front door opened. An imposing woman stepped out onto the porch. Her dark face held neither welcome nor hostility. Tall and slender, she waited, her hands folded across the midriff of her starched cotton housedress.

"Mrs. McKay?"

"Yes'm. You must be Miz Darling. Miss Dora called, said you were coming." She didn't smile. Her face was grave and thoughtful.

Annie recognized strength of character. Lucy Jane Mc-Kay would do what she thought was right—and the devil take the hindmost.

Annie was straightforward. "There's a girl missing—and it's tied up with what happened a long time ago—to Judge Tarrant and to Ross."

Lucy Jane looked at her searchingly. "Miss Dora says this girl is the daughter of Mr. Ross and Miss Sybil." A slow shake of her head. "Miss Sybil—even then she was too pretty for any man to resist, but I thought it would all come right. Mr. Ross, he could handle her—nobody else ever could." A faint, slightly possessive smile touched her lips. "Mr. Ross—he was a fine young man, a strong, fine young man." She nodded. Her decision was made. "You're welcome to come in, Miz Darling."

The living room was small but cheerful, and it shone from loving care. The gingham curtains were freshly laundered, the wooden floor glistened with wax, the red-and-white braided throw rugs were bright and clean. The smell of baking hung in the air.

Annie sat in a comfortable easy chair and accepted a cup of coffee and a fresh cinnamon roll.

Lucy Jane poured Annie's coffee, then sat on the sofa, her posture erect, her dark eyes somber.

"Did Miss Dora tell you what we learned last night?" A bite of cinnamon roll melted in Annie's mouth.

"Yes'm." Lucy Jane clasped her dark, strong hands together. Her face was troubled. "I always knew something was wrong—bad wrong—that day. I'd been in my quarters. It was afternoon and I was reading my Bible until time to go in the kitchen and set to work on dinner. I'd just looked up at the clock, to make sure time wasn't getting away from me, when I heard the shot. It was two minutes after four. I didn't know what to do. I know the sound guns make and there was no call for a gun to be shot off. Not that close. I went to my window and looked out and I saw Mr. Ross running across the garden toward the house. That relieved my mind. I knew Mr. Ross would take care of it, so I went back to my rocker. But pretty soon doors slammed and cars came and went. I went to see what was happening and Mr. Harmon met me at the kitchen door and told me to be fixin' food for all the family to come, that Judge Tarrant's heart had given out and he was dead." She pursed her lips, then burst out, "I knew there was more to it because Enid—she was the maid —she came to me the next week and showed me this charred bundle of clothes. She said they'd belonged to the Judge, and she'd found them out in the incinerator. I told her to hush her mouth and I would see to it. I gave the clothes to Mr. Harmon, and he told me he'd take care of everything. By then the funerals were over, and it had been in the papers how the Judge died from a heart attack when he heard the news about Mr. Ross's accident with his gun." She looked across the room at a table filled with framed photographs. "Mr. Ross never had an accident with a gun. Mr. Ross, he was always careful. He did things right." She smoothed her starched cotton skirt. "I knew it was wrong, all these years, and now the past has come due—and Mr. Ross's daughter is lost and gone. I tell you, Miz Darling, I feel low in my mind."

"You can help," Annie said quietly.

"Now? What can I do?" She was not so much reluctant as uncertain.

"Talk to me about the Tarrants." Annie held her gaze. "You knew them, really knew them. Tell me who was angry, who was afraid, who was threatened."

"The Tarrants." A smile transformed Lucy Jane's face. "Young Mr. Ross, he had a sense of humor, he did. Did you ever hear tell how he made a family shield? I suppose you know how prideful Miz Charlotte is, always talking about past glories and all the fine things the Tarrants have done and seen—and rightly so. Lawyers and doctors and preachers and good women keeping families going. Oh, there are many stories to tell. I used to hear the Judge talk to the boys when they were little, telling them about mighty battles and such. But Miz Charlotte, she riled Mr. Ross, and one day when he was home for the weekend from school, he and Miss Sybil were in the library giggling fit to kill. When they came out, they put this big poster up on the landing of the stairs, where nobody could miss it, and it was like those shields that knights of old carried. Above the shield, Mr. Ross had written THE TERRIFYING, TERRIBLE TARRANTS, and in each part of the shield, he'd drawn a huge hairy tarantula, and down below, he'd printed, THE FAMILY CREST—TARANTU-LAS RAMPANT. Course, it made Miz Charlotte mad as everything. She said he was making fun of the family, and Mr. Ross kept insisting he thought it was a lovely shield, very appropriate, probably the very name Tarrant came from tarantula, and that made her madder still." She chuckled, then slowly the laughter died away. "And not two weeks later, he was lying dead in his grave in St. Michael's. Just a boy."

Annie felt a prickle of horror: Ross Tarrant, having fun with his heritage and so soon to sacrifice himself for his family's honor.

"The Family." Annie shivered though the swath of sunlight spilling from the east window touched her with warmth. She drank more of the strong, hot, chicory-flavored coffee. "Tell me about the Judge."

"Mr. Augustus." If there was no great warmth in Lucy Jane's voice, there was ungrudging respect. The Judge apparently had earned great respect. Had anyone ever loved him? "He came to dinner every Sunday with his parents when I first came to Tarrant House. After his folks died, that's when Mr. Augustus and Mrs. Amanda moved in with their two little boys. Mr. Ross was born there. He was such a beautiful baby, blond curls and blue eyes, and always happy. Mr. Augustus was real strict with the boys. He expected them to do just so. I know it's a fact—I raised three boys and a girl—you have to expect a lot from children if they're to grow up right. But somehow, the Judge expected—" Her eyes were troubled. "—my heart told me he expected more than mortal boys could give. Even Mr. Ross. I don't know if I can rightly explain. I always thought the Judge never saw them—Milam and Whitney and Ross—as flesh-and-blood people. He saw them as . . . Tarrants."

"What else would you expect?" Annie asked.

The older woman nodded impatiently. "Yes. But they were Milam and Whitney and Ross, too. They had to pick their own way. That's it," she said firmly, "that's where it all went wrong. He never could see any way to be but the way the Judge believed a Tarrant should be—someone important and proper, the kind of men Chastain would look up to. That was real important to the Judge, to be looked up to."

Annie thought of the photograph of the Judge on the bench. The photographer, of course, had stood in the well of the courtroom, shooting up.

A stern judge. A demanding father.

"You see," Lucy Jane reflected, "Mr. Whitney, he couldn't quite do the things the Judge wanted and so he got in the habit of getting his friends to do his schoolwork for him. And his mamma, she protected him when the school found out and called. Miz Amanda never told the Judge. And once, when Mr. Whitney was in law school, there was trouble about a paper. I know his mamma went and talked to the dean and it all worked out. I think it was the next year that Mr. Harmon—that was Miz Amanda's daddy—he gave a big scholarship to the school." Lucy Jane's smile was dry. "You know how folks can work things around in their minds sometimes to where what happened didn't happen quite the way it was thought and so everything turns out all right."

Annie knew. It wasn't only beauty that depended upon the eye of the beholder. Funny how money could magically alter circumstances.

"Then when Mr. Whitney married, he picked a girl he thought the Judge would like, 'cause she cared so much about the old times and families and who married who. Miz Charlotte"—the cool, thoughtful eyes betrayed no emotion—"she cares more for dead-and-gone people than she does people here today. That's why Miss Harriet ran away. Miz Charlotte never would pay the child any mind. And Mr. Whitney, he was too busy with horses and golf and cards to notice. And when Miss Harriet acted up worse and worse, they just packed her off to school, and one day, when the school wrote and said she'd run away from there, Miz Charlotte was so busy with one of her history groups, she hardly took it in. Mr. Whitney sent Miss Harriet money when she took up living out in California even though Miz Charlotte said they shouldn't have anything to do with her until she started acting like a Tarrant should."

Would the Judge have been pleased with his daughter-in-law's total acceptance of Tarrant mores? Had he been pleased long years ago?

"How did Mrs. Charlotte and the Judge get along?" Annie pictured two faces, the lean, harsh, ascetic face of the man on the bench, the earnest, self-satisfied face of Charlotte.

Lucy Jane gave a mirthless chuckle. "Thing about the Judge, he was no fool. Ever. He saw through Miz Charlotte easy as pie, the way she simpered up to him, always wanting to talk about the Family and how much it meant to her and Mr. Whitney. The Judge, he knew Mr. Whitney didn't care a fig about the family. All Mr. Whitney ever wanted was to get along."

"And Milam?" Annie asked.

"Mr. Milam. He's a case, he is." But there was no admiring tone in her voice as there had been for Ross. "Lucky thing for him the Judge didn't live to see how he's turned out." She rose gracefully and brought the coffeepot to refill Annie's cup. "Course, it's plain as the nose on your face what Mr. Milam's up to. He wants to make people mad. Every time somebody here in town gets huffy over the way Mr. Milam acts or dresses, Mr. Milam's pleased as punch. One more time he's thumbing his nose at his daddy. If all he wanted was to be an artist and live like some artists do, he could pack up and go where folks like that is a dime a dozen. But that isn't what Mr. Milam wants." She sipped her coffee. "Even after all these years, Mr. Milam's angry with the Judge." She looked at the mantel and another set of photographs. "Sometimes young people get jealous when they see people in big houses having everything, but I always told my children that living in a big house can be a hard row to hoe."

Annie was struck not only by her wisdom but by the undercurrent of sympathy in Lucy Jane's voice. Annie was willing to bet few persons exhibited such charity toward Milam Tarrant, who seemed to have a genius for raising hackles.

"What about Julia?" Annie asked.

"Poor, little Miz Julia." Her voice was almost a croon. "So sad a lady." There was steel in her voice when she spoke next. "I do fault Mr. Milam there. He shouldn't have married, just to marry. But the Judge, as far as he was concerned, a man wasn't grown unless he married."

It was elliptical to be sure, but Annie thought she understood and she felt even sorrier for poor, damaged Julia than she had before.

"So Milam didn't really care for her." Annie didn't phrase it as a question.

"Poor Miz Julia. Like a little shadow when she came to

live at Tarrant House, and then—for a time—she was happy as could be. She loved her baby to pieces. Miss Melissa. Pretty little Missy. That child brought sunshine to Tarrant House. She made everybody smile. The Judge, too. Even Mr. Milam loved Missy. That was before Mr. Ross died. But when he and the Judge died, that was when Miz Julia's face was all pinched and white again." Lucy Jane reached out and touched the worn Bible that lay on the table beside her chair. "It didn't take more than a few days after the funerals for her and Mr. Milam to move out to the plantation. I know Miz Julia was never happy with Mr. Milam, but then I don't think she expected to be happy. And she still had Miss Melissa. It was when the baby was lost—almost the same time as Miz Amanda—that Miz Julia almost grieved herself into the grave—it might have been happier for her if she had."

"So Milam and Julia had a little girl." Annie frowned, picturing the family trees and remembering Charlotte's sharp insistence that her daughter Harriet was the only Tarrant grandchild. "What happened to Missy?"

"She fell in the pond." Lucy Jane didn't elaborate.

So the beloved baby died. That certainly made Julia's present-day misery easier for Annie to understand.

Julia Tarrant. She had been in Tarrant House the day the Judge was murdered. But why would she murder her father-in-law? "Did the Judge like Julia?"

Lucy Jane carefully set down her coffee cup. She looked out the window at the neat graveyard plots, many garlanded with flowers. She didn't look at Annie. "I don't think"—was she picking her words carefully? —"that the Judge ever understood Miz Julia."

"Why was that?"

Lucy Jane met her inquiring gaze with grave dignity. "I'm sure I couldn't say."

There was something here. Annie felt certain of it, cer-

tain and surprised and more than a little confused. Lucy Jane
had, to this point, seemed so straightforward. Straightforward, clear-sighted, sympathetic. Her face was still pleasant,
but now her lips were stubbornly closed.

Was the Judge involved with Julia? With his son's
wife? That moral, upright, judgmental man? Perish the
thought. But there was something. . . .

Lucy Jane gazed soberly out the window.

Annie looked, too, and saw the worn granite markers,
the tendrils of Spanish moss dangling down from the live
oak trees. Thick mats of grass covered all but one new, dirt-
topped grave. Many of the graves had sunk with time until
almost level with the spongy ground.

"They say trouble comes in threes," Lucy Jane murmured, "though it was a long year later that Miz Amanda
went to her rest. But her heart died that day with young Mr.
Ross. Oh, she grieved for him, her baby."

There was a good deal left unsaid. Annie raised an
eyebrow. "And for the Judge?"

Lucy Jane again smoothed her unwrinkled skirt. "A
woman couldn't help but feel sorry for a man struck down
without warning, but Miz Amanda and the Judge, it wasn't
a love match." Her gaze moved from the tombstones toward
Annie. "Sometimes families bind together for different reasons. I know her poppa thought the world of Mr. Augustus.
Miz Amanda, she was one you never knew what she was
thinking, but she had a sweet way and she was kind to
everyone around her. Never much to say."

A description of a gentle, even-tempered woman. But
there must have been moments when Amanda Brevard Tarrant was angry or afraid or unhappy. Surely Lucy Jane saw
other sides of this woman in all the years she spent in that
troubled household. "I understand Amanda and the Judge
quarreled on the day he died."

That was what Charlotte claimed at Miss Dora's dinner party. And there had to be some reason why Ross would have believed his mother guilty of murder, something more damning than finding her with the gun in hand.

But Lucy Jane's ebony face was shuttered and closed. "I couldn't speak to that," she said firmly.

"It would be unusual for them to quarrel?" Annie pressed.

"Yes'm." And not another word.

Annie felt certain there had indeed been a quarrel. But why? About what? And why on that day? And darn it, why was she pursuing this? If there was one certain fact, Amanda Brevard Tarrant had been dead, too, these many years, and, despite Laurel's belief in ghosts, Amanda assuredly could not have been involved in Courtney Kimball's disappearance or in last night's arson at the Tarrant Museum.

Annie decided to change tactics. "Lucy Jane"—she used her most beguiling voice—"I want you to think back to the day the Judge died and remember that afternoon before Mr. Ross died."

Lucy Jane's posture was still upright and formal, but her tense shoulders relaxed. "The Judge," she said ruminatively, "I saw him in the hall going to his study, oh, it must have been right on two o'clock. His face was white as a sheet. He looked like a man with a passel of thoughts. It was later —I was on my way out to my quarters—when I saw Miz Charlotte, and she looked worried, like she had a big burden to carry and didn't know what to do. Funny. Most usually, she was sure what to do. I didn't see Mr. Whitney or Mr. Milam until later that day, after they came and told me Mr. Ross was dead. Mr. Whitney, he looked upset as could be. Mr. Milam didn't show much concern. He was already talking about moving out to the plantation. I heard him tell Miz Julia they'd move pretty quick. He said, 'I can always get around Mother. We won't have to stay in this house much longer.' "

Lucy Jane paused.

"Mrs. Julia?" Annie prodded.

"She ran out to the garden, just before lunch."

"Ran out?"

"She was sobbing." Lucy Jane's voice was so soft, it was hard to hear.

"Do you know why?"

Lucy Jane clasped her hands together tightly. A breeze ruffled the curtains at the open window and brought in the sweet scent of honeysuckle. "I don't rightly know."

"Mrs. Amanda?"

Lucy Jane gazed at Annie almost in anguish. Annie thought she understood. Lucy Jane was a truthful woman. She didn't want to lie.

What could matter that much, after all these years?

Finally, reluctantly, Lucy Jane answered, because, like Annie, she knew the truth must be told. "Miz Amanda, she was coming down the stairs—it was just after Miz Julia went out to the garden—Miz Amanda was coming down the stairs and she looked like she was facing the end of the world."

Were answering machines a boon or a curse? The message light flickered like a pinball machine. Annie punched the button, then settled on the love seat with a mug of coffee and two peanut butter cookies.

Perhaps one's attitude toward an answering machine depended upon the messages being left.

And the messengers. Were there many people in this world who enjoyed one-on-one conversations with an answering machine? Annie hoped not. Surely Laurel's total relaxation and intimate tone were unusual, if not, perhaps, unique.

". . . *quite* depressing, actually, to realize the depths of depravity to which human beings are subject. Surely there can be no more sobering an example than that of the credulous slave girl at Belvidere Mansion, led astray by the immigrant English gardener, Timothy Wale. Wale had his own sorrows, of course, having lost his family and his dear sweetheart Clarissa to tuberculosis. But when he immigrated to South Carolina and obtained work on the plantation, he was bitterly envious of the wealth he saw there and hungry, too, for a woman. He persuaded the slave girl, also known as Clarissa, to meet him after dark. She begged him to take her away from the plantation, but he said there was no way to escape. And then she offered to steal the mistress's jewels, if Wale would carry her away. Wale agreed. One Saturday as Mrs. Shubrick, the mistress, took her coach to Charleston to shop, Clarissa slipped into the mistress's bedroom, unlocked the jewel case and took the brooches and rings and necklaces. That night, she crept out of her cabin and hurried down the moonlit path to meet Wale. He took the jewels but refused to take her too, and ran off into the darkness. The next day the girl feigned illness, then, in desperation, ran to the house and set it afire while the master and mistress were away at church. The Shubricks returned to find their lovely home in flames. Clarissa's odd behavior had been noticed and, when questioned, the slave girl confessed to the theft and the fire." Laurel sighed. "And so poor foolish Clarissa was hanged. And even now they say the lane that leads to the ruins of Belvidere is haunted at night by Clarissa's ghost, waiting for the English gardener to come and take her away. Do you know, Annie, I hope Timothy Wale never enjoyed his ill-gotten gains! Isn't it perhaps the greatest crime of all to take advantage of a trusting nature?"

The tape whirred. Laurel affording the listener time to contemplate the moral, no doubt.

The husky, unforgettable voice resumed just as Annie reached out to punch the fast-forward button.

"Have you considered a gathering together at Tarrant House of those involved that day? Just a thought, my dear. So *interesting* that Amanda's presence—ghostly, of course—is associated with the garden. I do find that frightfully significant. Do call me at your earliest convenience so that we may pursue this topic. Ta, ta."

Annie knew she should phone Laurel, but the likelihood of yet more recitations of ghostly South Carolinians was a powerful deterrent. Later. (Sometimes the fruits of procrastination were sweet, indeed.) Annie felt confident a lack of response would prove no discouragement to her unquashable mother-in-law. There would be other opportunities to ponder the variety of spirits who apparently throng the highways and byways (not to speak of the homes and hearths) of the great state of South Carolina. She wondered if the earthbound shades remained always *in situ,* so to speak. There was a question for Laurel to ponder. It might even keep her occupied beyond the boundaries of Broward's Rock for a good long while. Annie filed the query away for later consideration. Not, of course, that she was averse to Laurel's presence nearby. But a happily occupied Laurel at a distance . . . oh, there was a delectable prospect.

The mental picture of Laurel, once again ambulatory but at a far remove, distracted her. Annie lost the first part of the next message and was forced to rewind, which brought up the last of Laurel's: ". . . pursue this topic. Ta, ta."

Beep.

"Annie, Max, this is Barb."

Annie looked at the machine in surprise as she munched on the second cookie.

Barb's normally down-to-earth voice was a good octave higher than normal and softly dreamy.

"Certainly never knew *bowling* could be so much fun. Though, it wasn't actually the bowling. If "—the tone now was arch—"you understand what I mean. And I'm sure you do. You two of *all* people."

The tape whirred.

Annie grinned. How flattering to know that Barb saw them as romantic figures. The lock clicked and the room door swung in.

"Annie!" Her very own most romantic companion stood in the doorway, and she loved the unmistakable flicker in his eyes.

Annie held a finger to her lips, then pointed toward the machine.

Max nodded and shut the door softly behind him.

"Anyway"—there was clearly an effort here to return to everyday practicality—"everything's great here. Except Agatha got my sandwich at lunch. I'd fixed an anchovy sandwich—so I like salt—and anyway, there was a crash at the front of the store and I went racing up there and some-how"—her voice was loaded with suspicion—"the display on academic mysteries had been knocked over. I'd just fin-ished putting it all together, and I was really pleased. Not the most famous ones, but some very good ones, *The Better To Eat You* by Charlotte Armstrong, *The Corpse with the Purple Thighs* by George Bagby, *Death at Half-Term* by Josephine Bell, *The Horizontal Man* by Helen Eustis, and *Was it Mur-der?* by James Hilton. Isn't that marvelous? All knocked to kingdom come. So I put the display up again. It didn't take all that long, but by the time I got back to the coffee bar, there wasn't a single anchovy left in my sandwich. When I scolded Agatha, she looked at me with the most patronizing, amused expression! Annie, that cat's scary! Anyway, had another lovely note from Henny. She went to Fortnum & Mason and bought and bought, and said she kept looking for Nina Crowther" (in Margaret Yorke's *Find Me a Villain)* "and Richard Hannay" (in John Buchan's *The Three Hostages)*. "Gosh, just think, all that food and people you've read about for years! Anyway, you've got phone calls to the max." A quickly suppressed giggle. "Miss Dora wants you at her place *pronto.* Ditto Sybil Giacomo. I'd go to Sybil's house first; she's on a tear. And"—a pause, the sound of movement, the opening of a door, low murmurs of voices, and, finally, a hurried, almost breathless finale—"Louis just came. I'll fax you some stuff. Bye for now!"

"Barb sounds funny," Max observed, squeezing in beside Annie on the love seat. "Has she got a cold?"

Joe Hardy all grown up and sexy as hell but sometimes an innocent abroad.

Annie flashed a wicked grin and murmured, "Later," as the machine beeped again.

"Where are you people?" Sybil's deep contralto was sharp-edged and impatient. "I want to talk to you. Come here as soon as possible."

In the bedroom, the fax phone rang and the machine began to clatter.

But Max made no move—toward the fax.

Instead, he slipped an arm around Annie's shoulders and pulled her close. "Hey, we can't work all—"

A hard, impatient rapping reverberated against their door.

11:30 A.M., SATURDAY, MAY 9, 1970

The two women stood locked in a tight embrace, the auburn head pressed down against soft dark curls.

Julia trembled. "I can't go home. I can't. Oh, God, Amanda, I'll die if he touches Missy."

Chapter 15.

Miss Dora surged into the living room of their suite, her dark-gray cloak swirling around her, her silver-headed cane thumping against the heart pine floor. She stopped in the center of the artfully decorated room, planted her stick firmly in front of her, and raked them with those bright, malevolent eyes.

"Noon," she rasped. "Where have you been? What have you accomplished?"

Miss Dora deigned to accept a hard straight chair, her back erect, her head high. Annie sat primly on the love seat. Alone. Her posture was excellent. Max stood respectfully near Miss Dora.

As they made their reports, the old lady interspersed an occasional comment.

"Lucy Jane's no fool." The wizened face puckered in thought. "So she's skittish about Amanda. That's interesting. Don't quite see why, after all these years. Hmm."

She smiled sardonically as Max concluded. "So Whitney

tossed you out, eh? He's blustering. I'll fix his wagon. But, first things first. My own investigations, made this morning, indicate the fire was set either by Julia or by Milam." It was *almost* a modest announcement. And even Miss Dora was willing to accept appropriate praise. At their exclamations of interest, the sallow skin was touched by a faint pink glow. "It is quite clear that the blaze was fueled by gasoline. I confirmed that today when I spoke to our fire chief. Early this morning, I checked the garage at Tarrant House. The gasoline container used for the lawn mower was full. So, it was either replenished or not used. If replenished, I reasoned it must have been done this morning. I stopped at every gas station within the radius of several miles and inquired, presenting photographs of Charlotte and Whitney. All responses were negative. This done, I drove—"

Annie gasped. "Miss Dora, you drive?"

Miss Dora swept Annie with a furious reptilian gaze. There was a long moment of outraged silence, then the old lady snarled, "Are you questioning my competence, young miss?"

"Oh, no, no, no. I just thought . . . I assumed you had a driver."

Miss Dora permitted herself to be mollified. "Perhaps you might be excused for that presumption. But I don't believe in unnecessary frills. I've driven myself for almost seventy years, and I shall continue to do so. In any event, I drove to Wisteree Plantation. I went directly to the garage. What a rubbish heap! Milam should be ashamed—discarded boxes, tools in no order, messy, half-full cans of turpentine and paint. I finally discovered the gas container, flung carelessly in a corner. Not, I think, its customary location, for there was a distinct circular ring of sediment from gas and oil and dirt beneath some shelves along one wall. The container was empty. Milam and Julia's garage, however, is such an untidy, ill-run mess that an empty gas can would come as no surprise. More to the point"—she leaned forward, the bony hands tight on the knob of her cane—"I examined both Milam's truck and Julia's car. The truck"—her aristocratic nose wrinkled in disdain—"was rusted out and filthy. Milam could have transported the container without leaving discernible traces. But, in Julia's Honda"—the old lady's eyes slitted—"the floor carpet in the back behind the driver's seat was stained with a ring of oil, and there was a distinct odor, when the carpet was sniffed, of gasoline." She thumped her cane.

Annie wasn't trying to disagree, but the suggestion didn't make much sense to her. "Julia was just a young daughter-in-law when the Judge was shot. What could there possibly be either in the papers of the Judge or in Amanda's papers that could threaten her?"

Miss Dora glared. "Obviously, young miss, *that* is what we must discover. The question is, how do we proceed?"

"Turn right on Chestnut," Annie instructed.

Max flipped on the signal. "I was tempted to tell her to take the investigation and do it all herself." His voice didn't quite have the take-this-job-and-shove-it tone. But, it was close. "If it weren't for Courtney Kimball, I would."

"But Miss Dora *is* an asset." Annie kept her tone bland, the better to assuage the grumpy male beast. "I mean, she knows everything there is to know about Chastain. And everybody." Annie clung to the door strap as the Maserati screeched around the corner.

"Humph."

Annie tried to hide her grin. Max prided himself on his ability to charm any woman from eight to eighty. She contemplated pointing out that, of course, Miss Dora was only the exception that proved the rule, but decided that wouldn't improve matters.

The Maserati jolted to a stop on the dry dirt street, kicking up a cloud of gray dust.

Annie checked the address Miss Dora had given them. This was it.

The white frame, one-story house was beautifully tended. The thin soil didn't support a stand of grass but azaleas, wisteria, and amaryllis flowered in profusion, accented by a fragrant spill of daylilies, hyacinth, and jessamine. The sidewalk had recently been swept, the front steps were immaculate, the window panes gleamed.

And the shades were drawn and the front door closed, despite the lovely spring afternoon. And mail poked out of the letter box next to the door.

"Nobody's home," Annie cried in disappointment.

But Max jumped out of the car, and, after a moment, Annie followed him. They knocked. And rang. And walked around the house—to discover that the garden was as lovely in back as in front—and Annie's verdict held. Which, of course, had the contrary effect of making Max determined to find Enid Friendley, just as Miss Dora had charged them to do.

Max tried the neighbors on each side and returned to the front steps, where Annie had plopped down to enjoy the garden scents. "I found Enid's mother having coffee next door. She said Enid's at the church getting the parlor ready for a wedding reception. She didn't think it would do us any good to go over there because Enid wouldn't have time to talk." He pulled his notebook from his pocket. "We'll leave her a note."

Annie looked over his shoulder as he wrote:

Dear Mrs. Friendley,
Miss Dora Brevard has asked us to visit with you about the Tarrant Family. She believes you can be very

helpful to an inquiry she has asked us to undertake. My wife, Annie, and I will return to see you at nine A.M. tomorrow. If this isn't convenient, please call me at the St. George Inn where we are staying.

Very truly yours,
Max Darling

At Annie's suggestion, Max added the phone number in a P.S. and tucked the note on top of the waiting mail. "There. She can't miss that." He slipped the notebook back in his pocket. As they returned to the car, he pulled out a fax, the latest they had received from Barb. "Here's one name Miss Dora didn't come up with. As soon as Louis tracked this one down, I knew we could really be onto something." He was once again in his customary good humor. "Who knows everything in an office?"

It didn't take a marriage counselor to know the right response to this one.

Annie answered obediently, "The secretary, of course."

Odors of disinfectant and boiled cabbage mingled unpleasantly with those of honeysuckle and banana shrub. A nursing aide in a blue pinafore pointed down the wide corridor. "Go all the way to the end and you'll see the door to the screened-in porch. Miss Nelda spends most of the afternoon out there, reading. She's a great reader."

Warehoused human beings.

Annie made an effort not to look as they walked down the hall, passing open doors, but some glimpses could not be avoided.

An ancient woman in a bedraggled pink chenille bathrobe was bent almost double over her walker as she progressed with aching slowness down the hall.

A sharp-featured, grizzled old man slumped against the restraints that held him in his wheelchair.

A middle-aged woman leaned close to a bed. "Mother, it's Emily. How are you today?"

A wheelchair scooted past them, and its pink-faced occupant, her white hair in fresh, rigid curls, gave them a cheery hello.

Annie pushed through the door to the porch with immense relief. To be outside, to breathe sweet-scented air, to feel the easy grace of muscle and bone moving as bidden was, for an instant, a glorious reassurance.

Two elderly men hunched over a checkerboard at the far end of the porch. One of them looked up eagerly as the door squeaked, then quickly away. The sudden droop of his mouth revealed his disappointment. His companion never moved his glance from the red markers in front of him.

A small, birdlike woman with a beaked nose and thick glasses sat with her back to the game players, her wheelchair facing out toward the garden. She was immersed in a book, her face somber. The set of her mouth, Annie decided, was forbidding indeed. And she had to be Nelda Cartwright, who had served Augustus Tarrant as a secretary when he was in private practice and followed him to the courthouse when he became a judge.

"Miss Cartwright?" Max inquired.

Faded blue eyes, magnified by the lenses, peered up at him. "I don't know you." Her voice was reedy but decisive.

"No, ma'am," Max said quickly. "I'm Max Darling, and this is my wife, Annie. We are investigating the death of Judge Augustus Tarrant in May of 1970 on behalf of Miss Dora Brevard, who was—"

"Young man, I know who Miss Dora Brevard is." Heavily veined hands clapped her book shut—Annie was surprised somehow to identify it as *Collected Sonnets of Edna St. Vincent Millay*—and the expression on the old woman's face turned fierce. "What is there to investigate? The Judge died from heart failure."

"No," Max said gently. "If you will permit me to explain . . ."

As Max described the revelations by Julia Tarrant and the other family members during that remarkable gathering at Miss Dora's, Nelda Cartwright's unwinking gaze never left his face.

She spoke only once. "Augustus murdered! The devils."

When Max had concluded, Nelda Cartwright hunched in her wheelchair, the book in her lap ignored, her wrinkled face rigid with anger, her eyes blazing, her blue-veined hands gripping the wheelchair arms.

"Will you help us?" Annie asked.

"Augustus murdered. I should have known. I should have known! They all pulled at him constantly, wanting money, time, special attention, always making excuses." Her voice was cold and disdainful. "Whitney fancied himself as quite the man-about-town, too busy playing golf to get his proper work done. That's where he met Jessica Horton, of course. Whitney knew the firm was representing Alex Horton in the divorce proceedings, but did that stop Whitney? And you can't tell me it wasn't deliberate on Jessica's part. Who knows what she got out of Whitney? I saw them together, going into that motel. So I told the Judge. It was my duty." Her faded eyes burned with righteous fervor. "I said, 'Judge, did you know your son was meeting Alex Horton's wife in a room at the Hansford Inn? And I've heard Alex is being represented by Tarrant & Tarrant in his divorce action.' Oh, the Judge's face looked like thunder at that piece of news. He said, 'If that is true, Whitney will withdraw from the firm.' The Judge was a man who always did the right thing. And he was always so proud of the firm. His cousin Darrell was the senior partner at that time."

Annie didn't bother to ask how the Judge could have forced his son out of a firm in which the Judge no longer practiced. But she knew the answer to that. The Judge had only to speak to Whitney. His son would never have dared defy him. And, if he had, the Judge had only to pick up the telephone and call his cousin. The matter would have been attended to.

The secretary pushed her glasses up on her nose. "Later that afternoon—I know he talked to Whitney because he came out of the Judge's chambers and he looked like he'd had his comeuppance—the Judge told me that his son would be clearing out his office at the firm over the weekend." Her mouth twisted. "Augustus died the next day." Her cold eyes glittered. "I should have known!"

Annie was puzzled. "But Whitney didn't leave the firm."

"No. The week after the funerals, I asked Whitney if he needed any help clearing out his office. He looked shocked. Then he said of course not. I asked if there were any conflicts of interest that should be dealt with. I made myself extremely clear. He wouldn't even look at me, cutting his eyes like a bad dog. He said that particular matter had been attended to, that I needn't be concerned. I didn't like it, but what could I do, with the Judge gone? The week after that, he called and asked if I'd like to come back to the firm. The new judge would bring in his own secretary, of course. I accepted. I thought it was the least I could do for the Judge." A humorless smile touched her narrow lips. "For what it's worth, I don't think Whitney ever made that particular mistake again."

Max said dryly, "I doubt that Whitney would, with you on the spot."

Satisfaction glittered in her eyes. "Whitney's no match for me, I can tell you, Mr. Darling."

"Do you happen to know the provisions of the Judge's will?" Annie asked.

Nelda Cartwright did, and, after a moment's thought, elucidated them, crisply and succinctly. The balance of the estate had gone to Amanda, except for Tarrant House itself, which, in line with family tradition, always went in trust to the eldest surviving child.

"But that's Milam, isn't it?" Max inquired.

"Oh, yes, but Milam didn't want to live in Tarrant House." Nelda scowled. "He and Julia moved out to Wisteree almost immediately. Then, when Amanda died, Milam invited Whitney to stay on. Eventually, of course, Whitney and Charlotte's daughter will inherit the house, if Milam follows the family tradition. Who knows what Milam might do? But there are no other living descendants. In any event, that's far in the future."

Max redirected the old woman's thoughts. "So the Judge's death made a big difference for Whitney."

Nelda said bitterly, "It saved Whitney's skin, all right. He didn't have to leave the firm—and heaven knows who else would have wanted to hire him. Everyone would have wanted to know why he was leaving the family firm. He would have had a hard time explaining that. But with the Judge gone, Whitney had it all. And he never worked hard. He played golf every Wednesday and Friday. They tell me he still does. And, as soon as the Judge was out of the way, Amanda gave him and Milam whatever they wanted. If I'd had any idea—" Color flared briefly on her waxen cheeks. "I'll swear to this. I'll be glad to."

"So you think it may have been Whitney Tarrant who shot the Judge?" Max asked.

Nelda riveted him with a piercing, irritated glare. "Obviously, Mr. Darling."

"You said they all pulled at him." The scent of a mock

orange shrub added a softness to what Annie would always remember as a bleak scene—the crippled old woman, her face alight with vengeance, and the quiet checker players, still alive but so divorced from life. "What did the others do that upset the Judge?"

Nelda's thin lips pursed. "What didn't they do? That wife of his was always complaining because he worked so hard. I ask you," she asked scathingly, "what else is a man to do?"

Annie carefully didn't look at Max.

"A man's work is his life, and no one ever did better than the Judge. When he was on the bench, he did what was right and just. That's the way he lived too. A man of honor. A man of character." Her chin quivered with outrage. "What did Amanda want? A namby-pamby stay-at-home, like her two older sons? The Judge never said a word against his family—why, he wouldn't have done that—but it was as clear as clear that they were all a disappointment to him—all except Ross. Now that was a fine young man, a leader in his class. The Judge was so proud that he was going to be a military officer."

Annie wondered how Miss Cartwright would react if they told her that Ross had decided to refuse his commission and go to Canada if necessary, to avoid serving in a war in which he did not believe. Would she see a man of honor in that, a true Tarrant, or would she be enraged, as the Judge had been so long ago?

"What about Milam?" Max asked.

Nelda's eyes narrowed. "Milam." Her fingers tapped the cover of her book. "He was in trouble with the Judge that week. I remember now—I took a letter." Those faded eyes glittered. "Don't think I couldn't read between the lines." Her lips curled in distaste. "None of it surprised me. It was utterly transparent, both to the Judge and to me.

Milam took advantage of the family name to secure a historical restoration commission for this pretty young woman who'd come to town and opened up a decorating firm. No antecedents. Nothing to recommend her. To think Milam thought the Judge wouldn't realize what was going on! The Judge understood, all right. His voice was like a winter day when he dictated the letter asking that woman to resign the commission since it had been obtained under false pretenses —Milam told the board she had the confidence of the Tarrant Family and, of course, everyone thought that meant the Judge had recommended her. Why, this is too small a town to get away with something like that! Felicity Moore was president of the historical society. When Milam told the board that pack of lies, Felicity telephoned the Judge at once, asked why he wasn't in favor of continuing with Sheila Bauman. Sheila Bauman knew more about restoration than anyone else in Beaufort County! It was a scandal to think of throwing her over, after all the years she'd worked with the society, for this peroxided woman who'd moved here from Atlanta."

"A friend of Milam's," Max said carefully.

"You could call it that." Nelda's stare was icy.

Annie wanted to get it straight. "Milam recommended this woman for a restoration job, inferring that's what the Judge wanted?"

A sharp affirmative nod. Then a malicious smile. "Milam didn't win that one, even though the Judge died. I'd already sent the letter to the historical society. The Judge made it perfectly clear he wanted Sheila Bauman to be reappointed. Not that Crandall woman." The smile slid into a frown. "Of course, as soon as the Judge was dead and buried, Milam showed his true colors. He quit his job at the bank— I'll bet they were glad to see the last of him with his smart tongue—moved out to the plantation, and called himself a painter." Her tone oozed contempt. Nelda Cartwright apparently put artistic endeavors on the same level with panhandling and garbage collecting.

So how much of this diatribe should be attributed to malice?

Frowning darkly, the old lady gazed out at the lovely spring day. Delicate, wispy clouds laced the soft blue sky. Lovely, yes, but Annie still hungered sometimes for the clear, harsh brilliance of a Texas sky.

Max softly jingled some coins in his pocket. "Miss Cartwright, please, think very carefully for us, do you know of anyone—anyone at all—with a motive for murdering the Judge? Someone he had sentenced? Another lawyer whom he had bested? A client who was dissatisfied? Someone jealous of his prominence, his success?"

"Oh, there were many who were jealous of the Judge, I can tell you that." Her gray head bobbed in emphasis. "Sometimes I think a man's goodness can be measured by the number of his enemies."

That was a new proposition to Annie.

Nelda looked up at her and snapped, "Just you wait until you've lived longer, young lady, then you'll understand what I mean. Why, anyone would think good men would be revered, but they put others to shame, you see, show them up for what they are, and most people can't stand the light of day on what they really are."

Annie felt a pang of embarrassment. The old lady was right, of course. How well could anyone bear the spotlight if it focused on their shabby motives, their shameful desires, their petty jealousies, usually well hidden behind false social smiles?

How well, Annie wondered, could Judge Tarrant have borne such scrutiny?

"But the Judge—" Nelda's voice was soft. "He always

told the truth. He never made himself look big and important. And"—she poked a finger at them fiercely—"he did many a good deed that nobody ever knew about. Even I wouldn't have known, but I kept his files in order."

She didn't say it, but obviously she'd read letters the Judge had composed and sent himself. Read for her own happiness, read because she loved him.

"He paid for many a poor young man to go to school. White and black. He made anonymous donations to the Baptist soup kitchen, though he was a good Episcopalian. He . . ." Her voice trailed off, her thin shoulders slumped. Tears edged from beneath the thick glasses. "Struck down by a wretch in his own family. Who else could have gone into Tarrant House and not been seen by someone? They all lived there, you know, because he was generous, giving food and board to grown men with wives who should have worked hard enough to earn the money for their own residences. But not Whitney or Milam." She made no effort to wipe away the tears. Annie's heart contracted.

"Couldn't the Judge have helped his sons, made money available so they could have had their own homes?" Max inquired.

"What would that have taught them about standing on their own two feet?" she retorted angrily. "That would have been the worst possible thing to do."

Max was looking both bemused and appalled. Since he had never understood Annie's staunch devotion to the Puritan work ethic, it was unlikely the Judge's approach would impress him. As far as Max was concerned, money, which his family had and shared in abundance, was marvelous because it afforded freedom. The idea that a person's worth should be equated to how much money that person possessed or could earn was utterly foreign to him.

Annie offered up a silent prayer of gratitude for Laurel.

Dear, flaky, unpredictable, impossible Laurel, who had successfully inculcated her economic beliefs in her offspring. They were rich, yes. They enjoyed being rich, yes. But they never thought possessing money made them special or better or worthy of deference. They thought it made them lucky.

"Oh, no, you look at those lazy Tarrant boys," Nelda ordered. "Just one problem after another, the Judge had. Whitney and that graspy wife of his. Milam and that sad little woman he married. And the Judge's wife." An odd look crossed her face. She started to speak, paused, then said, "Funny, how things come back. I was thinking about the Judge on that last day, a Friday. Of course, I don't see how it could matter now, nothing came of it, and she's been dead so many years, too. But that afternoon, he put me to calling condominiums in Florida, to see about buying one for his wife, Amanda."

Sybil answered the door. "Where have you been all day?"

She didn't wait for an answer. Turning on her heel, she marched into the dining room. One full wall, including the Federal fireplace, and the wainscoting on the other three walls were paneled with rich red cypress. But little of it could be seen and little of the magnificent, equally richly red Chippendale table and matching chairs. Photographs, large and small, were propped on every level space and against the walls.

Annie felt her breath catch in her chest.

Photographs of Courtney Kimball, at all ages, from babyhood to the present. They captured the girl's beauty and the unusual, almost gaunt, configuration of her facial bones. She was elegant, elusive, fascinating.

As Annie looked from the photographs to Sybil, she realized that Courtney was very much her mother's daughter. The resemblance could be missed at first because Courtney was so fair. Her ash-blond hair, porcelain-white skin, and Nordic blue eyes were all a heritage from her father, Ross. But the reckless gleam in those sapphire-blue eyes was a spark of the unquenchable fire that burned in Sybil's and that remarkable, unforgettable bone structure was the legacy of her dark and dangerous mother.

Sybil stood, her arms folded across her chest, looking from one photograph to another: Courtney on horseback, playing tennis, as a baby, as a debutante, at Christmas, on Valentine's Day, her birthday, wielding a hockey stick, at slumber parties, as a cheerleader. "God. Isn't she beautiful? Isn't she wonderful?"

Despite her beauty, Sybil looked haggard. Tight lines etched the corners of that sensual mouth. Her cheekbones jutted too sharply, her velvet-dark eyes were red-rimmed. She was, as always, dramatically and exquisitely dressed. But her crimson blouse was partially untucked, and her white linen slacks wrinkled. Even her vivid makeup had the look of an afterthought.

She reached out tenderly and picked up a photograph. In it, Courtney must have been about twelve. She wore faded jeans, a pink T-shirt, and a mischievous grin. She leaned precariously out from a rickety, wood-slat tree house, high in an old live oak.

"I had a tree house once." Sybil swallowed and said gruffly, "They were good to Courtney, those people who took her." She looked at them piteously. "I would have taken good care of her."

"Of course you would have," Annie said warmly. She darted a helpless look at Max. She was out of her depth here. Nothing in her experience had prepared her to deal with this kind of anguish.

"They're looking for her, looking everywhere now." Sybil crooked the photograph in her arm and began to pace.

"I put the fear of God into Wells. They're really looking now." She stopped and gripped Max's arm with her free hand. "They can still find her, can't they? Maybe she was hurt and wandered away. That happens, you know. Sometimes."

Max put his hand over hers. "Sometimes," he said gently.

Haunted eyes clung to his face. "You think she's dead. I can tell. So does he. He said there's no trace of her, none. Her credit cards haven't been used, not since that day. No one's seen her. She hasn't cashed money out of her account. They think she would have—if she were out there somewhere. If she could."

Sybil jerked free, walked blindly to the mantel, and rested her raven-dark head against its rich rosy-red wood, the framed picture held tight in her arms.

"We're trying, Sybil," Annie offered, and knew it was forlorn.

"The fastest way to find out . . ." Max paused, then pressed on, ". . . what happened to Courtney is to find the person who killed the Judge."

For a long, long moment that dark bowed head didn't move. Then slowly it lifted, and Sybil turned to face them. The sight of her face brought a chill to Annie's heart. There was no mercy in it. And no avenging angel ever spoke with greater resolution. "I will know. No matter what it takes, no matter how long, no matter what I have to do, I will know. Old sins have long shadows, that's what my grandmother always said to me. I never knew what it meant—until now. There were so many sins at Tarrant House, weren't there? Whitney was lazy and weak. Charlotte—oh, I don't know that we can call her sinful. She's too insignificant, isn't she? Charlotte is one of those obstinate, boring, irritating people who don't have any core to them, so they have to fasten onto something other than themselves. With some people, it's religion. Or money. Or sex. But poor old boring Charlotte, it's the Tarrant Family. Oh, Christ, the almighty Tarrant Family!" The words were torn from her. "And then there's Milam. A lot more room for speculation there, you know. Milam's deeper than you think. He always seemed to acquiesce when the Judge was alive, whatever was demanded, but all the while, underneath, he kept worming and squirming for what he wanted. Julia—" Her voice was puzzled. "I never understood why Julia stayed. Why didn't she take Missy and leave? What could possibly have held her there? Milam's affair had started, even then, even when Missy was just a baby." She held out the picture in her arms, stared at it, her lips trembling. "Missy's dead. And Courtney—" She walked woodenly toward the table and put the picture down. "No. No." She whirled, her face ashen, and moved blindly past them. "No. Goddammit, no . . ."

"I know they're home," Annie insisted. The front of the mansion was immaculate, as always, which made the heavy scent of charred wood all the more disturbing.

Max knocked again. Rang the bell, kept his finger on the button.

They could hear the peal.

And see the lights blazing on both floors.

"Unfortunately," Max said grimly, "we aren't cops. We don't have a search warrant. Nobody has to talk to us."

Annie jerked to look to her left. Had the drapes moved at that second window on the ground floor?

But what if they had?

Charlotte and Whitney Tarrant were under no compulsion to permit Annie and Max Darling to enter Tarrant House.

But lights were also shining next door, at Miss Evangeline Copley's house.

Annie nodded her head decisively. "Let's see what Miss

Copley has to say. She's the one who heard Ross and the Judge quarrel that afternoon."

Max resisted at first. "We know all about that, Annie. And isn't she the ghost-lady Laurel talked to? Listen, Annie, I'm sure ghosts are fine, but they're no help to us. No ghost spirited Courtney away or set fire to the Tarrant Museum."

"Maybe Miss Copley saw something last night." Annie pushed away the memory of that flash of white, deep in the Tarrant garden. That was long before a hand splashed gasoline on the museum. "She's an old lady. Maybe she doesn't sleep much."

Annie led the way.

Max had just raised the knocker when the door popped open and milky blue eyes peered out at them.

"Miss Copley, we're here because Miss Dora Brevard—"

"I know all about you young people, and yes, I want to help. Come right in." White curls quivered as Evangeline Copley nodded energetically and held open the screen door. "To think that dear young man has lain a-mouldering in his grave all these long years, blamed for a heinous crime! Why, it sets my heart afire with anger." The soft voice rose indignantly. She was as tiny as Miss Dora but as different as a Dresden shepherdess from a witch's peaked hat. A fleecy white angora shawl draped her shoulders. Her blue linen dress matched her eyes. She clapped together plump pink hands. "Now, *I* know things that aren't generally known." She trotted ahead of them into a parlor that would have been a perfect setting for Jenny Lind. Two Regency sofas faced each other on either side of the fireplace. A magnificent French gilt mirror hung above the Adam mantel. The ceiling medallion that supported the glorious chandelier was also gilt. Golden brocade hangings decorated elaborate recessed windows.

Max gave Annie an I-told-you-so look and, when they

took their seats in matching curved-back chairs, he was poised for a quick escape. So he was brisk. "We know all about the quarrel Ross had with his father the day they died. But we wanted to ask if you knew anything about the fire last night, the one that destroyed the Tarrant Museum."

"Evil in this world, sadness in the other." She looked at them brightly, a link from one world to the next.

Max didn't roll his eyes, but he stiffened.

Miss Copley had no trouble divining his thoughts. With a sweet smile, she said matter-of-factly, "I'm almost there, you know. Ninety-nine my last birthday. The angel wings can't be long in coming. Perhaps that's why I was the one to see Amanda."

Max folded his arms across his chest and didn't say a word.

Annie would have pinched him if she could have managed it unseen. She and Max were going to have to have a chat about body language. But, for now, she knew it was up to her. "Uh . . . Amanda," she ventured. "You've seen her?"

Miss Copley eyed Max thoughtfully. "Now, now, young man, there are more things in heaven and earth than you know." But her tone was gentle. "Why, I've seen angels, too. Once when I was a young girl walking by the river on a summer afternoon, a group of angels went right by me, lovely girls in long white gowns with golden iridescent wings, talking, talking and there was such a sense of peace and happiness. . . . But that's not why you're here. Now, I do want you to understand"—she leaned forward, her china-doll face puckered earnestly—"ghosts are not angels."

Max looked helplessly at Annie.

Annie said heartily, "Of course not."

Miss Copley folded her plump hands and smiled approvingly at Annie. "Why not?"

"Uh." Annie took a deep breath. "Well, angels, of course, are"—she took a plunge—"happy?"

Miss Copley considered this seriously. "Well, my dear, of course they can't always be happy. But you see the difference. Angels are messengers of God, they come to do His bidding. Whereas, ghosts"—a faint sigh—"are tied to this plane. They can't be freed as long as they continue to suffer. But I hadn't seen Amanda in many years—not until this week. So I am quite concerned. Why is she walking again? What has happened to recall her to the scenes of her misery? Walking there at the back of the garden, just by the obelisk. I saw her again last night when I came home from dinner at my nephew's. Of course, I went out to see if she might be there, since I'd seen her the night before. And then for that awful fire to start. It brought me right up out of bed. But, of course, you know that Amanda had nothing to do with the fire."

The cloudy blue eyes clung to his face until Max gave an affirmative nod.

"A car drove up perhaps five minutes before the fire broke out. Someone set it, of course." Miss Copley nodded to herself. "But I know Amanda was nearby. For I've seen her twice now." Her sweet voice fell into a mournful singsong. "Each time, she was all in white. Just as Augustus liked for her to dress. Walking, walking. The swirl of white, the glint of moonlight, the sound of faraway footsteps."

It was one thing to deal with Laurel, who recounted ghostly tales somewhat in the same manner as a social climber toting up celebrity sightings. It was quite another, Annie realized, to discuss a ghost with an old woman as attuned to the next world as to this one.

"I'm very much afraid of what may happen." Cloudy blue eyes beseeched them. "You will try hard, won't you? Both nights that I've seen her, I've felt the mist against my face like tears. Amanda needs our help."

11:45 A.M., SATURDAY, MAY 9, 1970

The Judge's dark eyebrows drew down into a tight frown. "I'm busy, Milam." His glance was scathing, dismissive.

Milam had the old familiar feelings. He was too fat, too clumsy, hopelessly stupid. For how many years had he been humiliated, emasculated, diminished by his father? Always he had succumbed to the Judge, the imperious, superior, all-powerful Judge. Milam felt like he was choking. His hands shook. But he didn't mumble an apology and back out of the study. Not this time.

Milam closed the door behind him, stepped forward —and saw the surprise on his father's disdainful face.

No, he wouldn't turn back this time. This time the Judge was going to listen to him.

Chapter 16.

Miss Copley's front door closed behind them. They started down the steps, then Annie paused. The sound of the hounds baying raised a prickle on her neck. She gripped Max's arm. But she didn't have to speak. He took her hand, and they ran down the steps. They hurried to the side of the house and turned, heading for the river.

Dancing clouds of no-see-ums whirled around them, the closer they came to the river. Annie flapped her hands futilely and knew she'd soon be a mass of bites, but now they could hear thrashing in the thick undergrowth, and the throaty *aw-woo* of the hounds was closer.

"This way, by God, this way," came a shout.

They reached the path next to the bluff and not far ahead was Harris Walker, his face excited and eager, and a heavy-set dog handler with two bloodhounds straining at their leashes.

"Jesus, look at them go," Harris shouted. His shirt-sleeves were rolled up, his trousers dusty and snagged. "She came this way. Courtney came this way!"

"Max! Do you suppose Courtney's here?" Annie was poised to race ahead, but Max grabbed her arm.

He stared at the quivering bushes as the handler and dogs and Harris disappeared into the thicket at the back of Tarrant House. "Of course she came this way," Max said wearily. "Those dogs will find her scent here and at Miss Dora's. She came to both these houses—before she disappeared." His eyes were full of pity. "The poor bastard," he said softly.

It was almost closing time. The sun was sinking in the west, the loblolly pines threw monstrous shadows across the roadway, as they pulled into the parking lot of South Carolina Artifacts: Old and New. The small brick house was built in the West Indian style, with piazzas on the front and sides supported by heavy untapered white columns. The scored stucco exterior was a soft lemon-yellow. As she and Max walked up the front steps, Annie almost expected to hear the crash of waves from a turquoise sea and hear the breeze rattle tall coconut palms.

A bell rang softly deep inside as Max opened the door and held it for her. Annie always experienced the same sensation upon entering antique shops, a compound of delight at the artistry of all the lovely pieces and sadness that these were all that survived from lives long since ended.

That Chinese Canton ware in the Federal cabinet, what hearty sea captain carried those dishes across turbulent seas to Charleston? What pink-cheeked mistress, perhaps of a Georgian house on Church Street, welcomed guests to afternoon tea, using her new set of china? Who had commissioned that dark painting, a Victorian portrait of an oval-faced young woman with soft lips and warm eyes, and how had it come to rest half a world away from its origin? That glorious French Empire clock, topped with a gold flying griffin, who was the owner who looked up, perhaps from reading the latest novel by Dickens, to check the time? A merchant? A lawyer? A privateer who made a fortune in smuggling during The War Between the States? How many hours and days and lives had ticked away for its owners?

If Laurel wanted ghosts, ghosts were easy to find.

"Hello!" Max called out.

Steps sounded from the back of the crowded room.

The woman who walked out of the gloom to stand beneath the radiance of a red Bohemian glass chandelier was petite, with sleek blond hair and fine patrician features. Her face was saved from severity by merry blue eyes and a mobile mouth that curved easily into a friendly smile.

"May I help you?" Her musical voice was eager.

"Miss Crandall? Miss Joan Crandall?" Max asked.

"Yes."

"I'm Max Darling. And this is my wife, Annie. We'd like to visit with you about a friend of yours, Milam Tarrant."

Joan Crandall's expressive face was suddenly quite still. She flicked a cool glance between them. "Why?"

This wasn't going to be easy, Annie realized. This charming—or perhaps potentially charming—woman had her defenses up.

Max, of course, was undaunted. He said smoothly, as if there could be no question of the antique dealer's cooperation, "This goes back a number of years, Miss Crandall. Back to 1970. I understand Milam tried to help you win appointment as a restoration expert with the Chastain Historical—"

"Mr. Darling, forgive me, but I'm a little puzzled." She stepped past him, deftly flipped the OPEN-CLOSED sign with long, stained, graceful fingers. "I'm an antique dealer, an expert in the restoration of artifacts and in the reproduction of antiques. I am not an information bureau nor, on a baser level, a gossip. If you and Mrs. Darling are interested in South Carolina antiques, perhaps a rice bed or a plantation desk, I will be delighted to be of service, though it is now after-hours and I am officially closed. If you are not, then I will bid you good evening."

"Why don't you want to talk about Milam Tarrant?" Annie demanded.

Max waggled a warning hand.

Annie ignored that. Max was always urging her to think before she spoke, to remain cool, calm, and collected, but Annie was confident of her instinct here. No point in beating around the bush. They would have to break through Joan Crandall's carefully constructed reserve if they hoped to accomplish anything.

Miss Crandall reached for the knob and opened the door. "Good night."

"You could perhaps be helpful to Milam," Max said quickly.

"Would you want him to be accused of murder?" Annie asked.

"Milam? Murder?" Joan Crandall's voice was harsh. She looked from one to the other. "Murder? That's absurd. For God's sake, who are you people? What are you talking about?"

"We'll be glad to tell you, Miss Crandall. Let us have five minutes." Max unobtrusively gave Annie's wrist a warning squeeze.

It hung in the balance for a long moment. Finally, the dealer gave a short nod. Pushing the door shut and turning the key in the lock, she gestured for them to follow. She led the way through the crowded room to an office that looked out on a silent lagoon.

As they settled in wingback chairs that faced her desk, an American Chippendale card table, she said crisply, "All right, five minutes."

She listened without comment, her face unreadable, her hands folded together on the desk top. In the light from a Tiffany lamp, the large square-cut emerald in an ornate silver setting on her right hand glittered like green fire. The evening sun spilling in from a west window gave her hair the shine of gold.

When Max concluded, she relaxed back in her chair. Her lips moved in a faint, derisive smile. "Do you often put credence in twenty-year-old gossip, Mr. Darling?"

"This is especially important twenty-year-old gossip," Max replied temperately. "Someone shot the Judge. It may well have been Milam."

"Because his father humiliated him? Oh, come now, Mr. Darling. It takes more than that to engender murder." Her mouth thinned and ugly lines were etched at the corners of her lips. "Though I wouldn't have blamed him—and I was angry myself." She smiled wryly. "I assure you I didn't shoot the Judge." She lifted one hand to touch her temple. "God, it seems like yesterday. I was new in Chastain. I'd just finished a master's in art history, and I was so eager to get to work. Milam—I'd met him at some art shows—tried to help me get an appointment for some conservation work, work which I was eminently more qualified to do and oversee than the amateur plodder who'd been in charge for years. But the amateur plodder was from one of the old families, one of the right families, and I was an outsider. Everyone assumed Milam did it because we were lovers." For an instant, there was a genuine flash of amusement. "I was so shocked at that. Then. Now, of course, I've lived here for twenty years and I know that it's always assumed men do things because they love women—not because a woman might be smart or quali-

fied or capable. But I was new to Chastain." The smile
slipped away. "Do you want to know the truth?" There was
quiet honesty and a hint of regret in her tone. "Milam and I
are friends. We were friends then. And that's all, my dear
young people, despite what others assume. A very precious
friendship to both of us, but perhaps most precious to Milam.
We talk about art and life and beauty. How many people"—
she tilted her elegant head to look at them—"do you suppose
Milam can talk with about art and life and beauty in this
town?"

Milam Tarrant was a part of a family with long roots in
Chastain. No one could question his standing or his lineage.
But what good was that, Annie realized, if he didn't belong,
if he was a stranger on his own hearth?

"Are you saying Milam had no reason to be angry with
his father?" Annie asked.

"Reason to be angry?" Her eyes flashed. "Oh, I think
Milam had reason enough to be angry. It was another in a
series of embarrassments at the hands of his father. You see,
the Judge couldn't tolerate the idea that anyone would defer
to any opinion other than his. Oh, I remember that episode
very well indeed. The Judge didn't even bother to talk to
Milam, to ask why he'd recommended me. That didn't matter, you understand. The Judge sent Milam a letter—don't
you like that?—a *letter* informing him that it was beneath
the standing of a Tarrant to attempt to advance the career of
a person—meaning me—of questionable character, especially if there were suspicion of a personal relationship involved. So, yes, Milam was angry and humiliated. If the
Judge had lived, I don't know if the breach would ever have
closed. Milam said the letter was the final insult after a lifetime of degradation. That was how he put it, degradation.
Always, the Judge turned away from him because he was
different. All Milam ever wanted was for the Judge to see

Milam as he was, to love him as he was. But with the Judge, love was provisional—and only awarded when his sons performed as he demanded they should, as 'Tarrants.' "

"As soon as the Judge died," Annie said carefully, "Milam started acting very differently, didn't he?"

She gave an elegant shrug. "Different? No. That's not fair. But I think he finally felt free to be himself."

"And yet"—Max leaned forward—"you seemed astounded when Annie suggested Milam might be suspected of murder. It looks to me as though Milam had an enormously strong motive for murder."

For the first time, the dealer laughed out loud. "Milam as a skulking, conniving murderer? Oh, no. No. Milam is— oh, I know he has a waspish tongue. That's anger, of course, his way of trying to get back at those who have hurt him so badly all through the years. Milam has a great deal of anger. But he is—when you truly know Milam—such a gentle man. You never saw him with his little girl, did you? He adored Missy." Joan Crandall looked out at the lagoon turning purple in the fading light. "I almost thought he would succeed as an artist, that he would find himself, know what he should do . . . until Missy died. Missy's death destroyed his soul. After that, everything was derivative. Skilled, yes, but lacking heart. Poor Milam. That's all he ever wanted, to be loved. And that's all he ever wanted," she drawled bitterly, "from His Holiness, the Honorable Augustus Tarrant."

They stood at the edge of the bluff and looked down at the swift-flowing river rushing headlong toward the sea. In the glow of sunset, the darkening water glittered coldly, obsidian streaked with copper.

Max bent down, picked up a fused clump of shells, and lofted them high and far, out into the darkness.

Where they fell, it was impossible to tell.

The water would be cold. The river was deep, and the

current ran fast and dangerous. If Courtney went into the river (was she injured? was she conscious?), would she have had the strength to reach shore? If she didn't go into the river, where was she? What had happened to her? This was Friday night. Courtney Kimball had disappeared, leaving behind a blood-smeared car, on Wednesday night.

Annie shivered.

Max slipped an arm around Annie's shoulders, held her tightly.

She looked around the point. Theirs was the only car parked here. Where was Harris Walker? Had the hounds circled and circled? What would he do now?

Annie reached up to grip Max's hand, his warm and comforting hand. "If Courtney went over the edge, if she went into the water, they may never find her."

"We are going to find her," Max said stubbornly. "One way or another."

It was unlike Max to agree to eat fast food, very unlike him to be the proposer of fast food, and exceedingly unlike him to speed through dinner (though, of course, he opted for the healthy salad while Annie thoroughly enjoyed a Big Mac). That he had done all three was nothing short of astonishing. But Annie understood. Time, time. Every hour that passed made it less likely Courtney Kimball would be found alive. Max wanted every minute to count.

Their headquarters at the St. George Inn was beginning to seem homelike. She poured freshly brewed (Colombian decaffeinated) coffee into the thermos, arranged pens beside fresh legal pads, and eavesdropped on Max's side of a conversation with Miss Dora.

He was firm. "I consider it absolutely essential." He glanced at the clock. "It's just after eight P.M. You can call all of them now."

Annie settled comfortably in a chair at the breakfast

room table, picked up a pen, and began to doodle. It wouldn't have won a blue at an art show, but it was recognizable as a Southern mansion. Beneath it, she wrote *"Tarrant House."*

"That's right. Tomorrow afternoon at Tarrant House." Although he was barefoot and wore a pale-blue polo shirt and white shorts, Max didn't look relaxed. He hunched over the telephone with the intensity of Craig Rice's John J. Malone studying a dopesheet. "I'll handle everything else." Max looked up and gave Annie a big grin and a thumbs-up signal.

She scrawled *"Here we come!"* in bold letters.

It had a confident, aggressive ring. But Annie wondered just how eerie tomorrow afternoon's gathering at Tarrant House would be. How would you feel, she wondered suddenly, if you were a murderer, invited for a little exercise in reconstruction? But wouldn't a murderer have learned to school his face *(her* face?) through years of deception? Still, wouldn't it be a heart-pounding exercise?

As Max continued his brisk outline, Annie poured herself a cup of coffee and thumbed through the day's mail, which Barb had brought over in the afternoon:

The latest *Publishers Weekly:* An exploration of the market in Spain, the latest in computerware for booksellers, gossip about who really wrote a movie actor's bestseller, a nice assortment of mysteries reviewed.

MOSTLY MURDER: Fascinating and up-to-date reviews on all kinds of mysteries, from the most hard-boiled to the most genteel. A wonderful quarterly.

A brightly colored postcard brought a smile. Where was Henny now? Annie studied the sunlit picture of Charing Cross and the sandstone railway station named for it. *"Felt myself in quite good company today,"* the unmistakable backward-looping script reported. *"Irene Adler and Godfrey Norton caught their train here in* A Scandal in Bohemia. *And here's where Tuppence Cowley took a train in search of Tommy in* The Secret Adversary. *Dear Annie, wish you were here. But I'll be home soon—and eager to jump into the thick of things."*

Annie felt a pang of homesickness. Not, of course, to be in London, where she had never been, but to be back at Death on Demand, the finest mystery bookstore this side of Atlanta, to unpack books and check stock, to sell mysteries and pet Agatha, to respond good-naturedly to Henny's whodunnit one-upmanship and Laurel's unpredictable interests, to talk new books with Ingrid and look forward to after-hours and Max.

Dear Max.

He was sprawled back on the love seat now, the telephone balanced on his stomach, obviously pleased with the progress of his campaign. ". . . and one final point, Miss Dora. Ask Sybil and Chief Wells to come. That will put more pressure on the murderer."

A prickle moved down Annie's back.

She hadn't read mysteries since beginning with *The Secret of the Old Clock* without gaining a keen appreciation of some of the verities of the detecting life. Only the first murder is hard.

"Yes, we'll be prepared, Miss Dora." Max had never sounded more confident. "You can count on that." As he hung up, Annie popped to her feet.

"Max, what if the murderer gets too scared?" She managed to sound brisk. Inside, she still had that it's-midnight-and-I'm-alone-in-the-cemetery feeling. Like reading Mary McMullen or Celia Fremlin.

Max set the phone on the end table. He pushed up from the love seat, then stood and stared down at her, his hands jammed into the pockets of his shorts.

Annie saw a worry as deep as her own reflected in his eyes.

"I know. Someone out there"—he gestured toward the

window and the darkness outside—"is dangerous as hell. But we have to try and reconstruct that afternoon. We may be able to prove that someone absolutely *couldn't* have done it —just the way Ross was cleared. You see, Miss Dora didn't know the significance of the shot she heard until more than twenty years later. The fact that Ross was actually in her view at the moment she heard the shot—that changed everything. That's what I'm hoping for tomorrow—a breakthrough, something new that no one realized was important at the time. I know it's a volatile mix, but there's safety in numbers. And the chief will come. How can he refuse? So" —he clapped his hands together—"now we need to get to work. I'm going to—"

The phone rang.

Max picked it up. "Hello." A smile transformed his face, a smile Annie knew well, indulgent, amused, approving. "Oh, hi, Ma. Sure. We're fine. The fax? Oh, did Barb tell you about it? Yeah, that's right. They're terrific machines. Really link you up. Well, sure. Send it along, we'd love to see it." He had that hearty tone he employed when his words absolutely did not mirror his feelings. "Yes. That's great news. Annie? Oh, sure."

Annie was semaphoring *negative, no, not-me,* but to no avail.

Max handed her the phone with a bland smile, but she noted that his eyes avoided hers entirely and he damn near sprinted to the breakfast room table. He owed her one, that was for sure.

"Annie, my sweet, I do wish you were here . . . or I were there." The vibrant, husky voice held such a note of genuine fondness that Annie couldn't help smiling. She wasn't, however, beguiled enough to respond in kind. Instead, she murmured, "That's dear of you, Laurel."

Her mother-in-law burbled on. "That's not to say that *you* lack a sense of humor, dear Annie. Why, anyone who enjoys Pamela Branch books *must* have a sense of humor. That is what I've always told myself in moments of doubt . . ."

Annie glared at the receiver.

Max redoubled his flurry with papers and pens at the table.

". . . but we all do know that you can be quite, quite literal. And that seems to be a hallmark of many of the ghostly incidences I am studying. Now, I do feel that among those with a Southern heritage there is a similar devotion to what is explicit in a code of manners rather than to what surely any reasonable person would consider implicit and these commonly accepted tenets of conduct may be central to the issues you and Max are presently exploring. Take, for example . . ."

Annie's mind was whirling. Laurel on a metaphysical romp? Surely this was beyond the pale in any sense. Oh, God, was it catching?

". . . the celebrated case of Ruth Lowndes and her un-willing husband, Francis Simmons. It surprised all of Charleston when their engagement was announced and even one of the bride's own sisters never expected him to show up for the wedding. Everyone knew Francis had recently begun to pay attention to lovely Sabina Smith. Ruth Lowndes, who was determined to marry Francis, had noticed too, of course. Sabina was, presumably, Ruth's closest friend. One day Ruth told Francis that Sabina had promised to wed another young man. Francis was crushed. To change the subject, he pulled a handkerchief from his pocket, embroidered for him with love from his favorite sister, Ann. Poor, unwary Francis said, 'Wouldn't you love to have beautiful initials such as these?' The next day, word came from Ruth's father that he under-stood Francis had proposed marriage to his daughter, Ruth, and he was pleased to approve on her behalf.

"What was Francis to do? Tell the old gentleman his

daughter was a *liar?* A man must never sully a woman's name, must never speak of a woman without respect. Francis was trapped. He went to see Ruth's father and the marriage was agreed upon. And now, he had given his word. But his heart was shattered because Sabina was lost to him, promised, as Ruth had told him, to wed another.

"Imagine his despair, his fury, his anguish, when he paid a visit to Sabina to offer congratulations upon her engagement, to wish her every happiness, though his heart was breaking, and to learn from her own lips that no, she was not promised to another, that she never—now—intended to marry. The unhappy couple stared at each other, stricken, and the truth came out. Francis embraced his true love this one time only, then, bound by his word, he departed, betrothed to the scheming, meretricious Ruth Lowndes.

"Is it any wonder that he came to his own wedding looking like a man who had come for his execution? Francis participated in the vows, but never once looked at the bride. He remained aloof and grim through the reception. When it finally ended, he helped his bride into a yellow gilt coach that carried them to the home her father had given to them at one-thirty-one Tradd Street. Francis saw his bride to the door of her new house, formally bid her good-night, then departed in the coach to his own home on St. John's Island. He would return to the house on Tradd Street to preside at dinners and at parties, but he never once spent the night under that roof. Five years later, he built his own grand house in Charleston, perhaps to underscore his separation from Ruth. So it continued throughout their lives. Ruth never publicly gave notice to his anger; she was always cheerful and bright and smiling. So who in this bitter battle triumphed? No one, I'm afraid. One summer Sabina died of a fever, and then Francis was left with only memories until his own demise a few years later.

"Ruth Simmons's house on Tradd Street no longer stands, Annie dear, but sometimes late at night there is a clatter of coach wheels and old-time Charlestonians lift their heads, listen for a moment, then say, 'Oh, that must be Ruth Simmons's yellow gilt coach, driving her to her empty marriage bed.' " A sigh. "My dear, what a tragedy!"

Annie had this immediate (she knew it was unworthy) notion that Laurel, of all people, would surely be appalled by an empty marriage bed. Having, in fact, been married five times . . . Annie forced her mind into other channels.

"Damn shame," Annie said heartily.

Her mother-in-law's silence was a good indicator that Annie's response had—somehow—not been up to par.

What was expected?

Annie tried again. "Oh, certainly, I can see that honesty is the best policy." She felt like a walking bromide. Perhaps a dash of cynicism. "Well, I doubt that Francis spent all of his nights alone."

"Annie, Annie. Perhaps I should put aside my work here and join you and Max." Laurel's husky voice indicated a definite eagerness to put duty before pleasure. "The nuances of conduct, my dear, the subterranean rocks of existence which influence conscious action, these must be your concern. And I am certainly prepared to—"

"Laurel, Max and I know you would be very happy to join us"—she took a gleeful pleasure in Max's obvious discomfiture as he lunged to his feet and began to wave his arms wildly up and down—"but you must hew to your own course. The loss to our culture would be irreparable." At Laurel's sudden silence, Annie worried that she had overdone it. After all, she didn't want to hurt the old spirit-chaser's feelings. "Really, Laurel, we're managing just fine. In fact, we're very close to a solution. The case will probably be over before you could journey here . . . considering your present disabilities."

"Oh, in that event . . . well, I do have so many avenues to explore. I shall continue my vigilant pursuit of truth here and you shall continue your vigilant pursuit there. We *shall,* of course, keep in close touch. Ta, my dears."

Annie replaced the receiver. Before she could suggest to Max that, after all, this was *his* mother and next time it was his turn to embark upon spirited quests, the fax phone rang and the machine began to clatter.

Annie had poured fresh coffee for them both when Max returned, bearing a single sheet and looking absolutely mystified. He handed the sheet to Annie.

Annie turned it upside down. No, there were words scrawled on the sheet, so it must go the other way. She righted it and squinted.

A new kind of avant-garde art perhaps?

Made up of varying shaped splotches of black and gray?

She read the inscription. It, at least, she could identify without fail. She was exceedingly familiar with Laurel's surprisingly elegant script:

> Isn't this the most remarkable photograph you've ever seen? It shall certainly be regarded with the utmost excitement by the American Psychical Society!!!!
>
> L.

Max peered over her shoulder. "Mushrooms bouncing down dungeon steps?"

But revelation came to Annie in a flash. "Ruth Simmons's coach careening down Tradd Street!" she exclaimed.

"Oh, yeah. How could I have missed it?" Max frowned, glanced toward the room with the now-silent fax. "Yeah, well. I suppose the old dear's safe enough."

"Safe enough?" Annie asked.

"I mean," Max took the fax from her and waggled it, "this looks like she was out hobbling around making a photograph in the middle of the night. And God knows what this is really a picture of. But I don't suppose it matters."

Annie was steering him to the table as he continued to mutter.

As he sank into his chair, she took the fax, handed him a legal pad, and said crisply, "Would you want her to join us here?"

At his horrified look, she nodded and slipped into the chair opposite him.

"God, no," he said simply. "Okay, let's see where we are, Annie. Do you have the bio on Enid Friendley?"

Annie found it fourth in her stack and handed it to Max.

"Okay, okay." Max scanned the sheet. "Enid Friendley. Born February fifth, 1952, in Hardeeville. Mother Eloise an LPN, father, Donald, a short-order cook. Only child. Began working at Tarrant House while still in high school. Worked her way through community college while running a catering service. At Tarrant House for only two years, 1968–70. Her catering service, Low Country Limited, solidly successful, with gross receipts last year in excess of three hundred thousand dollars. Married in 1976 to William Pittman of Beaufort, one child, Edward, 1977, divorced 1979. Kept maiden name professionally. Extremely hard worker, seven days a week, ten hours a day. Her widowed mother lives with her, takes care of Edward. An innovative, original cook with a flair for catering successful parties from luaus to barbecues. A strict, demanding employer, no shirking allowed. On formal terms with both customers and employees. Rarely smiles. Intense. Always moves at high speed, impatient with those who don't move or think as quickly, but not unpleasant. A former assistant said, 'Enid's all business, but she's fair and she treats people right. You know how this kind of business goes, a lot of people work part-time, no health benefits, no pension, but if you're one of Enid's workers and you've done good for her, she'll help you out. Sam Berry got laid off from the cement company and he was about to lose his house and Enid helped him with the payments until he got regular work again. There's lots of stories like that. All she asks is you pay her back when you can.' Her ex-husband said, 'They ought to put Enid in charge of the world. It'd run a damn sight better. I'll tell you, she'd make everybody toe the mark. That's one tiger woman.' " Max grinned. "Sounds like a tired man."

But Annie wasn't interested in Mr. Pittman. "Hey, she sounds all right. I'll bet she's got some snappy views on the Tarrants." She glanced at the clock. Almost nine. But that wasn't too late. "Max, let's call Enid Friendley. Maybe she'll even see us tonight."

Annie was reaching for the phone when it began to ring.

11:55 A.M., SATURDAY, MAY 9, 1970

Judge Tarrant was a stickler for punctuality. Lunch at Tarrant House was served at precisely twelve noon daily. Shortly before noon, the Judge left his study. A moment after the door into the hall closed, the French door from the piazza swung in. The intruder moved swiftly across the untenanted room. It took only seconds for gloved hands to pull open the bottom left drawer of the desk and grab the Judge's gun. In a few seconds more, the French door clicked shut.

Chapter 17.

Charlotte Tarrant was a woman in a frenzy. "We're all going to be killed! That's what's going to happen!" Her head whipped from side to side as she stood beside the flowering wisteria—Annie would always remember the sweet violet scent and those wild, terrified eyes—and words spewed from Charlotte's trembling mouth, a red gash against a pasty white face. The yard light beaming down from the corner live oak surrounded the chatelaine of Tarrant House in a circle of radiance as neatly as a spot on center stage. "Who's doing this? I'll tell you who it is—it's that *girl*! Who says she's missing? Those people?" Her voice rose hysterically as she pointed at Annie and Max. "Why are they here? This is Tarrant property. *Tarrant* property." Furiously, she turned on Whitney. "Get them out of here. Make them leave. Maybe *they* broke in! Why are they here?" She clutched her husband's arm.

"Take Charlotte inside, Whitney." Miss Dora lifted her cane and pointed toward the steps. "She's distraught." The old lady peered up at the piazza and the squatting form of the police chief. A patrolman stood slightly behind Wells, holding a huge flashlight.

Shattered glass sparkled in the pool of light. The broken pane in the French door was beside the handle. The door was ajar. The cone of light illuminated a patch of Persian rug, pale gray touched with silver and rose, the russet gleam of mahogany, and, lying on the piazza, the chunk of brick that had been used to break the glass.

"Let's go back inside, Charlotte," Whitney urged. "The chief will take care of everything—"

Charlotte hung back. "We don't know who's in there. What if someone's in there—with the gun?" She dropped Whitney's arm and ran to the piazza steps. "Chief, hurry! They may be upstairs, waiting for us."

Wells remained hunkered down on the gray painted boards of the porch. He looked over his shoulder. "Miz Tarrant, was the gun the only thing taken from the room?"

"I think so. I saw it all at once," she said feverishly, "the broken window, the French door ajar, and the bottom drawer to the desk open. I ran and looked down into the drawer. When I saw the gun was gone, I screamed for Whitney."

"Didn't know what the hell!" Whitney came up beside her. "I found Charlotte scared to death. All she could do was point, first at the smashed glass, then at the drawer, then at the glass. Damn gun has disappeared. That's all I can tell you."

Charlotte peered into the darkness that pressed around them. The sliver of moon gave scarcely any light at all. The shadows in the garden were deep and dark. "Someone may be out there with the gun right now. Or waiting upstairs! They may be waiting upstairs to kill us both!"

Wells reached behind him for the flashlight. "Secure the

premises, Matthews." He stood, the flashlight pointed down at the porch. "Miss Dora, perhaps you could offer refuge to your kinfolk until we complete our investigation."

Miss Dora's head snapped up. Annie wasn't certain—the light was poor where the old lady stood—but, just for an instant, Annie thought she saw an odd expression. Uncertainty? Concern? Fear? But, in the next instant, Miss Dora was stepping forward. "My old Daisy would have a seizure, people tramping in my house at this hour of the night."

It wasn't long after nine o'clock, but Annie supposed that to Miss Dora and her no doubt aged retainer, the hour might be quite unseemly.

Miss Dora marched up to Charlotte. The wizened old woman was fully dressed in her familiar black bombazine, ankle length dress, and sturdy black shoes. So Miss Dora had not yet retired for the night when a siren sounded next door, announcing the arrival of the police.

Charlotte was in black, too, but hers was a stylish linen dress with a striped shawl collar. Pink pearl earrings and a two-strand pink pearl necklace added the only touch of color.

The contrast between the two women was startling, but Miss Dora didn't look absurd. Other-century and witchlike, yes, but not absurd.

Tossing her white head impatiently, Miss Dora snapped, "Try to show some control, Charlotte. Obviously, no housebreaker would remain on the premises after he was discovered. Moreover, it would take a demented burglar to await the arrival of the authorities. Had someone broken in to take the gun with the objective of attacking *you,* that attack would have occurred when you came into the study and found the window broken. No such attack occurred. And how would an intruder have reached the upper rooms? You and Whitney were both downstairs. Did anyone run past you and go up the stairs?"

Sullenly, Charlotte shook her head. Shaking fingers tugged at her necklace of pink pearls. "But someone could be up there," she persisted.

An expression of distaste crossed Miss Dora's aristocratic face. "The patrolman is now checking each room. As soon as that search is complete, you may feel quite safe to go inside." She sniffed. "Why in heaven's name would anyone want to shoot you, Charlotte?"

Chief Wells moved ponderously to the edge of the porch to listen to Charlotte's answer. One cheek bulged with a wad of tobacco.

Charlotte wrapped her arms tightly across her chest. Her voice shook with anger. "Why did someone shoot the Judge? Answer me that! Why did someone set fire to my museum? Answer me that! I'll tell you why! Someone hates the Tarrants!" Her eyes flicked venomously toward Annie and Max. "And why are *they* always here when there's trouble? He was the last one who saw that girl, too! That's what it said in the paper. Why are they—"

"Because I called for them." Miss Dora's bony jaw jutted obstinately. "Whatever happens here concerns all of the Family—and Mr. and Mrs. Darling are assisting the Family at my behest. Once you are somewhat in control of yourself, Charlotte, perhaps you can tell us what happened here tonight." The old lady's hands tightened on the silver knob of her cane.

Charlotte clasped her hands together, but they still trembled. "We were in the drawing room after dinner. Whitney was working with his stamps, and I was reading—a monograph on silver thimbles made in Charleston between 1840 and 1860. I wanted to check another source—a paper written by another authority—and I went into the library—"

A shout and a piercing whistle sounded out on the street.

Wells barked, "Stay here, all of you!" He thudded

down the stairs and loped around the end of the house. For a big man, he moved fast.

"Hey, you . . ." a man called hoarsely.

"Hold up there. Stop or we'll shoot!" Annie recognized Wells's deep voice. "All right, buddy. Hands up. Walk this way. Right. Keep right along."

Harris Walker, his arms lifted, his face stubbled with beard, stumbled around the side of the house. He blinked against the light hanging in the live oak. Then he saw Annie and Max. "What's happening here?" he demanded.

Charlotte Tarrant gave a little scream. "Who is he? Is he the one? Dear God, I knew it. We'll all be killed in our beds—"

"Hush." Miss Dora's tone was deadly and not to be ignored.

Charlotte subsided, but her wide, staring eyes never left Walker's haggard face.

Annie spoke first. "That's Courtney's boyfriend—and he's hunting her."

Charlotte took a step back. "Here. Here?"

Walker turned on Wells. "Listen, I got bloodhounds out here today and—"

Wells held up a meaty hand. "I know. There isn't much that goes on in this town that I don't know, Walker. But so what? I understand the young woman came to this house and to Miss Dora's earlier in the week. The hounds don't show us anything."

Walker's arms sagged. He swallowed jerkily. "They stopped dragging the river. Late this afternoon."

Wells didn't tell the young man to lift his arms again. Instead, he simply nodded, his craggy face somber.

"Does that mean . . ." Walker clenched his fists. "Where are you looking for her? Where are you looking now, dammit?"

The look on his face made Annie want to cry.

Wells tipped back his cowboy hat. "We have an APB out and—"

"That's nothing," Walker shouted. "There should be people out everywhere. When I got to town, all you talked about was him." He jerked a shoulder at Max. "But you know that's stupid. Something happened to Courtney because of the Tarrants, because somebody killed her dad. It's all tied up with them. Have you looked in this house? Have you?" He stood there, his young body tense, and he had the air of a soldier on attack despite his unshaven cheeks and dusty, torn clothes.

"There's an officer searching this house right now."

A tiny flicker of hope moved in Walker's sunken eyes.

"That's absurd." Whitney glared at Walker. "What's he saying? That we've done something with the girl?"

Charlotte swept forward, a shaking hand pointing at Walker. "Arrest him! You must arrest him—obviously, he's the one."

Wells rocked back on his feet. "Let's have some answers, Walker. What are you doing here?"

"I was driving by. Any law against that? I just keep driving, driving, driving. I think maybe I'll see her. . . ." He rubbed the back of his fist against his unshaven face. "I keep looking for her. . . ."

"Where's your car?" Wells demanded.

"Out in front."

The back door slammed.

Everyone looked up on the piazza at the patrolman.

Walker took a step forward.

Matthews reported to Wells. "The house is empty, sir. No sign of entry or exit elsewhere. Nothing else appears to be disturbed." He took the flashlight back from the chief. Wells didn't bother with a thank-you.

Nice man to work for, Annie thought.

Miss Dora thumped her cane. "Time is wasting." She

pointed the cane at Charlotte. "When was the last time you were in the library?"

The chief gave Walker a swift glance. "I'll deal with you later. Just stay right where you are." Wells shoved the light back at the patrolman and pulled out a notebook and a pen.

Walker glanced from the chief to the Tarrants, his eyes hard and suspicious. Annie knew nothing could have driven him out of that shadowy garden.

Charlotte gave Walker another hostile glance, then hurried to answer when Miss Dora waggled the cane at her impatiently. "Why, I suppose not since this morning. I returned several books from the drawing room—you see, we read in the evenings and there are always books about but we leave them until morning. That's when I straighten up. It must have been about ten this morning. I put the books up and closed the door. I didn't go back in until tonight."

"What time?" Max asked.

Charlotte looked at him resentfully, but answered before Miss Dora could intervene. "It must have been just before nine. Yes." She spoke with more assurance, looking toward Whitney. "It was just before nine, wasn't it?"

Her husband nodded, but he was staring at the piazza, with its scattering of broken glass. "Hell of a thing, to have someone break in. Never happened before. Never."

Wells wrote briefly in his notebook. "So, the brick could have been thrown through the French door anytime between ten this morning and nine tonight." He sounded profoundly unhappy.

Annie didn't blame him. That was a hell of a time span.

The chief glanced back inside the library. "Was the drawer locked?"

No one spoke.

Now Wells became impatient. "Mr. Tarrant, was that

drawer—the one where the gun was kept—was it generally kept locked?"

"No." Whitney sounded puzzled. "It's just an ordinary desk, Chief. I keep my important papers at the office."

"So you had this gun in a drawer where anyone could get at it?" His disgust with careless householders was apparent. Annie didn't blame him.

Whitney's head jerked up. "I beg your pardon. It isn't as though our library is a public thoroughfare. That weapon has been kept there for years and—"

"How many years?" Wells demanded.

The silence this time was distinctly strained.

Whitney and Charlotte glanced at each other.

Charlotte gasped. "Whitney, I never thought—was that the gun—" She whimpered and pressed the back of her hand against her mouth.

Whitney blinked nervously. "It was the Judge's gun from the War. It was always kept there until—oh, God, I don't know what happened that day! But that's the gun"—he swallowed convulsively—"my brother used. Granddad brought it to me months later and asked if I wanted it back. I said yes because somehow that made it seem as if it had truly ended."

"Loaded?" Wells asked.

Whitney's eyes fell away from the chief's cold stare.

That was answer enough.

"World War Two issue, that would be a forty-five-caliber Colt M-nineteen-eleven-A-one." Wells absently moved the wad of tobacco in his cheek. "All right. So somebody took it sometime today." He scrawled in his notebook.

Max stood with his hands jammed into his pockets, his face thoughtful. "Miss Dora, you called Mr. and Mrs. Tarrant tonight and arranged for tomorrow's gathering here. And you must also have called the others."

Annie expected another outburst from Charlotte Tarrant. But the harried woman satisfied herself with a silent, vengeful look at Miss Dora.

"I did indeed. And that meeting shall occur as I have decreed." Miss Dora ignored Charlotte. "Why do you ask?"

"It would be very interesting to know," Max said slowly, "if that gun was taken *after* your phone calls."

Chief Wells's heavy head turned toward Max. "What do you have in mind, Darling?"

Max looked toward the piazza. "I'm not certain, Chief. It's just that the murderer may be getting scared—and that worries me."

Wells's jaw moved rhythmically. His huge hand dropped to the butt of the pistol holstered on his hip. His message was unmistakable. "You don't need to worry, Darling. I'll be here."

The St. George Inn was lovely, but it wasn't home. There was no pistachio ice cream in the freezer. The pantry lacked brownies laced with raspberry, and the supply of peanut butter cookies was dangerously low. Coffee, of course, they had in abundance, and the thermos had kept the Colombian decaf hot. But there was something terribly unsatisfactory about coffee unaccompanied by edibles.

"Want a cookie?" Annie asked. She hoped her guardian angel was dutifully posting a gold star because there were only four peanut butter cookies left, and if Max took one now and so did she, that would leave only one for bedtime and one for breakfast and, as all peanut butter cookie lovers know, that would make a bummer out of breakfast.

"No thanks, sweetie. More coffee, though." Max held up his cup, but he never lifted his eyes from his papers.

Annie reached for a cookie. She was too cool, too disciplined to grab. Crunch. Pure pleasure. She looked up at the clock. Almost eleven. God, what a night. And she was still worried about pale, driven Harris Walker. At least he hadn't been arrested. Annie suspected Walker was free because he'd given the police permission to search his car and him. No gun turned up. So Wells told him to stay away from Tarrant House and left it at that. But, as Walker drove off, Annie knew he was looking back at the house.

There hadn't been, of course, any resolution to the break-in. The only certain fact was that the loaded gun was gone.

Not a cheerful prospect.

And she didn't share Wells's conviction that all would be well so long as he was present.

She finished her cookie, then poured the coffee and bent over to kiss the tip of Max's ear. Surely it was time to quit work for the night.

"Oh, yeah," he said positively. But it was rather more of an automatic response than she had hoped for, and he kept right on writing on his legal pad.

Annie refreshed his mug and her own, then dropped onto the chaise longue. She yawned. "Maybe Wells is the murderer. You know, maybe the Judge caught him out in something and the chief slipped into Tarrant House that Saturday afternoon and shot the Judge and slipped right back out. Then Ross came in and maybe his mother had got there just before him and he walked in and she was holding the gun and—"

Max finished writing with a flourish, ripped off the top sheet, and leaned over the coffee table to hand it to her. "Here's what we need to find out."

She looked at Max's list.

MAY 9, 1970

1. What was Whitney doing in the garage? He claims he didn't see anyone from the garage window,

so why did he look puzzled when we talked about it this morning?

2. Why was Amanda upset? Who might know? Why was the Judge buying her a condo in Florida?

3. Did Charlotte know about Whitney's involvement with the woman a client was suing for divorce? Did she know about the Judge's decision to force Whitney out of the family firm? Did Charlotte and the Judge have a disagreement?

4. Why was Julia crying in the garden?

5. How upset was Milam about his father's assumptions in regard to the nature of his relationship with Joan Crandall?

6. Where was each person in the house at the critical time (approximately four o'clock)?

7. How could the Judge's study be approached?

8. What did Ross see?

9. The authorities described Amanda Tarrant's death as an accident, while believing it was suicide. Who was the last person to see her? What happened the day she died?

10. Miss Dora alibied *herself* when she said she saw Ross in the garden at the time of the shot. Was she telling the truth—about herself? Could *she* have been in the study? Ross wasn't here to say where he was.

11. No one could prove where Sybil was. Could she have decided she wanted not only Ross but their rightful place in Chastain? Did Sybil even then give a damn?

Annie took a bite from her peanut butter cookie. Either the sugar or the list produced a spurt of energy. With a flourish, she gave Max an admiring salute. "Right on, Sherlock." He had certainly winnowed through what they'd learned and come up with a succinct, to-the-point list of all the questions raised by their new knowledge.

Max accepted her tribute with an almost modest smile. "A good detective has to discard the irrelevant."

Was there a hint, just a hint, of complacency there? A suggestion that others (and we all knew who that would be) were bogged in minutiae, unable to ascertain what was meaningful?

Although Annie would never admit to competitive feelings with her live-in sleuth, she was just a tad irritated. Her eyes slitted. Grace Latham might expect to be treated like a dimwit by Colonel Primrose; Annie wasn't having any.

Grabbing her notebook, she wrote furiously. In a moment, she ripped out the sheet and thrust it toward him.

Max studied her conclusions, which were, she would have admitted had she been pressed, not organized well in terms of time and space, but they got to the damn point. After all, what really counted in murder? Motives, of course.

MOTIVES IN THE MURDER OF JUDGE TARRANT

1. *Whitney—To prevent expulsion from the law firm.* Does Whitney have the guts? Was it the cornered-animal syndrome? In re the torching of Charlotte's museum, was there some written evidence that could have convicted Whitney? What kind of threat would Courtney Kimball be? (Was the attack on her, no matter by whom, a desperate effort to maintain the facade of suicide–heart attack that had survived through the years?)

2. *Charlotte—To protect Whitney.* (If she knew about the Judge's plan to have the firm expel Whitney?) Actually, did she give that much of a damn about Whitney? Their marriage certainly didn't seem like a passionate one. What was it like twenty years ago? Beyond concern about Whitney, she apparently had no personal motive. And it was beyond belief that she

would have torched her museum. Tarrant House and its occupants, past and present, were her only passion in life.

3. *Milam—Anger over his father's conclusions about his sponsorship of Joan Crandall.* Was that the final blow in a long line of emotional hurts? As for the museum, no doubt Milam would have enjoyed setting it on fire.

4. *Julia—*

Here, Annie's pen had faltered. So Julia was a drunk in a bad marriage; what did that have to do with the price of apples? There didn't seem to be any reason at all for her to shoot the Judge. Hell, Julia should have shot Milam and saved everybody a lot of trouble.

"It *has* to be one of them," Annie concluded. "Unless Miss Dora's conned everybody and she shot the Judge and for some reason wants to raise a lot of hell with the surviving Tarrants."

Max opened his mouth, but Annie barreled ahead.

"It couldn't be Sybil." Annie circled Sybil's name on Max's list. "That I wouldn't believe even if I saw it. She didn't care any more about social position then than she does now. She was going to elope with Ross. She was getting everything she wanted. And if she'd had any idea Courtney Kimball was her daughter, she would have moved heaven and earth to be with her. She certainly would never harm her."

"A little disconcerting," Max objected mildly as he rooted around in the fruit bowl on the kitchen table (Annie had assumed it was decorative), "this jumping back and forth between now and then." He picked up a pear and took a huge bite.

Annie liked pears poached in champagne. She studied the third cookie. Did she want it now or would it be better to save it for breakfast? Two for breakfast would be infinitely better than just one.

Max paused in his chewing. "But you've made some excellent points."

Annie was mollified by the admiring tone in his voice.

He grabbed the legal pad with his left hand and took another bite of the fruit. "The problem is, we still don't know enough about these people. Annie, where're the bios on Julia and Charlotte?"

Suddenly she found computer sheets in her hand, instead of a cookie. Was that an omen? Perhaps so.

"Here we are," she said briskly. " 'Julia Martin Tarrant. Age forty-eight. Born in Columbia, South Carolina. Father, Olin, a high-school chemistry teacher. Mother, Georgia, a primary-school teacher. Two brothers, Edwin and Arthur, and one sister, Frances. Julia made very little impression on those around her throughout her school career. Her brothers were both excellent students and held various class offices. They were also successful athletes.' " Annie paused.

Max prodded. "And?"

"What's the deal?" Annie said slowly.

Her husband looked puzzled.

She felt a rush of affection. Max of the three sisters and wacky mom had never encountered—and certainly never indulged in—the kind of sexism she sensed here. Annie waggled the printout. "Is this part of the old fifties syndrome? A woman's place is out of sight and out of mind? Or is this just Julia?" She resumed reading. " 'Frances was two years older than Julia. She died in 1960 (a drowning victim).' " Annie frowned. "Isn't that what happened to Julia and Milam's little girl?"

Max nodded.

"Isn't that—odd?" Annie asked.

"Yes. But surely—" Max looked appalled.

Annie had read enough Edgar Allan Poe to have an inkling of the dark depths in the human mind. But, as Max said, surely not. Julia was a drunk, but not a neurotic monster. Annie liked her. And felt sorry for her. The deaths of Julia's sister and daughter, both by drowning, had to be a hideous coincidence.

Annie cleared her throat. " 'Julia had a C average. Her brothers both attended the university full-time and were outstanding students. Julia worked part-time, lived at home (her brothers lived in student housing), and was a part-time student, paying her own tuition. She met Milam Tarrant in a photography course in the art department when he was a junior. They married after he was graduated.

" 'The high school counselor, Mrs. Humphreys, said: "Julia Martin? Oh, yes, of course. Olin's daughter. So funny, I almost never think about him having a daughter. The boys were so outstanding. Julia was a mousy little thing, always looked like she was scared of her shadow. I tried to encourage her to take part in class activities, but she always stood there tongue-tied and—why, I hate to say it—almost as if she were addlebrained. But her mother was kind of a washout, too. No personality at all. Not like Olin. He is such a charming man. And a very good teacher." ' " Annie rattled the sheet. "I'd say Mrs. Humphreys likes to back winners. I'll bet she's a great counselor."

Max took a last bite of the pear. "Doesn't anybody like Julia?"

"Apparently not." Annie skimmed the rest of it. " 'Julia didn't have a circle of friends in high school . . . a loner . . . "She walked around like a little ghost," her English teacher said. "I tried several times to strike a response. There was certainly trauma there. I was never sure why. Perhaps it was the death of her sister. Whatever it was, I was never able to break through, make a connection. I tried to talk to Olin about it once, but he refused to listen. He's one of these smile-all-the-time, you-can-do-it-if-you-try people. I'd say he was heavy into denial as far as Julia was concerned. But that's the way it is sometimes. He's a wonderful teacher. Loves kids." ' "

Annie paused, skimmed some more, then stopped, her eyebrows lifted. "Oh ho, here's the word from Olin. ' "Julia? I'm sorry, we haven't seen much of my daughter and her husband in recent years. We've tried to keep in touch. We don't know what's wrong, but we're afraid Julia's drinking too much. We've urged her to go into treatment, but a person has to want to get better, and I'm afraid Julia doesn't care. We survived the loss of our lovely girl. Why can't Julia face life?" Julia's mother, "I don't know, I'm sure. It's been such a long time. Julia won't talk to us when we call." ' "

Annie made a face at the printout. No sympathy for Julia. Anywhere.

Max grinned and tossed his pear core neatly into the wastebasket. "Found yourself an underdog?"

"Don't you think Julia's likable?" Annie appealed.

"Yes, I do," Max said soberly. "But we have to look at her closely. Remember the ring from the gasoline can on the carpet of her car."

"Even if she set fire to the museum, that doesn't mean she's a murderer," Annie defended.

Max grinned again.

"I am *not* a sap for underdogs," Annie said irritably.

"Of course not. Now, let's see. What do we have on Charlotte Tarrant?" Max poised his pen over his pad.

Annie thumbed through the pile of printouts.

"Here we go. 'Charlotte Carey Tarrant. Age forty-seven. Born in Greenville, South Carolina. Father, James, a bailiff. Mother, Lois, a secretary. Two sisters, Katie and Barbara. Lois Carey was from a fifth-generation family in

Greenville, the Bakers. The family was wealthy but lost all of its properties in the Civil War. Lois was a member of the Daughters of the Confederacy and the Daughters of the American Revolution. Charlotte, an outstanding student, received a scholarship to the university. A history major, she specialized in the American South. Always fascinated by family history. Pam Jergens, president of the high school pep club, said, "Charlotte was born old. She always had on white gloves, figuratively speaking. And she was so ladylike. God, that was a long time ago. What's Charlotte done, seceded from the Union again? Of course, you have to remember, I couldn't wait to get the hell out and see how the real world lived. I left twenty years ago and I've never regretted it for a minute." Zenia Phillips, a college sorority sister, said, "Boring. That sums up dear Charlotte, boring as hell." Betty Blake, who cochaired the Chastain house-and-garden tours with Charlotte several years ago, described Charlotte as ". . . absolutely marvelous to work with. Organized, responsible, enthusiastic. I'll tell you, we had the best spring tours our year that anyone's ever done. Charlotte was certainly the best president the Chastain Historical Society has ever had, and she is as knowledgeable about family history as anyone in the state. It's a terrific asset for a community when someone like Charlotte will devote herself heart and soul to preserving its heritage. I don't know what we would have done without Charlotte when they tried to get an exception to the preservation code and raze the old MacDougal House to make way for a parking lot for some apartments. Can you believe it? They wanted to destroy a lovely Greek Revival home built in 1848! Charlotte fought like a tigress. She wouldn't give up. Why, I'd say she almost single-handedly won that battle. We owe her so much." Cordelia Prince, president of the PTA when Charlotte and Whitney's daughter was in grade school, snapped, "That woman's a poisonous reptile. I'll bet the average snake of my acquaintance is a better mother. Cold-blooded? She was too busy to be a homeroom mother, too busy to drive on field trips, too busy to chaperon a dance. And on what? Dead and gone people who didn't need a minute of her time while her daughter turned angry and hostile. I don't blame that child for running away. Who would stay home with a mother like that?" '

"I *knew* I didn't like Charlotte," Annie said decisively.

"Being a lousy parent doesn't equate to committing murder," Max cautioned.

"I know," Annie said regretfully. "Besides, the woman's obviously scared to death."

When Max didn't immediately comment, Annie raised an eyebrow.

He looked at her with a gravity so foreign to his usual confident demeanor that she felt suddenly uneasy.

"Annie, the hell of it is, I think Charlotte's damned smart to be scared. I'm scared, too, about that roundup at Tarrant House tomorrow afternoon. It's almost twenty-two years to the day when murder occurred, and, you can bet on it, the murderer will be there." He jammed a hand through his thick, unruly blond hair. "I wish to God we knew where that gun was!"

2:30 *P.M., SATURDAY, MAY 9, 1970*

Ross listened tensely to the news through the crackle of static on the car radio. The station faded in and out, but he heard enough. Campuses were closing across the country, in California, in Illinois, in Massachusetts. Witnesses were saying no one had fired at the National Guard. Witnesses were saying the students, walking to class, were gunned down for no reason. The Guard was claiming an attack. Students were marching. . . . The station faded out. Ross turned the dial and Hank Thompson's mournful voice filled the car. Ross turned off the radio. He was almost home.

He'd made the right decision. He squared his shoulders, gripped the wheel tighter.

He could see his father's face, proud and arrogant. Always the Judge's somber eyes lighted for him.

What would his father say?

Chapter 18.

Annie gripped the door as the Maserati bumped down the deep-rutted, overgrowth-choked, dusty gray road. Cones from the slash pines crunched beneath the tires. Giant ferns glistened with dew beneath spreading live oaks. Holly and sharp-edged yucca, saw palmetto, and running oak flourished. Annie, for an instant, envisioned the land as it appeared to long-ago travelers: wild, untamed, inimical, with an almost overpowering fecundity.

The road curved left.

Max jammed on the brake at a flurry of movement in the foliage. Annie hung on tight. A blue-gray hawk zoomed across the road, swooping to pounce on a pinkish copperhead stretched in a sunny spot on a rotting log.

It was the only time Annie had ever felt sorry for a snake.

She wondered how much she would have loved the Low Country two hundred years ago. She wasn't altogether crazy about this present-day, off-the-beaten-path forest. She loved sassafras, sweet gum, and red bay trees, but nicely pruned and cut back, thank you. It was exciting to glimpse white-tailed deer, but the sudden thrashing in the undergrowth and the sight of bristly black hair and an ugly snout with razor-sharp tusks made her long for the confines of a well-kept clay tennis court.

Annie hunched tensely in her seat. Any kind of horror could occur in the midst of these longleaf-pine flatwoods.

"Do you think it's much farther?" She tried to sound casual.

Max, as always, wasn't deceived. "Don't worry, honey. As long as you don't step on a diamondback, you'll be okay."

She did not consider his answer especially reassuring.

"Oh, hell," Max swore, and the Maserati jolted to a stop.

One of last winter's nor'easters had toppled a dead pine. Breaking as it fell, a portion of the trunk blocked the road. A huge limb had splintered the wooden bridge over the sluggish stream.

Max glanced at the mileage counter he had punched when they left the blacktop. "It's about a half-mile farther. Look, Annie, you can stay here and—"

She was already opening her door. "In for a penny," she announced stalwartly, wishing she had put on hiking boots and jeans and a long-sleeved cotton top instead of white flats, a pleated pink-rose cotton skirt, and a delicate white cotton blouse with a lacy embroidered collar. She had considered it a fetching outfit (and perfectly appropriate) this morning at the St. George Inn. It was little comfort that she would be as out of place slapping away resurrection ferns and skidding on pine hay as that briefly spotted bristly black-haired wild boar would be reclining on the chintz-covered chaise longue at the inn.

Max retrieved a flashlight from the car pocket. They stepped out of the car into insect hell. The air was alive with whirring patches of no-see-ums. Mosquitos and biting flies attacked. Wasps buzzed angrily.

Annie waved her arms and broke into a trot, then almost slid into water scummed with green duckweed when her shoe soles skimmed over the pine hay.

Max caught her in time. "Be careful, Annie. Watch where you step. There will be plenty of snakes out."

Annie repressed a shudder. She knew she should reverence all God's creatures, but who could love a venomous pit viper?

She was glad she didn't have a video of their progress. Their careful, considered footfalls (rattlesnakes *always* have the right-of-way) were in stark contrast to the continued wild movements of their arms and hands as they tried to deflect the scores of starved or insanely bored insects.

The horde of biting bugs pursued them as they hopped from one remnant of the bridge to another to cross the stream. The buzzing cloud whirled around them as they hurried through the now thinning stand of pines. They came out onto a huge expanse of grass, covered with the vivid shades of spring wildflowers, the brilliant yellow of Carolina jessamine, the maroon of purple trillium, the bright red of crossvine. They'd reached the savannah, and there before them was the Tarrant hunting lodge.

Weathered wooden steps—the third sagged alarmingly —led up to a shallow porch. Although the paint had long ago peeled away, the square box building, well built, was still in good repair. As Max unlocked the front door, Annie did note a broken pane in the window on her left. She wondered how Miss Dora had obtained the keys. From Whitney? Yes, more than likely. She couldn't picture Milam here. She vainly swatted another mosquito and hurried inside as Max opened the door.

Max turned on the flashlight.

Annie followed the sweeping beam of light across the

single room: a rough-hewn fireplace with an open hearth, scattered chairs, a pinewood table, a sink, cupboards on one wall, and dust. Dust on the floor, dust on every surface, cobwebs on the walls.

A mournful, dreary, deserted room, musty and dank.

How long had it been since human voices had sounded here?

Max moved away, checking the windows and the back door.

Annie stood near the chair next to the rock fireplace. For the first time, painful as an unexpected blow, she felt the reality of Ross Tarrant's death. She stood very still, staring at the darkish upholstery. That irregular, barely visible, long-dried stain—

What would he feel now, if he knew about his daughter and the desperate search for her?

A man who lived and died that passionately would move heaven and earth to find his missing daughter.

"Max," Annie said abruptly, urgently, "let's hurry."

Enid Friendley studied them thoughtfully. Close-cropped, graying hair framed intelligent, wary eyes and a resolute mouth. She had an air of brisk confidence tinged with impatience. After a moment, she glanced at her plain gold watch. "I can give you twenty minutes."

In the immaculate living room, she gestured for them to take the couch, upholstered in plain blue linen. Enid sat in a straight chair, her posture excellent. The modern light-oak furniture was as angular and spare as its owner. No curtains. Pale-lemon blinds were the only window covering. No knickknacks broke the smooth expanse of the ocean-green, glass coffee table. The room was as cool and unrevealing as their hostess and her quietly tasteful but unremarkable black skirt and white, high-necked cotton blouse.

Perceptive dark eyes watched Annie. "I've seen enough

old furniture to last me a lifetime." Her tone was dry. "Where I grew up, we were lucky to have one real chair. Of course, the covering was ragged and the springs poked through. Cast off. Somebody hired my father to haul it away." Again, pointedly, she glanced at her watch.

Annie didn't need to look at hers. It was almost ten. Time raced ahead. The hours had piled up since Courtney Kimball was last seen, *three* days ago. Annie leaned forward impatiently as Max quickly described their mission.

Enid's face remained impassive. Even when Max mentioned the bloody shirt she had brought to Lucy Jane so many years ago.

". . . so we're hoping you can help us, Mrs. Friendley. We need to know what you saw that day and what you know about the Tarrants. But to begin, did you—"

Enid lifted a hand. She wore no rings, and her fingernails were trimmed short and unpainted. "Just a minute, Mr. Darling. I'll talk about that day and the Tarrants. I don't have anything to say about anything that happened later." She paused.

Annie looked at her, puzzled.

But Max nodded in instant comprehension. "Certainly, although I'm confident at this point that no one would accuse you of acting as an accomplice after the fact. After all, you were merely an employee following the directives of your superior. You had no reason to suspect that a crime had been committed."

The small, dark woman considered it, her suspicious eyes probing his face.

Annie had the feeling it could go either way. Enid Friendley would have no compunction about showing them the door. But perhaps she liked what she saw, or perhaps she, too, wanted to know the truth of that deadly Saturday. Whatever the reason, she finally nodded, grudgingly.

"All right. What do you want to know?"

"Have you seen or talked to Courtney Kimball?" Max didn't try to keep the eagerness from his voice.

Annie ached for him. He still felt responsible because he hadn't reached his young client in time.

"Wednesday afternoon," Enid said briskly.

Annie tried not to get excited, but this was as close as they'd come to Courtney Kimball in three days of searching. Wednesday afternoon!

"I was at work—we had two hundred chicken potpies due at the County Horticultural Building—that's out at the fairgrounds—by five o'clock. She insisted she had to talk to me. I told her straight out I was too busy. She didn't want to take no for an answer. You can tell she's always had her way." The resentment of a lifetime crackled in the words. "So I'm not surprised when you say she was Sybil and Ross's girl. It's in her blood." A meager smile curved her lips in reluctant tribute to the kind of personality that sweeps the world before it. "I couldn't help but kind of like her, bright, smart, brash—and pretty, very pretty. Yes, I can see Ross Tarrant in her face, now that I know. He was always the handsomest one. The best of the bunch. He saw me as a real person—talked to me about going to college and what a difference it could make in my life. I couldn't believe it when he killed himself. The only thing I could figure was that Sybil had thrown him over, and he took it too hard. Sybil's the kind of woman—and that was as true twenty years ago as today—who lives from her heart. That will hurt you pretty bad. She broke down at the funeral. I thought it was a guilty conscience. Anyway, that girl Courtney's got Sybil's wild streak, I can tell you that. I saw it in her eyes. Not afraid of the devil himself." She pursed her lips. "Maybe she'd have been better off if she'd had the sense to be afraid."

"What happened?" Annie urged.

"I don't put up with sass. Not from anybody. White or black."

Annie didn't doubt her for a moment.

"When she saw I meant what I said—I wasn't going to fool with her right then—she kind of laughed, and gave a shrug, and said, 'So you're upfront about things. Then answer one question for me and I'll leave. Of all the people who were at Tarrant House when Judge Tarrant and his son died, who can I trust?' " There was grudging admiration in Enid's dark eyes. "Not many people ever get around me. She did. I didn't have an extra minute to spare. Eliza Jones had called in sick. Probably her son'd beat her up again. My best driver had the mumps. Thirty-four-year-old man with the mumps! I was busy six ways from Sunday. But I took the time. I told her, 'Not a single one of them.' I told her if she wanted help from someone in the family, old Miss Dora was the only one I'd put any stock in. Then I shooed her out the door and went back to my chicken pies."

Had Courtney tried to contact Miss Dora on Wednesday? Obviously, she hadn't succeeded. Otherwise, Miss Dora would have told them, Annie was certain. But she made a mental note to check with their employer when they met her at Tarrant House in the afternoon.

"What time was this?" Max asked.

"Just after two. I was keeping a close eye on the time, I can tell you. I deliver on time. And I did on Wednesday."

Was that pride of ownership? Or was Enid Friendley trying to show she was too busy to have been involved in Courtney's disappearance?

Annie attempted to sound casual. "So you made your delivery around five. What time did you leave the fairgrounds?"

Enid took just an instant too long to answer. When she did, her words were clipped. "I finished the cleanup, still two short in my crew, about nine o'clock."

Max gave her his most charming smile.

There wasn't a quiver of response on Enid's face. Annie

wondered if Max felt a bit as though he'd smashed headfirst into a brick wall.

Undaunted, Max continued good-humoredly, "I suppose that like every business in the world, there's always some crisis—major or minor—in completing a job. Did you have to get back to your kitchen for anything?"

Once again, her response was just a beat too slow. "One dessert carrier was left behind. I went back for it, but returned directly to the fairgrounds."

Annie was pleased that Max let it drop. It was obvious that Enid read the newspapers and knew when Courtney had last been heard from and equally obvious that Enid had been away from the fairgrounds at about that time.

"You didn't see Courtney again?" Annie asked.

Enid bristled. "No. Why should I? I didn't have anything to do with her disappearance. You can look to the Tarrants for that."

"We are," Max said soberly. "As for the Tarrants, what can you tell us about the day the Judge was murdered?"

Enid smoothed her unwrinkled skirt. "That day . . . It was a lovely day, soft and warm. It smelled good, spaded-up dirt and honeysuckle and wisteria and pittosporum. I didn't usually work on Saturdays, but I'd had the afternoon off earlier in the week." Her narrow face was sleek and satisfied. "I'd enrolled for the summer session at Chastain College." She darted a quick glance at them. "If you've found out much about Judge Tarrant, you'll know he often helped students—poor people—to go to school. He gave me the money to start college. Actually, that was the last week I was to work there. But, because of what happened, I stayed on for a few weeks, after the funerals, to help with packing things away. That kind of thing. But that Saturday I was there, catching up on the ironing. So I was in the laundry rooms behind the kitchen." She scowled. "I hated being a servant." Her voice was controlled but Annie heard the resentment, saw it in the flash of her eyes. "Yes, ma'am, no, ma'am, scrubbing up after people like they were kings and I was a slave, all for barely enough money to buy a little food. And people so proud of themselves. The Tarrants. The kind of people who bought my people, bought them like a broom or a shovel and threw them away when they couldn't work in the fields." Now those slender brown hands were laced tightly together. "I started in Tarrant House, but I'll tell you this"—she lifted her chin—"I could buy Tarrant House now. I wouldn't want it, but if I did, I could buy it." Her eyes were cold. "People so proud of themselves, so used to telling people like me what to do. So high and mighty, but they had their secrets, all of them. The Judge—I wonder what all his fine friends would have thought if they could have seen the pictures he kept locked in the wooden box in his room." She flicked a glance at Annie. "Not the kind of pictures *you'd* know about—women tied up. And other things." Dark amusement glinted in her chilly eyes. "Such a high and mighty man. Just goes to show, you know, that white hair and a gentleman's face don't mean much. The next week, after the Judge died, I saw Miss Amanda slip out of the house with that box. She burned it up." Enid gave them a challenging glance. "Makes you wonder about the Judge. Doesn't it?"

"Pornographic photographs that he kept locked up?" Max asked innocently. "How did you happen to know about them?"

Just for an instant, Enid's face was utterly unreadable. Then she shrugged her slim shoulders. "One day I found the key on the floor near the closet." She lifted her chin defiantly. "I was curious. I'd noticed that locked box sitting up on his dresser when I dusted. It didn't hurt anything for me to look inside. I'll tell you, it was a shock. I was an unmarried woman. I'd never seen anything like that. I shut that box up quick as I could and put it and the key on his bedside table." Now she laughed. "I'd like to have seen his face when he found them there. I'll bet that gave him an almighty shock." The amusement slipped away, replaced with derision. "The big folks in the big house weren't quite so wonderful, you see."

"Folks," Annie repeated. "Were there others—besides the Judge—who weren't wonderful?"

Enid didn't hesitate. "He was a stern taskmaster; she spoiled them."

It was clear to Annie who Enid meant: the Judge and his wife, Amanda.

A brooding, faraway look settled on Enid's thin face. "Is it any wonder they grew up all twisted? They tried to stand tall for their father, but Amanda was sly and cunning and they learned that, too. Whitney always looked to her to fix things when they went wrong for him. And Whitney's wife—she sucked up to the Judge from the day she first set foot in that house. Going on and on about the Tarrants and how wonderful they were." A deep and abiding hatred burned in her eyes. "She didn't talk about Godfrey Tarrant, who beat a slave with his whip until he died—and do you know what for?" More than a century and a half's worth of anger sharpened her voice. "Because the slave—he was only seventeen and his name was Amos—lost one of Godfrey's precious hunting dogs."

"That's dreadful," Annie cried.

"That's dreadful!" Enid mimicked. "It is, isn't it?" Her eyes blazed. She took a deep breath, then spoke more quietly. "And that Milam's a queer one. He liked to hurt things, did you know that? On Sunday afternoons, I could take some time for myself. There's a pond not far from the bluff. Twice I watched him throw those heavy round balls—stones that they used for ballast in the sailing ships, you can find them everywhere—at the geese. He threw real well. Each time he hit two or three of the geese, hurt them. He didn't kill them. He watched them suffer. His face . . . it was all smooth and empty. He just watched." A tiny shudder rippled her shoulders. "The geese hurt, you know. They hurt real bad. I was behind a willow where he didn't see me. After he left, I killed them. If I hadn't—" She pressed a hand against her lips for a moment, then said very low, "My grandmother died of cancer. She hurt so bad. Nobody—not a bird, not an animal—nobody should have to hurt like that."

"What did you do about it?" Max demanded.

"Do about it?" She stared at Max in disbelief. "What could I *do* about? Enid Friendley's word against a Tarrant?" She gave a mirthless chuckle. "You didn't grow up black in Chastain, did you? But you want to know something?" Her voice rose. "I grew up better than any one of them. I sure did. I know how to work and make my way and not a single one of them can do that. They're hangers-on, clinging to a family name and to money someone else made. And more than that"—she struck a small fist against an open palm—"I may not have succeeded with my marriage, but I'm a woman and I know how a woman's meant to love. If you could see your faces! You don't know what I mean, do you? And you think you know so much about the Tarrants. So high and mighty, the Tarrants. Well, you just ask Julia Tarrant about the woman she loved."

When neither spoke, Enid continued angrily, "I saw them, whether you want to believe it or not! It's an old house —a house that's probably seen more living than you'll ever even know about—and when you walk down the hall on the second floor, there's a board that gives and when it does, sometimes the door to the southeast bedroom swings open, nice and easy. The Judge was home unexpected. I think it was that Thursday. He came up the stairs, walking fast. I was in the hall with a load of sheets in my arms and that door came open and I saw them, Julia and Amanda, and they were in each other's arms. I saw them, and so did the Judge."

Milam's wife and his mother?

"Well, don't you suppose—" Annie began.

"I don't *suppose* nothing," Enid snapped. "I know what I saw. And the Judge, he was right behind me." She jumped up. "Cover it all up if you want to. It's no skin off my nose. But if you really want to know the truth—if you really want to find out what happened that day—you'd better talk to Julia." Enid's eyes glinted maliciously. "If you can ever find her sober."

They argued all the way to Wisteree.

"Max, I don't believe it!" Annie recalled Julia on the night of Miss Dora's dinner party, frail, heart-shaped face, smudged violet eyes, the eyes of a child who knows no one cares.

Max gave her such a kind and gentle look that she blinked back tears. "I am *not* naive. I know all about that kind of thing."

His kindly nod undid her.

She exploded. "Dammit, Max, stop treating me like I'm twelve. I'm not dumb. I just think it would be weird—" She paused.

Max was nodding.

"Weird?" she asked.

The Maserati coasted to a stop at a ramshackle gate. A weathered sign dimly read WISTEREE PLANTATION.

"I'll get the gate," Annie muttered, hopping out. As she swung the gate wide—despite its unkempt appearance, the gate had recently been oiled and it swung open fast and without a sound—she continued the debate as the Maserati rolled forward between ivy-twined stone pillars. A stone pineapple sat atop one, a partial stump on the other. "Everybody dumps on Julia. It's damned easy to accuse her of just about anything. She's white meat." Annie pushed the gate shut. She hurried to the car and climbed in. She hardly took time to admire the enormous live oaks that marched along either side of the shell road. "Take a look at her accuser. Enid Friendley may be a model of independence and an accomplished businesswoman, she's also small-spirited and she has a mean mouth. Maybe we ought to look at how she went to college. Did the Judge send her because he wanted to help her—or did she take his money to keep quiet about that locked trunk?"

Max reached over and gave her hand a squeeze. "Okay, be Julia's champion. But remember, Annie, someone did shoot Judge Tarrant and that someone caused Ross's death, as surely as if they pulled the trigger that day at the hunting lodge. And the murderer's face is going to be someone you know—Milam, Julia, Whitney, Charlotte, one of the servants, Lucy Jane or Enid. Maybe Miss Dora. Maybe even Sybil. And that person knows what happened to Courtney Kimball."

The Maserati crunched to a stop in front of an old Low Country house that showed signs of neglect. A shutter hung askew on the second story, and paint flaked from the slender Doric columns supporting the sagging portico. The stuccoed walls were a faded, dusty rose, the shutters a dingy white. It was not a house that looked happily lived in. An arm was broken off one of the slatted wooden porch chairs. Weeds sprouted in the shell drive. Unpruned live oaks pressed too near, turning the air a murky green.

"Not *Sybil*," Annie exclaimed as they climbed out of the car.

They started up the broad, shallow steps. Max said gravely, "It could be. What if Sybil already knew she was pregnant that day? What if the Judge found out about Sybil and Ross's planned elopement and threatened to tell her parents?"

What might Sybil have done? Annie had seen Sybil fiercely angry, so she knew the answer to that one—anything was possible.

"But Sybil didn't know about Courtney, Max. I'd swear to that! And there's no way she would have hurt her own daughter."

"If she had," Max said it so low Annie almost couldn't hear him, "she would act just as she has—the distraught, vengeful mother. She hasn't been a mother, you know. How much does she *really* care?"

The porch was gritty underfoot. Twisted wires poking out of a small dark hole marked where there was once a doorbell. A tarnished metal knocker was in the center panel of a truly majestic entrance door. Above curved an elegant multipaned Palladian window, the panes streaked with dust.

Max rapped the knocker against its base.

Annie pictured faces now so familiar: Sybil, gorgeous and self-absorbed, a woman careless of her reputation, a beautiful creature accustomed to satisfying the desires of the moment; Whitney, a blurred reproduction of generations of Tarrants, his aristocratic face weak-chinned and unimposing; unremarkable, respectable clubwoman Charlotte, more interested in dead Tarrants than live ones; Milam with his earring and ponytail, showing an almost childish eagerness to flout society's conventions, but that could be a clever way to hide much darker, more sinister impulses; alcohol-sodden Julia clinging to dignity, but no matter how much she drank she couldn't hide the aching emptiness in her eyes; Lucy Jane, who so clearly knew something she didn't want to tell; waspish Enid, proud of her hard work, resentful of the Tarrants, and eager to drag them down; tiny, wizened Miss Dora— after all, they had only her word that she'd been in the garden with Ross when the shot that killed Augustus Tarrant rang out.

The front door to Wisteree Plantation slowly opened.

The Judge looked up eagerly as the French door opened. But—disappointment caught at his heart—it wasn't Ross, coming to say he was wrong. But Ross couldn't have meant what he said! Not Ross. As for the other, the matter was closed. "Yes," Augustus said brusquely, "what is it?"

His visitor spoke very quietly. "You've always been so reasonable and I hope—"

"Reasonable! Of course I am. But the right decision, once made, is final." It was as impersonal and abrupt as a ruling from the bench.

Those were the last words of the Honorable Augustus Tarrant.

The Judge's soundless oh *of shock was lost in the roar of the gun.*

Chapter 19.

Annie's nose wrinkled at the waft of acrylic from the paint-streaked rag in Milam's hand. He stood squarely in the doorway, blocking their entrance. In his stained, ragged sweatshirt and faded Levis, a calico bandanna bunching his scraggly hair out of the way, he looked like a working painter—and, at this moment, he looked damned irritated.

"Fuck. You two again."

Annie didn't have to look to know anger glinted in Max's eyes.

"Is painting this morning more important than Courtney Kimball's life? Or your father's murder?" Max demanded sharply.

Milam heaved an exaggerated sigh. "All right, all right. If I blow you off, you'll snivel back to Aunt Dora—and I don't want the old devil to leave her money to a home for abandoned cats. Be just like her. So, what the hell do you want now?"

"The truth." Max looked beyond Milam into the shadowy hall. "Is your wife here?"

"Julia's not in the house," Milam said indifferently. "She's out in the garden somewhere." He gestured vaguely toward the back.

"I'll go find her," Annie offered.

"Suit yourself." Milam started to close the door.

Max said quickly, "I want to talk to you, Milam."

Another exaggerated sigh. Milam shrugged. "Let's get it over with." He turned and started down the hall.

Max gave Annie a meaningful glance as he pulled open the door to follow Milam.

Annie understood. Max wanted her to take advantage of Milam's irritation. She'd find out a lot more if she talked to Julia alone.

As the door closed behind Milam and Max, Annie hurried down the steps and followed the oyster-shell path around the house. The unkempt appearance of the house didn't extend to the grounds, once beyond the uncontrolled grove of live oaks. She stepped out of the murky light beneath the moss-spangled oaks into a gardener's paradise. The perfumed scents of well-tended banana shrubs and mock orange mingled with the headier smells of honeysuckle and wisteria. There were no weeds among the golden-rimmed iris or carnelian tulips. Behind the house, glossy ivy cascaded down a brick wall. Annie pushed open a gate and stopped, dazzled by beauty. Azaleas, camellias and roses, hibiscus, lilies and Cherokee rose, lilac bignonia, Lady Banksia rose and purple wisteria rimmed or climbed the garden walls in a riotous explosion of colors that shimmered in the hazy morning sunlight. The central pool was dominated by a bronze cornucopia that had aged to the soft green of emerald grass in an Irish rain. Water spilled out to splash down softly in a gentle, cheerful murmur. Behind the fountain, a weathered gazebo offered a shady retreat. The loveliness of the scene was almost beyond bearing; the sense of peace, healing.

Julia Tarrant, a tomato-colored kerchief capping her dark hair, knelt beside a prepared bed, setting out pink and white impatiens from the waiting flats. Absorbed in her task, she looked young and almost happy, her lips parted in a half-smile.

Annie wished she could slip away and leave Julia adrift in private dreams.

But Courtney Kimball was missing. The Judge had been murdered. Ross was tricked out of life. Amanda fell to her death.

Annie steeled herself and stepped forward. Her shoes crunched on the oyster shells.

Julia's head whipped around. Any illusion of youth or happiness fled. Her face was fine-drawn and pale, the eyes dark pools of pain. Slowly, as if weary to the bone, she pushed up from the ground, leaving her trowel jammed upright in the fresh-turned dirt. Stripping off the encrusted gardening gloves, she stood waiting, looking vulnerable and defenseless in her too-large, faded work shirt, loose-fitting jeans, and earth-stained sneakers.

"Mrs. Tarrant. We met at Miss Dora's—"

"I remember." What might have been a flash of humor glinted in her sad eyes. "It hasn't been all that long ago." There was an element of graciousness; she would ignore the boorish assumption that she had been too drunk to recall, if Annie would.

There was graciousness, too, in her shy smile. "Shall we sit in the gazebo, Mrs. Darling? It's very cheerful."

As they settled opposite each other in recently painted, white slatted wooden chairs, the kind Annie always associated with a boardwalk along a beach, Julia ineffectually rubbed her hands against her pants. "It's hard to garden without getting muddy even when you wear gloves," she confided. Then she looked at Annie, her gentle gaze as direct and open as a child's. "You want to talk about the Judge, don't you?"

"Yes, please." Annie wished with all her heart that the Judge was all she had come to talk about.

Julia pulled off her kerchief and fluffed her hair. "I never liked him." She looked quickly back at Annie. "Does that shock you?"

"No." Annie's answer was truthful. "He must have been a difficult man to live with."

Julia stared down at her dirty hands. "I never felt that I ever really knew him. He was . . . so distant. Among us, with us, but never one of us. It was as if some kind of invisible wall stood between him and the rest of us." She looked out at her lovely garden, but her vision was focused in the past. "He was perfect, you know." She spoke softly, sadly. "So we all had to be perfect—and we weren't. Whitney's afraid. He's always been afraid. He can't do so many things. Charlotte hides behind the Family. I don't know why. But there are so many things I don't know. Charlotte feels bigger, better because her last name is Tarrant. I wish— I wish I could take comfort there. But it doesn't matter." She gave a tiny, revealing, melancholy sigh. "Nothing matters very much to me." She shaded her eyes and looked out at the shimmering colors of the flowers and shrubs. "It's better," she said simply, "when I'm outside, when I can smell the fresh earth and feel the sun on my face. I feel a part of everything then."

"Did loving Amanda make you feel a part of everything?" It was the hardest question Annie had ever asked.

Slowly, Julia's worn face turned toward Annie. Once again that bruised look darkened her eyes. She sat so still in the big white wooden chair, she might have been a part of it. She said, "Everyone loved Amanda."

Annie, hating every minute of it, said gruffly, "Someone saw you and Amanda."

Julia was silent for so long that Annie thought she wouldn't answer. But, finally, her eyes evading Annie's, she spoke softly, like the wind sighing through a weeping willow. "False witness. That's what you say when people lie, isn't it?"

Annie shifted uncomfortably, steeling herself. "Was it a lie?"

Julia's lips trembled.

The coos of the doves sounded a mournful requiem, and the sharp thumps of a red-cockaded woodpecker were as loud as drums beating a dirge.

"What do you want me to say?" Julia asked. "You've made up your mind, haven't you? Just like Judge Tarrant made up his—and it didn't matter what Amanda or I said to him." Tears glistened in her eyes. She swallowed, then said jerkily, "Have you ever—"

Annie leaned forward to hear that thin, tormented voice.

"—walked into a room and looked into someone's eyes and thought, 'I love you. I love *you*!' "

That poignant cry touched Annie's heart. And she understood. Yes. Oh, yes, she understood. A few years ago, she had walked into a room and a young man—blond with tousled hair and the darkest blue eyes she'd ever seen—had looked at her and smiled and she had been swept by a passion that would shape her life forever.

Julia's hands gripped the little kerchief, clutched it as if it were a lifeline. "That's how I felt about Amanda." The kerchief twisted in her hands. "But it wasn't wrong." She stared at Annie piteously. "It wasn't wrong, I swear it."

"What was the Judge going to do?" Annie gripped the arms of the garden chair so tightly her fingers ached.

Those bereft eyes slid away from Annie's. "The

Judge?" Julia's voice was as empty as an abandoned house. "I don't know. I'm sure we could have persuaded him."

"Persuaded him to do what?" Annie pressed.

"I don't know." It was the cry of a cornered animal. "I don't know. And what difference does it make now, after all these years?" She stared down at the crumpled kerchief in her fingers, then slowly smoothed it into a wrinkled square. "No one ever loved me except Amanda and Missy." It was a simple statement of fact. Not forlorn. Not angry. The anguish and rage had long since been spent.

Annie blinked back sudden tears. But it was too late to cry for Julia and Amanda. And much too late to cry for the Judge.

Softly, urgently, she asked again, "What was the Judge going to do?" Because that was the nub of it.

Julia lifted her chin defiantly. "I do not know what you are talking about."

Milam slouched on the worn couch, his legs thrust out in front of him, his paint-spattered arms spread wide on the upright cushions. This was not a living room that would be included in books describing the fine homes of the South. Old newspapers and magazines littered every tabletop, rested in stacks on the chairs and floor. The furniture was undistinguished, bland: rounded easy chairs and divans that could be found in countless department stores from Savannah to Pascagoula. The drapes must have been there for years, they were so faded, the green fronds of the weeping willows barely visible against the dulled lime background. The grime of many seasons dulled the windowpanes; handprints smudged the once-white panels of the doorways. Milam looked neither better nor worse than his frowsy, down-at-heels surroundings.

So far, Max hadn't succeeded in ruffling the painter's

nonchalant attitude. He tried again, his words sharper. "You admit you were angry, so how can you say you didn't have any reason to kill your father?"

"Look, Darling, I didn't want him dead. I wanted—" For the first time, Milam's voice wavered. "—I wanted him to love me. When he died, I felt empty, like somebody broke me open and all the stuffing spilled out. There wasn't anything out there, no direction to take. All those years I tried to get his attention. God, the things I did to get his attention. And it was always the same, those cool gray eyes would look me up and down and I always felt dirty. That's because he thought I was dirty. I can see that now. Whoever killed him, killed something inside of me. I don't know what exactly. But I was getting over it. Because of Missy. My life started to come together, because of her. I might have been a good artist, a really good artist. Missy was like a perfect spring morning. Have you ever had a little girl—a beautiful little girl—look up at you like you're God? She was so sweet and funny and kind. She loved everyone. Me. Her mother. Old people. Kids. Black. White. Everybody. And she woke up early one morning and went downstairs and outside and she walked into the pond—I found her floating there. And nothing's ever worked, since then." He balled the stained rag and flung it across the room, his face as empty as a broken heart.

"He was going to make Amanda leave," Annie insisted.

Julia shook her head in slow, stubborn negation.

Annie would have sworn to it. She felt, at this point, that she knew Judge Tarrant only too well—implacable in resolve, immovable in judgment, untouched by human appeal. Oh, yes, she could see it all. Amanda would have to go, sent away from the only home she'd ever had as an adult, away from her children and her infant grandchild. What kind of panic had seized Amanda?

And how had the Judge threatened his daughter-in-law Julia? "What did he say to you?"

Julia huddled in the big white wooden chair. She wouldn't look at Annie. She simply said over and over, "Nothing. Nothing."

"Then why were you crying that day?"

"I don't know," Julia said dully. "I cried a lot of days."

That was as much as Annie could bear. She couldn't stay here and badger this wretched woman. She had learned enough to know that murder may have moved in Julia's heart. Wasn't that enough for now?

But there was one more question she had to ask.

"Mrs. Tarrant, the fire at the museum . . ."

She didn't have to finish.

Julia looked up, her face so defenseless, so revealing. "All those letters," she said simply. "The ones I wrote to Amanda. Just notes, really." Her mouth quivered. "I even wrote her a sonnet once." Her chin lifted defiantly. "I wanted her to know . . ." Her voice fell away until it was little more than a whisper. ". . . how much I loved her. Was that wrong? To say 'I love you'? But people would make it ugly. I thought, maybe if it all burned up . . . I watched it burn." Her eyes were puzzled. "I wanted to destroy it—all those years and years and years of Tarrants. But it didn't help. You can't burn memories."

Annie stood. She hesitated, then bent and gently patted Julia's frail shoulder. "I'm sorry, Mrs. Tarrant. About everything."

As Annie started down the gazebo steps, Julia called out thinly, "Are you going to tell Milam?"

It was the last question Annie would have expected.

Why should Julia care?

Their marriage—Milam and Julia's—was so patently a failure. Why would she care at all?

Before Annie could answer, Julia struggled to her feet. "If you don't have to tell him," she said breathlessly, "then please don't. You see . . . Milam loved his mother so much. It's the one good memory in his life. Don't"—her glance slid away from Annie's—"ruin it for him."

Their suite at the St. George Inn wasn't home, but it was the next best thing. And it was a refuge. As the door closed behind them, Annie stepped into Max's arms. She wrapped her arms around him and gave him a huge hug. She didn't —and perhaps that was most important, most wonderful of all—have to explain.

"I know," he said softly into her hair. "Poor damn devils. God, we're lucky." And he held her.

The phone rang.

Annie had never mastered the precept (illustrated with such charm in Suzy Becker's enchanting book, *All I Need to Know I Learned from My Cat*) that it isn't essential to answer the telephone just because you're home. (As is often the case at mystery bookstores, Annie stocked a great many cat titles at Death on Demand. After all, reading mysteries and loving cats seem to go hand in paw.)

So, of course, she bolted from his arms with the same alacrity she would have shown had a boa constrictor poked a head from the jardiniere next to the telephone stand.

It was hard not to answer "Death on Demand," but Annie managed a simple "hello."

"My *sweet.*" Her mother-in-law's greeting burbled like bubbles in champagne. "I felt sure I would be conversing with your answering machine. A mixed blessing, don't you think?"

Annie was unsure whether Laurel was indicating a preference for her or for the answering machine, but it was better not to think along those lines. It could lead to a sense of anomie, which she had quite successfully avoided ever since forswearing the kind of literary fiction written primarily by English professors for other English professors.

"But I feel as if it were meant."

Annie had a sudden vision of a graceful hand with pink-tipped nails pressed against a bosom that was always shown to great advantage in low-cut ball gowns. Not, of course, that she begrudged Max's mother the opportunity to display her undoubted beauty, blond hair that glistened like spun gold, eyes as brilliantly sapphire as a northern sea, finely chiseled features, and a figure almost unseemly for a woman old enough to have four grown children.

"I am most concerned that you and dear Max be quite *cautious* in your pursuit of justice. There is so much *evil* in the world, my dear."

Annie managed a single intervening sentence. "Miss Marple never worried about her skin when she hunted for a murderer."

Max, thumbing through a batch of mail left by Barb, looked across the room, a question in his blue eyes. Annie covered the mouthpiece. "Your mom," she mouthed.

Max smiled fondly and walked a few paces to settle in an easy chair with the mail. The chair was rather handily out of reach of the phone cord.

Annie realized the pause on Laurel's end was still in force. One hell of a pause, actually. It indicated, without a single word, that dear Annie was regrettably callow to refer in such graceless prose to the greatest elderly female detective of all time.

Annie attempted damage control. "Not that Miss Marple would ever have thought about it in those terms. But, Laurel, you see what I mean."

"Of course, my dear." That resonant, husky, unforgettable voice *radiated* patience.

Annie's gaze fastened wistfully on a pair of crossed swords above the Adam mantel. It was a good thing Laurel had not progressed on the psychic plane to mind reading.

Mercifully unaware of the images—honestly, did it make her bloodthirsty to own a mystery bookstore?—cavorting in Annie's mind, Laurel swept on. "I quite take pride in your and Max's dedication to duty. I feel *impelled* to point out, however, that it has been brought home to me in a most shocking manner how ugliness begets heartbreak which not even the passage of a great many years can ease. Take the grisly episode at Fenwick Castle on St. John's Island. That imposing mansion is said to have resembled the castles in the family's English holdings."

Annie felt sufficiently embroiled in present-day heartbreak without adding dead-and-gone misery to her bag of emotions, but she knew that Laurel, once launched, was quite as impervious to deflection as Miss Climpson when in pursuit of information for Lord Peter Wimsey.

". . . and so Ann Fenwick fell in love not only with the spirited racehorse her father ordered from England, but also with the groom who arrived with the horse. Ann was a favorite of her stern father, Edward Fenwick, who had always treated her gently and lovingly. But Fenwick lived up to his reputation for anger and harshness when his daughter informed him that she wished to marry the young groom, Tony. Her father, a titled lord in England, was enraged. He swore that this would never happen, his daughter would not wed a groom. Ann protested that Tony was the younger son of a clergyman and her father could aid him in entering a profession. But Edward Fenwick, Lord Ripon, vowed he would rather see his daughter dead."

A delicate sigh wafted over the wire from Charleston. "My dear, *I* have loved as Ann loved."

Annie bit her tongue. It wouldn't be at all the thing to

ask Laurel if Ann Fenwick had also married five times. That would not be a proper filial response. Besides, Max was within earshot.

"It is," Laurel enthused, "as if dear Ann were here with me."

Annie also forbore to ask in which century Ann's problems occurred and whether the presence so near Laurel was moldy. And chilly. Graves did have a tendency to be both damp and moist. Especially in the Low Country.

"I feel her so *near*. Her tears have been mine as I contemplate the horrible fate which awaited her. Suffice it to say—"

Did Laurel fear Annie's attention might be wandering?

"—Ann and Tony continued to rendezvous, albeit secretly, of course, because of her father's furious prohibitions. Ann tried one more time to persuade her father and was rebuffed, with equal anger. So she and Tony eloped. They found a minister who wed them and they set out for Charles Town." (Annie got the clue; a long damn time ago when that city on the Ashley River still bore a double name.) "It was evening and too late to hail a boat to cross. They stayed their bridal night—I hope a *glorious* night—but when dawn came so did a search party headed by her father. It callously rousted out the newlyweds and placed them in a coach, with Tony bound in ropes, and set out for Fenwick Castle. When the coach arrived and jolted to a stop in the stable yard, Lord Ripon shouted for a horse to be brought. Then he ordered his men to place Tony on the steed and to take a rope, tie it to Tony's neck, then fasten it to the limb of the huge oak which Ann had climbed as a child.

"Ann, screaming and weeping, struggled with her father, pleading for the life of her new husband. Silent and grim, Lord Ripon placed a whip in her hand. Then, holding her tight, he lifted her arm and flailed down viciously on the horse's flank. As it bolted and her beloved swung by his neck in the air above her, twisting and turning, Ann gave a dreadful cry and collapsed."

"Laurel," Annie said faintly.

Max looked at her in alarm. Weakly, Annie waggled her hand that it was all right. But it wasn't all right. This dreadful story would haunt her sleep for many nights to come. Whatever possessed Laurel to—

"My dear, I know. Such nightmares I have had. But we must face the fact that evil acts create heartbreak that lingers through time. Poor little Ann never recovered. Oh, she regained consciousness, of course. But ever after, she wandered the halls of Fenwick Castle, crying out for Tony, searching for Tony. After she died, her spirit stayed. Even today, though Fenwick Castle lies in ruins, you can hear her footsteps as she paces halls that no longer exist and her mournful cry of 'Tony, Tony!' "

Annie shivered. On winter nights when rain hissed against the windows, did Sybil hear Ross's name? Or was the cry simply in her heart?

"I must say I now look forward to the day when I shall have completed my chronicle of South Carolina ghosts. As you know, dear Annie, I have never felt it my duty to wallow in tragedy. However, I—"

Actually, if Annie envisioned Laurel wallowing, it certainly wasn't in tragedy. In fact . . . Annie sternly corrected the drift of her thoughts.

"—must hew to the course as I find it, and I'm confident my insights shall be of *inestimable* value to you and *dear* Max. Ta."

Annie replaced the receiver and looked at her husband. As pleasantly as possible. "Wallowing in tragedy, but brave as hell."

"Now, Annie, you know the old dear means well." He got to his feet. "Lunchtime. Strategy time."

Annie wasn't altogether diverted, though she was ravenous. Was this the moment to point out to Max that he had a blind spot the size of Texas in his understanding of his mother, her motives and her actions? But, in this instance, maybe he had a point. Besides, how could Annie complain? After all, the old dear was in Charleston, not Chastain.

"So, trauma lingers," Max summed up as Annie concluded her report of the conversation. He put two plates on the golden oak table in their suite's breakfast room and began to unload the box lunches they'd bought en route to the inn. "Did you see the card from Henny?"

Annie rustled through the stack of mail and pulled out the postcard. She studied the Corinthian portico and baroque tower of an elegant church. Flipping to Henny's message, she read: *I thought I'd died and gone to heaven——this is St. George's, Hanover Square, where Harriet and Lord Peter were wed in* Busman's Holiday! *Annie, I do wish you and Max were here. But I shall be home soon. Duty calls. Love——*H.

As they raced through lunch—they had to hurry if they were going to be on time to meet Miss Dora for a guided tour of Tarrant House and its grounds—discussing whether they were prepared for the afternoon, Annie struggled to discipline her thoughts. Images whirled: Ann Fenwick's desolate cry for love and life destroyed, Julia's strangely passionate desire to protect Milam's memory of his mother, acid-tongued Enid's advice to Courtney Kimball that Miss Dora alone among the Tarrants could be trusted, a little girl waking early and hurrying outside to death, Lucy Jane pleating her apron and picking her words so carefully. . . .

Annie put down the last half of her sandwich. She checked her watch. Almost two. They mustn't be late to meet Miss Dora. She pushed back her chair.

Max looked across the table. "What's up?"

Annie hurried to the desk and grabbed the phone. "I need to make a couple of calls before we go." It was the first time in her life she'd ever left a smoked salmon/cream cheese sandwich unfinished. And she was hungry enough to devour a twelve-ounce T-bone. (As a native Texan, she fully subscribed to the ideal of real food for real people.) But the uneasiness that had plucked at her mind, conjuring up images of restless spirits and tragic losses, was too powerful to ignore. She had a dark vision that she desperately wanted to dispel.

Lucy Jane McKay answered on the first ring.

"Mrs. McKay, this is Annie Darling. We're still working for Miss Dora"—it wouldn't hurt to underscore their friend in high places—"and I wondered if you could give us some background information on Missy Tarrant's accident."

"Missy." The older woman's voice was soft. "One of God's angels, Mrs. Darling. That's why she went home to be with the Lord so young."

Annie could see the comfort behind this rationale, but theologically speaking it didn't appeal to her. "I know that she drowned in a pond, but do you know the circumstances?"

"Oh, Mrs. Darling, it was just so sad and it goes to show the evils of alcohol that every young parent should take to heart." Lucy Jane was firm, but her voice was thick with tears. "Now, there wasn't anybody who loved that baby better than her mamma and her daddy, but they liked to stay up nights drinking too much and then they didn't get up in the mornings like they should. A friend of one of my girls was helping out at Wisteree is how I know what happened. Missy lost one of her favorite toys, a big brown bear she called 'Bear-Bear.' How she cried and cried for him. Anyway, that last morning—it was a Sunday—Missy woke up early, but her folks didn't get up and Cathy, my daughter's friend, had a flat tire on her way out to Wisteree so she wasn't there to take care of the little girl—oh, still just a baby—like she would have usually. Missy got up and went downstairs and nobody locks doors—or did then—out in the country or in town either. So Missy let herself out of the kitchen door and she wandered down to the pond. When her daddy found her, she was floating facedown in the water and there was Bear-Bear floating beside her. Nobody knows how he got there. You'd think if she'd thrown him in the water when he was lost, she would have said so. And why didn't someone notice him floating out there? Anyway, they think Missy saw him in the water and went in after him. That's how it was when they found them, Bear-Bear and Missy."

"That's dreadful," Annie cried.

"It was awful." Lucy Jane's voice was low and grieved. "It broke Mr. Milam's heart and for a long time they thought it would be the death of Miz Julia."

But it was never Julia who died. Annie tried to push the thought away. Julia's sister. Her father-in-law. Her daughter. Her mother-in-law. But never Julia.

So? Annie demanded of herself. That could be said of them all, couldn't it?

No. Not quite.

But why would Julia—and the very thought sickened Annie's heart—murder her own daughter?

There could be no rational reason. But there might be many twisted reasons in the mind of a woman as miserably unhappy as Julia.

She passionately loved her little girl.

The same way she'd loved her sister?

Annie forced herself to pursue the phantasmagoria taking shape in her mind, a vision of a mind and heart engulfed by evil, the kind of evil Poe described with hideous clarity in "The Black Cat" and "The Tell-Tale Heart."

"Did Missy die before Mrs. Amanda fell from the cliff —or after?" Annie demanded. She saw Max's quick, curious glance.

Lucy Jane knew at once. "About a month before. They say death comes in threes. I thought we were all finished—what with Mr. Ross and the Judge and Missy all gone within a year—but Death wasn't satisfied yet."

Annie had a ghoulish picture of a dark-cloaked figure with a grinning skull face reaching out greedy fingers of bone.

"No wonder Julia was so stricken," Annie said softly. "Mrs. McKay, why didn't you tell us about Julia and Amanda and the fact that the Judge knew about them?"

There was a long silence; then, quietly, firmly, decisively, the receiver clicked in place.

Annie stared at the phone for a moment. She didn't feel good about it, but she had her answer. Julia had denied an affair and denied that the Judge could have known. Amanda wasn't alive to answer, but Lucy Jane McKay was an honest woman. She wouldn't lie—so she wouldn't answer.

Annie looked across the room at Max. "The Judge knew. About Julia and Amanda."

Max said quietly, "Julia would know where the gun was kept."

The telephone rang. Annie's hand still rested on top of the receiver. She snatched it up, glad to be connected to the here and now, not part of a shadowy, frightful world of imagined evils.

"Time to go." There was more than a hint of displeasure that the telephone had been answered. It was clear Miss Dora thought Annie and Max should at that very moment be en route to their rendezvous with her at Tarrant House.

As usual, Annie had to grab her temper and hold on. Now was not the time to tell the old harridan that she was rude, overbearing, and obnoxious.

"We're just getting ready to leave." It was an achievement to enunciate through clenched lips. Perhaps it was Annie's irritation that gave her the courage to snap a sharp query. "Miss Dora, did Courtney Kimball contact you the day she disappeared, last Wednesday?"

The sudden silence on the part of Chastain's most voluble and opinionated old lady caught Annie by surprise. And so did the rather odd answer that finally came.

"Wednesday?" It was the only time in their acquaintance that Annie had the feeling that Miss Dora was at a loss. "Why do you ask?" she demanded brusquely.

"Enid Friendley talked to Courtney on Wednesday. She told her you were the only person connected to Tarrant House that Courtney should trust."

"I see." Miss Dora cleared her throat. "Well, if Enid indeed did say that to Courtney, it's a shame the child didn't call on me. Now, I wish to speak with Max."

Annie wasn't unhappy to hand over the receiver.

But Annie had the damnedest feeling. Miss Dora had lied.

Why?

If Miss Dora had seen Courtney Kimball on Wednesday, why lie about it?

Miss Dora was an old woman.

That didn't mean she wouldn't cling to life, grasp it with fingers tight as talons, and do whatever she must to ward off death. Especially, perhaps, if she would die with murder on her soul.

If Miss Dora had lied about Wednesday, how many other lies might she have told?

4:04 P.M., SATURDAY, MAY 9, 1970

Ross Tarrant clung to the doorjamb for support. "Dad!"

Footsteps sounded behind him. A hand clutched his arm. "Oh, God, did she shoot him?"

"She?" Ross's voice cracked.

"She ran upstairs. Just now."

"Mother?" Ross's voice shook.

"Yes. Oh, God, what are we going to do? We have to call the police."

Ross shrugged off the hand. He ran to the desk and stared down at the gun for a long, anguished moment, then grabbed it up. As he brushed past the figure at the door, he said roughly, "Don't tell anyone you saw Mother. No one, do you understand?"

Chapter 20.

Tarrant House lay straight ahead, framed between the avenue of live oaks. On this cloudy, sultry afternoon, the plastered brick varied in shade from pale green to beige to misty gray, depending upon the slant of sunlight diffused through the clouds.

The air was moist and sticky, as humid as a July day. Not a vestige of wind stirred the shiny, showy magnolia leaves. Sharp-edged palmettos stood like sentinels on either side of the house. Gossamer threads of Spanish moss hung straight and limp on the low-limbed live oaks, their beauty as delicate as the brushwork in a Chinese landscape. Purplish clouds darkened the southern sky. It wasn't storm season, but a storm was surely coming.

This house had weathered more than a century and a half of storms and stormy lives. Tarrant House had seen happiness and loss, love and hatred, plenty and famine, peace and war. It seemed to Annie—though she knew it was fanciful—that the house had a wily, watching, wary appearance, drawing into itself in preparation for the promised winds, the coming tempest.

It was a day as fated for storm and death as the day Faulkner's Addie Bundren lay listening to the chock and thunk of her coffin being constructed.

What would this day see?

Without question, a murderer would walk the halls of Tarrant House once again before the storm broke.

Annie wondered if she and Max would be clever enough to determine the truth of May 9, 1970.

Miss Dora appeared suddenly, stepping out from behind a hedge of pittosporum. "I've been waiting." There was, as usual, no warmth in her greeting or in the midnight-dark eyes that looked at them so intensely, as if to rake out the secrets of their souls by sheer impress of will.

But, dammit, it was Miss Dora who had lied!

Abruptly, as they looked at each other, the young woman and the old, Annie glimpsed—for an instant that seemed an eternity—a welter of emotion in Miss Dora's gaze, uncertainty and terror and a terrible resolution.

Then the moment passed. Annie was left to wonder, as the old woman lifted her stick, gesturing for them to hurry, if that glimpse of agony in those implacable eyes reflected nothing more than the turmoil in Annie's own mind. Certainly, Miss Dora gave no other hint of distress as she led the way up the crushed-shell drive, using her cane as a pointer.

"That oak—the huge one to the south—was the site of a hanging in 1862. A Yankee spy. Redheaded, they say." The old voice was brisk, matter-of-fact.

How old was he, Annie wondered, and why had he come to Chastain?

As if she'd heard the unspoken query, Miss Dora continued: "Scouting to see about the fortifications and whether the harbor could be captured. Said to be a handsome young man. One of the Tarrant girls fainted at the sight, and everyone always wondered if there were more to his coming than was said to the world."

At least, Annie thought, it had not been the girl's arm, raised in the iron grip of an angry father, that struck the mount beneath the victim.

The scene before them darkened, the sun now hidden behind thick clouds. Annie looked up at the old house, at the double piazzas, at the four massive octagonal columns supporting the five-foot-high decorated parapet, at the four huge chimneys towering above the parapet.

"There are seventy-two windows," Miss Dora observed, as they started up the front steps. The stairway was necessary because the house was built one story above ground, supported by brick columns. A sour, musty smell rose from the arched entrances to the space beneath the house.

Cemeteries weren't high on Annie's list of places to spend time, but she felt certain no graveyard ever smelled earthier than the dark nooks beneath Tarrant House.

She was glad to reach the broad, first-floor piazza. Pompeian-red shutters framed the immense windows. An enormous fanlight curved above the double walnut front doors. The glass panes were clear as ice.

Miss Dora ignored the bell punch. Opening the door, she motioned for Annie and Max to enter. "Whitney and Charlotte know we're coming. Can't say they're thrilled." She gave a high cackle of malicious amusement.

Annie stepped into the entrance hall, a broad sweep of old wood flooring with occasional rugs. An elegant French chandelier hung from an intricate Adam plaster medallion.

So this was Tarrant House.

Annie's first impression, despite the gloom of the day, was of brightness and beauty. Archways opened off either side of the hall. A monumental grandfather clock stood near the cross hallway.

The soft rich glow of cypress, gloriously carved, dominated the drawing room, from the magnificent chimney breast and mantel to the archway decorated with surrounds of fluted Corinthian pilasters. Over the mantel was an oil portrait of a lovely woman with soft auburn hair and kind blue eyes. Her white ballgown was modestly cut. A pink sash curved around her waist.

Miss Dora saw Annie's glance.

"A lovely likeness of Amanda. She was," and the tart voice softened, "as good and kind as she looked. She deserved better than she got."

The dining room was equally beautiful. Other family portraits lined these walls. The peach walls made a gorgeous background for the Hepplewhite dining table and shield-back chairs. The drapes were of ivory silk. Crystal hung in delicate swags from the chandelier. Ivory and peach predominated in the rug.

Miss Dora jabbed her cane. "Drawing room to the left, dining room to the right. A cross hall opens to the side piazzas. Past the stairs, the sewing room, study to the left—"

The study. Annie took a step forward. Where the Judge was shot.

"—kitchen, wash areas to the right."

Miss Dora started down the hall. She was almost past the grandfather clock when she stopped. Her body went rigid. Then, slowly, she turned to look up at the clock face.

Annie and Max looked, too.

The hour hand stood at four, the minute hand at two minutes past.

The clock was silent.

"Four-oh-two." There was no mistaking the note of fear in Miss Dora's voice. Her silver head swiveled around, her eyes darted toward the stairs. "Dear God."

"Miss Dora, what's wrong?"

"The clock—that time—that's when Augustus died."

She leaned on her stick, as if, suddenly, she needed support. Her eyes gazed emptily at the clock. She spoke in a voice so low she could scarcely be heard. "The clock in my bedroom —this morning it was stopped. At four-oh-two." A shudder moved through her small frame. "What does it mean?" She looked at Annie, then beyond her. "Charlotte, have you seen?" The cane pointed at the clock.

Annie and Max turned to see Charlotte standing in the doorway of the kitchen.

Annie knew that if ever she had seen fear on a human countenance, it was at this moment. All the color had seeped from Charlotte's plump face. She tried to speak and no words came. She turned, and the kitchen door swung shut behind her.

She was gone, but the taste and smell of fear hung in that elegant hallway.

Miss Dora stared after her. Then, slowly, an implacable calmness spread over her sharp features. "What will be, will be," she intoned. "Come."

As Miss Dora moved on down the hall, Annie glanced back. She wished she'd insisted that they look more closely at the clock. Miss Dora apparently believed some ghostly force had summoned back the time of the Judge's death. That was sheer nonsense.

Of course it was.

They passed the staircase to the upper floors, and Annie welcomed the distraction. It was an absolutely gorgeous staircase, the elegant banister and balusters carved from rich red mahogany.

The study was a warm and welcoming room with a broad fireplace and more cypress paneling. Two walls were filled with books. Many, with leather bindings and faded gilt titles, were obviously old. The desk glistened with polish. There wasn't a smudge upon it. It may have been a desk for work when it belonged to Judge Tarrant. Today, it was part of a room for show. The only hint of anything out of the ordinary was the broken window in one of the French doors that opened onto the back piazza. The pane was temporarily replaced by a piece of plywood.

Max walked to the desk and sat behind it. His eyes scanned the room, the back piazza, and the cloud-muted flame of flowering azaleas in the garden.

A scholar's room. A retreat from the world of action to the world of ideas. How often had the Judge stood beside the bookcases to choose a volume? Dickens perhaps? Chesterton? Montaigne?

"If the gun was kept in that drawer—"

Max reached down, slid open the lower left-hand drawer.

"—and if the Judge was sitting there," Annie asked, "how did the murderer get it?"

She came around the desk to stand beside Max. But, as she looked down, her glance was caught by the porcelain clock on the Queen Anne table between the French doors.

This clock, too, wasn't running.

The hour hand pointed at the four, the minute hand at two past the hour.

Annie scarcely heard Miss Dora's comment.

"Quite a pertinent question, young miss." Miss Dora gave her a grudging look of respect.

"It certainly is." Max's look of admiration wasn't the least grudging.

But Annie hardly noticed. She pointed at the silent clock.

Max's lips curved in a soundless whistle.

Miss Dora's eyes widened. "Again." The old lady touched the ruby brooch at her throat. "Dear God. It can only mean that the hour of judgment is drawing nigh."

Max said gently, "Miss Dora, don't be frightened. Someone's playing tricks."

"I only wish that were true." Her voice was somber.

"Maybe the point is to keep us from thinking—but it isn't going to work. Now"—he pointed at the drawer—"how did the murderer get the gun? The Judge wouldn't have sat here and let someone reach into the drawer, take out the gun, and shoot him! That means the killer took the gun out of the desk earlier in the day and came into the study with it. So the murder was premeditated."

After a final lingering look at the clock, Miss Dora said soberly, "Augustus was not a fool." She stared at the desk and Annie was certain her eyes beheld another figure there. "However"—and her tone was full of reluctance—"if one of his sons came in to see him—not Ross certainly after their fiery quarrel—but either Whitney or Milam and the talk led to hunting and guns, would Augustus have been suspicious if his visitor professed interest in that relic from the War and asked to see it?"

Max pushed back the desk chair. "If a man has murder in mind, it would be a little foolhardy merely to assume that the gun was in working condition. How could he count on it being loaded?"

"That could have been determined earlier," Miss Dora replied dispassionately. "Besides, loaded guns are no rarity in Chastain."

Max walked toward the French doors and looked out into the garden. "Would these doors have been locked that afternoon?"

"No. In Chastain, locked doors, of any kind, *are* a rarity." The old lady too looked out at the garden. "So, of course, the murderer could easily have entered from the piazza."

Loaded guns and unlocked doors. And someone with murder in his heart. Or hers.

On the way out of the study, Annie glanced back at the tranquil room. Murder had occurred there, at that desk. Nothing today remained of that moment— except the time captured by the silent clock on the beautiful old Queen Anne table. Annie shivered.

Her sense of horror grew as they climbed the magnificent staircase. This was a house teeming with violent memories. The bloodstain just before the landing was evident, a dark discoloration of the wood. It was obvious that the step had been scrubbed and scrubbed, but no amount of effort had washed away the last vestige of Robert Tarrant's blood. Annie skirted that uneven splotch and hurried after Miss Dora. Max gave her elbow a squeeze.

"Plenty of room up here." Miss Dora stood at the top of the stairs like a tour guide. "That door leads out to the second-story front piazza." She turned, pointed her stick the opposite way. "That door at the end of the hall goes out onto the second-story back piazza.

"There are six bedrooms upstairs." Her silvered brows drew down in thought. "It's been a good many years since I've been upstairs, but I believe the master bedroom is in the southeast corner."

She stalked down the wide hall. Annie hoped her cane wouldn't snag the carpet runner. Miss Dora rapped the knob of her cane against the door, then opened it. "Hmm, yes. As I thought. This is the master bedroom."

Annie and Max peered over her shoulder. Annie definitely felt like a trespasser as she scanned the room, home now to Whitney and Charlotte. A pair of trousers in a pants press. An ornate silver jewel case on the dressing table, the lid open to reveal a handful of antique rings with stones of opal or carnelian or jade. A book of poetry—Longfellow—facedown on the pale gold of the bedspread, which matched the linen window hangings and the delicate background color of the Chinese wallpaper. Acanthus leaves decorated the posts of the four-poster bed. Past the half-open closet door, Annie glimpsed a row of Whitney's suits and shirts.

Miss Dora thumped her cane to the floor and gripped the silver head. "Now you've seen it. Much as it was twenty-two years ago. Let's go to the garden."

When they came out on the first-floor piazza at the back of the house, Annie felt sweat trickling down her back and thighs. What had happened to their usual crisp, clear, dry days of spring? She took a deep breath and felt as though she'd gulped mist from a sauna. The storm couldn't come too soon to satisfy her. As if in answer, lightning crackled to the south, followed almost immediately by a low growl of thunder.

"Charlotte has a green thumb, no doubt about that. Amanda would be pleased. She loved this garden." Miss Dora waggled her cane. "She spent a good deal of time working the borders toward the back wall."

In the murky light, the garden had the greenish, watery glow of an aquarium, the bright reds and pinks of the azaleas and camellias softened into smudged impressionist tints. Beneath the scent of coming rain and freshly turned earth was the darker, angrier odor of fire. The charred remains of the museum dominated the garden, drawing the eye away from the superbly tended plantings. The garden's design—separate components scattered around the structures—was still evident. Rosebushes in formal beds circled the fountain and its brick patio. Scarlet tulips formed a brilliant necklace around the obelisk. Bunches of flowering azaleas curved and flowed around nooks and crannies with benches. Honeysuckle and bougainvillea cascaded over the garden walls. Willows ringed the pond near the bluff. An herb garden thrived near the kitchen. An arbor thickly covered with climbing roses kept the potting shed out of sight. It would be quite possible—it was planned for that effect—for several persons to enjoy solitude in the garden without intruding upon each other.

But the effects of the fire—the charred structure tumbled inward to create uneven heaps of debris, the trampled-down iris beds where the firemen had labored, the muddy spots where water had collected on the ground—gave the garden an aura of desolation, made even bleaker by the gray and cloudy day.

Faintly, a bell rang within the house.

Miss Dora's pale lips tightened. "It is time," she said grimly, "for the curtain to rise."

Quickly, as if impelled by urgency, Miss Dora orchestrated the cast of survivors. In scarcely a quarter of an hour, each person was standing—if truthful—where he or she had been at approximately four o'clock on Saturday, May 9, twenty-two years before.

In the central hallway of Tarrant House, Miss Dora shrugged as the last unwilling participant straggled out the back door. "Can't prove who was where, after all this time. But only one person has reason to lie. Now, before we start" —wizened fingers scrabbled in the black reticule hanging from her left wrist—"I've some notes here." She pulled out a tiny notebook, opened it to a page of crabbed writing, and said briskly, "Amanda was in her room. Missy was asleep in the northwest bedroom—that belonged to Milam and Julia. Sam—he died about six years ago." She paused, looking pleased. "Ninety-seven and he walked two miles to church the day before he passed away. Sam was in his room in the servants' quarters. Just like Lucy Jane. Ross was in the garden. And the Judge was in the study. Clear?" she demanded.

Annie and Max both nodded and the old woman started up the mahogany steps.

Milam lounged in a wooden-slatted white chair on the

second-story back piazza, a sketch pad in his lap. He didn't rise as they walked out on the piazza. He didn't look quite so much sullen as sardonic and bored. "Nice to see you keeping interested in the world, Miss Dora."

She eyed him coldly, her disapproval evident, but she made no response.

Milam tried again. "I can see it now, the parlor game to end all parlor games. Re-create the day dear old Pater died—"

"Milam."

The single snapped word silenced him and brought an unaccustomed tinge of pink to his plump cheeks.

Max tried conciliation. "Milam, don't fight us. We're not the problem. The problem is what happened to your father twenty-two years ago. We need your help."

"Look, Darling, if I knew what really happened, I'd tell you. But I don't have any f—" He paused, looked at Miss Dora, then continued, "I don't know. And I don't think this afternoon will tell you anything."

"Maybe not," Max said agreeably. "Let's talk about your father."

Milam's face was still and guarded.

"And your mother." Max's blue eyes were intent. "Did you know they were going to separate?"

"I think you've been misled," Milam drawled. "That would be out of character. For both of them."

His eyes dropped. He stared at his tightly clenched hands.

Annie felt a rush of excitement. Milam *did* know. The question was, did he know why?

"What kind of marriage did they have?" Annie asked.

Those graceful hands, artist's hands, slowly relaxed. He flicked her a derisive glance. "I was their oldest son. Not their confidant. I don't have any damned idea. They were polite to each other. Very polite. They never quarreled. What they did—or didn't do—behind closed doors, I don't know. But what difference does it make? Mother's not here to take the rap."

"If," Max said slowly, and Annie knew he wanted to be careful in what he said, "your father intended to force your mother to leave Tarrant House, would you have any idea why?"

"No."

There was no way to know whether he spoke the truth.

"About your mother's fall from the bluff—"

For the first time, anger laced Milam's voice. "Wait a minute, Darling. Are you suggesting I gave my mother a shove off the path?"

"Somebody did." Miss Dora's gravelly tone was certain.

Milam's head jerked up. This, obviously, was an altogether new thought—and an unpleasant one—to Milam. Or was he simulating shock?

"Why?" he demanded harshly, his voice raw with disbelief.

Max rocked back on his heels. "Somehow she discovered that Ross wasn't guilty—"

A sharply indrawn breath brought silence. They all looked at Miss Dora.

"If only Amanda had told me, shared—" Miss Dora gazed somberly at Milam. "I came to see her. One year to the day of your father's death. You must remember that I had not been told what happened. I knew only the story that had been made public: Ross dead of an accident, the Judge collapsing with a heart attack. Amanda and I sat in the drawing room, with tea. It was a rainy afternoon. We talked about the Judge. And about Ross. It must have been fate—or the hand of God—or of the Devil. I don't know. I said that I would never forget Ross, moving so quickly at the sound of a shot that afternoon and he himself to be dead so soon in an accident with a gun. She looked at me strangely, but I thought it was grief, the pain of remembering. She said, 'You and Ross heard a shot?' And I replied—I had no reason not to do so—I said so carelessly, never dreaming how much harm I was doing with those words, 'Oh, yes, about four o'clock. I was at the gate. I could see Ross standing in the garden.' Amanda looked quite faint. So I poured her more tea and then she thanked me for coming but said she must go upstairs, to rest. Don't you see? That's when she realized—and then she began to think."

It could, Annie realized, have happened exactly like that. Or it could have been some other memory entirely that re-formed Amanda's picture of that day. Perhaps on the anniversary of the Judge's death, she remembered the click of a cane in the hall or perhaps she remembered the glimpse of a long, old-fashioned dress. . . .

"You think Mother went from that to accusing someone of the Judge's murder?" Milam frowned fiercely. "That wouldn't be like her. She would have come to me or to Whitney."

"Or perhaps to Julia?" Annie asked quietly.

"Maybe." The suggestion apparently didn't bother Milam. "Or even to Charlotte, though I never thought Mother liked her overmuch."

Miss Dora was nodding, her shaggy white hair flying. "Of course. Don't you see? She *did* tell someone. But it was the wrong person."

"Murder piled upon murder?" Milam's lips curved down in ugly amusement. "You've been reading too much family history, Aunt Dora."

Max lost patience. "You seem to think all of this is amusing. But you weren't laughing the day your father died. You were upset."

Milam let the pad slip into his lap and folded his hands

behind his head. He looked insolently up at Max. "Sorry if I let the Family down, showing emotion and all that. But it's quite a shock, to have your little brother blow away your old man. At least, that's what I thought at the time. Believe me, it was a hell of an afternoon. I suppose I—"

"You were upset *before* your father died," Annie interrupted irritably. "We have it on good authority." Was it stretching the truth to consider Enid Friendley a good authority?

Milam's arms dropped. His expression smoothed out as if all thought and emotion had been wiped away with a sponge. "Do you now?" he asked silkily. "And who would that be?"

No one answered.

A sour smile stretched his lips. "Enid, probably. Well, that's fine. Maybe so. It was a long time ago. If Enid told you that, ask her what else she knows."

"We will," Max replied. "Look, Milam, you were upset that morning. Long before someone shot the Judge. Why?"

Milam looked down at the sketch pad in his lap.

So did Annie.

It was just the merest hint of a sketch. A child's face. A wispy ponytail. That's all it was.

Milam traced the outline of a delicately drawn cheek. "I don't remember. It's been too damn long ago."

When they walked—the three of them—into the downstairs laundry room, Enid Friendley watched them approach, her arms folded across her abdomen, a curious expression on her face.

"We appreciate your coming," Max said briskly.

Her unfriendly eyes remained wary. They moved from Max to Annie to Miss Dora. It was to the latter that Enid spoke. "Hello, Miss Dora."

"Enid, we need your help." Miss Dora's glance was

compelling. "What happened that last day? Who did the Judge talk to? What did you see?"

The caterer hesitated.

"Come now." Miss Dora was impatient. "Max and Annie told me what you said about Amanda and Julia. I can't say I believe you were right, but we'll leave that for now. Tell us what you actually saw or heard."

"I know what I know," Enid said mulishly. "If it isn't true, then why were Amanda and Julia scared to death that day, quaking in their shoes? And Amanda—well, she came out of her room that morning and there was a bright-red mark on her cheek where he'd slapped her. And I can't say I blame him. Two women—" Her face wrinkled in disgust. "And later, Julia came running down the stairs and out into the garden and she looked like the hounds of hell were after her. And maybe they were! And rightly so. But they weren't the only ones upset. Milam came downstairs a little after that and he had an ugly look on his face when he went into the study. I was still in the hall when he came out. He stopped in the door and threatened his father. He said, cold and clear, 'I won't stand for it. You don't run the world.' He walked by me like I wasn't there. He left the door open and in a minute the Judge came and pulled it shut and his face was hard as the stones in the cemetery."

Milam's story.

Enid's story.

"What happened next?" Max asked.

Enid shrugged. "I was out in the kitchen to help with lunch." A look of surprise touched her face. "Funny. I hadn't thought about it for years. But he was the only one who came to lunch."

"He?" Annie asked.

"The Judge. Ate all by himself, and he was mad as a wet hen. Later, after he died, I thought he'd given his heart a beating that day sure enough. Quarreling with first one, then another. It was after lunch—oh, more than an hour—that Ross came home. From school. He wasn't expected. I was surprised when I heard his voice—and he was upset, upset as he could be. I didn't understand all of it, but he was standing in the door of the study—just like Milam—and he was saying that he wouldn't go, that it was all wrong. It wasn't till later that I knew what he was talking about." Her eyes filled with anguish. "My cousin Eddie died over there. Just three weeks before it was all over." Unquenched anger burst out. "That's when I knew the government lied to us. They said we had to be there, that if we didn't stay, didn't fight, that all those countries over there would go Communist and we couldn't let that happen, that it would be bad trouble for us. But when the war ended, nothing happened! And finally I saw it for what it was—a big lie. All those soldiers died for nothing. That's when I stopped believing the government—ever." Tears glistened in her blazing eyes. "They put Eddie's name on a wall. Like that helped."

To Annie, that long-ago war was the stuff of history. And here was raw pain and unhealed bitterness flowing from that history. For the first time, Annie understood on a personal level something of the misery and anger of those days. The shootings at Kent State crystallized the emotions of many Americans, including Ross Tarrant, who made a fateful decision.

"So Ross said he wouldn't go—he wouldn't die for nothing. Then he died anyway. And he was the Tarrant everybody loved. I can tell you, the tears in this house were for him. Not the Judge." Her voice was harsh.

"Do you think everybody knew about Ross's argument with his father?" Max asked thoughtfully.

"Oh, yes. You could have heard them from here to Bathsheba. The Judge's voice was terrible, like a winter wind." Enid didn't even try to mask her dislike.

"It must have broken Augustus's heart." Miss Dora's

face softened with pity. "Ross was his favorite—because Ross always did everything right. To have Ross refuse to serve his country—I can imagine how Augustus felt."

But Annie wasn't focused on Augustus Tarrant and whatever disappointment he had felt over his son's decision. She was studying the bitter twist to Enid's mouth, the fury in her eyes. "Enid, when did the Judge offer to send you to college?"

Enid stood still and straight, her face suddenly empty of expression.

Annie attacked. "Was it before you found the key to that special box—or after?"

Annie would have sworn there was a flash of satisfaction in Enid's eyes, but it came and went so quickly she couldn't be certain.

"I came here to help," Enid snapped, "not to take the blame." She grabbed up her purse from a table crowded with wash powders and bleach and brushed past them.

Miss Dora called after her, "Wait now, Enid. We need you."

The only answer was the slam of the front door as it closed behind Enid.

"She blackmailed him!" Annie said urgently.

"It could be," Max said grimly. "It very well could be."

Whitney, his brows drawn in a tight frown, stood stiffly by a post in the garage, irritation in every line of his body.

It was a three-car garage. A dark-green Jaguar was parked in the first space, a blue Chrysler in the second. The third was empty.

Max edged between the west wall and the Jaguar, past the first window to the second. He looked at Whitney across the hood. "As you recall, you were cleaning out your car from a picnic the previous day?"

"Yes." He clipped his answer. His mouth was a thin, tight, hostile line.

Max waited.

Whitney might not be the world's best lawyer, but he wasn't stupid. He didn't say a word.

"Why don't you demonstrate what you did?" Max suggested.

"Oh, for Christ's sake, Darling, I've had enough—"

"Whitney." It was a command, punctuated by a single crack of his aunt's cane on the cement floor.

He resisted for a moment, his head down, his shoulders hunched, then, grudgingly, he stepped closer to the Jaguar. His face was sullen as he pantomimed opening the trunk, removing materials, placing them on shelving against the wall. Then Whitney walked to the rear door of the automobile, pretended with exaggerated motions to open it, and mimed removing and carrying more objects to the shelves. He finished and stood, arms folded, and glared at them.

Max ignored his hostility. "Let's see, you were putting things away. That brought you up and down the length of this wall which parallels the garden."

"Yes." Whitney sounded bored.

"So you passed both of these windows."

"Yes."

Max walked to the second window, past the hood of the Jaguar. He looked out, but he couldn't see the house. His view was blocked by the wooden arbor covered with climbing roses. The arbor was obviously designed to keep the garden shed out of sight from the house.

Max pointed out the window. "Was the arbor here twenty-two years ago?"

Whitney glanced out the window. Slowly, after a glance at the shed, he nodded.

Max retraced his steps, stood by the backseat and

looked out the first window. This was a different story. The entire back of the house was in full view, plus the drive along the side of Tarrant House. Max's eyes settled on the steps to the back piazza onto which, of course, opened the French doors to the study.

Max swung sharply about. "What did you see that day, Whitney, from this window?"

Whitney stared at the first window for a long time.

Annie tensed. Was Whitney going to help? Did he remember something?

Then, with an odd note in his voice, Whitney finally spoke. "I didn't see a damned thing."

No matter how Max went at it, Whitney stubbornly repeated his denial.

Annie broke in. "You're lying." She saw Max's quick frown. But sweet words would do no good with Whitney, and he might as well know they weren't taken in.

Whitney ignored her, shaking his head, but his eyes had a distant, faraway look.

Annie started to speak, but subsided at Max's stern look.

Max stepped to the first window and looked out again into the murky light. "Anyone coming from Miss Dora's or the back of the garden or the servants' quarters would be visible to you."

"Sure," Whitney agreed. His answer was ready, but his tone was still abstracted. Then he spoke more briskly. "Thing is, I didn't see anybody at all, so let's drop it. Okay?"

"Whitney, this is a very serious situation." Miss Dora poked her head at him, like an irascible turtle. "You must tell us what you saw. Don't you understand, you could be in danger!"

Something flickered in his eyes, but he just shook his

head. "Aunt Dora, don't worry about me. I don't know anything that has to do with the Judge's murder. Look, I was out here, out of the way. The first I knew there was a problem was when Ross slammed into the garage, white as a sheet, the gun in his hand." He paused and genuine sorrow touched his voice. "God, to think he blew his brains out for nothing!"

Or was it, Annie wondered, simulated sorrow? Had Ross been manipulated by an older brother he trusted? She said briskly, "Of course, there's another reason you might not have seen anything out the windows."

"What is that, young miss?" Miss Dora demanded.

Annie's eyes locked with Whitney's. "You wouldn't have seen a thing—if you weren't here."

Whitney's face hardened. "If I killed the Judge, that's what you're saying. No. I didn't do it. Why the hell should I?"

Max went right to the point. "Jessica Horton."

For an instant, Whitney's shock was naked—the widening of his eyes, the quickly indrawn breath, the sudden stillness.

But only for an instant. Then, he shrugged. "Horton," he mused. "Jessica Horton. I don't think I—oh." The dawn of phony remembrance was almost a caricature. "Oh, yes, of course. She was killed in a plane crash a few years ago."

Dead men—and dead women—tell no tales. Obviously, that was Whitney's conclusion.

"Your father was furious that you got involved with Jessica when the firm was representing her husband in a divorce action against her," Max persisted.

Whitney's lips curved in a smug smile. "Really? That's very interesting. I don't know a thing about it."

.   .   .

Charlotte stood stiffly in the doorway of the gardening shed, too upset to even try to hide her uneasiness and fear. Her chin quivered, and her voice shook. "I can't stand this. It's all so awful, so dreadful."

"But why are *you* afraid, Charlotte?" Miss Dora peered at her with troubled eyes.

"The gun," she whispered. "Someone took the gun. Why?"

Leaves skittered in a tiny dust devil near them. The wind soughed through the limbs of the live oaks and magnolias. The storm could not be far away. The dark sky lowered over them. The shed behind Charlotte was as dark as a cave.

Annie shivered. Charlotte's fear was contagious. The woman was consumed by terror.

"The best way to be safe is to tell us all you know," Max urged.

"But I don't know anything!" Charlotte wailed. "If it weren't for the gun being stolen, I'd think you were wrong, that there must have been another shot, that Ross killed the Judge like we've always thought. But the gun—" Frightened eyes stared at them.

Max looked at the rose-laden arbor that stood between the shed and the back of the house and then at Charlotte. "Could you show us where you were that afternoon, what you were doing?"

Like a sleepwalker, Charlotte stepped inside the shed. She switched on the light and turned to the worktable. She was clearly visible through the open doorway. But when Charlotte faced them, it was obvious she would have seen nothing. The arbor blocked her view.

Just to be sure, Annie asked, "Did you see or hear anyone go past, just before four o'clock?"

Charlotte shook her head. "I wasn't looking toward the house. I was snipping and cutting, working on the flowers for the hall table and for the dining room. If anyone passed by, I didn't notice."

"Charlotte"—Miss Dora was getting good at blunt questions—"did you know that Whitney was in trouble with the Judge?"

"Whitney? Why, that's silly. The Judge thought Whitney was wonderful."

Did she really believe this, Annie wondered, or had the passage of time dimmed her memory of the Judge's strained relations with his older sons?

Annie would have challenged her, but once again Max caught her eye. Annie chafed at the restraint. Charlotte may have thought her young husband was wonderful; it was pretty clear Augustus Tarrant didn't share her vision. But Max was right. There was no point in raking up long-ago escapades to trouble Charlotte now.

"The Judge and Whitney quarreled that morning," Max said.

"I don't believe that!" Her lower lip jutted out. "Who said so? I'll bet I know. Enid! Enid's trying to cause trouble. That wretched woman has always hated all of us. She's such an ingrate, after all the Judge did for her. I've never understood why she's so hateful."

Annie stared at the older woman's suddenly spiteful face. No, Charlotte didn't understand Enid's anger. Even if Enid's fury at poverty and second-class treatment were explained, Charlotte wouldn't—with the myopia of her background: white, prosperous, landowning, and steeped in a mystic past garlanded with heroes—have understood.

"I wouldn't believe a word Enid says," Charlotte said harshly.

Lucy Jane McKay stared somberly at the ruins of the Tarrant House Museum. "Ashes to ashes," she murmured. "I don't rightly know what's right or wrong, but it's a bad thing to drag the dead out of their graves. Leave the dead to themselves."

"That might be the thing to do," Max agreed quietly, "but we must find out what happened to Courtney Kimball."

Thunder exploded with an earthshaking roar. A sheet of brilliant white lightning cut a jagged rent in the black clouds. Wind spurted against them. Leaves and dust swirled in the heavy air.

The former Tarrant cook lifted her face to look up at the storm-freighted sky. The wind flattened her dress against her. She spoke above the growing clamor of the wind. "It's wrong that a young girl should be taken away." She turned to Annie. "On the telephone, you asked me about Miz Amanda and Miz Julia. I don't know the truth of it, but that morning the Judge told Miz Julia she would have to leave Tarrant House and take Missy and go back to her parents. I saw Miz Julia's face. It was . . . so pitiful."

Thunder crashed nearby, followed immediately by a cascade of sheet lightning. Julia, clutching a shabby umbrella, huddled on a wooden bench near the back wall in a shady glen surrounded by azaleas. She looked up blankly as Miss Dora, followed by Annie and Max, ducked beneath overreaching branches of vivid crimson-flowered shrubs.

Miss Dora planted her cane firmly on a stepping stone. "Julia, why didn't you go to lunch—the day the Judge was murdered?"

"Lunch?" Julia fingered the tassel to the umbrella. "I don't know. I wasn't—I suppose I wasn't hungry."

"What did the Judge say to you?" Annie asked.

Julia worked the umbrella tassel between her thumb and forefinger, faster and faster. Her face was slack. The dark smudges in the hollows beneath her eyes gave her an abandoned, neglected look. "He was so angry. Amanda tried to tell him—and he wouldn't listen." She spoke in a rapid, dull monotone, never once looking up. "I didn't know what I was going to do. I came out to the garden, and I dug and dug. Later, I went back and there was a hole"—her hands spread until they were two feet apart—"and I dug it." Surprise lifted that monotone for an instant. "I *dug* it. Maybe I thought I could dig my way to China—anywhere. Anywhere but home. I wasn't going to go." Now she did look up. Her voice was suddenly childlike, but her face was older than time. "I wasn't going to go. No matter what happened. I'd already decided that." A quirky half-smile tilted her lips. "Everyone's so ugly about Milam. But he promised me. He said Missy and I didn't have to go."

Max leaned forward. "Go where, Julia?"

"Back . . . home." A shudder racked her thin body. "I couldn't do that. If I did, then Missy—" Tears welled in her eyes. "Everything was always good for Missy. Nothing ugly ever happened to her. We all loved her. And Milam did, too. But the right way. The *right* way."

The three of them looked at her in silence. Max crouched on one knee by the bench and took Julia's hand, quieting the spasmodic quiver of that hand working the tassel. "Your father—" Max's voice was gentle. "It wasn't right, was it?"

Those dark, pain-filled eyes stared at Max, then tears began to streak her cheeks. "Not Missy." Her voice was hoarse. "I would have died first."

Max loosened his grip and reached into his pocket. He handed his handkerchief to her.

She took it and held it tight, but made no move to wipe away the tears. "Not my baby."

Annie and Miss Dora leaned closer, straining to hear

that soft, agonized voice over the rustle of the leaves, the whipping of the branches, the growl of thunder.

"When I heard he was dead, I was glad." She lifted her head and glared at them defiantly. "Glad. Glad!"

For a crackling instant, Chastain House stood out against the lightning-white sky. The vivid explosion of the storm limned Sybil, too, her dark hair whipping in the freshening wind as she stood with the wild arrogance of a Valkyrie beside the gleaming bronze gates at the foot of the Chastain drive. Beside Sybil, his clothes crumpled now from having been slept in, his eyes red-rimmed from exhaustion, stood Harris Walker, his face bleak and hopeless.

"Tell us," Sybil shouted over the crash of the thunder. "Who, dammit, *who?*"

4:16 P.M., SATURDAY, MAY 9, 1970

Just short of the end of the drive, Ross Tarrant slammed on his brakes. He sat, his shoulders heaving, gripping the steering wheel. Then, with an unconscious moan, he threw open the door and ran to the brick wall he'd climbed so many times when he was a little boy. He pulled himself up, tearing away swaths of ivy, but pulling and climbing until he could see over the top.

He hung there and looked and looked, for this was the glimpse to last him a lifetime.

Sybil stood beside the bronze Chastain gates, her raven-black hair stirred by the breeze, her lovely face lifted to the sun, her mouth curved in a smile of joy, her eyes glowing with happiness. She walked up and down in front of the gate, not anxious, but eager, so eager. Then she glanced down at her watch, cast a quick look at the suitcase on the sidewalk, and turned to hurry back up the drive.

. . . something borrowed, something blue . . .

Ross landed heavily on his feet and ran to his car.

All the long drive out to the hunting lodge, he held tight to the sprig of ivy in his hand.

Chapter 21.

Miss Dora lifted the mallet and swung at the bronze temple gong that sat opposite the silent grandfather clock.

Charlotte straightened the rose scarf at her throat. "Great-grandfather Jemson Tarrant brought it home from Ceylon. Such an interesting life he led. The captain of his own ship, of course. He was lost in a hurricane in 1891."

The mallet swung again and again, the somber tone echoing in the hallway.

As they came—from outside, from upstairs, from other rooms—Miss Dora pointed with her cane toward the drawing room. Sybil came with white-faced Harris Walker at her side. Miss Dora looked at him searchingly, then nodded in acquiescence. Milam was the last to appear, swaggering insolently down the stairs.

Miss Dora followed him into the drawing room.

In its dramatic and scarred history, the drawing room of Tarrant House must have welcomed many unlikely visitors. But Annie felt certain that in its century and a half of existence, this Saturday afternoon gathering was perhaps strangest of all.

Chief Wells, hands behind his back, stood next to a dainty Chippendale piecrust table, dwarfing it. His white hat, the curved rim undented, rested next to a Spode clock. In deference to his surroundings, the ever-present hunk of tobacco was absent from his cheek. He glanced at Max, then at Annie. As usual, his icy dark eyes evinced no joy at seeing them.

But Annie ignored him. Her eyes kept returning to the Spode clock. It didn't surprise her that the hour hand pointed to four, the minute hand to two past the hour.

Miss Dora, so tiny she didn't even reach the chief's elbow, stood beside him. But she gave him no heed. Her gaze, too, focused on the clock. Slowly, she lifted her cane and pointed at the delicately tinted china clock.

"The hour has come. I have summoned you here to conclude my inquiry into the death of Augustus Tarrant." There was a terrible dignity in her voice. "But I am not alone. Augustus and Amanda demand justice."

The tiny old woman looked around the drawing room.

The glistening chandelier with its brilliant pinpoints of light emphasized the gloom beyond the storm-darkened windows. Thunder rumbled almost incessantly, a reminder that nature is inimical, untrustworthy, dangerous. Annie thought of Courtney Kimball, last seen on a soft spring night receding in time, and put away her last hope for Courtney's survival. How could they continue to believe Courtney would be found when there was no reason to hope? Three full days had passed since Max found her half-open purse flung to the ground in St. Michael's Cemetery. The steady rumble, the rattle of wind-whipped branches, the sighing of wind through the eaves sounded a requiem. Was Courtney's killer listening in this room? Who struck Courtney down? And why?

Whitney and Charlotte sat on the silver-brocaded Regency sofa. There was no sense of a united front against the world with this couple. They sat as separately as two people could sit. Charlotte cringed at every crash of thunder, her eyes moving restlessly around the room, her fingers pulling and picking at her rose scarf. Whitney's face was stolid and thoughtful. A fine dark stubble coated his cheeks. He looked like a seedy aristocrat who had gambled the night—and his birthright—away.

Julia was in the room, but not a part of it. Her frail shoulders hunched, she gripped the sides of her armchair as if only that tight handhold kept her in place. Her smudged, lonely eyes looked into a past where no one could follow.

Milam stood behind Julia, one hand touching the back of her chair, but she didn't seem aware of him. He watched her, pain and worry in his eyes.

Sybil, her lovely face pale and haggard, paced like a lithe and dangerous animal, back and forth, back and forth, in front of the fireplace.

Harris Walker leaned against the mantel, his eyes, angry, hurt, dangerous eyes, probing each face in turn.

Lucy Jane sat in a straight chair near the archway to the hall. Her posture was regal, and her face impassive.

Miss Dora thumped her cane against the heart pine floor. "Our investigation is done."

Chief Wells shifted his weight.

Annie sensed terror abroad in that room. One of those listening was the quarry, feeling now the hot breath of the pursuing hounds, beginning to weary, quivering with desperate lurching fear, hunted with no place to hide.

"Twenty-two years ago Death walked in Tarrant House, setting in motion events brutal enough to sear our souls." Miss Dora's tar-black eyes touched each face. "Tonight, let us find peace."

A long, quiet silence pulsed with feeling.

"Let us," she said softly, "finally lay to rest the ghost that has haunted us since that dreadful day."

Julia's chin sunk on her thin chest. She began to shake.

Miss Dora's gaze focused on Whitney. "Whitney, what did you see from the window of the garage?" All of the impress of her formidable personality was contained in that simple question.

Whitney was not her equal; he had never been her equal. His eyes shifted away from her. The hand he lifted to his chin trembled. "I didn't"—he paused, took a deep breath —"I didn't see anything. Or anyone."

Oddly, unexpectedly, Annie believed him. There was a ring of truth in Whitney's voice, yet, at the same time, a tone of abject despair.

What kind of sense did that make?

Miss Dora pursed her lips. Her face was as empty of expression as a skull, but Annie knew she had failed. This was Miss Dora's moment. She had wielded her power—and lost.

What now?

"Very well." The arrogant voice was as confident as ever. "I would have welcomed your assistance, Whitney, but I shall prevail. I know what happened. I know who committed murder. Not once, but twice. This chapter must be closed. I know, and tomorrow I shall inform the authorities."

"Grandstanding!" Annie poured fresh coffee, but even their best Colombian couldn't warm away the chill in her heart.

Thunder crashed, drowning out Max's reply. Lightning exploded, and the lights quivered, dimmed, returned to full strength. Wind-driven rain lashed against the windows.

Max tried again. "Relax, Annie. You can bet the chief has men upstairs and down at her house. He's probably in the old monster's boudoir himself, right this minute." His tone was irritated. Max, too, wasn't pleased with their aged employer's calculated indiscretion.

"Doesn't she have any confidence in us?" Annie demanded, her mood swinging from worry to fury.

Max grinned. "What do you think?"

Unwillingly, Annie grinned, too. "So, okay, she decided to short-circuit her way to a solution. She's going to be damned lucky if she doesn't short-circuit her way into the family plot at the cemetery. See how she'd like that!" Annie demanded obscurely.

Max was accustomed to Annie's thought processes. He kept to the point. "No sweat, honey. It's the hoariest ploy in the world."

Annie muttered, "Right out of Edgar Wallace."

Max bypassed a peanut butter cookie for a shiny apple. He took a bite and, between crunches, said, "Only an old-time melodrama fan would even try it. There's no danger. Chief Wells isn't my favorite cop, but he's not stupid. The security around Miss Dora at this moment is right on a par with the patrols at Kennebunkport, you can count on it."

Annie picked up two peanut butter cookies and stared moodily at the welter of papers on the golden oak breakfast room table. "Dammit, Max, we ought to know. We ought to *know*!"

The fruits of two hours' intensive labor lay before them. She took two bites, finishing off the first cookie, and picked up Max's motive sheet.

MOTIVES TO KILL JUDGE TARRANT

WHITNEY TARRANT—If the Judge lived, Whitney was out of luck and out of his cushy job in the family law firm.

CHARLOTTE TARRANT—Tarrant House and the Tarrant family were her life. And the Judge's death?

MILAM—All he'd ever asked for was his father's love. How angry was he when his father orchestrated a public embarrassment? And what was he willing to do to make certain Julia and Missy weren't sent home to Julia's parents?

JULIA—She was determined not to take Missy home to her father. Determined enough to kill?

LUCY JANE—She was the soul of rectitude. Everyone admired her. When she didn't answer the questions about Amanda and Julia, that refusal spoke volumes.

ENID FRIENDLEY—Tart-tongued, tough, tenacious. Tough enough to blackmail? What if the Judge decided to brave the consequences and bring charges?

SYBIL CHASTAIN GIACOMO—Tempestuous, wildly in love. Did she already know she was pregnant? She was ready to run away with Ross. What if she decided that Ross wouldn't have to run—if the Judge died.

MISS DORA BREVARD—Amanda was her beloved niece, as close to her own child as she would ever have. Did Amanda tell her aunt that her husband was forcing her to leave? After all, no one knew whether Miss Dora was standing in the garden with Ross when the shot sounded. She could have been in the Judge's study.

A montage of unguarded moments whirled in Annie's mind: Charlotte's eyes suddenly shifting, Julia's tight grip on the chair arms, Whitney looking out the first window in the garage toward the back piazza, Milam standing behind his wife's chair, the click as Lucy Jane replaced the receiver, Enid's angry eyes, Sybil standing like a Valkyrie at the Chastain gates, Miss Dora gazing down toward the river and saying, oh so conversationally, "That's when they see Amanda, dressed all in white to please Augustus," Enid's tart comment about Courtney Kimball, "She's got a lot to learn."

"It looks bad for Julia." Max's voice was heavy. He pointed at the drawings spread out on the table. Annie was really rather proud of her depictions of Tarrant House and its surroundings.

Annie studied the map. Max had circled the numeral marking Whitney's location.

"It seems obvious." His voice wasn't happy. Max, too, liked Julia. "If Whitney saw the murderer from that first window in the garage—well, it has to be Julia, Lucy Jane—or Miss Dora." He stared morosely at the map. "And Julia's the only likely one."

"What about Sybil?"

Max leaned closer. She smelled the nice scent of fresh soap. She reached up and touched his cheek and liked the prickly feel of stubble.

"Oh, yes," he agreed. "Yes, we can't forget Sybil. But why would she burn down the Tarrant Museum?"

"She didn't. That was Julia." But Annie's answer was automatic, unthinking. She was concentrating on the map—and suddenly she knew.

Oh, God, of course. Whitney looking out—and seeing no one.

All the pieces shifted in Annie's mind, clicking irrevocably into place. Tarrant House. The Judge dead. Milam and Julia and Missy at Wisteree. Missy's birthday party. The teddy bear. Amanda hearing Miss Dora's chatter and discovering her youngest son was not guilty of patricide. In her happiness at clearing Ross's name, had Amanda followed that truth through to its lethal conclusion? Or was she so elated at Ross's innocence that she'd talked too much and to the wrong person? Years passed, and Courtney Kimball demanded to know what happened on May 9, 1970. The his-

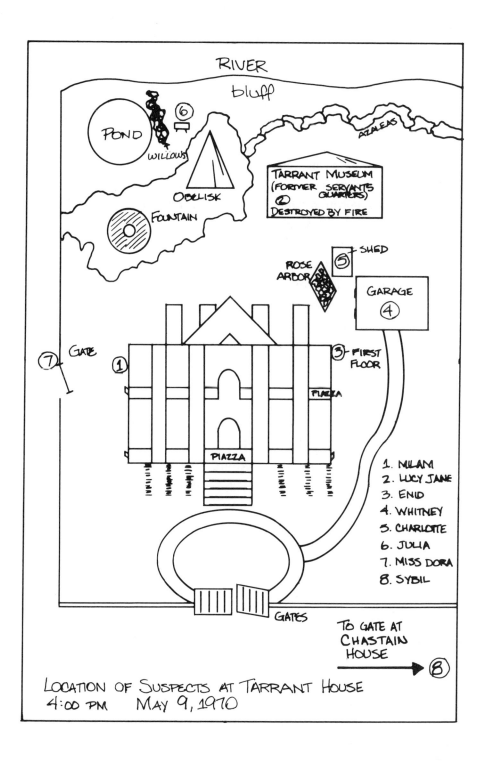

LOCATION OF SUSPECTS AT TARRANT HOUSE
4:00 PM   MAY 9, 1970

tory of the Tarrant Family. So much good and so much bad, but Charlotte included only the good.

"Max—"

The phone shrilled.

Annie was nearest. As she reached for it, another burst of thunder was followed hard by a sheet of lightning. *It was a dark and stormy night*—The familiar refrain flashed in her mind. It almost brought a smile because it was such a perfect time for Laurel to call with macabre descriptions of ghostly peregrinations. Annie wondered, did ghosts get wet? That was an absorbing metaphysical puzzle.

But the voice on the other end of the line, hoarse and strained with worry, was not Laurel's.

". . . I tell you, she's gone! I tried Aunt Dora's. She's not there. We've got to find her. She's out in the storm. She hates storms!" There was panic in Milam's voice. "She left a note."

A note. Annie tensed. "What did she say?"

Static crackled on the line.

" '. . . sorry for everything. We never had a chance, did we? But you were always kind. You hated Tarrant House, too. And you loved Missy. Don't follow me.' "

Annie's hand tightened on the receiver. "Did she say where she was going?"

"No. No. Oh, God. And my gun's gone."

Annie felt a chill. "You had a gun, out there at the plantation? Are you sure Julia took it?"

"Yes. Because . . ." Static crackled again. ". . . this morning and now it's gone. Listen, you've got to find her. You've got to. Do you hear me? It's all your fault, coming to Chastain, meddling, scaring her. You've got to—"

Lightning exploded.

The line went dead.

"Max," she cried, "Julia's gone. She has a gun." Julia

with a gun—but that was all wrong. Wasn't it? Annie had worked it out—but the face she had pictured wasn't Julia's.

The Maserati crawled, Max straining to see through a windshield awash with rain. A half-block from Tarrant House, the low-slung car floundered, rolled to a stop, its engine flooded by the water running hubcap-deep in the old, poorly drained street.

They battled through a nightmare world, the rain a blinding deluge, the wind a brutal, tearing force. Branches twisted and cracked. Old trees toppled. Thunder and lightning intermingled in an explosive, blinding cacophony.

In a sizzling, eye-shocking instant of light, they saw Julia's shabby car parked in front of Tarrant House.

Annie broke into a run, but Max was faster.

He pulled open the driver's door.

Annie peered past him. The car was empty.

Max slammed the door. They darted across the sidewalk and through the open gate. They began to run up the drive. The house was a blur of darkness with the faint gleam of light almost obscured by the pelting rain. Above them branches creaked and swayed.

Then, between blasts of thunder, they heard the sharp, unmistakable bark of gunfire.

The front door was locked. Max knocked and pounded and rattled the handle; then, feet skidding on the slick wetness of the drenched piazza, he and Annie flung themselves out into the night and ran around the side of Tarrant House.

And found that Death had been there first.

It was the only time Annie ever felt sympathy for Charlotte Tarrant. Her chenille robe plastered against her, her hair lank against her head, Charlotte cradled Whitney's bloody head against her breast and moaned, a low, wild, desolate cry.

It was a tableau Annie would always remember. Then movement broke the nearby darkness, and Miss Dora darted into the pale circle of light from the fixture above the back steps.

Suddenly Chief Wells was there, too, and Sergeant Matthews.

Miss Dora had come first. Alone. That seemed important. Annie clung to that piece of knowledge.

Chief Wells and Miss Dora knelt by Charlotte and made her loosen her grasp. Matthews swept the surrounding area with a huge flash that was puny against the rain and night.

The chief eased Whitney gently to the ground. Charlotte whimpered and reached for his limp hand.

Miss Dora caught her arm, and Annie remembered the strength in those wiry old fingers. "Come now, Charlotte. We must take shelter."

Chief Wells nodded. "Take her to your house, Miss Dora. I'll come when I can." He shouted at Matthews. "Stay with them."

It was a nightmare walk through that storm-battered garden to the open gate in the wall and up the rain-lashed path to the house next door. Max and Annie supported Charlotte between them. Every few steps she halted and tried to twist free and turn back.

But, somehow, they reached the house, wet, numb, shaken.

Miss Dora led the way to the drawing room. Water dripped from their clothes, splashing on the gleaming heart pine floor. Annie could take no comfort now in the *bois-de-rose* silk hangings or the costly Georgian furniture. Rain spotted the rose Aubusson rug.

Charlotte stumbled to the nearest sofa. She looked up, dazed. "It's cold out there." She shivered. "Whitney . . ."

Annie could imagine her feelings. Whitney was still in their garden, the cold rain washing away his blood.

Miss Dora busied about, bringing blankets and whisky. Annie helped.

A door slammed at the back. Matthews put a hand on the butt of his gun.

Sybil stormed into the drawing room.

Harris Walker was close behind. "Jesus Christ," he demanded, "what's going on?" He jammed his hands in his pockets and stared at Charlotte.

"Who shot Whitney?" Sybil carried a crimson umbrella, now closed, but her silk raincoat was dark with rain. She strode to Miss Dora. "Have you found Julia? Milam called me."

"Julia?" Milam's voice carried from the hall, rising with excitement and hope. "Julia?" He rushed into the drawing room. His clothes were sodden. He wore no raincoat, no hat. His eyes swept the room, seeking, seeking, then his shoulders slumped. He appealed to Miss Dora. "Tell them to look for Julia. They'll listen to you."

"They are looking." Her voice was toneless. "Sit down, Milam." Her skin was waxy, and the hands tightly clasping the silver knob of her cane trembled. Her old black bombazine dress glistened like wet raven feathers. "When did you get here?"

"Just now. It was hell driving into town. A bridge was out and I had to come the long way round. They've got a barricade up at the end of the street." His eyes blinked. "I couldn't get through the police line at Whitney's. But I saw him. Is he . . ."

"Yes."

Milam threw back his head. "Julia didn't do it. I tell you, Julia didn't do it. She's out in that storm—" Tears glistened in his eyes.

Charlotte blazed out of her stupor. "She killed Whitney! It must have been Julia. There was a banging at the back door. I begged him not to go downstairs, but he did—and then I heard the shot and I ran—but there was no one there but Whitney." She shuddered, her mouth quivering. "His blood. Oh, God, his blood, everywhere." Charlotte pulled herself to her feet. "Julia! You've got to catch her. She's killed Whitney—and she killed Amanda and the Judge and—" Charlotte broke off. She took a step back, but the sofa blocked her way. One hand clutched at her throat.

"And?" Julia's voice was harsh. She stood in the doorway from the hall. Her green poncho glistened, but it didn't drip. She stood with her arms folded, her hands tucked into the floppy sleeves of the raincoat.

Annie wondered how long Julia had been there, how she had avoided capture by the men at Tarrant House where Whitney lay dead.

"Who else, Charlotte?" Julia demanded. "You almost said someone else, didn't you?"

Charlotte's lips twitched. "That girl, the one who came, the one who disappeared—what did you do with her?"

Harris bolted across the room. He grabbed Julia's arm. "Where is Courtney?" It was a hoarse and maddened shout. "You're going to—"

Julia came alive, twisting free of his grasp, slipping around him, crossing the room to the fireplace. And she now held a gun in her hands and faced them all.

She looked at Harris first. "Leave me alone. I didn't hurt Courtney. I would never have hurt Amanda's grand-daughter."

Harris's hands dropped to his sides. He stood very still.

Julia's hand moved, and now the gun was aimed at Charlotte. "I want to talk to you, Charlotte. It's time now."

"Policeman!" Charlotte squealed, cutting her eyes toward Matthews, who stood in shock, his hand fumbling with the holster snap. "Do something! She's going to kill me, just like she killed Whitney!"

The poncho was too big for Julia. She looked like a lost child. Except for the gun in her hand. "It's no good, Charlotte. I was almost sure before I came tonight. Now I know. Because only you needed to kill Whitney. He didn't look through the window toward the back of the house. If he had, he would have seen me. And Whitney had no reason to protect me—certainly not if he thought I'd killed his father. But he didn't look through that window—"

Annie was nodding. Yes, oh, yes. That was what she had decided. Not the first window. Whitney had looked through the second window, the window with no view of the house because of the rose arbor, but a clear, unobstructed view of the potting shed.

"—he looked through the other window at the garden shed—and you weren't there, were you? I thought about it and thought about it tonight and I was almost sure. You see, I started toward the house—I was going to make one last effort to talk to the Judge. I was going to tell him about my father. Not even the Judge would have sent me there—if he knew. He wouldn't have wanted my father to touch Missy. I was going to tell him—but I was afraid. I kept standing there, trying to make up my mind, then I heard a shot. I didn't know what had happened, but I was frightened. I turned and went back to the bench where I'd been. But you see, I was midway up the garden, so I would have seen Miss Dora or Lucy Jane. They had a much longer way to go. Only you and Whitney were so close to the back piazza. It was only a few feet from the arbor or the garage to the back steps. So it had to be you—or Whitney. And now there's only you."

Charlotte's eyes were wide with panic. "You're insane," she hissed. "I wouldn't kill Whitney. Never."

Julia took a step forward. "I have to know." She raised the gun, aiming it at Charlotte's heart.

Chief Wells stood in the archway, his hands loose at his sides. "Miz Tarrant, put down that gun. You can't get away."

But, Annie realized with a thrill of horror, Julia didn't care.

It was as if Julia hadn't even heard him. She took one step closer to Charlotte. "All because you are obsessed with the Tarrants. That's almost funny, isn't it? To kill and kill and kill for a house. An old, hate-filled, heartless house. That's why you killed my baby, isn't it? To be sure that someday your daughter would be the Tarrant of Tarrant House. Harriet was born the next year. Did you know you were pregnant? You did, didn't you? So my baby had to go. Did Amanda figure that out, too? Did she know that Missy's teddy bear was left at Tarrant House, after the birthday party? Did she wonder aloud how it could have been found in the pond—where you led my little daughter? You told her Bear-Bear was waiting, didn't you? That he was swimming out in the pond and she could swim with him. Did you pick her up and throw her?" Julia's unearthly voice broke and then she screamed, a shriek of pain and anguish and bitter, unrelenting fury. "Did you throw my baby in the water?"

"Miz Tarrant—" the chief bellowed.

Julia held the gun out straight. Charlotte screamed. Then, sobs racking her wasted body, Julia turned away. The gun clattered to the floor. She walked blindly across the room, into Milam's arms.

Charlotte Tarrant struggled to regain her composure. "She's sick, don't you see? Sick. I didn't do any—"

The lights flickered, dimmed, went out.

A flurry of movement sounded in the hall. Then, all at once, there was a dim and smoky shaft of light from the hall and a flickering image moved toward them. The scent of lily of the valley was almost overpowering.

Annie struggled to breathe.

Amanda Tarrant.

It was vague and pale and insubstantial but the features were those of her portrait, and high and ghostly came the cry: "Charlotte, Charlotte, I'm coming for you."

Charlotte began to back away, her hands stretched out in front of her. And then she screamed, "Amanda, no, no. Amanda, I had to kill him, *I had to!*"

Chapter 22.

Chief Wells tried, but Charlotte's demonic plunge through the archway caught him off guard. And then she was out of the house. They all ran after her. Even Miss Dora thumped her way out into the wild night.

Everyone except Julia and Milam.

The storm still raged. One patrolman almost cornered Charlotte near the ruins of the museum, but she ducked away into a deeper shadow.

But everyone heard her final, despairing cry as she jumped from the bluff, down, down, down into the flood-raging water below.

Harris Walker stood by the obelisk. Rain beat against him, his face full of despair.

Miss Dora came up to him. "We'll go back to my house now."

He stared down at her, his eyes empty. "We'll never know. Oh, God, we'll never . . ."

"Come along now." She jerked her head, the silver hair

plastered against the small skull, at Sybil. "Bring him. And you, too. We must close the chapter." Her eyes summoned Annie and Max.

As they entered the quiet house, they could hear the sounds of searchers near the river bluff, faint shouts, and the wail of a siren.

Once again, a wet, bedraggled, numbed group gathered in Miss Dora's drawing room. It was empty. Milam and Julia had gone. Revenge would not bring Missy back. But did they drive through the dark night home to Wisteree with some kind of peace in their hearts?

Annie kept hearing Amanda's voice. *"Charlotte, Charlotte . . ."* But how had she known it was Amanda's? Oh, yes, Miss Dora had once lifted her own voice in imitation of the dead woman's and it had had the ring of truth.

But Amanda?

What caused that shimmering light in the hallway and that insubstantial but unmistakable apparition?

The lights were all on now, the glare almost shocking after the coal-black of the stormy night.

"We will lay our ghosts to rest this night." Miss Dora's face was haggard but composed.

Sybil pushed back her wet hair. "So it was Charlotte, respectable, conventional, oh-so-proper Charlotte, the keeper of the flame for the Tarrants of Tarrant House." Sybil stared at the portrait of Joshua Brevard, whose granddaughter Amanda had married Augustus Tarrant on a lush summer day fifty-five years before. "My daughter. Whitney. Missy. Amanda. The Judge. Ross. For Christ's sake, Aunt Dora, why? For that bloody goddamn house?" Eyes reddened by weeping began to fill.

"Tarrant House was the symbol to Charlotte, the symbol, the treasure, ultimately, the obsession," Miss Dora said wearily. "And killing became easy. When she shot Augustus, it could be said that she was emotionally distraught, over-come by the fear of losing the world that made her life meaningful, being a Tarrant in Tarrant House. But passion gave way to calculation. How hideous to imagine her slip-ping through the halls to Missy's room, waking her, enticing her out of the sleeping household and down to the pond. Happy, laughing, beloved, trusting Missy."

How had Charlotte lived with that hideous act all these years? Annie wondered.

Miss Dora gripped her cane. "And Amanda had no chance, of course, once she began to question and wonder and worry about what happened to the Judge and to Ross. That's why when Courtney came to me—the night of her disappearance—with a flesh wound in her shoulder from a shot out of the bushes, I made my plan."

Harris Walker jumped to his feet, but Miss Dora made an imperious gesture. "You will listen, all of you."

If ever listeners were held spellbound, Miss Dora's audi-ence of Sybil, Harris, Annie, and Max were.

Sybil's eyes flared. She stood absolutely immobile. Har-ris hunched like a sprinter waiting for the gun.

"I didn't know, of course," Miss Dora continued, "whose hand had held the gun, but I feared that Courtney's life would be in danger forever. She was raising a ghost that someone was determined to keep buried. But, you see, I was determined, too. I would not stand by and see Amanda's granddaughter lost. The resolution had to be now. And now it is, finally, ended. Charlotte's death closes the account." The old lady's face was implacable, her hooded eyes merci-less. "Tonight Courtney was the avenging spirit who came for Charlotte." Miss Dora grabbed a bellpull and yanked hard twice.

Annie had seen bellpulls in historic homes, had their purpose explained. Could this be one that actually worked?

In answer, running feet sounded on the main staircase.

Sybil whirled toward the hall, her face white from shock.

Harris's face was transformed, despair replaced by incredulous joy.

"Courtney—" A lifetime of love and yearning rang in Sybil's cry.

The girl burst into the drawing room, her face alight. She stopped in the doorway, young and slim and blond and lovely, her hands outstretched. She smiled tremulously. "Mother . . . Harris . . ."

They came together, mother and daughter, dark head and blond. Then Harris Walker slipped strong arms around them both in an embrace that brought tears to Annie's eyes.

Chapter 23.

Max leaned against the coffee bar at Death on Demand. "Come on, Agatha," he admonished the glossy black cat, "don't sulk."

Agatha ignored both Max and Annie as her pink tongue delicately lapped the milk.

Annie reached down to stroke glistening black fur, but drew back at a deep, warning growl. "Dorothy L. was glad to see us," Annie snapped. She did not go on to share with Agatha the intelligence that Dorothy L. had been equally disturbed by the several days' dearth of adoring *Homo sapiens* and had demanded almost constant attention since they'd arrived home that morning.

"I guess Barb doesn't have the magic cat touch," Annie concluded as Agatha settled on her haunches and began to wash her face while continuing to pretend Annie and Max didn't exist. "How long do you suppose we'll be in the doghouse?"

Max grinned. "Long enough to make her point."

Annie reached up and pulled down mugs *(Cat of Many Tails* by Ellery Queen and *The Transcendental Murder* by Jane Langton). "You'd think she'd appreciate our coming into the store on a Sunday." She poured the freshly made coffee and checked the cupboard devoted to people food. Hmmm, fresh raspberry brownies, her favorites. Barb might not be an all-time favorite with cats, but Annie appreciated her.

As they settled at one of the tables near the coffee bar, Annie looked around appreciatively. "I'm so glad to be back!" She felt as though she'd been away from Death on Demand for weeks instead of days. It made her appreciate living in a happy house, and spending her days in a congenial pursuit, notwithstanding the difficulty of enticing publishers into offering co-op money to help publicize author signings or the never-ending juggling of paperwork, book unpacking, and inventory or the despair in dealing with an industry where every publisher's ordering form differed or the other myriad tribulations of booksellers. She was home, and that assuredly was where her heart thrived. Especially after the time she'd just spent, immersed in an unhappy family's miseries. But perhaps now, at last, that family could look to happy days.

She gave her husband's hand a squeeze, which hardly took her fingers a jot from the most direct path to the raspberry brownies. "It's great about Courtney. I know how badly you felt." Hmm. Was there, this side of heaven, anything quite as wonderful as a mixture of chocolate and raspberry? Well, of course—but she meant food!

"I sure as hell did feel bad." Max's tone lacked its usual geniality.

Annie understood. "They *could* have told you," she agreed sympathetically.

"I suppose I was a chump who came in very handy,

thrashing around Chastain, stirring everybody up." Max forgot himself and picked up a raspberry brownie.

It was a down-in-the-dumps declaration if ever Annie had heard one.

"Now, Max. How could we have known it was a put-up job? The purse in the cemetery. The empty apartment, the doors open, the television on. Blood in the driver's seat of Courtney's car. Why, I'll bet Susan Rogers Cooper's Milt Kovak would have fished, too."

He shrugged disconsolately and ate half a brownie.

"Look, Max—"

The bell at the front door pealed.

Annie looked around in irritation. Darn it, it *was* Sunday. Everyone knew Death on Demand was closed, but she heard the door opening and closing, and pushed her chair back.

Then she heard, too, the quick, unmistakable tap of a cane. Miss Dora came down the central corridor.

"Thought I'd come see you." For once the bright dark eyes avoided their own.

Max's look was distinctly frosty.

Miss Dora's hat today was a dramatic purple velour with a topknot of orange feathers. Annie wouldn't have wished it on a derelict parrot. Thankfully the old lady's dress was also purplish, not orange. Her sallow skin wore an unaccustomed flush. "Came to explain. Not apologize. Had to do what had to be done. Told Courtney she'd have to trust me absolutely. Set her to work being Amanda's ghost." There was a touch of defensiveness in her voice. "I've seen Amanda, you know. On misty spring nights. Down there near the river. But I called her to come—and had Courtney play the role. Set the clocks at four-oh-two, sprayed some scent Amanda loved—lily of the valley." A high cackle hung eerily in the quiet bookstore. "People are such fools, believing things like that. But ghosts do walk. Their hearts hurt too much to find peace. Maybe now Amanda will be able to rest. Ross did his best and his girl is safe with her mother and her young man. A fine young man." The dark eyes looked mournfully at Annie and Max. "Lost Whitney. I'm sorry about that. Not a perfect world, but better than it was." She cleared her throat. "Want you to know I wasn't playing the two of you for fools, but I had to have help, had to get the feeling out that the hounds were loose, loping closer, sniffing, pushing, pressing."

Annie remembered Charlotte's terror. Oh, yes, Miss Dora's plan had worked, worked very well indeed.

Miss Dora held out an old gnarled hand in a black-lace half-glove. "Bury the hatchet?" she asked Max.

Max took that tiny, withered hand. "Of course, Miss Dora."

The quick, sharp cackle sounded again. "Heard about how the chief came over here to the island, started in on Annie about your girlfriend. Teach you not to be so close-mouthed next time." She gave another satisfied chuckle, then darted past them to peer up at the paintings. "Too easy," she sniffed.

Annie tried not to take umbrage, but she couldn't resist a quick retort. "If they're so easy—"

Miss Dora pointed at the paintings in turn.

"The Great Mistake by Mary Roberts Rinehart, *Murder with Southern Hospitality* by Leslie Ford, *Sister of Cain* by Mary Collins, *Madam, Will You Talk?* by Mary Stewart, and *Search the Shadows* by Barbara Michaels."

What could Annie say?

Annie held her breath as Miss Dora tapped toward the section of collectibles. If that old hag thought she was going to get a rare book for—

The bell pealed at the front door.

For heaven's sake. It was Sunday!

Annie started up the center aisle but stopped at the sight of the speeding wheelchair. Laurel careened toward them, beaming. "I am so glad to be home! Much as I *love* Charleston. And those *dear* ghosts! Did I tell you about Mrs. Latham? Not that she was a ghost. Though, of course, the dear woman may be by this time. She's long dead!"

Annie gave Laurel a bewildered glance.

Her mother-in-law beamed at Miss Dora. "You're look-ing just lovely today, Miss Dora." She then braked beside Annie and Max and squeezed Annie's hand. "This *isn't* diffi-cult, my sweet. Not even for you."

Some of Annie's bonhomie seeped away.

Max tried not to laugh.

"You see, Mrs. Latham was hired to come to Charleston to be governess to four dear little girls at Old Goose Creek Plantation. She was given a *very* nice room upstairs. Now, she loved to read romances. And the next morning was a Sunday but she stayed in her room—that was, after all, her free time—and didn't come downstairs for devotions but cozied herself in her four-poster to read *The Turkish Spy.*" Laurel clapped her hands. "Isn't that a wonderful title, An-nie? Can't you just imagine the story? In any event, Mrs. Latham was thoroughly enjoying her story when the door to her room opened and this old lady in a black gown with a muslin neckerchief crossed on her breast and wearing a close-fitting white cap on her head glided into the room and stared, with obvious disapproval, at Mrs. Latham's book. And Mrs. Latham felt a hideously cold draft of air. Then the old woman turned, still frowning, to leave. Mrs. Latham tried to follow, but the woman receded from her and then disappeared into a wall. Well, you can imagine"—Laurel gave a sympathetic head shake—"how this upset Mrs. Latham. Why, it would upset anyone, wouldn't it?"

Annie felt constrained to murmur, "Of course."

"Dear Annie, you have such a high-strung nature. Well, I know Max is *very* good for you."

Annie contemplated Laurel as she might have a grinning alligator. She almost replied, "And you have so many teeth, my dear," but was afraid Max wouldn't understand. Or, worse, might understand only too well. Instead, she bared her own teeth in what she hoped resembled a good-humored smile.

Max gave her an approving pat.

Annie suddenly had an inkling how Agatha felt about unsolicited attention.

"Mrs. Latham was so upset she rushed downstairs and disrupted the service, pressing everyone to join her in a search for the old woman. But no one was found. Now, the truth of the matter was, those downstairs couldn't have missed seeing an intruder, but they couldn't convince Mrs. Latham that she had imagined the episode. Then, the next Sunday"—Laurel leaned forward portentously—"the mistress's brother-in-law arrived and Mrs. Latham went into shock, crying that he was just the image of the old woman she'd seen. Then everyone understood." She sat back triumphantly.

"They did?" Max encouraged.

Annie would have kicked him had he been close enough.

"Why, yes. It was the mistress's deceased mother-in-law, old Mary Hyrne, and the family understood at once. Mrs. Hyrne was very pious and she must have been upset by Mrs. Latham reading frivolous fiction instead of observing the Sabbath. Do you know what?"

Annie knew it was her turn. "What?" she snapped.

Laurel wasn't daunted. "It had the most *profound* effect upon Mrs. Latham. Why, she never missed a Sunday service for the rest of her days at Old Goose Creek Plantation. So, you see, ghosts sometimes have a very good effect!"

"Without doubt," Miss Dora seconded.

"But I feel that I've spent enough time with those residents of another plane." Laurel gave each in turn a most beguiling smile.

"Really?" Annie perked up. Perhaps Laurel was contemplating a trip to Addis Ababa.

"Yes. Much as I mourn their inability to be freed from this world of woe and heartbreak, I feel that I have a greater call upon my good offices."

Miss Dora's eyes glittered with amusement.

"A nunnery?" Annie muttered. Preferably one atop Mount Ararat.

A trill of delighted laughter. "Dear Annie. Such a sense of humor. No, it is much more of this world, of the here and now, and actually, very very here!"

Annie's heart sank.

"I have the most exciting news." Laurel clasped her hands to her heart. "Henny, our own dear stalwart, outspoken, progressive Henny is going to run for mayor! Annie, Max!" Laurel flung wide a graceful hand, the pink-enameled fingernails shining. "The rallies! The campaign! The excitement! Oh, it will be a campaign such as has never before been seen on Broward's Rock!"

"Huzzah!" Then Miss Dora broke into an odd, unmusical hum. It took Annie a moment to recognize "Yankee Doodle Dandy"!

Chapter 24.

The strains of a Strauss waltz lilted on the soft summer night air. Annie accepted another glass of champagne and looked through the festive crowd for her husband. Then, she gave a good-humored shrug and drifted down the flagstoned path toward the river. It would be lovely in the moonlight.

It was a wonderful party—and such a dramatic change to see love and youth and happiness at Tarrant House. It helped wipe away the memory of that dreadful spring night. The party was fabulous, of course, as would be any celebration planned by Sybil Chastain Giacomo. And she had spared no effort or expense for her daughter's engagement dance: Japanese lanterns winked cheerfully throughout the grounds, a striped tent housed a superb buffet, a portable dance floor enticed eager couples, and the symphony orchestra from Savannah provided the music.

Annie smiled, recalling Courtney Kimball Tarrant's vivid smile and the pride on Harris Walker's face.

She came to the end of the path and looked out at the river, shining like a silver band in the moonlight.

The bushes rustled nearby and she had the sense of another presence, a happy, cheerful presence.

Had Max . . .

She glimpsed, just for a moment, a breathtaking instant, a swift sweep of white, she smelled lilies of the valley, and she felt a welling up of happiness.

Annie smiled and whispered, "God bless, Amanda," and then she turned to run lightly back toward light and laughter.

I am indebted to the following authors for their wonderful tales of South Carolina ghosts:

Charleston Ghosts by Margaret Rhett Martin, University of South Carolina Press, 1963.

South Carolina Ghosts from the Coast to the Mountains by Nancy Roberts, University of South Carolina Press, 1983.

Southern Ghosts by Nancy Roberts, Sandlapper Publishing Co., 1979.

Ghosts and Specters of the Old South by Nancy Roberts, Sandlapper Publishing Co., 1974.

More Tales of the South Carolina Low Country by Nancy Rhyne, John F. Blair, Publisher, 1984.